The Inquisitor's Niece

by
Erika Rummel

For Jim, with a warning:
suppress your academic
persona when reading
this!

Erika

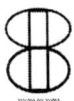

Copyright © 2016 Erika Rummel

Published by:
Bygone Era Books, Ltd
7665 E. Eastman Ave. #B101
Denver, CO 80231

This book contains material protected under International and Federal Copyright Laws and Treaties. Any unauthorized reprint or use of this material is prohibited. No part of this book may be reproduced or transmitted in any form or by any means, electronic or mechanical, including photocopying, recording, or by any information storage and retrieval system without express written permission from the author.

Book cover design and layout by
Bygone Era Books, Ltd. using artwork from
SelfPubBookCovers.com/yvonrz

ISBN: 978-1-941072-38-7

Printed in the United States of America

ALL RIGHTS RESERVED

I would like to thank my friends Gisela Argyle, Karin MacHardy, Charlotte Morton, and Barbara Spiller for reading the manuscript at various stages. I've greatly benefited from their advice and insightful comments. I am also grateful to Daniel Willis for his editorial help and for keeping the historical novel alive and well

CHAPTER 1

Seville, 1514

"COME IN, FRAY NATALE," DOCTOR MALKI SAID TO his visitor. He couldn't help smiling at the sight of the plump little Franciscan who greeted him with a flutter of his fingers and entered the house with mincing steps.

Alonso Malki had no liking for the Franciscan Order. They were a boorish lot of hypocrites making a show of their piety and devotion, but Natale was the exception to the rule. He was a man of rare accomplishments who could turn out polished Latin phrases and recite Homer in the original Greek. He was a fellow book lover who shared the doctor's interest in ancient manuscripts.

He ushered Natale into his study.

"So you are off to Alcala, my friend, depriving me of your learned company?"

Natale dropped into a chair and stretched his legs. "I would have preferred to stay, but my skills are not valued here."

"And Alcala offers you greener pastures?"

"Only if Cardinal Cisneros takes me into his service."

At the mention of the Cardinal's name, the doctor's blood ran cold. Cisneros was a patron of learning and a scholar in his own right, but he was the Inquisitor General and a bitter enemy of the Jews. It was at his prompting that King Ferdinand and Queen Isabella had passed the infamous decree that forced Jews to convert to Christianity or be exiled. The law had driven Alonso's family underground. After submitting to baptism, the Malkis moved to Las Palmas and quietly practiced the religion of their fathers there. They thought they could escape the watchful eye of the Inquisition in the outlying territories of Spain, but the Church had a thousand spies, and the Malkis were under investigation now.

Alonso suppressed his private sorrows and recalled himself to his duties as a host. The servant had brought in a carafe of sweet Malaga wine. The doctor lifted his glass and drank to Natale's health and prospects in Alcala.

"I wish the Cardinal would employ me on his great project," the Franciscan said. "Heard of his plan to publish a polyglot Bible?"

Alonso nodded. "A Bible with parallel columns in Hebrew, Greek, and Latin. It's an ambitious undertaking."

"He has hired a team of scholars to put together the text on the basis of old manuscripts. His library is well-stocked, but his agents are scouring the bookstalls for more. Don't you have an ancient Hebrew Bible in your possession, Alonso?"

It was a delicate question to put to a *converso* who was supposed to forget his Jewish past.

"You mentioned an old codex to me once," Natale said. "Cisneros would pay a good price for it. If you want to sell the manuscript and are willing to entrust it to me, I could take it to Alcala and present it to the Cardinal for inspection."

Alonso forced a laugh. "I know what you are thinking, my dear Natale. An ancient codex would serve you as a better introduction than any letter of reference."

"You caught me out," Natale said with a grin. "The thought has crossed my mind, I won't deny it. Still, it would be money in your pocket. The Cardinal is a generous man when it comes to buying books, especially Hebrew texts which are rare in our country now. But perhaps you are too attached to your heirloom to let it go?"

The Bible in question had been handed down from father to son for many generations. When Alonso left Las Palmas to study medicine in Salamanca, his father gave him the Bible together with a signet ring. "May God be with you, my son," he said. "May the ring protect your body, and may the Bible guide your soul to heaven." After completing his course of studies, Alonso set up his practice in Seville. The precious manuscript was concealed in a recess behind his bed, wrapped up in a prayer shawl. He had no intention of parting with the book or letting on that it was still in his possession. Times were perilous, and a man's devotion to a Hebrew Bible might be construed as an act of heresy.

Two months ago, Alonso had made his way through the crowded market square of Seville, when he felt a tug on his sleeve. He turned and saw an old Arab standing behind him. He recognized the man as a friend of his father's and was about to greet him, but the Arab's eyes flashed an eloquent warning. He slipped a letter into Alonso's hand and quickly walked away through the throng. Heeding the man's silent warning, Alonso concealed the letter under his cloak and hurriedly walked home. When he reached the safety of his house, he unfolded the single sheet. It bore neither address nor signature, but Alonso recognized the handwriting of his father. "I have been cited before the tribunal of the Inquisition," the note said. "I have good hopes of fending off the charges, but lie low in the meantime and do not write to us until you hear from me again. Remember, a Jew has no friends among Christians. Trust no one."

No, Alonso could not afford to take a risk.

"I no longer have the codex," he said to Natale. "When we converted to Christianity, my father cast the *tefillot* and *machzorim* and *selichot* into the bonfire, together with all his books."

"What! He cast the Old Testament into the flames? I would have thought that the Word of God was sacrosanct even when written in Hebrew characters."

"The bishop thought differently."

Natale groaned. "That man is a barbarian, don't you think?"

"It would not be right for me to pass judgment on a bishop."

"Ah, you are a cautious man," Natale said, "and perhaps better so."

The bells of Santa Maria de la Sede began to toll. Through the windows of his study, Alonso could see the solid walls and flying buttresses of the cathedral. His house was next to the Patio de Naranjas, a little plaza that had once been the *san* of a mosque, and was now the forecourt of the cathedral. The bells rang out a victory message: Christ has triumphed!

"The bells are tolling for the heretics, an invitation to repent before they are burned at the stake," Natale said, heaving his rump out of the seat. "Are you coming to see their punishment?"

"I prefer to reflect on their fate in private."

Natale wagged a plump finger at Alonso. "Where is your caution now, my friend? My advice is: go and show your face even if you feel sorry for the sinners."

"I dislike the carnival atmosphere surrounding executions. The common people behave like animals and take a beastly pleasure in the suffering of others."

"So you *are* sorry for the heretics," Natale said.

The doctor bit his lip.

Natale gave him a probing look. "And now you are sorry that you opened your mouth."

"I have no reason to regret what I said, and I'm not afraid of speaking my mind."

"You need not be afraid of *me*. But think of your neighbours, Alonso. You don't want them to say: Why is the doctor staying home? Is he in sympathy with the heretics?"

"In that point you are right," Alonso said. "We live in a wretched age when it is not enough to *be* honourable. One must *appear* to be honourable as well."

"Then come along," Natale said and led the way to the Plaza Mayor.

Public executions always fetched a good crowd. People craned their heads to see the expression on the faces of the trio of heretics, an old Jew and two youths, his sons presumably, bareheaded and shirtless, their backs bloodied by the lash, their hands and feet shackled. They were transported in an open cart for all to see, to vilify, curse and spit on. The crowd was in a holiday spirit, merry and boisterous. Boys were hawking chestnuts, dried fruit and sugared almonds. A band of blind musicians was playing their guitars. A juggler performed tricks with coloured balls. A harlot was sidling up to Alonso, looking for business, brushing his arm, giving him flirtatious looks. She smiled at him with more than professional interest perhaps, because he was young and handsome and had passion in his eyes, even if his bearing was grave as became a practitioner of medicine.

The crowd was jostling for the best spots from which to watch the spectacle. There was excitement in the air when the heretics were dragged to the pyre and tied to the stake. A joyful shout went up when the executioner put a torch to the kindling, and for a moment the cheers and jeers drowned out the agonized shrieks of the men at the stake. The crowd watched them writhing as the smoke and the licking flames enveloped their bodies, and the fumes and the pain overcame first the old man and then his companions. Their bodies slackened, the roaring fire ate through the ropes that tied them to the stake, and they dropped to the ground. For a while an updraft of air made it look as if they were waving their limbs in desperation, then the bodies turned into a darkly glowing heap, shapeless lumps seen through a curtain of fire.

The flames had hardly died down before souvenir-seekers started raking the hot ashes for keepsakes and carried off the bones to grind up and hawk as magic powder. Alonso watched them in cold horror. The spectacle made his skin crawl. It was an evil omen. Was this the fate that awaited his father? No news had reached him from Las Palmas after the letter delivered by the Arab. Perhaps he should make discreet inquiries through the Franciscan. *Trust no one*, his father had written. No one? Nor even a fellow scholar? Surely Natale would not turn on him. Surely he would not blame him for worrying about his family. No one could twist a son's love for his father into an act of heresy, or could he?

Alonso turned to his companion. Natale met his eyes calmly.

"You look shaken," he said, "but what we saw here was divine justice. Those men relapsed into Judaism and refused to recant. It is the first concern of the Inquisition to bring the lost sheep back into the fold of the Church, but if they are unrepentant..."

"And if they were innocent? If the accusations were false? If they were denounced by malicious neighbours?"

In Seville, as in other cities of Spain, the Inquisition appealed to the faithful, inviting them to come forward and denounce those who sinned against the Holy Catholic faith. The appeals were posted on every church door, striking the fear of God into the congregation.

And all you, who conceal heretics, will be proceeded against as abettors, excommunicated and cursed. The wrath of the Almighty God will strike you down. Your possessions will be enjoyed by others, and your children will be orphans, and your wives widows. And likewise the houses you inhabit and the clothing you wear and the beds upon which you sleep and the tables upon which you eat: let them be cursed and ruined, and may your wickedness be remembered on the Day of Judgment.

It was a powerful warning and posted together with a list of suspect behaviour: changing into clean linen on Saturdays, kindling lights on Friday evening, eating unleavened bread and bitter herbs, standing up before a wall when saying prayers, shrinking from eating pork, hares, snails or fish that had no scales, cutting sinews out of meat, taking a morsel of dough when baking and throwing it into the fire – those were the practices that betrayed Jews who had relapsed into their old religion.

"If those men had been falsely accused," Natale said, "the tribunal would have acquitted them. The *Suprema* makes no mistakes."

No, I cannot confide in Natale, the doctor thought. I will heed my father's warning. *Trust no one.*

***

A week went by before Natale called on Alonso again.

The doctor was leafing through medical books, reading up on a rare condition he had detected in one of his patients. Four tomes were laid out on the oaken table in his study, ready for consultation: the *Recepta Varia*, a collection of essays on blood-letting, surgery, and diagnosis by pulse and urine, Avicenna's *Canon of Medicine,* an all-encompassing work, Isaac Israeli ben Solomon's *Liber Pantegni,* and a volume containing the writings of the Greek physician Galen.

Natale stepped up to the table, eyed the books, and in passing brushed his fingers against the *Liber Pantegni.*

"If I were you," he said to Alonso, "I'd put that book away. Or are you so fond of the old rabbis that you cannot let them out of your sight?"

"I honour them for their knowledge, and you too may thank the old rabbis one day when you seek my medical advice and benefit from the skill their books taught me."

"May that day be far off," Natale said. "My health is excellent, thank God." His florid com-plexion and his wheeze, as he lowered himself into the chair, told Alonso otherwise. The man enjoyed food and drink a little too much for his own good.

"It's not me I'm worried about," the Franciscan said. "It's you."

"And what is the reason for your concern?"

"I hardly know how to tell you, my dear Alonso. I wanted to give you a piece of information that came my way yesterday. No, *wanted* is the wrong word, for what I heard will come as a great shock to you. I very much regret being the bearer of grave news, but I felt obliged to come and tell you nevertheless. Better to hear it from a friend who can console you, I thought, than from an official who does not care about your feelings or your livelihood."

The Franciscans' words filled Alonso with dread. He was afraid for his family ever since he had heard that his father was caught in the web of the Inquisition. Natale's long preamble did not bode well, and the doctor prepared himself for sinister news.

"A visitor from Las Palmas told me that your father has been condemned to death for relapsing into Judaism, and that the customary punishment will be visited on your family."

The words entered the doctor's head like a ruinous noise, a thunderclap shaking his core. In a flash he saw his father tied to the stake and relived the scene he had witnessed in the Plaza Mayor, the fiery death of the three Jews. He fought the hallucinatory flames and forced himself to attend to the Franciscan's words, *and the customary punishment will be visited on the family.* Yes, he knew the punishment meted out to the family of relapsed Jews. The goods in his father's shop would be sequestered to pay for the cost of his incarceration and trial. His female descendants were barred from wearing silk or jewelry, his male descendants from practising any profession for the duration of ten years. The judgment would leave his mother impoverished, his sisters shunned, and himself unable to offer them help because he could no longer practice his profession. He had lost his livelihood at the stroke of the inquisitor's pen, the same pen that had deprived his father of his life.

He felt Natale's hand on his arm. The tips of his fingers were soft and warm. Alonso looked into the Franciscan's pudgy face, but his expression was opaque. It wasn't compassion that lit his eyes. It was a curious watchfulness, almost as if he was observing an alchemist's experiment and recording the outcome. But what was he recording –Alonso's grief?

"Don't despair," Natale said, squeezing his arm. "There is nothing you can do for your father now except pray for his soul, but you can do something for yourself. Come with me to Alcala and petition the Inquisitor General for an exemption from the judgment. It isn't impossible. I've heard of cases in which the Cardinal granted immunity."

"And I have heard that he is an inveterate enemy of the Jews."

"But you aren't a Jew, my friend. You are a Christian." Natale let the words hang in the air between them, as if they were a question. Are you a Christian?

"A dispensation will protect me against legal harassment. It will not shield me from prejudice. If as much as a rumour of the judgment reaches my patients, they will desert me. And if they continue to patronize me, the parish priest will bully them and threaten them with excommunication for associating with a man whose father has been declared a heretic."

"Discretion is necessary, of course," Natale said. "There is no reason why the judgment should become common knowledge. My informant is no longer in town, and he mentioned the matter only because I inquired about your family. I told him that a man of my acquaintance had moved to Las Palmas. Did he by any chance know Isaiah Malki? The man said he had heard of him, but in a most unfortunate context, and told me about the trial."

"Then what is your advice?"

"Don't wait until you are officially notified. Use a dodge. Announce that you have decided to go on a pilgrimage to the shrine of Santiago de Compostela. Say you are fulfilling an old pledge. Then come with me to Alcala. We'll have plenty of time on the journey to talk about your affairs, the judgment of the Inquisition, and whatever else is on your mind, and plenty of time to devise a strategy how best to approach Cisneros."

Alonso shook his head. "Asking for a dispensation feels like a betrayal, as if I wanted to dissociate myself from my father and acknowledge that he committed a crime."

"Are you saying that the Inquisition was wrong to condemn him?"

That is exactly what Alonso was thinking, and it took a great deal of self-discipline not to blurt it out. Instead, he silently shook his head and lowered his eyes, afraid of what Natale might read in them.

"Then think about my advice," Natale said. "But don't delay. I'll be leaving in four days with a caravan of merchants. It's the safest way to travel, as you know, and time is of the essence in your affairs."

Alonso accompanied his visitor to the door and stood under the porch, watching him saunter away. It was an overcast night, and the receding figure of the Franciscan was soon swallowed up by darkness and melted into the night. Alonso turned back into the house and tried to shake off the desolate thoughts going in his mind like winding sheets around a corpse. Natale's advice is sound, he thought. I must not let despair get the better of me. He tried to overcome his grief with logic. What was the next practical step? Make the rounds of his patients and explain that he was going on a pilgrimage, supply them with a stock of potions and salves and arrange with an apothecary to take his place for a period of, say, two months. Discreetly convert his valuables into ready money, since there might be a need to grease palms. Pay the owner of the house the quarterly rent in advance, although, God knows, rumour and prejudice might force him to leave Seville even if he was successful in obtaining an exemption from the judgment.

Planning ahead calmed Alonso, but reason loses its power after midnight when the shadows of darkness descend on a man's soul. Alonso prided himself on being a man of science and not easily overwhelmed by fantastic dreams, but that night he fell prey to a disturbing vision.

He found himself wandering through a place of echoes and shadows. Suddenly the murky darkness lit up, and two figures appeared in a halo of crackling flames. He recognized his father and, beside him, a mysterious young woman whose beautiful pale face was streaming with tears. Flames threatened to engulf the pair. The old man's hand glowed like iron softened on an anvil. He placed it on the girl's head in a gesture of blessing. "Don't weep, my daughter," he said. Soon both were caught in a vortex of flames, but before Alonso lost sight of them, his father raised a finger to him in caution: "Remember Rashi's advice," he said: "first prayer, then bribes, and lastly combat." But perhaps it was the woman who said the words, for surely his father would have quoted Rashi in Hebrew.

Alonso was awoken by the clanging bells from the cathedral, dinning a message into his ears: "Al-ca-la! Al-ca-la!" He opened his eyes and stared in confusion at the gray light of dawn filtering through the shutters of his bedroom window. Regaining possession of his senses, he realized that he had heard only the metal tongues of the church bells, a sound without words, and that the young woman had been a dream image. The fumes of an unsettled mind, he told himself, and yet his heart was pounding, and the figure of the dream woman was haunting the room. The echo of his father's voice quivered in the air. Alonso would have pushed aside the nocturnal vision as empty vapours, had it not been for filial love. Alonso's father had been a firm believer in prophetic dreams. Respect for his memory would not allow Alonso to dismiss the dream out of hand. Could it be that the souls of the departed were able to communicate with the living, that a father's love transcended death? Was the ancient poet Lucretius right when he said that the world consisted of atoms in constant flux, never decaying, forever reconstituting themselves? And who was the young woman, weeping for his father – or was she weeping for him? Alonso pondered these questions, but could find no logical answer and was obliged at last to suspend judgment. He had a more pressing question to solve: how to preserve his livelihood. But the dream held him in thrall, and the bells tolling Al-ca-la were like a confirmation: Natale's plan of action was right for him. I will go to Alcala, he thought, and petition the Inquisitor General for an exemption from the judgment.

***

Three days later Alonso departed, wearing a wide-brimmed pilgrim's hat, and carrying a pilgrim's staff and bundle containing a coat, blanket, and provisions for the journey. But, tightly wrapped up and hidden in the folds of the bundle, was the family Bible. His father had hoped it would preserve Alonso's soul. Alonso hoped it would preserve his livelihood as well. He thought of his father's dream counsel: *First prayer, then bribes, and lastly, combat.* He had said his prayers. Now it was time to offer a bribe to the Inquisitor General. The Bible was a handsome present and might persuade Cisneros to grant Alonso's petition. It seemed his only hope at the time, although the dream also mentioned combat. Will it come to that? he thought. I am ill equipped for fighting, but if I must, I will fight for my livelihood, for my honour, and for the memory of my father.

Anyone observing Alonso on the journey would have been surprised to see him stop in Carmona, exchange his hat and staff for a plain cape, buy a gray gelding, and continue his journey in a different direction, riding toward Alcala – anyone would have been surprised except Natale who was in the doctor's confidence and greeted him with alacrity when he arrived at the inn where the merchants had stopped for the night.

The next day, an unvarying landscape of freshly ploughed fields and pastures stretched before the travellers as they rode along the open road and passed through sleepy villages. Alonso was glad of Natale's company. The Franciscan was a master in the art of conversation. He could talk on any subject, mundane, scientific, or sublime, but it was diversion that Alonso wanted rather than serious discussion. Natale seemed to have gauged his mood. Bobbing along on a little mule, as stout as the rider, he made light conversation. He talked about his childhood and youth and told Alonso more about himself than he had told him in all the years they had known each other. *He is making a special effort to lighten my mood*, the doctor thought. *He wants to tell me that I am not alone in my misfortune, that I have a friend in him, that he is my ally.* Alonso certainly needed a friend, but he could not erase from his mind the warning his father had given him. *Trust no one*.

Before the sun had reached its zenith, Natale had recounted the story of his life – a version of it, at any rate, for it sounded rather well rehearsed and did not lack rhetorical embellishments. He had been raised in a wealthy household, he said, and owed his education to his Neapolitan father, a courtier in King Ferdinand's service. He learned from him a love for ancient literature but also a love of luxury.

"I developed a palate for dainty food, a liking for soft beds, and a gentleman's refined taste for objects of beauty," he said. "I lived a dream of wealth and expectations, and had a rude awakening. When my father died, I discovered that he had run through his fortune and lived on borrowed money. I was a poor man. What could I do but seek refuge in the arms of Mother Church? Entering the church requires less capital than entering a business."

"Less capital, perhaps, but large collateral in piety," Alonso said.

"My dear friend," Natale said with good humour, "if you mean chastity, that is a habit quickly acquired."

Chastity may indeed come easy to a capon like Natale, the doctor thought, observing the Franciscan's peachy complexion and beardless chin. "And poverty as well?" he asked.

"Ah, there's the rub," Natale said, fluttering his fingers and puffing out his cheeks. "I did find it hard to resign myself to poverty. And I am still fending off dreams of opulence, of a library full of ancient manuscripts and cabinets full of beautiful objects, chiseled silver, carved ivory, fine porcelain from China. I covet beauty, and that desire is not easy to uproot. Nor is the temptation to follow one's own will. The vow of obedience I took as a friar has always been a challenge."

"Was your Superior hard to please then?" Alonso asked.

"Oh, he was satisfied as long as I gave due consideration to his rank," Natale said. "It's the ritual that I can't bear. There are a thousand rules a Franciscan has to obey to demonstrate the discipline of his mind and the purity of his faith. I for one do not wish to have my faith defined by the hours I spend on my knees in prayer, by the colour of my habit, by the knots in my cingle. Faith is an inner quality, don't you think? It must not be made subject to man's scrutiny and judgment."

Natale had never spoken so freely, and Alonso was astonished by his candor. He heartily agreed that conscience should not be subject to human judgment, but a man in his circumstances could hardly afford to question the practices of the church. Yet he could not help saying:

"But isn't that exactly what the inquisitor does? Scrutinize men's hearts and pass judgment on them? And did you not reprove me for doubting the Inquisition's judgment?"

"I wish there was no need for the Inquisition," Natale said. "For centuries Moors, Jews, and Christians lived together peacefully – what, I ask you, happened to the principle of *convivencia*, which has been hailed by our forefathers? Why can't we live together in peace? I would go as far as asking: Is it so important to celebrate the Lord's Day rather than the Sabbath, to recite the gospels rather than the psalms? Is not the God of the Old Testament the same as the God of the New?"

Natale's shrewd eyes rested on Alonso's face.

"I'll leave those questions to you," he said. "I don't know anything about theology." In truth, he had no taste for theology, the science that reduced God to a set of barren rules and curtailed the freedom of men to think.

Natale gave him a cherubic smile. "You are too modest, my dear Alonso. I've heard you argue theological questions very competently."

"I wouldn't call it arguing. I am not knowledgeable enough to give a decided opinion. I may have cited the opinion of Thomas Aquinas or some other authority." Alonso knew very well: Arguing about theology was a dangerous game. Dare to question any article of faith and the theologians will call you a heretic. Alonso's quest for the truth was an interior journey, hidden from the tyranny of the church.

"All I know about the subject is what I learned from a student of theology," he said. "We shared a room when I was at the University of Salamanca. He believed that reading aloud was the best way of mastering his subject. Night after night, he rehearsed the answers to the questions on which he expected to be examined. By the time he obtained his license, he had dinned the whole of Aquinas' *Summa Summarum* into my ears."

"Then you are living proof for your roommate's theory that hearing is memorizing. Or else you are a natural theologian."

"Hardly natural. I was required to study dialectics and hone my debating skills like every other undergraduate, but I never had a taste for subtle questions. And today my logical exercises are confined to the diagnosis of illness: if symptoms A and B are present, it follows that the patient suffers from condition C. And my observations do not concern the soul but much coarser materials, indeed the coarsest of them all: blood, urine, and feces."

And he began to discourse at length on the qualities of the stool, its consistency, rapidity of desiccation, odor, form, and frequency, hoping to put an end to Natale's questions which might have led a less cautious man into the thickets of heresy. But in the days that followed, the Franciscan often reverted to the subject of theology. It was as if he was testing Alonso's faith. He was clearly enjoying the game, if that's what he was playing. Every question he posed seemed to lead into turbulent waters, and Alonso was often reduced to seek the safe haven of silence.

The convoy reached the flat terrain of the meseta, which heralded Toledo. Riding along the grassland dotted with grazing livestock and the plantations of gnarled olive trees, the two men fell once more into the kind of conversation Alonso liked best. They talked of their common love of books and their admiration for the classics. Natale praised the ancient Roman poet Ovid and entertained his companion with quotations from his immortal verses. He knew them by heart and recited them with glee.

"You remember the poem of Thisbe straying into a cave and catching sight of a lion," he said and intoned in a husky voice: *"Vidit et ob-scu-rum."* He puckered his mouth and drew out the dark vowels to intimate the yawning cave. *"Timido pede fugit in antrum,"* he trilled, echoing the quick steps of the fleeing girl.

The man is a born actor, Alonso thought. A slight misgiving entered his heart. Was Natale's cherubic face just a mask? But he dismissed his suspicions. The cruel fate of my father has shaken my confidence, he thought, and makes me fearful of every shadow. I sense danger where there is none.

Natale came to the end of his recital. "Not to your taste?" he asked, seeing Alonso's clouded face. "I'm afraid I have no medical writers in my repertoire, doctor, whereas you are laying in a good supply, I see." He pointed to Alonso's saddle bags. "Or are you trying to weigh down your horse so it won't gallop away with you?"

"Yes, the book stalls of Cordoba have yielded a rich harvest," the doctor said. "I've come away with an obstetrical treatise by Trota of Salerno and a Latin translation of Galen. And to sweeten the deal, the bookseller gave me a volume of Prudentius' verses. I hope to find the book stores of Toledo equally well stocked."

They had reached the outskirts of Toledo and, after crossing the Tagus River, passed into the city through a gate braced by thick stone walls. The vestiges of history were everywhere, the Roman aqueduct, the Moorish alcazar, and the grand synagogues converted into churches now.

"Let us spend the night at the monastery of San Juan de los Reyes," Natale said. "The abbot has a splendid collection of manuscripts and may allow us to inspect his library – unless, of course, you are averse to narrow beds and scant dinners, for a monastery does not offer the comforts of an inn."

"I shall gladly trade a comfortable bed for a view of the abbot's treasures," Alonso said. Indeed no lodging, however luxurious, could assure him of a good night's sleep. It made no difference to him whether the mattress was stuffed with straw or horsehair, the pillow hard or soft as eiderdown, the blanket rough or smooth. His rest was disturbed, not by rough bedding, but by grief over his family's misfortunes and by apprehension for his own future. He often woke in the dead of night with a feeling of oppression and foreboding, his mind tortured by images of death. Every night, phantasmagoric dreams descended on him, gruesome visions of his father engulfed in flames, his body writhing, his skin breaking open and exposing his bones, his blood boiling, and by the side of the pyre a weeping woman, her exquisite face pale and translucent, her eyes blazing and her black hair smooth and shiny like a wet stone. Sometimes she stretched out her arms and awoke in Alonso a burning desire for her embrace. At other times she spoke in a low sweet voice and filled him with longing. He wanted to follow her, to fulfill her every wish, but he could not make out her message. Her loving words were carried away into the roaring inferno. A lingering memory of the dream woman followed him in his waking hours and hovered about him like a shadow. But of this he said nothing to Natale.

CHAPTER 2

THE MONASTERY OF SAN JUAN DE LOS REYES HAD been built only recently, according to the plans of the architect Juan Guas. Natale and Alonso stood in the high, light-filled nave of the church and marveled at the flamboyantly carved stone pillars. The hexagonal tower with its delicate lacework of stone was still awaiting the final touches of the workmen.

From the church, they walked through the courtyard to the cloister of the Franciscans. The abbot welcomed them and, after a dinner of watery stew and coarse bread, brought out a more generous repast, indeed a royal feast for their eyes: his books. Once he saw the keen interest of his visitors, he took the most precious manuscripts from the tall shelves that lined his study and laid them out on a table: the works of Jerome and

Augustine, Ambrose's treatise on resurrection, Gregory's dialogues, and the biblical commentaries of Thomas Aquinas. As the abbot proudly pointed out the finely stencilled bindings and rubricated edges, Natale's eyes narrowed. He looked at the manuscripts hungrily, with the concentration of a thievish magpie. His nostrils were dilated, inhaling with relish the scent of parchment pervading the room. Alonso observed him silently and once again felt a tingling in his breast, a silent warning against a man who showed such gluttonous delight, such abandon, such unrestrained passion. There is murder in the heart of such a man, he thought, but immediately rebuked himself for the irrational leap. The fact that Natale coveted books did not make him a murderer. He did have a thievish glint in his eyes when he looked at the abbot's treasures, but he wasn't the man to translate such thoughts into action. He was harmless, a talker, not a doer.

"But here is a manuscript I don't bring out very often," the abbot said, smiling mysteriously, as he unlocked an iron-bound chest and unfurled a scroll. The ancient parchment was covered with Hebrew letters.

Natale licked his dry lips and nodded with-out looking up. All his senses were occupied. His eyes caressed the scroll.

The abbot gave Alonso a sideway glance. "I thought *you* might be interested in this," he said. "It contains the first five books of the Old Testament. I am told it is called a Torah and venerated by all Jews."

He looked at Alonso with barely concealed suspicion. Alonso groaned inwardly. It was as if his face bore the mark of Cain.

"The Torah is used in prayer services," he said, concealing his anguish and keeping his voice level. "But my family converted to Christianity when I was a child, and I have long ago discarded the old customs."

"Oh?" the abbot said. "Is it that easy to abandon the traditions of one's forefathers? I for one would find it hard to exchange one religion for another." He turned his attention back to the scroll. "The Hebrew language itself is perverted. The words are written from right to left, I am told. Is that true?"

"It is."

"I, for one, do not trust that diabolical script. I have never shown it to any of my monks. Who knows – the ungodly letters might infect their eyes even if they cannot read the words. For none of us here knows Hebrew, thank God."

He looked at the scroll darkly. "If it were up to me," he said with severity, "I would do away with Hebrew books; burn the whole lot of them."

"Would you destroy such beauty?" Natale said like a man awaking from a dream. He ran his fingers over the polished wood of the scroll and sighed.

"If you have such grave misgivings about Hebrew books," Alonso said to the abbot, "I would advise you to show the scroll to Cardinal Cisneros and let him decide whether your library is a suitable repository for the manuscript. He is surrounded by theologians and will be able to put your scruples to rest. Fray Natale and I are on our way to Alcala. Allow us to take the scroll to the prelate and inquire into his views on your behalf."

The abbot looked at Alonso with palpable relief and was about to hand over the scroll, when hesitation overcame him. "It is a precious object, and part of the monastery's treasures," he said. "I loathe the thing myself, but I would not want to deprive the monastery of a valuable asset."

"I cannot blame you for refusing to entrust a treasure to a man you hardly know," Alonso said. "Perhaps it would content you if I left behind a gold florin as surety. If His Eminence, the Cardinal, decides that there is no harm in keeping the scroll in your library, I shall return it on my way back and redeem the gold piece. If he should decide that it is unsuitable, I am willing to reimburse you for the loss and regard it as a treasure laid up in heaven."

"And I," Natale said, recovering his wits, "can vouch for the Christian character of my companion."

The abbot made feeble protestations, but Alonso knew he had won his case. When they departed for Alcala the following day, the abbot had accepted the florin, and the Torah was stowed in Alonso's saddlebag with his other books.

"A fair bargain," Natale said with an ironic grin. "You have acquired a rare manuscript, and the abbot has been relieved of his anxieties. It was a clever move, doctor. I wish I could have made that offer myself, but then I do not have gold florins at my disposal, and the abbot would have looked askance at a Franciscan who did."

***

They reached Alcala and made their way through the narrow streets where riders jostled for space with carts and oxen, and the sharp cries of street hawkers mingled with the guffaws, haggling voices and boisterous shouts of passers-by. It was time for the two men to go their separate ways—Alonso to procure a room at an inn, Natale to report to the house of the Franciscans—but before they parted, the doctor took from his saddlebag the volume of Prudentius' poems. There aren't many Franciscans who will stand by a Jew, he thought, and handed the book to Natale.

"A small token of my friendship," he said.

The Franciscan's eyes lit up. "This is unexpected kindness!" he said. "You are most generous." But he hesitated to accept the gift.

"If you have scruples, and the possession of a book of poetry violates the rule of your Order, regard it as a long-term loan."

"Ah," Natale said. "You are a man of understanding, Alonso." He took the slim volume from the doctor's hands and looked at it lovingly. "I cannot thank you enough," he said and hugged the book to his chest. "I wish I could express my gratitude in some tangible form, and perhaps I can. I shall keep my ear to the ground at any rate, and if I hear of anything that might promote your cause, I shall let you know."

Seeing Natale's great pleasure, the doctor felt he had done the right thing, and they parted with mutual good wishes and a promise to meet again in a day or two.

It was the feast day of Corpus Christi, and the city was in a celebratory mood. The houses along the route of the Corpus Christi procession were hung with precious tapestries. Tables had been brought out onto the pavement displaying silver statues and vermeil ornaments for the greater glory of Christ.

After arranging for his lodging, Alonso joined the spectators that thronged the road, waiting for the procession to pass. Twelve choirboys clothed as angels and four postulants representing the evangelists came first. They were followed by the canons of the cathedral of Alcala, carrying the relics of saints in jeweled cases. The decorated float bearing the Holy Sacrament came next, shrouded in the perfumed mist of frankincense. Behind the float and the altar boys swinging censers, the Cardinal and his retinue walked in measured steps.

The balconies and loggias on both sides of the street were dressed with embroidered cloth and crowded with onlookers. Alonso's attention was caught by a slender young woman. She was sitting by the side of her aya. She lowered her fan when the aya reached across to drape a shawl around her shoulders, and with a shock Alonso recognized her exquisite features. She was the young woman he had seen in his dreams, who had appeared by the side of his father in a halo of flames. No, surely his eyes were playing him a trick!

A chill ran through his body. There was something mesmerizing in the young woman's eyes. He could not stop looking at her luminous face. He was stricken with her beauty and the wonder of seeing the woman of his dreams in the flesh. She fastened her gaze on Alonso—or so it seemed to him—and smiled a bewitching smile. As he was staring at her with a strange longing, the procession suddenly came to a halt and the celebrants parted in confusion. A man wearing the Franciscan garb had sunk to the ground and was lying on the pavement, unconscious. Two friars lifted him up and carried him to the side of the road.

With difficulty, Alonso turned his eyes from the dream woman's face. She had risen from her seat and was looking down on the unconscious man with pity. Her mouth was drawn into the shape of a rosebud, breathing a soft Oh!

The sick man shuddered and moaned as if he had been pierced by an arrow.

The crowd parted to make way for him and his bearers. A woman standing beside Alonso stepped back hastily, held a handkerchief to her mouth and murmured: "God have mercy on us and protect us from the sweating sickness."

Alonso recovered his bearings and remembered the Hippocratic Oath which obliged all practitioners of medicine to come to the aid of the sick.

"I am a physician," he said to the friars and offered his help. He gave directions to carry the ailing man into a shop. The owner admitted the bearers with ill grace, but on Alonso's insistence permitted them to lay the sick man on a bench.

Alonso pulled open the man's robe to allow him to breathe more freely and saw that he was wearing a coarsely woven hair shirt and a spiked metal belt that had pricked his waist. His emaciated body bore marks of the whip.

A flagellant, Alonso thought, and pitied the man. He was one of those unhappy creatures tormented by self-loathing and the nagging sensation of worthlessness, from which only severe penance could release them. They thought they were diminished by their carnal desires and mortified their flesh with lengthy fasts, prayers and floggings to bring their sinful mind to heel.

It was not difficult to diagnose the man's condition. His body was weakened by the self-inflicted injuries and the austere regimen he had imposed on himself.

Alonso loosened the spiked belt and listened to the patient's breathing return to normal. The man regained consciousness, opened his eyes and tried to sit up, but sank back exhausted.

"You have dangerously weakened your body, my friend," Alonso said.

"No," the Franciscan answered, "it is the Devil who has weakened and tempted me, but I have recovered from his onslaught. Still, I thank you for your kind attendance when others, naturally enough, would shrink from me, fearing I had a contagious disease."

In the meantime one of the friar's companions had fetched a mule to carry the ailing man home. The Franciscan rose with determination and declined all further help. "I can manage by myself," he said to his companions. "See that the doctor is compensated for his services."

Alonso let him go reluctantly. He urged one of the man's companions, who had stayed behind, to keep an eye on the patient. "He must rest and keep warm, and gradually strengthen his body with broth and mulled wine."

"Martin Casalius will hardly take instructions from me," the friar replied.

"Then perhaps I should follow him to the monastery and give instructions to whoever is in charge of the kitchen."

"I see you are a stranger in our town," the man said. "Fray Martin does not live at the Franciscan House. His rooms are in the Cardinal's palace, and I can assure you he will receive proper care there."

***

The inn where Alonso had obtained lodgings was comfortable enough, but it did not keep away his nightmares. The next morning he woke up from another foreboding dream of dark sepulchers and fiery angels and a pale vision of the woman he had seen on the balcony, stretching out her arms to him and begging him to stay by her side. With the echo of her pitiful cries still ringing in his ears, he made his way to the Cardinal's palace. He puzzled over the intricate connection between dreams and reality, the woman he had seen at the Corpus Christi procession and his longing for her embrace, but he was too fatigued to pursue the connection. His body felt bloodless, and his stomach weighed down by the stones of grief, as he set out on his errand to obtain an audience with Cisneros.

    The great walls of the Cardinal's palace looked grim in the early morning light. Alonso passed through the wrought-iron gate leading to an inner courtyard. The square was already crowded with petitioners, resigned to waiting out the day in weariness. Two stray dogs were nosing around as if they had a secret order to sniff out heresy.

    Alonso approached the guard stationed at the door, stated his business, and was admitted to a cavernous foyer. The heavy oaken doors closed behind him, shutting out the din of the courtyard. Crossing the echoing marble floor, he handed his petition to an usher and saw it placed at the bottom of a stack of similar papers. No doubt he had a long wait ahead. He recalled that the Franciscan he had attended lived at the palace and, on the spur of the moment, decided to look up his patient and pass the time in a useful manner at least.

    He asked to see Martin Casalius.

    The usher eyed him skeptically.

"Do you have an appointment?" he said, and Alonso understood that the Franciscan was a more important man than he had realized.

"I would like to inquire after his health," he said. "I am a physician and was in attendance on him yesterday."

The usher took his name upstairs and returned with a message, which he delivered with a respectful bow. Martin Casalius regretted not being able to see the doctor at once, but requested the pleasure of his company at noon.

At the appointed hour, the usher conducted Alonso up a flight of stairs to the Franciscan's office. He was at his desk, bent over a stack of letters. When Alonso was shown in, he laid them aside and rose to greet the doctor.

"I am sorry I could not see you earlier," he said. "My work is pressing. Letters, assignments, and contracts awaiting the prelate's signature, budget items to be approved, details of a building plan gone awry – it's a never-ending stream of business. But as you can see, I am following your advice and breaking my fast."

He conducted Alonso to a table set for two in an alcove of the room. A servant placed bowls of barley soup and thick-cut bread before them. The Franciscan dipped a crust into the soup and ate with the contentment of a man who had earned his daily bread. Alonso joined him in his frugal meal and brought the conversation around to the Franciscan's health.

"I am better," Martin Casalius said.

"And you sleep well?"

"Unfortunately not. I am plagued by ominous dreams. What do you think is the root cause of nightmares, doctor? Do you have a theory to explain them?"

Alonso started at this unexpected question. The subject of nightmares was one on which he needed advice himself. He was hardly qualified to counsel others. "It is difficult to make a general pronouncement," he said, "but they often ac-company a fever."

"The Bible says: It is in dreams that *God reveals unto his servant the things that must come to pass.* But perhaps Satan is tempting me, and my dreams are a case of *Be wise and beware of the wiles of the Devil.*"

Alonso shook his head. "I am a physician, Fray Martin. I deal with men's bodies, not their souls."

"That is why I value your opinion. I have told my dreams to a confessor. He granted that they might be prophetic visions. After all, the prophets saw the truth through a veil of dreams, but the Old Testament was given for a time only. We are people of the New Testament. The Word is revealed to us clearly through Christ. We have no need for dreams and soothsayers." Martin sighed. "That is what my confessor said. His answer gave me no comfort, and so I am taking a two-pronged approach to my troubles. I pray to God to heal my diseased soul, and I consult you, a physician, in case a bodily disease is playing a role here as well."

If I cannot rid myself of my own nightmares, Alonso thought, how likely is it that I can cure this man whom I hardly know? But he fetched a deep breath and said: "Very well. I'll try my best. Tell me about your nightmares."

"It is a repetitive dream, a vision of two persons in a room full of shadows. One is a young woman in great distress. Suddenly a man in priestly robes appears beside her and says as if pronouncing a verdict: *Sponsae vita nuptiis tollenda.* It is an ambiguous phrase since the Latin verb *tollere* can mean either to raise up or to erase. The verdict could therefore be *Marriage will destroy the bride*, or *Marriage will uplift the bride*."

"The message of nightmares is often ambiguous because they flow from a disturbed mind," Alonso said. "But in the case of marriage, the ambiguity is in the nature of things, is it not? A good husband may uplift his wife. An evil man may cast her down and even destroy her. We need no prophetic dreams to tell us to be careful in choosing a husband for a young woman. It is common sense. The ominous dream may reflect your own worries if you know the young woman in question and care about her future."

Martin hesitated. Clearly he knew the woman who haunted his dreams. At last he said: "I care for the salvation of her soul, as I care for that of every man or woman. But the dream has a sinister aspect. Is it my duty to warn her, I wonder, and would speaking up put an end to my nightmares?"

Perhaps he is enthralled with his dream woman as I am with mine, Alonso thought, but his vows forbid all passion. Perhaps he tortures and beats himself to atone for his sinful thoughts. In that case, talking to the object of his infatuation will not cure him of his nightmares.

"If your fears for the woman are grounded in reality and you think she is about to marry an unsuitable partner, speak up by all means," he said. "Otherwise I see no need to act on your dreams. If they are the consequence of an illness, rest and a healthy diet will alleviate the symptoms. But if you believe that your dreams are prophetic, I cannot advise you. I leave such things to theologians."

"I will have to give the matter more thought," the Franciscan said. He got up and rang for his servant to clear the table. "It was kind of you to look me up, doctor. I hope I haven't taken you too far out of your way."

"Not at all," Alonso said. "In fact, I have business here. I have come to Alcala as a petitioner and in the hope that His Eminence will grant me an audience."

"In that case, I can repay your kind attention. I am the Cardinal's private secretary. There are many petitioners, and the wait for an audience with His Eminence may be long. I shall write a note on your behalf, and ask the usher to admit you in a timely manner."

***

Alonso made his way back to the entrance hall and handed the secretary's note to the usher. It had the desired effect. The man conducted Alonso to an antechamber and assured him that his wait would not be long.

The room was deserted except for a bearded man with rugged features, clad in the black robes of a scholar. He stood in the embrasure of the window, looking out on the courtyard. He gave Alonso a glance, nodded, and turned back to his silent watch. The usher returned, and the scholar stepped forward in the expectation of being called, but the summons was for Alonso. The man arrested his step, allowing the doctor to pass. His forehead was wrinkled in surprise and dismay.

Alonso was shown into a long, high-ceilinged room with an apse at the far end. He had envisioned the Cardinal surrounded by books, but his study was bare except for heavy ebony chests lining the walls and concealing their content behind thick paneled doors. No carpet cushioned the caller's step. The stone floor was worn and polished by the feet of a thousand supplicants. Three tall windows illuminated the desk where the Cardinal sat, bent over an open book. The slanting rays gave him a saintly aura. The remainder of the room was enveloped in dusky obscurity.

Cisneros received his visitor without rising from the desk or taking his eyes off the breviary before him. He went on reading, tracing with his finger a passage in the book. When he reached the bottom of the page, he looked up, nodded curtly in Alonso's direction and asked him to state his business.

"My name is Alonso Malki." The doctor spoke hesitantly, unable to keep a tremor out of his voice. He was standing before the man who held his fate in his hands. "I have been told that Your Eminence takes a scholarly interest in biblical manuscripts," he said. "I have in my possession two ancient codices and would regard it a great honour if they found a place in Your Eminence's library."

He had brought with him the family Bible and the Torah from the abbot's library and was ready to submit them to the prelate.

The Cardinal made no answer but motioned Alonso to advance.

He placed the two manuscripts before the prelate, stepped back and waited respectfully for his response. The Cardinal examined Alonso's family Bible with an experienced eye, paged through it, lifted it up to peer at the colophon, and finally raised his head to look at Alonso. His eyes were narrow-set and sunken. His lips may have been capable of a smile once upon a time, but a habitual look of severity had deepened the lines around his mouth and gave his face the chiseled look of stone.

"How did these manuscripts come into your possession?" he asked, and Alonso told him of their provenance.

The Cardinal rose to his feet and walked up and down the length of his study in deep thought. He was an oddly proportioned man, with narrow shoulders and a long, low-shanked body. The hem of his gold-embroidered robe curled as he walked, revealing plain leather sandals. Alonso remembered what he had been told of Cisneros. He wore ornate robes to honour God, and beneath them a coarse linen tunic and sandals to honour St. Francis, the founder of his Order.

Cisneros stopped abruptly before the doctor and said in a voice betraying neither interest nor hostility: "Do you expect a favour in return for the manuscripts?"

Alonso looked at the Cardinal uneasily. His porous eyes, reflecting only the sacral light of the room, gave no hint of his meaning. Alonso let out a hard breath and said: "If I may speak candidly, yes, I have come to ask a favour of Your Eminence."

The Cardinal's features softened. "Candor is what I require in a man," he said. "What is your request?"

Alonso explained his predicament. "I am a physician," he said. "My father was condemned by the Inquisition. The verdict includes the usual punishment, depriving his descendants of the right to practice their profession. This means the loss of my livelihood. I have come to plead with Your Eminence for an exemption from the judgment."

The cardinal returned to his desk and opened the Hebrew Bible. Pointing to a passage, he said: "Read these lines and interpret them."

Alonso thanked his good fortune for having shared quarters with a student of theology, but even so the tongue in his mouth went soft with fear as he read out the passage and began the exposition. "The prophecy," he said, "foreshadows the coming of Christ and was fulfilled by him." And he quoted in support of his interpretation the authority of the Church Fathers and of Thomas Aquinas.

The cardinal's stern look changed to one of kindness. "I see you are a Christian and a man of erudition," he said when Alonso had finished his exegesis. "You deserve the exemption for which you have asked. I shall direct my secretary to prepare the necessary papers."

Alonso began thanking him, but the Cardinal held up his hand. "A thought has occurred to me. You are a native speaker of Hebrew. I have need of a man with your skills for a project I have in hand: a polyglot edition of the Bible."

Alonso bowed. "I have heard of the great endeavour. It is in the mouths of all learned men," he said, "but I fear I have little to contribute to such an undertaking. I am not a biblical scholar."

"Your modesty is commendable," the Cardinal said, "but I am not asking you to do the work of a philologist or a theologian. I want you to assist others with passages that require a native speaker's sensitivity to idiom. The work I have in mind will not occupy much of your time or engage you in the long run. The project is well advanced and will, I hope, come to fruition within a year or two. I expect you to continue working in your profession now that I have granted you an exemption. Offer your medical services to the citizens of

Alcala and, who knows, you may find the city a congenial place to set up a practice."

"In that case I am happy to oblige Your Eminence and serve the cause of scholarship," Alonso said. The task appealed to him, and Alcala might indeed be a better place to practice medicine than Seville, where his family was well known and rumours of his father's condemnation might surface and ruin his career. But what determined Alonso to stay was his desire to see the dream woman again, to speak to her, to hear her voice, to bathe in the light of her eyes. That desire outweighed all other considerations. "It will be a great honour to serve Your Eminence as best I can," he said.

"Then I shall introduce you to the man who is in charge of the Greek text and will be your colleague," Cisneros said. He rang the bell for the servant: "Ask Philotimus to join us," he said, and the bearded man who had been waiting in the antechamber was shown in.

He made a deep obeisance to the Cardinal, but even before he had straightened up, he said in a blustering voice: "That servant is an insolent fellow, Your Eminence. He kept me waiting a good half hour..."

The Cardinal cut him short. *"Complain not about another that ye may not be judged* – James 5: 9," he said severely.

The Greek shrunk under the Cardinal's gaze and the force of the biblical injunction. "I beg Your Eminence's pardon," he said, "but I've brought the text of Matthew for your review, and I thought Your Eminence's interest would take precedence over everything else." He gave Alonso a withering glance, but his speech—an absurd mixture of Latin and Spanish—was so droll that the doctor could not take offense.

The Cardinal made desultory intro-ductions. His mind was already on the bundle of sheets Philotimus had handed to him. He sat down at his desk and began leafing through the pages. "You will oblige me by taking Doctor Malki to the university and showing him the library," he said to the Greek. "Explain our modus operandi, tell him what has been done and what needs to be done. The rest we shall discuss another time."

The audience was at an end. Without ceremony, the Cardinal turned his back on the two men and began his study of the text. They bowed and were conducted out by the usher.

CHAPTER 3

"HE IS A GRUFF OLD MAN," PHILOTIMUS SAID IN HIS pidgin Spanish when they were back in the street and making their way to the university. "You won't find him easy to deal with. Nothing about the project is easy." He described the task, speaking with a quirky liveliness, rarely pausing, giving his words a desperate and breathless quality. Alonso was glad nothing much was expected of him in the way of answers or explanations. The sudden reversal of his fortune, from lowly petitioner to member of a respected scholarly team, the prospect of living in the very city that was home to the woman of his dreams – these precipitous devel-opments left Alonso queasy. His mind was crowded with thoughts. He had to force himself to listen as Philotimus explained the task awaiting him.

"The work seems straightforward enough," the Greek said. "You compare the standard Vulgate text with the old manuscripts in the Cardinal's library. You jot down the differences. You ask yourself: which is the correct version? What was in the original text? You make a guess and enter the correction. It sounds simple, doesn't it?"

"Simple perhaps to a grammarian," Alonso said, "but I can already hear the howls of protests from the theologians. They will tell you: the Bible is divinely inspired and does not admit of correction."

Philotimus nodded his head rapidly. "You've put your finger on the spot. They will cry: Heresy! And the parish priests will complain: We've always recited the text that way, and now someone comes along and tells us it's wrong, and we must change it." He took a quick breath and held up his index finger: "That is Problem Number 1: how to make the necessary changes palpable to the theologians and the clerics, and to the Cardinal, who is sensitive to their objections." He held up two fingers: "Problem Number 2: the assistants on the project, who are supposed to produce a clean text for the printer. They are a lazy and incompetent lot – as useless as monkeys!" He looked around and scowled at the street urchins who had been attracted by his loud voice and were following them, mimicking his accent with glee.

"Scat! Get along, you!" he said to them, but he took the precaution of switching to Latin, the international language of scholars, before thrusting three fingers in the air and proceeding to explain Problem Number 3 to the doctor.

"The Cardinal's secretary, Martin Casalius, is supposed to supervise the assistants," he said, striding along now with determined steps, elbowing milkmaids and beggars out of his way and carrying Alonso along with him. "Supposed to supervise them! But he comes by only once in a while. He is overworked and in poor health – young in years, old in body and spirit. If you ask me, the elements in his blood are not properly mixed. Too much black matter, too much acid. One look at his dour face and you know everything. You are a medical man; perhaps you have a prescription to sweeten his nature."

"If I had such an elixir, my friend, I would be the most sought-after physician in the world," Alonso said, and Philotimus gave him a sardonic smile.

"Well, those are the problems concerning the transcription of the Latin text," he continued. "Then there are the errors in the translation – yes, you heard me right. I dare to call them errors, doctor. If you listen to the theologians, you'd think God himself held the translator's pen, when he turned the original Greek into Latin. But that's nonsense."

"You are indeed a bold man to call them mistakes," Alonso said.

"I know I should watch my words," Philotimus said. "I more than anyone else, because I am a Greek. People don't trust an émigré from Constantinople. They say my thoughts have been corrupted by the schismatics!

But I suppose your case is worse. You are a Jew, and you must put your light under a bushel. You must learn to button your lip." He gave Alonso a look of sympathy, the pity of the one-eyed for the blind, and went on with his complaints, irrepressible and theatrical. "The man in charge of the Latin text is spared that difficulty at any rate. He is born and bred Catholic, and if anyone should take it into his head to make difficulties for him, he will soothe them away with honeyed words. You may have heard of him: Deodatus Rijs. He teaches rhetoric and poetry at the university."

"Ah, the man who rivals Cicero in eloquence, or so I'm told! I certainly look forward to meeting him."

Philotimus rolled his eyes. "And you'll soon wish you hadn't. He is a hypocrite of the first order. Truckling to those above and kicking those below. His skill to parlay his talents into money is amazing. Absolutely amazing." He began to mark out another series of complaints with his fingers: the occasions on which Deodatus had bested him. Occasion Number 1: When King Ferdinand visited the university, and the scholars were presented to him, Deodatus brought out a poem in praise of Spain, copied on soft vellum. He presented it to the King with great flourish and was handsomely rewarded in gold. "He made me look like a fool," Philotimus said, huffing and sucking his lower lip. "I never thought of preparing anything. Here I was, stuttering out extempore praises for Spain. The King gave me a crooked smile and allowed me to kiss his hand, but his hand was empty."

They reached the entrance of Ildefonso College, but the Greek would not allow Alonso to enter before he had explained Occasion Number 2: "The Christmas celebrations gave our man another opportunity to enrich himself. He prepared half a dozen translations of Plutarch's essays and handed them out as presents to the heads of the noble families in Alcala. That elicited a veritable golden shower! Mark my word, friend! Deodatus has an uncanny skill to make money and insinuate himself into the company of the great." He took hold of the doctor's sleeve and twisted it violently. "He is the star of the university. Do you know that he earns a stipend in excess of what jurists and theologians are paid?" he asked. "The Cardinal thinks the world of him. And now the King has appointed him royal historian. Add in that honorarium, and the total is a tidy sum."

His voice seethed with jealousy. "I would have left long ago," he said, "but what is a fellow to do who can't go home?" The rhetorical question seemed to sober him. His beefy shoulders sagged, the lines in his rugged face deepened. "I have no choice but to stay. I no longer have a home. Constantinople, my beloved city, the jewel of the Black Sea, has passed into the hands of the barbarous Turks."

He sighed deeply, helpless with wonder at the vagaries of fortune, but Alonso was no longer listening to his words. His eyes were riveted to the facade of the house they were passing. This was the street where he had first laid eyes on the dream woman. And there was the balcony from which she had watched the Corpus Christi procession. It was empty now except for a cast iron chair. The door leading from the loggia into the house was ajar, drawing his gaze to the darkness beyond, to a room where *she* might be watching him at this very moment. Alonso was overcome with longing to see the young woman's face again, not filtered through a shimmering dream, but clearly in the light of day. He wanted to gaze into her eyes and discern their colour. He wanted to witness again the small gesture of her hand when she dropped her lace fan. He yearned for a spark of contact, for a smile, a word. What was her name? Alonso wanted to know more about his dream woman, to see how her lips moved when she talked, how she gestured, how she walked – was it with a light or a deliberate step?

Timotheus had come to the end of his lament and following Alonso's gaze, looked up at the facade of the house that concealed the dream woman.

"A handsome building," Alonso said, to explain his interest. "Who owns it?"

"Ramon Cardosa," the Greek said. "He is one of the wealthiest men in town, and married to a cousin of the Cardinal."

Cardosa. Alonso savoured the name and allowed it to linger on his tongue like the taste of a ripe pomegranate. And what was her first name? He wanted to hear more about the Cardosa family, but the Greek had already walked through the gate of San Ildefonso College. He beckoned to Alonso, led the way to the library, and ushered the doctor into a high-ceilinged room.

Rows of parchment volumes lined the shelves and manuscripts were spread out on a long table, their pages quivering in the draft of the open door.

Two young assistants rose from their writing desks in a move that could have been choreographed. They raised their faces to Philotimus and greeted him with the deference and ill-concealed loathing of whipped schoolboys.

"And what have you been up to?" he said crusty-voiced. "Nothing good, I warrant."

***

Natale eyed his narrow cell. The Franciscan monastery La Penitencia was no better than its name. The meal that welcomed him on the day of arrival was penitential. It consisted of a thin gruel seasoned with beans and gristly bits of pork. The chaff that filled the mattress of his plank bed had turned to dust, leaving it as flat as a communion waver. He woke with a sore back and made his way to the Cardinal's palace stiff-legged and aching in every joint. A clerk received him and requested an account of his journey, but Natale asked to present his report to Cisneros in person, hoping for an opportunity to mention his aspirations and humbly ask for work, however menial, on the great Polyglot project.

The clerk, to whom he presented his letter of introduction, grumbled.

"The Cardinal is a busy man," he said.

"But this was a special mission," Natale argued and put on a mysterious air. A special mission, indeed, he thought. It had not been easy to keep talking about theology to the doctor and drawing him out without arousing his suspicion.

"Still," the clerk said, "the Cardinal can't be expected to lend an ear to every *familiar*, every lowly servant of the Inquisition."

Natale persisted, however, and in the end the clerk relented and agreed to send word to Cisneros. An orderly took away his letter of introduction and returned to say that he had delivered it into the Cardinal's hands, but His Eminence was too busy to see him.

"Not today," he said, blocking access to the great staircase like the angel of Eden.

Natale left, uncomplaining.

"I shall come back tomorrow," he said and sauntered off on a little reconnaissance trip. What else was a spy of the Inquisition to do with his time? He wandered through the streets of Alcala, snooped around the shops, struck up conversations in the market place, and ended up at the Capilla del Oidor, offering to relieve the parish priest in the confessional. It was good policy for a man new in town. There was much to learn from matrons relieving their conscience to a confessor. Natale even went to comfort a verger on his deathbed. There was nothing to be had from the dying man. In coin, that is, but the verger entrusted to him a secret that could be turned to advantage if used judiciously: a scandalous story of adultery. The most curious case he encountered that day, however, was that of Deodatus Rijs.

Natale had met the famous scholar at the Cardinal's palace when he made his fruitless attempt to obtain an audience with the prelate.

"I couldn't help overhearing that you are from Seville, Father," Deodatus said as they were crossing the courtyard together. He was elegantly dressed. The black silk of his cope was lustrous, his tunic of the finest wool, his boots of the softest leather. "How long will you be staying in town?"

"Not very long, I hope, at least not at La Penitencia, where I am quartered now." Natale looked at the scholar with the faint hope of receiving an offer of hospitality. But Deodatus wanted a favour himself.

"I have a request, Father," he said. "May I make a confession to you in private? I am too well known to kneel in the confessional at the cathedral. There are always people milling around the nave, hoping to overhear an interesting tidbit, something to satisfy their taste for salacious stories. You understand me, I hope."

Salacious stories? Natale gladly granted the favour. Of course he would hear the scholar's confession in private. He understood perfectly. The man was afraid of being overheard, and naturally shied away from confessing to a priest who would recognize him through the screen, with whom he might be rubbing shoulders the next day at the house of an illustrious patron. There was no risk of a friar from Seville being invited to the houses of the rich and powerful. A man staying at La

Penitencia! Deodatus lived in a grander world. He was a celebrated scholar, a man who had caught the eye of the court. Not everyone admired him. That much Natale had already discovered in conversation with the townspeople. Some people called him selfish and grasping, a social climber and a hypocrite, a man who spun straw into gold. But they were jealous perhaps of his success. Natale was prepared to rejoice in Deodatus' good fortune, especially if his influence might be brought to bear on his own aspirations and bring him closer to his goal of joining the Polyglot team.

That afternoon, Deodatus came to Natale's cell. His countenance, which had been smooth as marble in the morning, was now somber and overcast.

A pose to go with confession, Natale thought and wondered whether the charge of hypocrisy was true. He put on a purple stole, made the sign of the cross and said the prayer that would transform their conversation into the sacramental act of confession.

"Begin," he said, "and may the Lord be with you."

The room was so small that their knees almost touched as they sat on hard-backed chairs, facing each other.

"I am a scholar," Deodatus said – a peculiar way of beginning the recital of his sins. "I have read the books of learned men, but I am no wiser than before. I have failed to apply their moral lessons to my life."

All that lecTorinog has given the man a didactic voice, Natale thought. There was nothing confessional about Deodatus' confession. His gestures were fluent, his expressions impeccably correct.

"It is good to recognize one's weaknesses," Natale said. "But to examine your conscience is not an intellectual exercise, my friend. You must begin by humbling yourself before God." It was always good to put a sinner in his place. The more abject he was made to feel, the more generous in the end. That was Natale's experience. And although his vows obliged him to live in poverty, they did not require him to reject favours.

"I have humbled myself before God many times," Deodatus said. "I have shed bitter tears thinking of the occasions when I yielded to my desire for glory and reveled unduly in my accomplishments, looking down on those less fortunate than myself, on those who are lacking in intellectual gifts or toiling in obscurity. There was a time when I denied my sin and said to myself: I am merely taking pleasure in my achievements. But pride is a deadly sin. I made excuses. The desire to excel is a natural inclination, I told myself. But my ambition is wicked, a monstrous thing roiling within me, driving me on relentlessly to seek perfection, to surpass everyone."

No wonder the man was a popular lecturer. He was a star performer. He was playing the penitent to perfection. But that didn't serve Natale's purpose. He could not allow Deodatus to be the hero of his own story. Heroic characters did not pay well, as a rule. The man must be pulled down from the pedestal and made to weep and gnash his teeth. Natale cut short his performance.

"You are, then, confessing to the sin of pride?"

"I am, with a repentant heart. And the sin of pride is, alas, only one of my failings. Many times I have prostrated myself before the cross in my room and lamented my moral lapses. Even now I feel the sharp pricks of remorse and promise to do penance with a sincere heart. I wish to be at peace with God and with myself."

Deodatus trailed off into a conventional formula of remorse and asked for absolution, but Natale would not let him off so easily. His recital of sins had been only a list of commonplaces, his words of repentance too round, too well balanced to amount to anything. So far Natale had heard nothing that could not have been said in the confessional, in the hearing of all. Where were the salacious tidbits? The bits Deodatus was afraid to whisper in the Cathedral?

"Remorse is a first step toward obtaining forgiveness," he said, "but I cannot absolve you until you have enumerated your sins. Of what kind were your moral lapses?"

Deodatus hesitated. He let his eye travel upward. His gallantry began to die.

"You must not be embarrassed to name your sins to me," Natale said. "I am only God's vicar. It is He who hears your confession."

"I have committed the sin of fornication," Deodatus said. His lean jaw worked involuntarily.

Natale pressed on. "The laws of the church command me to inquire into the circumstances of your sinful behavior. You are in God's court. The penance must match the crime. I need to know whether you have taken advantage of a person's innocence or have been seduced yourself. With whom have you committed the sin of fornication?"

Deodatus blinked into the small square of light coming from the window above Natale's head. "With no one," he brought out with difficulty. "I have committed fornication in my thoughts only." He sank into a melancholy silence. There was true suffering in his eyes at last. "That is, I loved a man once a long time ago, but he died, and my love died with him. Still, I experience temptation when I look at the firm limbs of young men."

So that's it, Natale thought, and entered the final round. Now that the penitent's heart was softened and made pliable, a little understanding was needed to bring out his gratitude, and indeed he felt sorry for the man. Sinful desires of that sort were a common enough failing, especially in those who were barred from female company by custom or by their solitary life. In prison, men pleasured other men. In outlying places, they practiced incest and bestiality. Deodatus' sin was paltry by comparison.

"A more severe confessor than I might counsel you to wear a hair shirt," he said, "or to prick your flesh with thorns to overcome all carnal thoughts, but I say there is another remedy: marriage. St. Paul counsels those who experience the flames of lust 'to marry rather than burn.' It is likely that your unnatural desire has been caused by repressing the natural and God-given faculty of procreation and that you will find happiness in a legitimate union, in the arms of a loving wife and helpmate."

Deodatus compressed his lips as if he wanted to keep his inner life from vibrating and betraying his thoughts, and Natale wondered at the man's tricky soul. He gave Deodatus a fatherly smile. There now. Surely such understanding warranted a generous donation to the poor and goodwill toward the confessor.

"Perhaps you are right," Deodatus said at last. "I have tried to subdue sinful thoughts with work, but in the fateful hour between waking and sleeping when my soul is weary, I stumble and fall into the pit of despair. Can a woman save me from despair?"

"Provided you make the right choice, of course," Natale said.

Deodatus plucked at the sleeves of his tunic. "My choice is limited," he said. "Family connections are at the top of every matchmaker's list, and I shall be found lacking in that respect." He went on, choosing his words carefully. "There is, unfortunately, a blot on my lineage." He paused and gave Natale a bitter smile. "What man of honour, what man of standing, would give his daughter in marriage to a bastard—a bastard, whom the laws of the church do not permit to make a lawful will and thus provide for his wife and children? What father would consent to such a match?"

More secrets coming out, Natale thought. But Deodatus' admission puzzled him. An illegitimate birth placed many obstacles into a man's path. And yet Deodatus was a star lecturer at the University of Alcala. "Don't the canon laws also prevent such a man from teaching at a university?" he said to him. "Have you concealed your impediment?"

"I mentioned the impediment to the Cardinal, as I was in duty bound, and he gave me a dispensation which allowed me to accept the appointment."

"If the Cardinal already knows of your problem," he said, "why not consult him in the matter of marriage as well? You may even obtain papers in Rome legitimizing your birth, if the Cardinal is willing to set things in motion for you."

Deodatus nodded. "I will take your advice," he said, "and go to the Cardinal."

"I in turn shall pray to God on your behalf," Natale said and concluded the penitential rite, giving Deodatus absolution. There was nothing more to be gained. For a penance he assigned him three Hail Marys and a donation to the poor. Unfortunately he could not prescribe the granting of a favour. He would have liked to ask Deodatus about the Polyglot project and beg him to further his chances of becoming a member of the team, but the man looked like he needed a respite, and Natale decided to wait for a better time to press his cause.

***

The light in the window had turned lavender by the time Deodatus left the friar's cell. Natale was well pleased with the day's work. He made himself as comfortable as the circumstances permitted, lit a thin taper and began reading the book of poetry Alonso had given him. It was a fine present, even if Prudentius was no match for the ancient poets. What was the physician up to now, Natale wondered, as he looked into the amber halo of the candlelight. Should he have trailed him a little longer? But why waste time on Alonso when he had other, more promising leads—the verger's story of adultery, the hint of Deodatus' taste for young men—leads that would obtain him favours and comforts. Favours and comforts, but no riches. Natale was heartily tired of working for the Inquisition. It might be profitable for a layman who was paid to spy on heretics, but a friar received no compensation for his labour in the service of faith. He was just a cog in the *Suprema*'s vast machinery, and Fonseca—the man to whom he reported—was a slave driver. It never occurred to *him* to do a favour to Natale; treat him to a sumptuous meal or a fine bottle of wine or put in a good word with his Superior.

    Natale made up his mind: he would let Alonso Malki off the hook and repay his gift (no, loan!) with an innocuous report. It cost him nothing to say that the doctor was a pious man. After all, he had no proof that he was a Judaizer. Alonso had avoided all pitfalls and dexterously answered the many questions Natale put to him. Indeed he admired the man's native intelligence. Pity he was born a Jew!

Of course, Fonseca would be furious. He wanted results. He wanted convictions. He had handed Natale the dossier the Inquisition had compiled on the Malkis and told him to read the trial records.

Natale dutifully leafed through the interrogation. At first Alonso's father had denied everything, but then he was put to the question. Nice turn of phrase, wasn't it? *Put to the question.* Much more elegant than saying *tortured.* Natale only wished the records were more specific about the procedure. *Taken to the cellar in the presence of the prosecutor and assessors* left a lot to the imagination. They used the standard procedure presumably: strapping the accused to a trestle table, pinching his nose with an iron clip, gagging his mouth with a linen cloth and pouring water on it until the accused began to choke and started fighting for breath. The records only noted the number of jugs poured. Isaiah Malki didn't last long. One jug of water forced down his throat, and he signaled his willingness to confess. He admitted that he had relapsed into Judaism, but he refused to recant, and was burned at the stake. As a consequence his son was barred from practicing his profession for ten years.

"And this is where you come in, Natale." Fonseca had said. "I understand Alonso Malki is a friend of yours."

"An acquaintance," Natale corrected him. "There's no such thing as being friends with a Jew."

"Right," Fonseca said. "But you are on visiting terms with the doctor. Keep him under observation and report back to me."

"You want me to make sure that he stops practicing his profession? Has he been notified of the verdict?"

"No, we are holding off. My hunch is: if we notify the man, he'll pack up and leave the country."

"So? Good riddance!"

Fonseca shook his head. "Why should we let him off scot-free? He is a Judaizer like his father. Here is what I want you to do, Natale. Watch him closely. Make conversation. Ask leading questions. Close the trap on Alonso Malki."

But it wasn't that simple. Fonseca didn't understand what was involved. The doctor wasn't a Judaizer. He was another kind of troublemake: a philosopher, a doubter, a searcher for the absolute truth. He was too subtle to be caught in the coarse net of the Inquisition. Close the trap on Alonso Malki? Hah! Easier said than done.

***

The next morning, at last, Natale was summoned into the presence of the Cardinal and entered the semi-obscurity of the study, where Alonso Malki had pleaded his case the day before. Looking at the bare walls, Natale thought: What's the use of being powerful if you aren't allowed to enjoy the good things in life? And for the hundredth time he regretted taking the monastic vows.

Cisneros was at his desk with Fonseca's letter of introduction before him. He raised his face to Natale and said in a chill voice: "Report your findings."

The old man will be hard to humour, Natale thought, wreathing his lips into a pleasant smile. "Miguel Fonseca asked me to follow a man by the name of Alonso Malki," he said. "He comes from a family of relapsed Jews and is suspected of heresy himself. I kept a close eye on him all the way from Seville to Alcala and conversed with him whenever opportunity offered. The suspicions are unfounded, Your Eminence. Malki was a child when he converted to Christianity. He has all but forgotten the language and customs of his fathers and takes no interest in theology at all. Indeed he is an ignorant man and barely knows his catechism. He merits no further attention from the *Suprema*, in my humble opinion."

The Cardinal's face remained blank. "You are indeed the man Fonseca portrays in his letter," he said. "Do you want to hear what he says about you?"

"If Your Eminence would deign to enlighten me," Natale said, expecting to hear a bit of gentle flattery, the kind usually found in letters of introduction.

"He writes: Natale Benvenuto is unreliable. He does not exercise due diligence in his work for the *Suprema*. Although I have no firm proof of misconduct, I suspect he is open to bribery. He has at any rate been lax in the pursuit of his duties. I suggest Your Eminence terminate his employment as a *familiar*. In his favour, I may say that he has considerable learning and is an excellent Latinist, although he takes more interest in heathen poets than in the writings of the Holy Fathers. He may serve as a tutor or a scribe, but he is a poor soldier in the army of the Lord, etc." The Cardinal looked up. His lips were compressed into an unforgiving line.

Natale's heart had begun to palpitate at the first words of the Cardinal. Beads of sweat were glistening on his forehead now. Fear made his legs buckle. It was no mere gesture of submission when he fell on his knees, knocking against the hard stone floor.

"Your Eminence!" he cried, raising his arms in supplicant prayer, "Fonseca is wrong. I have been unflagging in my efforts. I've kept my eye on Malki. I suggested the journey to him so I could keep watch on him day and night, and I barely slept for fear of missing out on any information of value to the *Suprema*. Fonseca has misjudged me. Your Eminence!"

"It is your judgment that is amiss," the Cardinal said. "I have met Alonso Malki. Far from being an ignorant man, he is well versed in biblical exegesis, and I have taken him into my service."

That's what I get for being kind to a Jew, Natale thought. On the other hand, if I had called him a heretic, it might have been worse, seeing that he has won the Cardinal's approbation.

"My judgment may have been wrong in this case," he wailed, "but I have accepted no bribes.

Fonseca has mistaken mercy for venality. If I have ever held anything back it was out of reluctance to injure the reputation of the church." He was shaking with fear, but he still had a card to play: the secret entrusted to him by the verger. It was a trump card. "I have pursued another case," he said, cringing under the prelate's hard look, "and would present my findings, if I did not shy away from giving offence to Your Eminence."

"There is no need to shy away from telling the truth," the prelate said severely.

"And if the sin of one woman should blacken the name of a prominent family and tarnish the reputation of the Franciscan Order? Should I not shy away from telling the truth?"

The Cardinal looked at Natale sharply. "What do you mean?" he said. "Make your case, and be prompt about it. I have no time to listen to circumlocutions."

"May I speak with impunity then?" Natale said, looking up humbly.

"Say what you have to say," the prelate answered tersely. "And get off your knees this instant. I loathe grovelers and sycophants."

Natale scrambled to his feet. "A few days ago," he said, "I heard the deathbed confession of a verger. He told me that he served for many years at the shrine of Santa Maria de la Vega. One day, he said, he arranged a tryst between a Franciscan and a member of your illustrious family." Natale's voice steadied as he saw the blood draining from the Cardinal's cheeks. "The lady concealed her face under a thick veil, the verger said, but a curious pair of earrings gave her away, and he recognized her among the pilgrims in the guesthouse. He heard that the lady gave birth to a daughter nine months later and foisted the child on her unsuspecting husband." The prelate's face was ashen. Natale saw that his words had hit the mark. "The verger named the lady to me," he said, looking at Cisneros steadily now. "Alas, the name he whispered to me was that of your cousin, Catalina de Cardosa, but compassion urges me to expunge the name from my memory."

"Compassion and the hope of a reward," the Cardinal said bitterly.

"The hope of kindness, Your Eminence," Natale said adroitly.

"What is it that you want from me?"

Natale made a quick calculation. His ambition was to work on the Polyglot, but he did not want to push his luck too far and be refused. A more modest plea, on the other hand, might be successful. "I have heard that the Cardosas are looking for a tutor," he said. "A word from Your Eminence will obtain the post for me."

Cisneros' jaw tightened. He eyed the friar with disgust, but necessity was forcing his hand. "I shall see what I can do since Fonseca vouches for your skill as a Latinist," he said. "But I will not exert undue pressure on your behalf. Until I have an answer from my cousin, you will report to my secretary, Martin Casalius."

Natale bowed. A smile began to flicker across his face, but he took care to keep his head down. "I am at Your Eminence's service," he said meekly.

It has turned out better than expected, he thought as he followed a servant to the secretary's office. What a scare the Cardinal had given him, reading out Fonseca's letter! That man was a snake in the grass, friendly to his face and slandering him behind his back. But never mind Fonseca. Natale was on to better things now. The position of tutor in the Cardosa household was his, he was sure of that. And Doña Catalina would see to his comforts once she understood that he was the keeper of her little secret. Then there was the record of the Malki trial, which Fonseca had given him. The file was in Natale's luggage now, neatly wrapped, tied up with string and sealed against the eyes of curiosity-seekers. There might be a paying customer for the parcel: Alonso Malki. Now that the physician was in the prelate's employ—a wonderful coincidence, surely—he would not want to see the trial records go astray. I will offer the file to Alonso, Natale thought, at a discount of course, since I regard him as a friend. It will be the last advantage I get from the *Suprema*, but I'm glad I'm out. The waters were getting too deep for me. In any case, perhaps it's time to build up a secret cache and buy a dispensation from my vows. Everything is for sale in Rome, I am told.

Chapter 4

It was Sunday. The midday meal was over, and Luisa Cardosa was resting in her room. The louvers covering the windows shut out the merciless brilliance of the sunlight and left the room in shadowy repose. A sluggish breeze made the curtains move and rippled the fringes of the canopy on the poster bed.

"I can't sleep," Luisa said to the aya who was folding up her Sunday clothes, putting away the puff-sleeved gown, corselage, and silk stockings. "It's too hot."

She felt for the ribbons of her lace chemise and touched her breasts, frowning. They are too small, she thought, and hard like plums. She was suffering the qualms of a teenager. She lifted her arms: too thin! She thought with envy of the kitchen maid. Maria's arms were brown from the sun, but well rounded, and the backs of her hands were dimpled.

Luisa slid off the bed, lowered her naked feet to the cool tile floor, and took a hand mirror from the bedside table. Dropping back on the bed, she inspected her face. "I wish I had Mama's creamy complexion," she said.

"Then you should stay indoors like Doña Catalina. Sunlight coarsens the skin."

"But the garden looks so nice just now."

The aya puckered up her face. "You should let me put cucumber milk on your face, sweetheart."

"I can't stand the smell. It reminds me of wet fur."

The aya dropped into a chair by the bed and folded her hands over her plump stomach. A drowsy stillness filled the room. In the yard below, a high, clear voice was singing *Ya te espero, mi amor*.

"I wish I could be with Maria and help her shell peas," Luisa said.

"Shelling peas is for kitchen maids and little girls, sweetheart. Young ladies keep siesta."

Luisa sat up and leaned against the headboard. "I don't want to rest. It's boring."

"I don't know what's to become of you, sweetheart!" the aya said. "You are a capricious young lady. You don't sleep when you are supposed to sleep. You run when you are supposed to walk. You speak when you are supposed to be silent. You gawk, when you are supposed to lower your eyes. You have no respect for tradition or etiquette."

Luisa leaned over and gave the old woman a quick kiss. "I can't help it, nanny." She caressed her wrinkled cheeks. "Don't be cross with me."

The aya took her hand and stroked it. "I'm not cross, my lamb, but your parents want to find you a good husband. Your papa will provide you with a respectable dowry, and everyone says you are beautiful. But who wants to marry a wilful girl?"

"Am I wilful because I can't sleep?"

The aya shook her head. "If you can't sleep, my dear, read Fray Ferrero's book." She picked up a booklet from the dresser and held it out to Luisa.

"*The Duties of Wives and Mothers* – you are right, nanny, that will put me to sleep."

"Show respect for your tutor's book, Luisa. Why don't you read a bit, just for me?" she said in a cajoling voice. "One short chapter. You like reading aloud, don't you, sweetheart?"

Luisa sighed. "But I know Fray Ferrero's book by heart! Mama has made me read it a thousand times." She took the book from the aya's hands and opened it at random. "*Advice to the young Mother*," she read.

The aya patted her arm, plumped up a pillow and stuck it behind her back. "There, my pet. Now you are comfortable," she said.

"*Never entrust your daughter to a wet-nurse who is not of impeccable character, for with her milk the child will imbibe a certain disposition. The proverb is right that says that he who was nurtured with the milk of a sow will roll in the mire like a sow.*

Luisa stopped and looked at the aya. "If I said 'roll like a sow in the mire', you'd tell me to use more delicate language."

"It's a proverb, sweetheart. Fray Ferrero knows what he is saying."

"Take special care that your daughter is not defiled by immoral and dishonourable conversation or behaviour. Chastity and virtue are a woman's greatest good. Guard your daughter well and keep her in your presence, so that you may regulate her pastimes and direct her mind to goodness and virtue. But I'm hardly ever with my mother. She is always tired."

"In your aya's presence or in your mother's presence, it comes out to the same thing, dear. Your Mama trusts me. I've served her family for a long time."

"Anyone of the male sex should be excluded from your daughter's presence so that she will not become accustomed to find pleasure in the company of men. I can't believe that. Alejandro keeps me company sometimes, and he has done me no harm."

"I am not sure about that," the aya said. "He is too wild. Girls should be kept away from their brothers."

"Alejandro will be gone soon enough. Papa wants him to go to Salamanca in the fall."

"I don't know why he doesn't send him to the court with Duke Manrique's son."

"Because a Duke's son is expected to lead the King's armies, and for that he must attend the court and learn fencing, and the like. Papa wants Alejandro to study law," Luisa said and lowered her eyes to the pages of Ferrero's book again. "*Subject your daughter to strict discipline to guard her innocent and untainted natural disposition against being warped by sinful tendencies. Especially guard her against the proclivity to talk too much. Let her dolls be clothed modestly so they do not arouse in the girl a desire for finery. Better yet, give her instead of dolls toys representing household objects. At the earliest possible age train her in the care and management of the home, which should be a matter of prime concern for women. Not even a princess or queen should be ignorant of working with her hands. Idleness is the devil's playground. Our own Queen Isabella wished her four daughters to be experts in spinning, sewing, and needlepoint.* Spinning. Sewing. Needlepoint." Luisa sniggered. "How is that different from shelling peas?"

"Don't snigger, dear. It makes your mouth go crooked. A face should be like the surface of a pond on a sunny day, smooth and unruffled. You should practice in front of a mirror."

Luisa took up the hand mirror lying beside her on the bed. "Spinning, sewing, needlepoint," she said, looking at her reflection. Her nose wrinkled up, and her features dissolved. She broke out laughing. "Spinning, sewing, needlepoint!" She snuffled. "It's too silly, aya."

"How can it be silly if it's a fit occupation for the Queen's daughters? You have a head full of unruly thoughts, dear."

Luisa swallowed her laugh. *"You must also train your daughter's mind,"* she read. *"But beware: the devil lurks in many a book. And too much learning spoils a woman's character."*

The aya settled back into her chair and rested her feet on a stool. Her eyes were half closed.

"Choose books that will fortify your daughter's mind with precepts and moral counsel. Let her read the Bible, the Church fathers, and the Lives of the Saints."

The aya began to nod, and Luisa trailed off.

The Bible, the Church Fathers, the Lives of Saints. Yes, Luisa had read the Lives of the Saints as a child, and conceived a wild ambition of becoming a famous saint. She made up her mind to enter a nunnery, a dark and mystical place it would be, where she could spend her days in the contemplation of God and be seized by an ecstasy of joy as her soul became one with the Maker. The thought had intoxicated her. She saw her assumption into heaven, a glorious scene in blazing sunset colours: Santa Luisa in a cloud of white gauze, being swept up by the hand of God, higher and higher until the fields were only golden smudges, the manor a toy house, and the garden a square covered with green and red dots. "Child!" the aya exclaimed when she told her that she was ready to enter heaven. "May God forgive your sinful pride! You are far from sainthood."

The aya's head had sunk back. A light whistling sound came from between her half-open lips.

Luisa thought of the troupe of players that had come to Alcala during Carnival. They dispelled all her saintly ambitions. She so much wanted to trade places with Maria and attend a performance of *Amadis*. As it was, she had to listen to the maid's breathless account, telling her of the burning passion of Calisto and reciting the famous lines describing his lady love, the beautiful Melibea. *Her hair was like the skeins of golden thread spun in Araby, her skin so smooth and white it darkened snow.* Luisa was at once consumed with passion, charmed and terrified by a nameless knight swearing eternal love to her in a moonlit garden. The aya would have been scandalized if she had known of her day dreams.

    The old woman started and opened her eyes. "That's right," she said as if she had heard every word Luisa had been reading and guessed her scandalous thoughts.

    Luisa took up the book again: *"Our age has seen the four daughters of Queen Isabella, each of them well accomplished. Alas, her oldest daughter Juana, who was much admired for her ability to answer in Latin the Latin speeches of the ambassadors, is now suffering from nervous prostration.* You see the Queen made mistakes, too," she said, turning to the aya.

    "May her soul rest in peace," the aya said. "Don't speak ill of the dead, Luisa. Read on."

    "Juana's illness, I fear, is the unfortunate consequence of overindulgence in studies unsuitable for a woman. I myself would not counsel a woman to learn Latin, even if it is the language of Holy Writ. Do not forget that woman is the weaker vessel, and her powers

may easily be overtaxed. Only if they have to read boring books by boring old men like Fray Ferrero!" Luisa cried and clapped the book shut. "Thank God, Papa has decided to pension him off. The new tutor can't possibly be worse than Fray Ferrero."

"Child!" the aya said. "Your mood changes like the weather in August. Sunny one moment, stormy the next."

"Well, I won't read on," she said. "I'd rather sleep." She lay back on the bed and closed her eyes. Her thoughts drifted to the morning mass at the cathedral. She had been watching the Manrique women taking their seats in the ornate family pew across the aisle. Duke Manrique was standing behind his wife's high-backed chair. His daughters were dressed most elegantly, wearing corded silver belts and daintily embroidered dresses with sleeves turned back to reveal pleated cuffs.

Mass began. The altar boys in their red frocks and lacy surplices came into the nave in rows of two, carrying bells, candles, and censers, and the choir chanted the entrance hymn as the priest walked up to the high altar.

Luisa's eyes had strayed back to the Manrique pew and to a gentleman in the Duke's retinue. His features were refined, and his movements elegant. His gaze settled on her face. He looked at her with melting eyes. She raised her fan, and smiled at him, her mouth half hidden by the lace. He bowed.

The choir was singing Kyrie eleison. Luisa acknowledged his bow and lowered her eyes, allowing herself to be stirred by the mystery man.

"Nanny," she said, shifting on the bed, "who was the gentleman bowing to me in church – the one wearing the scholar's cape?"

"Deodatus Rijs," the aya said and gave her a quick, inquisitive glance.

"I knew it! I knew it! Alejandro told me all about him. He lectures at the university, and Alejandro thinks he's a genius. Is he eligible?"

"The matchmakers have him on their lists, sweetheart, but he is a Fleming."

"There is nothing wrong with being a Fleming. Princess Juana married one."

"Yes, but Prince Philip was a Habsburg and the son of the Emperor. No one has ever heard of Deodatus' family."

"And I suppose he is too old for me."

"He is about thirty, the best age for a husband. But if you aren't interested, Luisa, why did you nod to him? Because don't think I didn't notice that you smiled and nodded at him."

"I was holding up my fan all the time, nanny."

"You shouldn't even have looked at him, sweetheart, because you have magnetic eyes. If you fix them on a man's face, you will draw him in. Don't even think of him. Even the eyes of your mind will attract a man."

Luisa waved her off. "I don't believe a word you are saying." She wished it was true, and she could summon a lover just by thinking about him, but no knight *with valiant and unvanquished arm* had appeared in the garden, when she dreamed of Amadis and breathed a storm of sighs. No handsome cavalier with heroic eyes had ever materialized, no matter how passionately she longed to be adored.

"Mark my words, little one. Your eyes are magic. It's the sacred truth."

"I suppose it wouldn't be a bad thing if I attracted Deodatus Rijs," Luisa said pertly. Now that Alejandro had told her of the scholar's consummate learning, the moonlit garden of her dreams had been replaced by book-lined shelves. A new vision of a learned Luisa was crowding out the saintly heroines and noble ladies in her mind. "If I married Deodatus, I would read all his books and become Spain's first woman scholar," she said.

"Who put that nonsense into your head, Luisa?" the aya said sternly. "You are full of wild dreams and confused ideas. Whoever heard of a woman scholar? You mustn't indulge in such fantasies, my child. One day you will conjure up an image, and it will become flesh and blood..."

"Stop it, nanny. I can't sleep at night when you tell me ghost stories."

"They are not ghost stories, sweetheart. The world is full of spirits, and they are not to be trifled with. You call them up at your peril."

"Nonsense," Luisa said. And yet the Cardinal's secretary fainted when she looked at him during the Corpus Christi procession, and he did resemble the confessor of the abbey she had dreamed up when she wanted to become a saint. Perhaps the aya was right, and she could invite Deodatus into her life with dreams of scholarship. The idea gave her a disturbing sensation around the heart.

***

In the master bedroom, Ramon Cardosa was lying stretched out on his back, looking up into the burgundy-coloured canopy of his bed. Time was stagnant. The dark red brocade seemed to intensify the heat in the room. Sweat was stinging his eyes and making his hair stick to his forehead. Sweat glistened on his bare chest. He wiped his face on the cover of the pillow and looked hopefully toward the double doors connecting his room with that of his wife's. They remained firmly shut.

He rang the bell. His valet entered, carrying a basin of cold water. Ramon sat up and allowed him to sponge his chest, neck, and back. He towelled off and slipped into the fresh batiste shirt the servant held out to him.

Crossing the room he opened the dividing doors and looked with distaste at the silk tapestries in his wife's room. Fluttering birds of paradise. Catalina's fantastic taste! On the bed, he could see his wife's body outlined under a sheet, a moribund hump. How could she stand being wrapped up in a sheet when the room was brooding hot?

Catalina's little maid rose from a chair in the corner of the room and curtsied to Cardosa.

At the sound of the chair scraping on the tiles, Catalina stirred and raised her head. Her eyes were puffy with sleep. She gasped for air like a drowning woman breaking the surface of water. "Is it time to get up?" she said.

"It's time," he said gruffly. "I want to speak to you."

"What is it?" she said in a languid voice.

"A matter of importance," he said. "I'll wait for you downstairs."

He retreated to his own room and completed his toilet. He had a vague sense of dissatisfaction. But why should he be dissatisfied? He thought of his rich farmlands, the hectares of arable fields, the handsome country house in Arelate, the leaseholds in Toledo and Alcala. He had a wife who came from an excellent family, a son to carry on the Cardosa name, and a daughter, who had blossomed into a great beauty. The matchmakers were praising the fire in Luisa's eyes, her dancer's step, and her voice which had the flavour of ripe berries. There will be many suitors, they said.

If you asked Ramon what he considered his greatest asset—wealth? reputation? family?—he would not hesitate to tell you: "It is impossible to choose among them. Take away one of them, and I can no longer call myself a happy man."

He went out into the corridor and walked down the curving staircase under the ancestral portraits blackened with age. The hall below was gleaming with silver ornaments, their sheen doubled in the full-length mirrors flanking the entrance. He had every reason to be content, and yet he was dissatisfied.

The interview with the Cardinal had left him disgruntled. Perhaps he should have consulted Duke Manrique instead. But the duke was so haughty it made your blood boil. He looked down on anyone whose forefathers had not fought the Saracens and won their laurels on the battlefields of yore.

There weren't many people Ramon could consult about family matters. He was careful not to get too close to the men in his own circle: merchants and landowners. That way he was under no obligation to do favours, a wasteful practice that had ruined many a household. It was enough to entertain lavishly. Ramon spared no expense to see his business associates, his relatives and neighbours well fed and served with choice wines, but there was no sense in indolent lingering and aimless conversation, which some people considered the marrow of friendship. Cardosa knew very well what they said of him: he had no anecdotes to make another man laugh, he had no heart to share another man's grief. He was too proud. Cardosa shrugged his shoulders: he had reason to be proud. He had managed life a great deal better than his so-called friends.

He certainly had done the right thing when he married Catalina. She brought him a rich dowry, and she came from an old Galician family that had produced many luminaries, but there had been faint hints of impropriety on the part of the bride that made the terms of the marriage contract not quite as advantageous as they seemed at first glance. Nothing definite could be ascertained, or Ramon would not have married Catalina even if her family was superior to his, even if the land she brought him was fertile and adjoining his own estate. There had been talk of feelings between Catalina and a cousin. And what were "feelings"? Ramon asked. Did she exchange lascivious glances with the man? Did she speak endearments or allow him to press her hand? No one could bring such accusations against Catalina, let alone prove them. The rest was empty noise and nonsense. It didn't keep Ramon from signing the marriage contract.

Feelings, indeed! Perhaps Catalina wasn't in love with him. She spent the wedding night weeping, but in the end, weeping in his arms. And all was well when she informed him that she was with child. She was overcome with emotion when she gave him the good news, and wept copiously. Ramon soon came to accept tears as a contingency of talking to his wife. Her eyes were brimming with tears when she contemplated the beauty of a fine summer morning, when she looked up from reading one of her silly romances, when she held Alejandro, their first-born son, in her arms. Tears were sure to disfigure her cheeks if Ramon as much as raised his voice. But Catalina also had the most exhilarating laugh: a warm, panting laugh, at least in those first swooning months of their marriage.

For a time after Alejandro's birth, it seemed the couple would not be blessed with another offspring. Two years later, however, Catalina gave birth to a healthy girl whom they named Luisa after her maternal grandmother. Catalina credited a barefoot pilgrimage to the shrine of Santa Maria de la Vega outside the town of Toro with the fulfillment of her prayers. She had undertaken the pilgrimage on the advice of her confessor, Fray Ferrero. Naturally Ramon rewarded him with a handsome gift and entrusted him with the direction of the children's education. It was better in any case to take the boy out of his mother's hands. She treated him like a lapdog. Alejandro had grown into a rambunctious boy and was clearly beyond her control. Catalina did not object. As for the baby, she refused to let her go. She cried and cried, the little fool, but in the end she submitted to Ramon's judgment. Luisa was put into the care of an experienced aya, who did not mollycoddle the child and did not laugh and weep and carry on like her sentimental mother. And now that Alejandro was a young man, it was time to replace Ferrero with someone who understood the ways of the court. But it had been a bad idea to consult the Cardinal. Never take a woman's advice, Ramon thought. Go to the Cardinal, Catalina had said to him. He is Alejandro's godfather, after all, and an important man at court. And so Ramon talked to the Cardinal and was introduced to a tutor: a man he did not like at all. And one thing leading to another, they talked about Luisa next. She has celebrated her sixteenth birthday, he said to Cisneros. Her mother and aunts are putting their heads together to find her a suitable husband. Of course they will consider family, social standing and wealth, the Cardinal said and wrinkled his nose as if there was something wrong with that. They should make it their business to match hearts and minds as well. Ramon could hardly believe his ears. Hearts and Minds!

It will be troublesome to explain it all to Catalina, he thought as he watched her descending the stairs with the maid in tow. Her robes rustled faintly with every step. Poor Catalina! Time had not been kind to her. When they married, she was a woman who gave a dinner a great air just by attending. Her beauty drew admiring glances from everyone, but soon she turned into a matron of dull respectability, listless, languid, her flesh softened by indolence. Her Celtic fair hair, a great source of pride to Ramon, took on the sallow colour of chamomile tea. And her fine bosom turned into a shapeless billowing mound resting on her stomach. Such is life, Cardosa thought, contemplating his wife's double chin. The little maid was no doubt a more pleasing sight, but Catalina was the mother of his children.

"Let's take a turn in the garden," he said to her.

"But the sun..."she objected.

"Bring your mistress a parasol, Elena," he said to the maid, and she hurried off.

"We could sit in the library," Catalina said, giving him a trembling smile.

"No," he said. "The walls have ears."

The maid brought a parasol of sea-green taffeta, and Cardosa took his wife's arm. Together, they walked along the pebbled path, through an arcade of mingled white and red roses, to a stone bench at the far end, where the burbling of a lion-headed fountain muted all sound, and their conversation could not be overheard by curious servants.

"I talked to Cisneros," he told his wife. "I wish to God I hadn't! I have the very man for you, he says, and introduces me to a fat little friar with a sly face and a slippery tongue, a man to whom I would not entrust a lame mule, let alone my children. His name is Natale Benvenuto. Of Italian parentage, I assume. He talks like an Italian, at any rate, spinning out sentences as long as an emperor's funeral cortege."

"Will you hire him?" Catalina asked anxiously.

"I have no choice. I'll think it over, I said to the Cardinal, but he wouldn't let me get away with that. You will be well advised to take the man into your service, he said, and I recognized the tone. I had asked for advice, and the Cardinal was giving me instructions. I'm afraid we are stuck with the tutor. I don't like his grovelling manner or his oily smile, but I'll hire him to oblige the Cardinal. Then he gives me another bit of advice. Let the friar instruct Luisa in Latin, he says."

Catalina gasped. "Latin!" she exclaimed. "Fray Ferrero would never..."

"I don't care what Fray Ferrero says or does," Ramon said. "For all I know, the Cardinal, the old fox, may be on to something. In my time, it was enough for a young woman to know her prayers, but nowadays suitors are looking for something more. Duke Manrique engaged a tutor of Latin for his daughters. I thought him rather a fool at the time, but the Cardinal tells me it's the fashion at court. The late Queen had her daughters instructed in Latin."

"I suppose there is no harm in it, then," Catalina said. "A girl may say her prayers in Latin." But her voice was shaking.

"The Manrique girls are reading the Seven Sages and the Florilegia of Virgil with their tutor. The very books I read as a boy."

"Virgil!" exclaimed Catalina. "Is a Christian girl to read pagan verses?"

Ramon nodded dolefully. "I don't know where this will end, although I found Virgil dull stuff, let me tell you, and more likely to inspire sleep than sinful thoughts. But if the fashion catches on, we mustn't short-change Luisa. I myself don't understand why anybody would want to saddle himself with an educated wife, but let it be. And that brings me to the subject of suitors. Luisa is an exceptional girl, the Cardinal, the old meddler, said to me. I intend to see her married to a man who values her gifts and will make her the companion of his soul."

"It's only right that he should be thinking of her soul, Ramon," his wife said.

"And it's only right for me to think of her position in the world."

"There is something to be said for a marriage of love."

"Sentimental nonsense is the only thing that can be said."

"But you didn't -"

"No, of course I didn't say that to the Cardinal. What do you take me for? I said Luisa is young and malleable. She will adapt to the man we choose for her and fix her affections on him. Then the Cardinal said: But a bully may break a horse's mettle and spoil it for the hunt, and a sullen husband may break a high-spirited girl and ruin her for life."

"Oh dear! What a horrible thing to say. What can he mean?"

"I'll be damned if I know. I told him it's up to the husband to shape his wife according to his wishes. Then he said: Luisa has a fiery spirit and a thirst for knowledge unusual in a woman. She will blossom under the tender care of a man of learning and sensibility."

"Perhaps the Cardinal has someone in mind for her."

"He does. He hinted he would like to see Luisa married to a protégé of his, Deodatus Rijs. He is a famous man, he told me. Famous for what, I said. His books are widely read, he said."

"You mean the Fleming we met at the Duke's house?" Catalina said. "He seemed very pleasant and well-spoken."

"Being pleasant and well-spoken doesn't make the Fleming a desirable suitor. He has been the Duke's guest on several occasions, but that's because the old fool yearns to see his name immortalized in one of Rijs' books. Such are the useless fancies of our betters."

"What will you do?" Catalina said, her eyes filling with tears of apprehension.

Ramon glared at her. "I don't know yet, but weeping doesn't make it any better. The Cardinal is rather pressing about it. He has appointed Deodatus Rijs to a chair at the university. The King has made him royal historian, and he is being received in the best houses."

"That is something at any rate," Catalina said.

"That's what I thought. So I said to the Cardinal: I'll take your recommendation under advisement. Quite so, he said, and let me add that I am willing to contribute to Luisa's dowry if she marries a man of whom I approve. The sly devil!"

Catalina nodded. "Then, perhaps you should consider Deodatus Rijs."

"I have humoured the Cardinal in the choice of tutor," Ramon said, "but I'm not about to humour him in the choice of a husband for my daughter unless he makes it worth my while and comes up with a substantial wedding present. I guess he has a stake in this marriage. He wants that protégé of his to stay at the university, and marrying him to a local woman is one way of tying him down. So if he has an interest in this marriage, let him pay."

"I'm sure he will be generous to Luisa," Catalina said, and her eyes flooded with tears once again. "He loves her dearly."

"Love is one thing, and money is another. The Cardinal is a skinflint in anything except buying books. I would stand up to him, but it's dangerous to balk a powerful man."

"And what does he tell you about Deodatus Rijs' family?"

"Very little. He comes from an honourable family, merchants in the Low Countries, the Cardinal says. Nothing more. His reticence on the point made me uneasy."

"My poor child!" Catalina wailed.

"Your headstrong child!" Ramon said. "She will give us trouble at the first hint that the man is undesirable. You must depict him in flattering terms. Don't say a word about his family."

"What do you wish me to say about him?"

"Tell her..." Ramon faltered. "I don't know what the deuce we can tell her. He is neither young nor handsome. He reminds me of Prince Philip: pale lips and shapeless brows. It must be a Flemish trait."

"The prince's looks were not prepossessing, but his wife was madly in love with him."

"She is mad in every respect. That's why they call her Juana La Loca, and yet she will be queen after King Ferdinand's death. May God have mercy on our country! We should do away with female succession."

"Fray Ferrero says it was learning that unhinged Juana. She read too many books."

"Never mind Ferrero. We have other things to worry about: what to tell Luisa about Deodatus Rijs."

"Inform her in plain terms," Catalina suggested timidly. "And if she cannot be induced to accept him, even the Cardinal – especially the Cardinal who is a scrupulously pious man – will not insist. A marriage lacking consent is no marriage in the eyes of God."

"I don't know about that," Ramon said, "but you may have something there. For once, Luisa's stubbornness may be useful. At the very least, we'll gain time, and I may discover the reason for the Cardinal's reticence about Rijs' family. He cannot expect us to accept him as a son-in-law if there is a blot on his name. And if we do accept him, the marriage contract will reflect our reservations. In any case, I want to see the Cardinal's contribution before I sign anything."

They returned to the house, Ramon in better humour and Catalina placid, comforted by his improved mood. They summoned Luisa. She came into the drawing room with a light dancing step.

Like a high-spirited filly, Ramon thought. A little thin, perhaps, but she holds herself gracefully. There was a pleasing hint of chestnut in her hair. And her eyes – truly fetching.

***

"Come, my dear," Ramon said and led his daughter to a high-backed chair. He rarely treated her in this formal manner, but he wished to convey to her a sense of the grand occasion. She looked at him expectantly, ready to be spoken to.

He sat down on the sofa beside his wife. Silence descended.

For a moment Luisa had the curious feeling that she was a guest in her own house. She noticed the spacing of the objects on the console tables. It was as if she was looking at them for the first time. A rattle of crockery came from somewhere in the house. A door was shut. The sound fell away, and her father leaned forward.

"The time has come to think of a husband for you, Luisa," he said ceremoniously.

"Yes, Papa," she said, trying to look demure. Her hands were resting in her lap, but she could feel a spring-like tension in them. She aligned the tips of her satin shoes to form a perfect parallel. "But you promised to respect my choice, Papa," she said.

He looked at her sternly. "You are a pampered girl, Luisa. Few fathers would make such concessions to their daughters, but I have given you my word, and your wishes will be taken into consideration."

"I am very grateful, Papa," she said and gave him an inquiring glance. "Do you have a suitor in mind?"

Her father's eyes followed the beam of light slanting across the wall, and wandered to the window panes gathering the retreating fire of the sun. "I consulted the Cardinal on your behalf," he said. "He has suggested to me a man of great erudition, Deodatus Rijs. He is not a young man, but it's an honour for a woman to be sought out by a famous scholar."

Luisa gave him a compliant smile. "Like Paula being sought out by Jerome," she said.

"Paula? Jerome?" her father said crossly. "What are you talking about?"

His wife put a soothing hand on his arm. "She means Saint Jerome and his pupil, the noble Paula. Fray Ferrero believes that their letters exemplify the ideal relationship between a man and a woman."

Ramon looked at her, irritated. "Ferrero again?" he said. "What's he got to do with the business at hand?"

"I only wanted to explain...," his wife began and stopped. Her face had the pasty look of indisposition.

"I know all about Deodatus Rijs," Luisa said. "He is the most popular lecturer at the university. Alejandro said he would much rather take a course in rhetoric from Deodatus than go to Salamanca and study law, as you want him to. He says there hasn't been an orator like Deodatus since the days of Cicero. And he has written an amusing book in which he praises folly..."

"You must have gotten it wrong, Luisa," her mother said, interrupting her. "No one praises folly."

But Ramon had already heard of Deodatus' book, *The Trouble with Lady Wisdom*. It had recently been translated from Latin into Spanish.

"It's all the rage at court," he said, "but it is not seemly for a young lady to know about a book that speaks with such liberty of foolish lovers and with such irreverence about society." He knitted his brow. "What has Alejandro told you about the book? The aya should know better than letting you talk to your brother. Young men of his age are full of the wrong kind of ideas. He is bound to have a bad influence on you."

"Oh, but everyone thinks it is a very good book," Luisa said. "It begins by amusing the reader and ends up by edifying him." She warmed to her subject. "I'll give you an example," she said, rising and striking up a speaker's pose.

"Luisa!" her mother breathed, but she ignored her and began to recite with fearless enthusiasm: *Then there are the philosophers. They blot their pages with unadulterated rubbish. They read and reread it...*"

"That will do, Luisa," Ramon said, suppressing a smile.

His wife had shut her eyes in mute objection. She opened them now and started nervously picking at the folds of her clothes. "The things you say, Luisa!" she said disapprovingly.

"But they aren't my words," Luisa said. "They are the words of..."

"That will do!" her father said.

She sat down and compressed her lips for a moment, then perked up again.

"Will there be an exchange of presents, Papa? I could send Deodatus a locket with my picture."

"We are far from the stage of exchanging presents. Negotiations haven't even begun yet. And it would be better if you were not seen in public while those negotiations are ongoing. I want no one whispering in your ears, Luisa."

"You don't want me to go out, not even to church?"

"Papa has hired a new tutor," her mother said. "He will say private mass for us in the chapel."

Luisa's hopes were high for the new tutor. "What's his name? What is he like?" she asked. She was tired of Fray Ferrero. She wanted someone with fresh eyes, soft-spoken and understanding.

"His name is Natale Benvenuto," her mother said. Her lips were twitching. Was there something wrong with the tutor?

"Enough questions, Luisa," her father said. "You may go to your room now and write a letter of thanks to Fray Ferrero and think of words to welcome your new tutor. Perhaps the aya can help you with that."

"She doesn't have any words, and her spelling is awful."

"Luisa! How can you talk like that about the dear old woman!" her mother said.

"She is a dear, but she can't spell."

"Then you will show the letter to your Mama, and she will tell you whether it is appropriate," her father said. "And now you are excused, Luisa."

She rose and took a step forward to kiss him, then remembered that she was a young woman about to be married, and curtsied. "Thank you, Papa," she said. "I will show the letter to Mama."

CHAPTER 5

RAMON CARDOSA THOUGHT HE WAS WELL armed for the marriage negotiations. He had sent a courier to the Low Countries to ferret out any family secrets, and here was the report the man had sent him:

> *Deodatus' mother was the only child of a merchant in Mechelen, who disowned her when she ran off with a musician. Some say that the pair married in a clandestine ceremony. Others say that they weren't married at all when Deodatus was born. In any case, the musician died of the plague, and his widow returned to Mechelen, gravely ill. An uncle, the headmaster of a Latin school, took her in. When she succumbed to her illness, he became the child's guardian.*

I visited the schoolmaster, but the conversation was hard going. He is the only surviving member of the family now, a very old man, half-blind and ill-tempered. He told me that Deodatus entered the service of a courtier and accompanied him to Italy. He lost contact with Deodatus after that and last heard of him when he wrote to say that he was teaching poetry and rhetoric at Alcala. "He would teach poetry," the old man said. "He always had the spirit of perversion in him. And to prove that he had made his way in life, he sent me a foolish little book with a title as contrary as the author. The Trouble With Lady Wisdom – *that was the title, if you please. And he signed himself Doctor. What pseudo-university would give a man like him a doctorate, I don't know!" That's all I could get out of the old man. It was his suppertime, he said, and practically threw me out. I asked if I could come back at a more convenient time. No, he said, we had talked enough about that ingrate. I then made inquiries about Deodatus' doctorate and was told it was an honorary degree from the University of Torino, and might be given to a man in recognition of his exceptional learning but also for ready money or to gratify his patrons.*

Ramon was satisfied. The report was worth the money he had paid the courier. The bit about Deodatus' parentage would certainly serve as a bargaining tool. The questionable academic degree provided additional leverage. The rest was well enough. Deodatus was the Cardinal's protégé. He had attracted the attention of the royal court. He was a popular lecturer and had a devoted following among his students. Not long ago one of them stole Deodatus' lecture notes, cut them into strips and sold them to his classmates as souvenirs. They folded the bits of paper, tied them with ribbons and wore them around their necks like amulets. Ramon heard about this novel fashion from his son. He shook his head and despaired of the young generation. But Deodatus had enthusiasts also among the elite of Alcala. He was wined and dined by wealthy aristocrats in the hope that he would dedicate his next work to them. He was a famous author. His books sold well. They all wanted a piece of Deodatus' fame and were bribing him with silver goblets, signet rings, ermine collars, and cloaks lined with satin. Really, his own generation was just as foolish as the young people!

Ramon Cardosa thought he had discovered Deodatus' secrets. But he had not penetrated to the core of the man, to his thoughts and feelings. He knew nothing of the beast eating away at Deodatus' heart, his sinful inclinations, the malaise of his gloomy thoughts, the dark moods that overtook him at night. He had met Deodatus at the Duke's palace once or twice and knew him only as an urbane man always ready with a quip or a learned quote, a man who gave life to any gathering he attended and who cast a spell over his listeners with the grace and eloquence of his words.

Cardosa never asked himself why Deodatus sought the hand of his daughter. It was all too obvious: Luisa had a good dowry and belonged to the elite of Alcala. Clearly money and prestige is what determined Deodatus' choice. Cardosa would have been astounded to hear that Deodatus felt he had made no choice at all. He was being carried on by destiny. Three times Fate had spoken. When he made his confession to Natale, the priest had imposed on him a most severe and lasting penance: marriage. The Cardinal seemed an agent of fate as well. When Deodatus asked for his help, he at once proposed a match with his niece.

"Luisa's happiness is dear to my heart," Cisneros said. "She is an excellent young woman. I am too fond of her to allow the matchmakers to sacrifice her on the altar of wealth and standing. Luisa must have a husband who cherishes her mind as well as her beauty and does not allow her soul to wither in the shade of ordinary household cares. She is made for extraordinary things."

"I wish I were deserving of her hand," Deodatus said, "but Your Eminence knows my predicament. Cardosa will not accept a bastard as his son-in-law."

Cisneros brushed aside his misgivings. "I will write to the Spanish ambassador in Rome. He will obtain a document legitimizing your birth," he said.

"I hardly deserve such kindness, Your Eminence," Deodatus said with a deep bow. "But even if I obtained a papal dispensation, a marriage contract requires full disclosure and would be an embarrassment to Cardosa."

"I shall instruct the ambassador to insert a clause that allows you to keep silent on that point in legal transactions. Cardosa will have to be informed of your status in private, but he will make no difficulties if the matter can be kept off the public record. He is a man of reason and always listens to my advice."

The Cardinal's words fired the ambition that was ever smouldering in Deodatus' heart: a lasting connection with the Cardinal, a well-dowered wife, kinship with the prestigious Cardosa family was awaiting him. Still, he had qualms until fate spoke to him a third time when he saw Luisa in the cathedral of Alcala. Someone in Duke Manrique's retinue pointed her out to him.

"That's Cardosa's daughter," he said. "They say the stonemason who sculpted the statue of St. Catherine used her as a model. It's a silly story. When the Cardinal commissioned that statue, Luisa Cardosa was a child. But now that she has grown up, she does look remarkably like the saint, don't you think?"

Deodatus looked across the aisle to the Cardosa pew. He saw a slim figure in the first blush of womanhood, exquisitely dressed in a silk gown, her head modestly covered by a lace mantilla. Her skin was so translucent that the veins beneath seemed to cast shadows. Conscious perhaps of being observed, she sat very still and upright, a lovely figure to be adored from afar.

Deodatus' eyes wandered from Luisa to the marble statue of St. Catherine, the patron of scholars, shimmering in the light of votive candles. The saint extended her arms to the faithful, with the palms of her stigmatized hands upturned. Her head was adorned with flaming letters: The Word of God.

"They do indeed look alike," Deodatus said. As he gazed at the statue with wonder, a poem began to form in his mind. St. Catherine's features began to change. The folds of her garment billowed, her arms turned to soft flesh, and a rosy hue enlivened her cheeks. Her countenance was no longer illumined by mystical sainthood but glowing instead with the fresh beauty of a young woman. Her outstretched hands were smooth and unmarked now. She seemed to invite Deodatus to draw near and seek comfort in her embrace, in the embrace of learning. Was it a miracle or poetic inspiration? He couldn't tell, but looking once more at Luisa Cardosa, he bowed to her, and she smiled. At that moment he became convinced that she was his destiny. She was the incarnation of St. Catherine. Dread and foreboding mingled in his heart with anticipation. A deep sense of the inevitable overcame him.

The Cardinal presented a formal proposal on his behalf. In the first exchange of gifts Deodatus gave Luisa a gold-stamped copy of *The Trouble with Lady*

Wisdom. To read a man's book was to read his mind and soul. I shall lay myself open to her, he thought.

Luisa in turn sent him a medallion with her portrait. The painter had given her eyes a curious iridescent quality, as if she was a creature from another world, a nymph escaped from the Homeric woods. No, Deodatus thought, looking at the miniature. She is no pagan creature. She is St. Catherine descended from heaven. We shall lead a life of learning and be a comfort to each other in times of tribulation. The words became his mantra. She will be my St. Catherine. He said them over and over again, until he became a believer.

***

The intricate bartering that precedes marriage began in earnest. Cisneros was a match for Cardosa when it came to negotiating terms. To begin with, they both played for time. Cisneros had to manage the tricky business of legitimizing Deodatus' birth, the diplomatic dance of obtaining a plenary dispensation from the Roman curia. Ramon in turn needed time to investigate his prospective son-in-law's family connections. At last the two protagonists were ready to put their cards on the table. Each of them thought he held the trump.

"I have an offer from a nobleman in Barcelona," Ramon told the Cardinal as they sat down in the privacy of his study, "and a nobleman seems to me a more desirable connection than a scholar."

"My dear Ramon," replied the Cardinal. "I have made my own inquiries and know the man in question. Now let me ask you: are you prepared to give the dowry he demands?"

That round went to the Cardinal. Ramon knew he could not meet the nobleman's expectations without impoverishing himself, but aloud he said: "I am in negotiation with him about that point. And there is another suitor for Luisa's hand. He is the son of a wealthy merchant from Toledo, a very pleasant young man who shows the kind of enterprising spirit I appreciate."

"A man after your taste, no doubt," said the Cardinal. "But he offers you no social advantages. He comes from a family of no distinction."

"And you think your Flemish scholar is the more prestigious match?"

"Nobility of mind counts for something, you know," the Cardinal said.

"I understand that," Ramon said, and decided to play his trump card. "But it does not make up for an uncertain birth."

The Cardinal's expression did not change. He knew how to keep face. "You have heard rumours, I see."

"Never mind rumours. I have had a letter from a correspondent in Antwerp. He tells me that Deodatus' mother ran off with a musician. Does not the church frown on clandestine marriages – if it can be proved that there was a marriage at all?"

"I have always admired your business acumen, Ramon," said the Cardinal. "I am not at all surprised to see you have come to the negotiating table armed with information, and I'm not so foolish as to deny what cannot be denied."

"And you wanted to marry Luisa to a bastard?" Ramon said in a tone of outrage. He did not feel outrage. After all, no one knew of the circumstances of Deodatus' birth. It was a matter of being compensated for taking a risk on him. Showing outrage might induce the Cardinal to make financial concessions.

"I have as much respect for your family – and mine—as any man in my position. I would not have suggested Deodatus, if he did not have a dispensation from Rome, which legitimizes his birth and allows him to remain silent about the matter in legal transactions. There will be no need to mention his illegitimate birth in the marriage contract and expose the information to the eyes of the witnesses. Does that satisfy your concerns?"

It did. If the law permitted Deodatus to suppress the facts, Ramon was content, but it was better to hedge his bet a little longer. "That depends," he said in answer to the Cardinal's question.

Cisneros took the bull by the horns. "What does it depend on, my dear Ramon? Money?"

Ramon held one more trump. "You say that Deodatus is an illustrious scholar," he said, "but are you sure his degree is genuine?"

"Since when are you interested in academics, Ramon?" the Cardinal said. "I can assure you that his learning is genuine. As is the universal admiration for his books."

The Cardinal's answer had not been straightforward. Ramon could tell he had put his finger on a weak point. "However that may be," he said smiling, "what counts with me is the fact that Deodatus is your protégé." Cisneros had hinted that he was prepared to make Luisa a generous gift if the negotiations were concluded to his satisfaction. "If I accept Deodatus as my son-in-law, I do it only to oblige you," he said.

"Most gracious of you, my dear Ramon," the Cardinal said. "You expect to be compensated for your good will, of course."

The time had come to speak of money. "May I remind you of your promise to add to Luisa's dowry and to preside over the wedding ceremony?" Ramon said. "If I can count on you throwing your prestige behind the affair, I am prepared to make allowances for the shortcomings in your protégé."

"I stand by my promise," said the Cardinal. "Deodatus' financial resources will permit him to maintain his wife in the style to which she is accustomed and which the honour of the Cardosa family demands. He is the descendant of a respectable family, and there will be no public embarrassment. I understand that the fact of his illegitimate birth remains, however, and calls for an adjustment in the dowry. If you are agreed to the marriage in principle, we may as well call in the lawyers and discuss the exact terms."

Ramon listened to the Cardinal's summary with an unmoved face. He knew better than to show his satisfaction. "If that is your wish," he said unhurriedly, "let us call them in."

"I have instructed my lawyer to draw up a preliminary document," said the Cardinal. "I understand your man, too, is waiting below. Shall we summon them?"

The lawyers were called. They sat down and haggled over the fine points. Clauses were altered and crossed out and put back in again, but at last a document was drawn up on which all parties could agree:

> *In the name of the Holy and Indivisible Trinity, of the Father, the Son and the Holy Spirit, of the most glorious Mary ever-virgin Mother of God, of the blessed apostles and the entire celestial court triumphant,"* the contract read. *"Be it noted that the respected Ramon de Cardosa promises to give his daughter Luisa to the worthy Deodatus Rijs as his lawful spouse and wife, and the two parties have agreed as follows: Ramon de Cardosa will give him in dower and by the way of dowry of the aforesaid Luisa 700 florins in this wise: that is, a house in Arelate built of masonry with an upper story and with an orchard and wood and outbuildings of stone with a paved yard, with all its appurtenances, valued at 350 florins. Item: jewels and pearls to the value of 150 florins. Item: clothes and other adornments and*

possessions of the aforesaid lady to the value of 50 florins. Item: moneys of account, 150 florins. And the bridegroom pledges that, having received the dowry, he will draw up a document promising to leave the said sum or property and goods to the value of 700 florins to his wife should he predecease her. And thus shall both parties subscribe, and may Jesus Christ permit the couple to live in happiness, prosperity and joy, and grant them sight of their descendants even unto the third and fourth generation, and at the end the paradise of life eternal. Amen.

Ramon was satisfied. Deodatus (or rather, the Cardinal on his behalf) had started out by demanding a dowry of a thousand florins. Had it not been for his illegitimacy, a man of Deodatus' standing would not have accepted anything less than nine hundred florins. And here the whole affair cost Ramon no more than five hundred and fifty. Cisneros had agreed to contribute the 150 florins in moneys-of-account. Yes, it was an excellent bargain.

Ramon called for wine to celebrate the conclusion of the talks and sent a servant to fetch his wife and daughter and the relatives who had been awaiting the outcome of the meeting. The Cardinal in turn sent for Deodatus. A festive table had been laid in the dining hall in the expectation that the negotiations would be fruitful, and Ramon once more congratulated himself on having brought a difficult business to a successful conclusion.

***

The company was waiting. Cardosa introduced Deodatus as his future son-in-law. Deodatus shook hands with the men and bowed to the ladies. At the end of the reception line he spotted a face he had not expected to see in Cardosa's household: a man who knew too much, the Franciscan who had heard his confession. Deodatus had confessed his sins to him because he was a stranger to the city. He expected him to be gone long ago, but here he was – introduced as Luisa's tutor. Natale gave him an ingratiating smile. No recognition showed on his face, no sign that they had met before.

At dinner, Luisa and her mother were seated across from Deodatus. He thought of the portrait she had sent him in the first exchange of presents. The painter of the miniature had gotten it wrong. There was no iridescence in Luisa's eyes. They were black like a bottomless well. Deodatus was overcome by vertigo. He had to look away to steady himself.

It had been madness to sign the contract. How could he be a husband to Luisa? The love poems he had published were a romantic conceit. He knew nothing about women. He had been to brothels long ago, in his student days, but he no longer remembered the touch and feel of women's bodies. He knew only how to make love to men.

Luisa had the slim body of a boy. There was no softness about her, no dimples, no yielding flesh. Is that what saints were like? I might adore her from afar, he thought, but that would not do. She will demand more. Her family will demand more at any rate: an heir.

Luisa was biting her lips. Her mouth was working as if feelings were pulling her this way and that, as if she longed to speak, but was afraid to say the wrong thing and was looking to him for guidance.

He pulled himself together. "I am told you are studying Latin," he said.

"I am trying my best, but there is so much to learn."

"And what have you learned so far?"

"Oh, just silly stuff. The declensions and conjugations."

He gave her a smile meant for a child. She had answered him like a child. "Why is that 'silly stuff'?"

"Because you can't say anything of importance with it. Just *terram video*, 'I see the country' and *puellam videt,* 'he sees the girl' and the like."

"And *puellam amo*, 'I love the girl'?" It slipped out. An easy quip. He shouldn't have.

Luisa blushed. "That, too," she said, and looked down on her plate.

He must try and find the right attitude toward her. Fatherly-stern? Husbandly-earnest? Wit was too dangerous. He was afraid of slipping into satire or sarcasm.

They looked at each other in silence.

"Forgive me," she mumbled, ill at ease. "You are a scholar. You must find me dull."

"Not at all, my dear."

"I want very much to be a learned woman," she said. "Natale – my tutor – says you approve of learned women."

She leaned forward and looked down the table at Natale to assure herself.

"Your tutor is right," he said. "Erudition is a great treasure."

"Natale is teaching me a wedding song by Catullus: *Vesper adest, iuvenes*," she said with a sudden surge of confidence.

"My dear," her mother said, "don't speak Latin at the table. It's not polite. Nobody can understand you."

"Deodatus understands me," Luisa said defiantly.

Catalina squirmed. "Luisa," she said with emphasis, "why don't you tell Deodatus how pleased you were to receive his book."

"How pleased I was to receive your book!" she said, parroting her mother's tone.

"Even though it is in Latin, and nobody can understand it?" he said.

And they both laughed, to Catalina's utter confusion. Perhaps it was possible to be witty with Luisa.

At the end of the meal, they were allowed a moment of privacy, a turn in the garden.

"You are as eloquent as everyone says you are," Luisa whispered.

Next, she will confess her love for me, he thought. And he did not want to make a confession in turn.

"I am so glad you've come into my life," she said, looking up into his face with trusting eyes. "I have always wanted to be the wife of an illustrious scholar." She put her arm on his. "No, that's not quite true. When I was younger, I wanted to be a saint. I wanted to be like St. Catherine."

"St. Catherine?" he echoed, shaken by the confirmation of their fatal bond.

"Yes, a learned saint," she said. "But that was long ago." Her arm remained firmly on his, as if she was afraid he might escape the romance she had planned for them. She held up her face to him, and it was impossible not to kiss her.

He felt her body tensing as she thrilled to his chaste touch. He was baiting calamity. He had no idea how to go on with this charade, how to go on with the story of their mismatched souls.

Chapter 6

It was a long evening. At last he made his escape and walked home through the dark streets of Alcala. A sighing wind arose and broke up the clouds, revealing the wandering moon.

A shadow crept up on Deodatus and settled alongside.

"A splendid dinner," the shadow said. "One feels the need for a digestive walk. You don't mind if I join you?"

Deodatus recognized the shadow. "Not at all, Fray Natale," he said. "It was a pleasant surprise to see you at dinner and discover that you are Luisa's new tutor."

"It was very pleasant, yes, but an occasion that spells the end of my employment."

"You will be leaving the Cardosas?"

"They will have no further use for me after Luisa's marriage and her brother's departure for the University of Salamanca in two months' time."

Deodatus made a quick calculation. It might be best to oblige the Franciscan, take him into his employ and ensure his discretion.

"Luisa is young and has much to learn," he said. "I would not want marriage to put an end to her education. Why not join our household, Fray Natale, and continue with Luisa's instruction? I in turn will continue to benefit from your spiritual counsel."

Natale's face broadened into a smile. "I am most grateful for your offer and glad to accept it," he said. "Let us hope my counsel will be as beneficial in the future as it was in the past."

"Indeed," Deodatus said. "You counselled me to marry and you quoted St. Paul: *It is better for a man to marry than to burn*. But I am not certain I have escaped the fire. Marriage is not without its dangers."

"Especially marriage to a sphinx like Luisa," Natale said. "You know what Cardosa's servants say about her? That she has magical powers. She can attract people as a magnet attracts iron."

Deodatus looked at the Franciscan side-ways. "I grant you Luisa has the power of attraction, but there is nothing magical about the charm of a young woman."

"And if her powers are a divine gift?"

Deodatus laughed uncomfortably. "I don't know whether I would go as far as that, Fray Natale. I agree that Luisa's eyes can be enchanting. But at other times they are the eyes of a child, full of trust, inspiring only love and affection."

"Then I hope you will love her," Natale said.

Deodatus heaved a sigh.

"The prospect of marriage to Luisa does not seem to make you entirely happy," Natale said.

"There is a deep unhappiness in me that nothing can eradicate."

"Not even the love of a divinely gifted woman, a *beata*?"

"You will be calling Luisa a saint next," Deodatus said, and trembled inwardly.

"Oh no, my friend, I wouldn't go that far. The Inquisition might take an interest in me if I did. I leave canonization to the authorities."

"But what is the difference between a *beata* and a saint, I ask you?"

"There is a great difference, my dear Deodatus. *In essentia et in definitione*, in essence and in definition. Not to mention that my proposition was framed in the form of a question rather than a positive statement. Have you forgotten your scholastic training, Doctor Rijs? Or, to quote your uncle, the respected schoolmaster of Mechelen: What pseudo-university would bestow a doctorate on a man who does not know the rules of dialectic?"

Deodatus stopped in his tracks. "My uncle?" he said sharply. "What do you know about my uncle?" He looked into Natale's smiling face and knew that his reaction had been a tactical mistake.

"I know only what the man told me whom Ramon Cardosa hired to inquire into your antecedents," Natale said. "He is a diligent father. You can't blame him for investigating his future son-in-law, can you?"

Deodatus held his breath and allowed his heartbeat to slow before he said calmly. "To answer your question about my degree, or rather my uncle's question—if he really asked it—I obtained my doctorate at Torino. And I believe Italian universities command as much respect in the academic world, if not more, than Spanish universities."

"Oh, indeed, the Italians are highly respected," Natale said. "I did not mean to impugn your credentials. Nothing can be further from my mind."

"And what other innuendoes, or should I say lies, did the man spread about me?" Deodatus said. He had regained his composure. His voice was firm.

"Only that you have the spirit of perversion in you. That is how your uncle put it, I'm afraid."

Deodatus could feel cold sweat gathering on his brow. He wished he had never confessed to Natale. "The old man has as much justification to question my character as I have to question your orthodoxy for believing in *beatas*."

"You are tweaking my nose, and I deserve it because I have spoken too freely," Natale said. His voice was amiable. "As for my orthodoxy, the belief in *beatas* is well received in the church and as old as mysticism itself. Sodomy, I grant you, may be an old tradition in the church as well, but it is not well received, or at any rate not approved by the Pope. But come, Deodatus, these are quibbles. You need not worry about my discretion. I respect the secret of confession."

They had arrived at the gate of the university, where Deodatus had rooms. He could not very well bid Natale good bye on that note. Unfortunately he had confessed the attraction young men held for him. It was only a small step from sin to crime, from expiating a wayward thought with a penance to paying for wayward behaviour with public humiliation and incarceration. He forced a smile.

"The night is young. Why don't you come in, Fray Natale, and join me for a glass of Malaga?"

***

They drank to each other's health and talked about their avocations, Natale's love of books, Deodatus' love of words.

"My uncle never approved of my literary efforts," he said to Natale. "We did not part on good terms. He never could forgive my refusal to follow in his footsteps and take over his school."

"Your literary talents would have been wasted on schoolboys," Natale said. "Your uncle must be a cross old man not to acknowledge your success. Alcala resounds with your praises." He launched into a list of Deodatus' successes. "You are the Cardinal's protégé.

You have been appointed court historian. Your books are admired everywhere."

"Yes," Deodatus said, "I have risen in the world. But does it add up to happiness? When my students applaud or my friends express their admiration for my writings, I feel safe in the womb of their approbation. I listen to their praise with pride, but when I am alone, my happiness drains away. My spirits sink as I contemplate the long night ahead. I lie on my bed sleepless."

"Insomnia is a great affliction. It can drive a man to the brink of insanity," Natale said full of solicitude. "But if that is all that's keeping you from happiness, my friend, a sleeping draught will take care of it. You know about Chavez the alchemist? He has the remedy for your troubles. He plies his trade in a shack by the city wall."

Deodatus said nothing. It was risky to associate with an alchemist. Was the Franciscan baiting him?

Natale smiled nonchalantly. "I went there to satisfy my curiosity about a man whose services are so highly appreciated by society. The visit was rather unpleasant. The place is a hovel half sunk into the earth and windowless. I must say I felt nauseous at first. The air was stifling, thick with acrid vapours from the furnace. The sights made me queasy as well—shelf after shelf packed with jars of frog legs and shrunken lizards, crooked teeth, eyeballs, foetuses suspended in murky liquids. My stomach was churning. But after a while, I got used to the fumes and the lurid sights."

"I have no desire to associate with an alchemist," Deodatus said. "The Inquisition has probed his activities and accused him of necromancy."

"And acquitted him."

"In exchange for supplying the names of his customers?"

"More likely, because he has friends in high places. I know of a grand lady who asked him to cast a horoscope for her new-born child. You would not be the first man of good standing to ask him for a sleeping draught, believe me. His concoctions are quite effective, although they work an irregular magic. Sometimes the coloured dreams turn into nightmares."

"As a bridegroom, I should perhaps worry more about perking up than about going to sleep," Deodatus said. He tried to smile, but the smile turned into a grimace. The wedding night weighed heavily on his mind, more heavily than the wakeful nights he had suffered in the past.

"I see," Natale said lightly. "You want a spell of virility for the wedding night. I suppose Chavez does that kind of thing as well. I have heard he sells scented lamp oil which makes men and women delirious with passion, and pomades to be smoothed on lips and fingertips to arouse a lover with one touch, and of course the usual potions to turn you into Priapus."

"That is the kind of prescription a bridegroom needs," Deodatus said. His lips stretched into a ghastly grin.

"Perhaps we should pay him a visit together," Natale offered.

"I cannot risk my reputation."

"You worry too much, my friend. Even Jesus walked among the publicans and sinners."

Deodatus was writhing with embarrassment. "You would not oblige me by..." He dared not finish his request.

Natale smiled ironically. "Going to Chavez on your behalf, you mean?" He paused and left Deodatus in suspense before continuing. "I would not do it for just anyone. But I sympathize with your plight, my friend—I may call you friend, I hope. So be it. I shall visit Chavez and inspect his wares and buy an elixir to quicken your reflexes. It will be my wedding present."

Deodatus knew it was the wrong thing to do. He should not accept favours from a man like Natale. I must not be in his debt, he thought. I will have to make it up to him. Thank God, he is a venal man, and I can buy his silence.

He thanked Natale and bid him goodnight and sat down at his desk, calming his fears the way he always did. He took up pen and paper to write down his thoughts. But he was too upset even for that and had to settle for a schoolboy's exercise, writing out a sentence in a dozen variants.

I can buy his silence. I can procure his silence. I can obtain his silence. I am able to buy his discretion. I am able to buy his secrecy. I can hush him up. I can make him hold his peace. I can stop his mouth. I can bribe him to keep silent. I will induce him to keep my secret. I shall buy him off.

The possibilities were endless. Deodatus felt reassured.

***

The day began as glorious as Luisa had imagined it. The house was adorned with garlands of flowers, the doors festooned with canopies, colourful tapestries fluttered from the balconies. Her mother was resplendent in a golden chaplet set with gems and pearls, her father regally austere in black velvet. They exchanged greetings and embraces with the wedding guests. The servants offered trays of delicacies to the well-wishers: sweetmeats of honey and pine nuts, coloured and decorated eggs, rice pudding cooked in milk of almonds. Masked players were performing mimes and dances, actors recited love poetry; it was just the way Luisa had imagined it. But in other respects, the day did not go according to her dreams. Deodatus wandered off to talk to the guests. Their hands did not stay entwined, their eyes did not stay locked in a yearning gaze. She tried to reason with her discontent. It was as it ought to be, she told herself. The bridegroom must entertain his guests. Maybe I, too, should be more solicitous, she thought, and join the maids and matrons of the family to gossip about who would be the next bride. But her attention wandered. She looked across the room trying to catch Deodatus' eye. "You need only look at a man to attract him," the aya had told her, but her magical powers were in abeyance. It seemed as if her strength had ebbed with the exchange of rings. Are my charms only a temporary gift, she thought, a gift lost the day I stood before the altar and promised to love and obey? Perhaps that's what it means to grow old. One day, she thought, I will be as limp and drained of life as my mother.

When she finally caught Deodatus' eye, there was no melting love in his gaze, nothing that said he wanted to sweep her up in his arms and carry her to a secret bower, as the poets promised in their verses and she had pictured in her dreams. Deodatus gave her a look of adoration, yes, but as if he wanted to put her on a pedestal and touch the folds of her gown for good luck or say a prayer to her. He has strayed into the wrong dream, she thought, the one I had long ago, when I wanted to be a saint.

In the evening, Luisa was allowed to touch his hand again as they sat down to a sumptuous dinner of fifteen courses with musical interludes. There were trumpet players, sackbuts, hornpipes, and mandolins. Her father had spared no expense to make the wedding an elegant celebration. After dinner, Luisa handed out mementos to the ladies: small oblong baskets containing silver tongs, cases filled with needles from Damascus, and silver thimbles covered in fine filigree work. The house rang with laughter and good cheer, but the tableau did not match Luisa's dreams. Deodatus' face was a little too grey; the wine and the laughter had failed to warm him. At the second hour of the night, a giddy entourage of cousins led them to the master bedroom. They teased the groom. Could he handle so beautiful a girl? They bantered. After so much wine, was he up to the task? Luisa blushed and did not know what to say, but Deodatus parried every pun with one of his own, and gave as well as he got. She was glad he was so witty, but wit was not the same as happiness, and elegance not the same as youth and beauty.

Luisa had foolishly dreamed of a moonlit garden, of reciting poetry in a bower, of being crowned with a wreath of spring blossoms, but it was a different kind of magic that filled her wedding night – black magic. The door closed on her laughing cousins, and Deodatus' charm turned to stone. A glum silence descended on them. Her great embarrassment, her awkward embraces and diffident kisses were unmitigated and not consoled by sweet wonder. She did not know what to expect, but when Deodatus' embroidered robe fell open and exposed his body to her curious eyes, she shrunk from touching his thin chest, averted her eyes from his stringy arms and trembled at the thought of the veins in his neck. Did all embroidered cloaks, pleated silk robes, and all fine cambric shirts conceal such ugliness? Did God compensate the poor for their deprivations with beautiful bodies? She thought of the smooth brown cheeks of the stable boy and the sturdy sunburned arms of the men in the yard. How handsome they were! But she had promised to love and obey Deodatus.

She watched Deodatus take a vial from a carved ebony chest on the bedside table. He smiled at her, but there was a deadly sadness in his eyes. "Natale's wedding present," he said and raised the vial to his lips. "To your health, my lady love." For a moment he stood beside the bed with his shoulders stooped, as if in defeat, then he lay down beside Luisa. There was pain in his eyes as he brushed his lips against her shoulder. She shut her eyes tightly and stiffened as he lowered his body onto hers. She could not help thinking of the painting above the main altar: the body of Christ being lowered from the cross, the stiff limbs, the crown of thorns pressing on his pallid forehead, the blood mingled with water welling up from the gash in his side, the suffering face of the Virgin as she enfolded the lifeless corpse. It was as if Deodatus' groans were uttered by the grieving onlookers at the foot of the cross, and she received his body in sorrow.

A macabre dance of death began. He heaved and panted. Luisa wanted to cry out, but her voice was locked within her. The senseless wrangling continued, until he stopped suddenly, rolled off her, and roughly directed her to turn on her stomach. She obeyed, and he began to belabour her furiously, slapping his body against her back like one possessed. She felt a searing pain, shrieked and arched her back to throw him off, but he brought his weight to bear on her and rode her like a demon. With a muffled cry he collapsed at last, shedding sweat and tears. He lay beside Luisa, very still, his face so close to hers that she could feel his breath on her cheek. Luisa's body was throbbing with pain. She put her hand to the small of her back and came away with a sticky substance. The blood of a dying man has entered me, she thought. He moved away, and she could see his damp, glistening face.

"Forgive me," he said humbly.

A great wave of pity filled Luisa's heart. She was willing to forgive him. She was willing to weep with him, but he was looking up into the dark canopy of the bed, and she sensed that he was speaking to another. She felt a tremor passing through her body, like a musical vibration. An unseen presence stood between them, a matte radiance, a silver coating in the air, a blurred image in the corner of her eye. Then she understood: a lover, someone who was taking up her place in his heart. She wanted to run, to hide, to be back in her own bedroom with the aya stroking and soothing her and crooning a lullaby. I must be brave, she told herself, I must win him over, but fear of the unknown seized her, beating its wings in her heart like a caged bird.

CHAPTER 7

LUISA WAS MISTRESS OF HER OWN HOUSE now, an elegant villa with a flagstone court, a sun-dappled stucco front and red-tiled roof. It sat on a hillside overlooking the village of Arelate and the fields of their tenant farmers. The walls of Alcala and the spire of the cathedral formed a jagged line on the horizon, shimmering in the hazy morning sun. A terrace at the back of the house led to a walled garden with orange and lemon trees, square flower beds in full spring bloom, and fragrant herb borders. It was an idyllic setting for her unhappiness. How could a man be so changeable, she wondered: urbane and witty by day, grotesque and monstrous by night?

When her mother came to pay her first official visit, Luisa looked into her lethargic eyes and despaired of getting advice. Her face will crumple when I tell her that I am unhappy, Luisa thought. She will dissolve in tears. Her mother had brought along the aya. If anyone would come to her aid, it was the nanny. Luisa had always thought of the old woman as a family treasure, a legacy from her mother, but it turned out she was a borrowed jewel and, on Luisa's marriage, reverted to the original owner. She was hovering around her mother now, clucking and fussing over her mistress as if she was a little girl again.

Luisa led the two women into the drawing room. Her mother, dressed in shimmering silk of pewter grey, sank into a settee and allowed the aya to arrange the folds of her dress. She looked around the well-appointed room with satisfaction and patted the seat beside her.

"Come, my dear," she said to Luisa. "Sit by my side."

The aya discreetly excused herself to allow them a heart-to-heart talk. "I'll take a turn in the garden," she said.

Luisa had played the chatelaine bravely and kept up a painted smile, but now that she was alone with her mother, she allowed the corners of her mouth to droop. A look of alarm came into Doña Catalina's eyes. She was not prepared to deal with unhappiness. When she asked "Are you happy, my child?" she expected to hear no more than a polite affirmation: Yes, mother, I am.

Luisa said nothing of the sort. She asked a question in turn: "Tell me, Mama, why did you and Papa decide on Deodatus as my husband?"

"He was the Cardinal's choice," Catalina said. Her cheeks wobbled. The question disturbed her.

"The Cardinal's choice?" Luisa said. She trusted the Cardinal. He had never disparaged her dreams. When she told him of her wish to become a saint, he promised to pray for her. When she changed her mind and told him she would rather be a wife and mother, he smiled kindly and said: Then we must find you a husband. And when her mother complained about her unruliness, he gently defended me: She is young, Doña Catalina. She is a spirited girl. He had her interest at heart, and he was admired and respected by everyone. His judgment could not be wrong.

"But why do you ask?" her mother said.

She blushed when Luisa told her: "Because Deodatus does not love me. He makes me suffer."

"It is our lot as women," she said, giving her a helpless embrace. Her eyes were moist. "You must be patient, Luisa. In time, God willing, you will be with child, and the pleasure of dandling a baby on your knees will make up for all the sorrow and suffering Eve has brought upon us women." She recommended to Luisa her own marital arrangement. She always submitted to Ramon's demands, she said, even if they were distressing.

But Luisa was not done with her story. She told her mother things she did not want to hear, the dark ritual of her bedroom. Doña Catalina raised her hands to ward off Luisa's words. She would have liked to stop her ears. She pretended not to understand, and her eyes widened with relief when she saw the aya standing at the door.

"You are back in time, my dear," she said to the old woman. Her voice was thin and panicky. "Luisa needs your advice."

The aya plodded across the room on her flat feet, eased her broad thighs into a chair, and politely waited to be taken into confidence, waiting to be told what she had likely overheard already.

"We need to consult a priest," Doña Catalina said, sniffling back tears. "I wish I could talk to Fray Ferrero!"

"He would be more useful than Fray Natale," the aya said. She looked at Luisa probingly. "I can't think why your husband has kept him on. I wouldn't entrust my soul to a priest like him. He has no dignity. He dodges to the right and left like a puppy dog."

Catalina sighed. "Don Ferrero was a very different kind of man."

The aya nodded. "He lived like a man of the cloth. Fray Natale, I am told, carries on like a gentleman. The maid says the chairs in his room are padded, the floor covered with a rug. Fray Ferrero never indulged in such luxuries. He prayed, kneeling on the stone floor like the rest of us, humbling himself before God. A cross was the only ornament he permitted. Fray Natale, I hear, has filled his room with heathen things: a headless statue and a shell shaped like a trumpet. Whoever heard of such things? And he has books with strangely shaped letters.

The maid is afraid of dusting them. They look like black magic to her."

"Nonsense," Luisa said. "What does a maid know about books? And what has all that got to do with my troubles?"

"Luisa is right," her mother said to the aya. "You should speak more respectfully of Fray Natale, my dear."

The aya pursed her lips and looked defiant. "In any case," she said, "if Fray Ferrero were here to advise you, he would tell you the same thing as I: you must speak to Don Ramon about Luisa's troubles."

Catalina blanched. "I can't possibly tell him what Luisa said," she wailed. "I would die of shame."

"It is your duty, Doña Catalina," the aya said firmly.

Catalina's shoulders sagged. "If it is my duty," she said, dabbing at her eyes, "and if you think Don Ramon can help Luisa..."

"He will at any rate remind her husband of the holy purpose of marriage. God said: go forth and multiply," the aya said.

Catalina looked at her daughter teary-eyed. "I think no one should come between husband and wife," she said. "My advice is: bear with Deodatus. He may yet learn to love you. Once you present him with an heir-"

"But that's the difficulty," the aya said sharply. "There will be no heir if things go on like that. No, there is no way around it, Doña Catalina. You must talk to your husband."

Doña Catalina went away trembling and in tears, leaning heavily on the aya's arm, but she did not shirk her duty. She informed her husband: Luisa was being used unnaturally.

***

Luisa was standing at her bedroom window when she saw the groom open the gate to her father. He dismounted and crossed the courtyard. His face was black with rage. Luisa went downstairs to receive him and was told that his business was with her husband. As the two men went into the large drawing room, Luisa withdrew to the library next door. She hesitated a moment before stepping out on the terrace. The French windows of the drawing room stood ajar. The men's voices drifted across to her. She flattened her back against the wall and looked down on the dusky rose tiles of the terrace, her face hot with embarrassment. It was shameful to listen in on the men's conversation, but Deodatus' behaviour was equally shameful.

She heard her father's booming voice. "It's a sin against God and the laws of marriage!"

Deodatus' response was measured and barely audible. "You are putting the worst construction on the words of an inexperienced girl," he said evenly. "What, exactly, has she told you?"

"She has told me nothing," her father conceded. "She complained to her mother that things were not as they ought to be."

"And you give credence to the tales of two silly women," Deodatus said, "instead of supporting my authority as a husband? How would you like it if I undermined your paternal authority?"

"I shall support your authority," her father said, "when I see proof that you have acted like a husband."

"And if Luisa is incapable of bearing children?"

"And if you are incapable of fathering children?" her father retorted.

"I suggest," Deodatus said, "you go home and cool your heels. We shall resume our conversation another time, when you are prepared to honour the conventions observed in polite society and when you can muster the good will that should govern family relations."

"You are very good with words," her father said, "and have the cunning of a lawyer, but we shall see whether you can back up your words with deeds."

Luisa had heard enough. Deodatus had not demanded an apology from her father for impugning his honour. Among gentlemen, that was as much as admitting guilt.

She slipped back into the library and withdrew to a window seat. A few minutes later, her father took his leave. She heard Deodatus bidding him an icy farewell. He crossed the hall and stopped at the door of the library. Luisa was hoping to remain unnoticed, but Deodatus had already caught sight of her in the window recess. Their eyes met. Luisa felt her cheeks flame up.

Deodatus looked through the open window to the terrace.

"So you have been listening," he said.

"I could not help overhearing your conversation."

"Indeed your father raised his voice to me in a most unbecoming manner," he said. "I understand you have been complaining to your mother." He tossed it off like a casual observation, but his eyes were watchful.

"I did not complain. I merely asked my mother –
"

"No need to justify yourself, Luisa. I shall not trouble you again."

"You think I betrayed you."

"You are so very innocent, my child." He sighed. "Life always punishes the innocent."

"I don't understand you."

"And it is better that you should not understand me," he said.

The macabre nights ended. So did the amicable days. Deodatus treated Luisa with polite indifference. He looked at her with eyes that refused any obligation. A wall arose between them, of beautiful words. The conversations Luisa had imagined, full of wit and laughter and learning, became like the exercises in a handbook of style, full of measured, practised phrases. Their sequence did not matter much. You could string them up any way you wanted. They always yielded half-meanings and innuendoes and fragments of thought, not quite disjointed, not quite well fitting either, enough to carry on pleasantly and never say anything in particular. She began to regret her father's involvement. Her mother had been right after all. It was a matter that should be settled between husband and wife. It was the wife's task to gain her husband's love. Luisa looked in the mirror and bit her lips: who could love a scrawny creature like her? Her face was thinner and her hands bonier than ever. She thought of the many times she had been reprimanded for being wilful and obstinate. No wonder Deodatus could not warm to her. She should never have complained. She should never have allowed her father to interfere. Of course it was the aya's advice that had caused all the trouble. She had urged her mother on: you must tell Don Ramon. It is your duty. But it was the wrong advice. The aya had gotten her into trouble, and she must get her out again, Luisa thought, and sent a note to her mother. "Dearest mother," she wrote. "Can you spare the aya for a few days? I need her advice on the management of the household and would like her to go over the routine with me."

  A few days later the aya came. She sat with her hands folded in the lap of her black cotton dress. Her grey hair was neatly pulled back and covered by a starched wimple. Luisa took a seat beside her and felt like a child again, safe and protected. The warmth of the evening sun coming through the half-closed shutters of the bedroom mellowed her heart. She was reluctant to begin on the unpleasant subject.

  "Nanny," she said at last, breaking the peaceful silence, "I despair of ever making Deodatus love me, and

Papa's meddling has made things worse." She wanted to say: it's your fault, but she settled on a milder reproof. "I wish you had given my mother better advice."

The aya lowered her eyes, but refused to take the blame. "It was the right thing to inform your father," she said.

"I don't know about that. It didn't endear me to Deodatus. Fray Ferrero's book, which you and mama pressed on me, had nothing to say on the subject of winning a husband's heart. And you made it seem so easy. You talked a great deal about the 'magic' of my eyes. You said I could attract any man I set my sights on, but I do not find that magic efficacious in the bedroom."

"My dear child," the aya said, "perhaps I was wrong, and you need a different kind of magic."

"And what would that be?"

"There is a woman in the village who knows how to mix love potions. I won't name names, but one of the ladies in the Duke's family gave her husband a draught, and he was besotted with her in no time. Ten months later she gave birth to a baby boy, and her grateful husband presented her with a pair of fine ruby earrings – but I won't say more, or you'll guess who she is, and I've been sworn to secrecy by her maid."

"I have heard talk about the *bruja* of Arelate, but no one can tell whether her knowledge comes from God or from the devil."

"The devil could not have produced such an angelic child, Luisa. He is the sweetest boy you have ever seen, with cheeks as round and soft and glowing as peaches. I would thank God and all the saints and light a hundred candles in the cathedral if I could see you with such a child in your arms, my pet. Would you like me to consult the *bruja* on your behalf?"

"I should want to talk to the woman myself before I use any of her potions."

"Don't be stubborn, Luisa. It would not do for a lady in your position to visit a *bruja.*"

"I'll risk it," Luisa said, a little breathless and caught out by her own recklessness.

The aya wagged her head. "Say rather, *we*'ll risk it, my pet, for I cannot let you go on your own. But if as much as a whisper reaches Don Ramon's ears that I have taken you to see a *bruja,* he will dismiss me, and I will end my life in poverty and shame."

"I will look after you, don't worry," Luisa said. She kept her voice firm, but her eyes pleaded with the old woman. "You will do it for me, nanny?"

The aya sighed. "I will risk anything for your happiness, my sweet child," she said.

And you owe it to me, Luisa thought. It was your bad advice that got me into trouble with Deodatus.

"Here is what we'll do," the aya said. "We'll wait until everyone is asleep. Then we'll slip out through the little gate in the garden. God willing, we'll find what we want and get back without being caught."

After the house had fallen silent, the two women went out into the garden, veiled and wrapped in black mantillas. It seemed to Luisa that the rustling of the skirts must give them away, and the crunch of the gravel under their feet must wake up the whole household. But everything remained still. All but invisible in the deep shadow of the trees, they passed through the back gate into the road. Luisa gathered up her skirts and hurried after the aya, feeling hot and sticky despite the cool night air. Once she saw a shadow in the road, and her insides liquefied with fear, but it was only a stray dog slinking and nosing about. Just before they came to the first houses of the village, the aya took Luisa's arm and turned into a narrow lane leading to a dilapidated hut. She knocked on the window. The ramshackle door opened almost at once, and an old woman peered at them from the threshold. She did not seem surprised at the late visitors. She was dressed in rags. Her sagging bosom spilled out of her tattered dress and revealed long nipples like decaying berries. She eyed the fine material of Luisa's mantilla and beckoned the two women into her hovel.

"Come in, come in, my dear ladies," she said, bowing and scraping. The only light in the room came from a heap of fitfully burning sticks in the hearth, illuminating a packed dirt floor. Smoke rose from the hearth to the black rafters in a hazy swirl. A burlap curtain shielded the back half of the hut from sight. Luisa heard raucous voices and inarticulate groans mingled with laughter and heavy breathing as if a fight was going on in that quarter. The old woman gave off a stale odour of sweat and urine with every step, and a more spicy scent that reminded Luisa of the *corrida*. She had never imagined such a sordid existence.

"What can I do for you, my dear ladies?" the old hag said, leering at them. Luisa lost courage and hid behind the aya's stocky frame, leaving the explanation to her.

"You've come to the right place," the woman said with a rotting grin after listening to the aya's request. "Love charms are my specialty. I've been of service to many ladies, and every one of them has come back to thank me. Let me show you what I've got, my dears."

She rummaged under a bench by the wall and produced three small packages tied with twine. She unfolded them and revealed their contents: tiny bleached bones, speckled beans, and white powder. She dove once more under the bench and returned with a candle, a piece of rope, and a flask containing a murky liquid.

"That's what you need if you want a man's love, madam," she said to Luisa. "It took me a deal to get all the ingredients together, so I can't let you have them cheap."

"Don't worry," said the aya brusquely, "you'll get what you deserve, in this world and the next."

The old woman only cackled in response. "This is the rope of a church bell," she said, cutting off a short piece. "It cost me a pretty penny to get it from the sacristan, and it has never failed me yet. If you want a man's love, you need a consecrated rope. There's no way around it." She lit the candle, burned the ends of the rope over its flame, and extinguished the smoldering wick with a sprinkling from the flask. "Holy water," she explained, "from Jerusalem, every drop worth its weight in gold." She cast the piece of rope together with some of the bones, beans, and white powder into the fire. It flared up in a momentary blaze and died down again. "And now the magic formula, to be spoken by the spirit of an innocent child," the woman said, clapping her hands.

The curtain parted, and an adolescent boy appeared, pretty and slim hipped. He did not strike Luisa as an innocent. He was filthy and turned on her a roving eye that betrayed an equally filthy mind.

"My angel," the old woman said to the boy, nodding and giving him an insider's wink, "I thank you for coming to our aid. Now say a prayer on behalf of this unhappy woman and send her lover the three good messengers!"

The boy gave Luisa another insolent look, raised his arms and intoned:

"I am sending you three good messengers: the bell, the bean, and the ashes of St. Daniel. I pray they will bind you and squeeze you and inflame your loins to make you lovesick until you do my bidding. I conjure you by the power of this holy trinity. Amen."

After the prayer, he held out his palm to Luisa, pocketed the coin she gave him after a whispered consultation with the aya, and ducked back behind the curtain. He was received with a great cheer, and shut up his unseen companions with a coarse command. The voices in the backroom fell silent.

"Begging your pardon, ladies," the *bruja* said. "It's hard sometimes to keep the spirits down."

"Evil spirits, by the sound of it," the aya said.

"They have never yet failed me," the old woman said and looked at her visitors boldly. "I have them all at my command." She took an iron poker and drew a circle with it on the dirt floor of the hut.

"We are almost done," she said. "Step into the circle, my dear lady, and think hard of your lover."

Luisa had clasped the aya's hand and let go reluctantly. She stood in the circle, waiting. She had lost all nerve after looking into the eyes of the *bruja's* helper. No good could come from that depraved beggar boy and his filthy dame.

The old woman sprinkled the hem of Luisa's coat with water from the flask of Jerusalem water and announced: "It's as good as done. Your lover is in your hands now, madam."

Luisa paid the woman, dropping the coins into her palm gingerly without touching the unclean hand, and quickly turned to go. But the pay was perhaps too generous because the old woman followed her out into the lane eagerly and pressed on her a piece of paper, folded into a square.

"And to keep the spell working, madam," she said, "you need only apply this magical square, the use of which I shall gladly teach you the next time. For I hope you will honour me with another visit soon."

Luisa tucked the gift away unwillingly and said nothing. When they were safely out of earshot, she whispered to the aya: "I shall never go back. The woman is a charlatan, I am sure."

"Don't be so sure, my dear," the aya answered. "It did look bad, but wait and see if the magic works."

Was this the nurse on whose lips she had hung as a child, the constant companion whose sagacity she had never questioned? Luisa pursed her lips and said nothing. She had eaten from the tree of knowledge. The return to the Eden of her childhood was barred. I am truly alone, she thought. I cannot expect help from a woman who is a credulous fool.

They reached the house without incident. Luisa threw off her cape and bid the aya good night. Alone in her room, she inspected the grimy bit of paper the *bruja* had foisted on her. It contained a line of writing, or rather mysterious signs she could not decipher. On the outside it said: "Capnio's use of the powerful name of Christ." She was about to toss the paper into the fire, but respect for Christ's name made her hesitate, and she put it away in her writing desk.

***

The next evening, as Luisa was about to go to bed and knelt at prayer, Deodatus came to her room and, for a moment, she wondered whether it was Capnio's use of the powerful name of Christ that had brought him, but she reprimanded myself and discarded the superstitious thought. There was no affection in Deodatus' eyes. He offered her no endearments. He took a seat by her bed, keeping his distance.

"I have brought you a present," he said and placed a manuscript on the bedside table. "A book I have recently completed."

A peace offering? Or an opening gambit in another round of marital strife? Luisa glanced at the title: *How to live one's life. Three Dialogues.*

"I have made you a character in the book," he said.

"Again?" Luisa said lightly. "I thought I recognized myself in *The Trouble with Lady Wisdom.*"

He ignored her bantering tone. "You have always been my inspiration, Luisa," he said in a serious voice. "Ever since you appeared to me in a dream."

"A dream or a nightmare?"

He looked at her gravely. "A poetic dream. I was attending mass at the cathedral when the statue of Saint Catherine seemed to me to come to life. The stone turned to flesh before my eyes. Instead of the saint I saw a young woman who beckoned me to embrace her. When I recovered my senses, I pondered the meaning of this miracle, or shall we say, poetic inspiration. St. Catherine is the patron saint of learning, I thought. She asks me to embrace scholarship. She wants me to understand that learning will be my salvation. Then I met you, Luisa, and recognized St. Catherine in you."

"And I have disappointed you, because I am no saint," Luisa said.

He did not reply and looked at her sadly.

She knew not what to make of his words, but he seemed to be speaking from the heart, and she did not want to discourage him. "Tell me about the book," she said.

"It is a book of dialogues," he said. "The first one is called 'The abbot and the lady'. He advises her to put aside romantic dreams and turn her attention to the household. She advises him to put aside worldly desires and turn his attention to books."

"I see, they are giving each other valuable advice," Luisa said. Disappointment crept into her voice. The sincerity was gone. Their talk had reverted to a game of words. "Never mind the abbot and the lady," she said impatiently, "let us speak instead of Deodatus and Luisa."

"I meant the two characters to represent you and me," he said. "I find I cannot live in the material world, which brings me only unhappiness. I hoped we might reach an understanding and divide our spheres of action. I shall withdraw into the world of books. You will immerse yourself in the government of the household. Of course, I do not mean you should neglect the training of your mind."

"Only to forget my romantic dreams." Luisa could not keep the passion out of her voice. "No, my dear Deodatus, you must revise your book and write in something about love if your characters are to represent you and me."

"I am afraid I cannot revise my book, Luisa."

The manuscript sat on the side table, a bundle of leaves, loose and untidy like their lives. They stood, mutely looking at each other. If only he kissed me, Luisa thought. If only he took me into his arms. But he is who he is. Fate has written the dialogue, and he cannot revise it.

"I have interrupted your prayers," Deodatus said and stepped back. "I should not have come so late in the day."

They said good night without looking into each other's eyes, without touching.

Capnio has no knowledge of divine power, Luisa thought when Deodatus had left. She opened her writing desk, searched for the paper with the mysterious words, and tore it to pieces. The *bruja* had no magic. She played on the despair in the hearts of her customers, imposing on fools and tricking the minds of the credulous. I must look for another counsellor, she thought, someone who can support his advice with reason. Perhaps I should confide my troubles to Fray Natale.

At first Luisa had not thought much of the fat little man. Next to Fray Ferrero, he seemed inconsequential. Ferrero had been a tacit and stern old man who commanded fear and respect. No one could possibly be afraid of Natale. He was always smiling, always anticipating her wishes. The pain behind Luisa's forehead eased when she thought of Natale. She was glad he had moved into their house at Arelate, glad that Deodatus asked him to continue as her tutor. He had a knack of mingling his lessons in Latin composition with lessons in the ways of the world. Natale would make a good sounding board. There was no need to confess her troubles. Under the guise of rhetorical exercises, she could hint at what could not be said outright. And Natale was in Deodatus' confidence as well. Perhaps he could serve as their go-between, and the book of life might be revised after all.

CHAPTER 8

NATALE WAS PLEASED WITH HIS NEW position. The Cardosas had been a disappointment to him. Ramon was a brute, his wife an imbecile. As the keeper of Catalina's guilty secret, he had expected to be indulged by the mistress, but Catalina was in no position to hand out favours. She made no decisions. She had long relinquished the reins of the household to the aya, a sullen old woman. And she had no influence over her tyrannical husband. Or perhaps it was truer to say, no one had influence over him. No one could bend his will or shake his sense of self-importance.

    Natale was happy to leave the Cardosas and join the young couple at Arelate. He settled into a comfortable routine there. He said morning mass in the private chapel, and then sat for an hour or two reading his breviary, or at any rate keeping the open breviary in his lap. Sometimes he attended Luisa when she gave her instructions to the housekeeper and listened to their discussion of the purchase of victuals, the airing of linen presses, the turning of mattresses, and a thousand other details necessary for the smooth running of a household. At other times he walked in the garden or read in his room. At noon he sat down with the couple to an elegant dinner. Deodatus regaled them with amusing anecdotes and learned opinions if there was company present. With only the three of them around the table, he allowed Luisa to run on, correcting her diction from time to time and smiling indulgently. Sometimes he lost patience with her and said to Natale: "She is a charming prattler, our dear Luisa, isn't she?" Then Luisa blushed and fell silent. After the meal Natale retired to take his siesta. At four o'clock, punctually, he went to the library to tutor Luisa. At six, refreshments were served. And so the day passed very pleasantly into evening, ending with supper and devotions before bedtime, when the whole household assembled in the drawing room and knelt in prayer.

In Cardosa's house Natale had been assigned a miserable room hardly better than a hermit's cell – cold, lightless, and ill-furnished. At Arelate he was provided with comfortable quarters. Deodatus did not begrudge him the elegancies of life. "Make yourself comfortable in our house," he said. "Let me know if there is anything you need, my dear Natale, and it will be looked after." True, Deodatus was in no position to balk him. He had given himself into the friar's hand by confessing his taste for young men, but so far there had been no need for Natale to make undue use of his knowledge. Deodatus indulged him in every way because he was indispensable to his master. Who else would run his secret errands for him? Deodatus was dependent on Chavez' art now. Natale watched him take the alchemist's concoctions, slip into languor, wake from a drugged sleep to new determination, work calmly for a while, plunge into needy despair again and start the evil cycle over. Watching him, Natale feared for his master and for his own idyllic life at Arelate. And as if Deodatus' habits weren't bad enough, there were dark clouds in the marital heaven as well.

***

The library was Natale's favourite room. It was airy and well-proportioned, and the dark red and moss-green spines of the books in the glass-fronted cases glowed like a forest in mellow autumn colours. It was a comfortable room if you disregarded the painting above the writing desk: Mary Magdalene penitent, raising her tearful eyes to heaven, but Natale did not dwell on the dreary scene and did not allow his eyes to rise above the mahogany desk, a beautiful piece of craftsmanship and very calming to the soul. He had already advised Deodatus to replace the cheerless image of Mary Magdalene with something more inspiring – Socrates teaching in Athens or Scipio Africanus releasing a slave girl. Deodatus quite shared his objections to sentimental horror, but the painting was a wedding present from an aunt of Luisa's and must be kept in sight for a year at least.

Luisa was waiting for Natale at the desk. He took a seat by the window, which offered a pleasant vista of tidy flower beds and fruit trees, black-green in the soft afternoon light, a welcome diversion to the eye if the lesson should become too tiresome. He took up Luisa's notebook and cast an eye over her homework.

"My dear," he said pleasantly, "there is a little mistake in the second line, but otherwise the summary is very well done. You will be a star in the firmament of scholars one day."

"You are too kind, Fray Natale," she said.

"Shall we go on with our definitions of the emotions?" he said, and she nodded eagerly. "We shall consider three pairs of antitheses: Love and hate, happiness and sadness, greed and generosity."

"Let us begin with love," she said. "Love is..." She hesitated. "Attraction? Good will?"

The door of the library opened, and Deodatus entered. Natale greeted him amiably.

"I see you are at your books," Deodatus said. "I shall return later." His face was pale, his step hesitant like an old man's.

"Don't go, Deodatus," Luisa said quickly. She rose from her seat and took his hand impulsively. "You are not well," she said.

Indeed, Natale thought, he looks more haggard than ever, and there is glittering desperation in his eyes. He will send me on another errand to Chavez soon.

"I have a slight cold, that's all," Deodatus said, pulling away from Luisa.

The tension between husband and wife was palpable. Natale smoothed over the awkward silence descending on them. "I have set Luisa the task of defining love," he said. "You might give her some hints, Deodatus."

"Ah, love." Deodatus said. "What is love? Admiration of an idol one has set up in one's mind? God's generous gift to man? A humble offering from man to his Maker? The outpouring of a mother's heart to her child? A sense of intimacy between equals?"

"A feeling of intimacy between husband and wife," Luisa said, "even if they are not equals."

"There can be no intimacy except between equals, my dear, if you consider the meaning of the term proper," Deodatus said and launched into a lecture. "As Plato says, using a wonderful simile, we have been split apart by a God who wished to humble us and we are now forever searching and yearning for our alter ego, for the other half that is our match and will make us perfect."

"I cannot hope to be your match," Luisa said, "but..."

"But," said Deodatus holding up his hand: "Allow me to anticipate your thoughts, my dear, but, you wanted to say, one must aspire to the ideal. We have a sacred duty to make the utmost of our potential. As Pico della Mirandola tells us in a charming story, when God created the world and had given each beast its distinct quality, he created man, and having no peculiar quality left to give him, he endowed him with potential only. You may raise yourself up to the divine heights of wisdom, or you may lower yourself to the depth of a soulless beast. It is up to us, Luisa. That is why I wish you to study hard and apply yourself to the lessons Natale prepares for you."

"Luisa needs no reminder," Natale said with a smile. "She is an exemplary pupil. The powers of her mind are astonishing."

"You mustn't allow her to become too self-satisfied," Deodatus said, "or make me too conceited for being the husband of such a paragon. And now I shall leave you to your labours."

He shook his head at Luisa's pleas to stay a little longer and took his leave.

Natale looked at Luisa's pouting lips and feared an ugly scene. He tried to ward off her anger with a little flattery.

"It is as I said: you are the perfect pupil. We must give thanks to the Lord for endowing you with such a happy disposition," he said effusively.

She drew back. "I am wretched," she said. Her voice was peevish.

"Wretched, my dear Luisa! But why?"

"I cannot put it in words," she said with burning cheeks.

"Well, then, let us pass it over in silence and continue with our lesson. Now that Deodatus has defined love for us, we shall do a rhetorical exercise on the theme of love."

"Yes," she said. "'A husband's love for his wife' will be a most appropriate topic."

"Shouldn't we begin with 'A wife's love for her husband'?"

"But then it wouldn't be a rhetorical exercise. I would be speaking from the heart, and there would be no difficulty finding appropriate arguments and figures of speech."

Natale resigned himself to the inevitable. He would have to listen to a marital complaint. "I see," he said. "Let us talk about 'A husband's love for his wife,' then. Begin with a definition."

"Love is intimacy between equals," Luisa said and stopped, waiting for his approval.

"That's Deodatus' idea at any rate," Natale said.

"But St. Paul says that men are superior to women," Luisa continued. "*The man is in charge of the woman* – 1 Corinthians 11. If love is intimacy between equals, there can be no love between husband and wife."

"*Quod erat demonstrandum*, that needs proving," said Natale. "There is a logical fallacy in your argument, my dear. Neither 'Man' nor 'Woman' is a simple concept. They are made up of parts and cannot be compared *generaliter*. *Ergo*, you must compare the individual traits of men and women: as children of God they are equals, in the procreative function they are equal. In physical strength man is superior to woman; in moral and spiritual qualities woman is superior to man, *et cetera*. Love is therefore possible in the areas in which they are equal, *ergo*, love between husband and wife is possible."

"Ah," she said. "I see I made a mistake. Let me begin again. Intimacy is possible only between equals, and in so far as husband and wife are equal, their love can be defined as intimacy."

"Very well," said Natale. "Proceed."

"Plato says we have been cleaved apart by a jealous God and are forever searching for our alter ego, the matching half that will make us perfect. Every man is therefore searching for a wife that resembles him and, in marital love, will perfect him."

"*Quod erat demonstrandum*," said Natale. "This time you have made a mistake of interpretation. For Plato is speaking of cylindrical beings, some consisting of two males being joined back to back, others consisting of two females, and a third variety consisting of a male and a female. After God sundered them, they went around searching for their other half. *Ergo*, some men are searching for wives that will perfect them; others are searching for their alter ego among their own sex, and similarly, some women are searching for husbands that might perfect them, while others are searching for a mate among the members of their own sex."

Luisa looked perplexed. "And is Deodatus searching for a man or a woman?"

"My dear, what has Deodatus got to do with it? You did propose a rhetorical exercise, didn't you?"

"I did," she said, lowering her eyes.

"Then you must not descend to particulars or use arguments *ad hominem*."

Luisa recovered herself. "Let me say, then: according to Plato, some men find their alter ego only among the members of their own sex and will therefore never love their wives intimately."

"Stop," said Natale. "You have made another mistake of interpretation. Plato did not speak of real men and women. He used a simile. And similes do not correspond to reality in all aspects."

"It seems I cannot get anything right today," Luisa exclaimed.

Natale smiled peaceably. "Perhaps the theme is too difficult for you."

"You mean I cannot grasp the subject of a husband's love for his wife?"

"You have the ability to grasp it, Luisa, but you need more experience than you have at present."

"Oh, Fray Natale!" she burst out. "Deodatus does not love me! He has grown cold. He shows no affection for me."

"I am sure you are mistaken, my dear."

"He does not keep me company. He does not care to be close to me."

"My child, he is a busy man."

"I am his wife. A husband has duties toward his wife."

"My dear Luisa," Natale said soothingly. "You are thinking perhaps of the young passionate gentlemen in romances and their breathless professions of love. In real life..."

"In real life, too, women enjoy the lawful embraces of their husbands, but he does not love me." Luisa's tears were flowing copiously now. "Help me, Fray Natale! Talk to him! Tell him I am dying for want of affection."

Natale looked at her, taken aback. He had no intention of importuning his employer. "Calm yourself, my child," he said. "We will talk about your unhappiness at another time when we have more privacy. The servants will be around with the refreshments at any moment, I believe." And he made his escape, but he could tell there was no escaping the unpleasant situation. Luisa would insist on making him her confidant.

Natale knew enough about Deodatus' inclinations to guess at the root of her unhappiness. He knew enough also about Luisa's stubborn mind to predict that she would give him trouble. To add to the difficulties, Don Ramon had meddled and shouted insults at Deodatus. And now Luisa was trying to involve him in the quarrel as well. It was an ill wind blowing, a gale that might destroy his comfortable berth.

***

Natale's diplomacy was of no avail. Things went from bad to worse. Luisa took to her bed, sulking and sending away the trays of food taken up to her room after she failed to appear at the dinner table. Her unhappiness was much discussed in the councils of her aunts and cousins. Why, in heaven's name, was Luisa unhappy? A young woman living in comfort, married to a husband who commanded the admiration of all? They counted the months that had passed since the wedding and thought they had found the answer. What she needed was a child, they said wisely. A procession of friends and relatives descended on the house, but Luisa refused to speak to anyone and fended off their attempts at conversation with broken sobs and banshee cries. One by one they fell away again, peeved at having their well-meaning advice spurned. Only Doña Catalina kept up her daily visits, weeping at the bedside of her daughter, who was lying curled up and silent or vapourish and quivering, as the mood took her.

  The stale air of the sick room seemed to infect the whole house. The servants became listless and indolent, going about their work in a careless manner without anyone reprimanding them. Deodatus was in a feverish prostration, his skin bloodless, his eyes alive with desperation. When Natale ventured a discreet question about his master's health, Deodatus answered him with a groan.

  "I should not have married," he said. "I have broken a sacred vow: to consecrate my life to learning. I look into the mirror and no longer see a rational man. I see an abject creature, a caricature of a man." There was a sob in his voice, although his lips were distorted into a ghastly grin, the bare-toothed, gum-showing grin of a dying man. "I have brought retribution on myself for falling in with the ways of the world. Where will I find peace now? I long to be released from this world." He compressed his lips to a thin line as if he was holding back a shriek that might burst out any moment like a whistle.

There is nothing I or anyone else can do for him, Natale thought. He is in the last agony of self-destruction. Natale's trips to Chavez' den became more frequent as his master's anxieties mounted. He expected to be sent on another such errand, when Deodatus called him into his study. On the table beside his desk was an exquisitely painted miniature of the Tower of Babel, a gilded ziggurat rising to an azure sky. Natale cast a covetous glace at the little treasure.

"I see you are admiring my latest acquisition," Deodatus said. "Perhaps I should make you a present of it. I am eager to oblige my friends, you know."

Natale bowed. "And I in turn am eager do anything in my power to oblige you," he said.

"Then I will be bold enough to ask for your help at once," Deodatus said, but he kept his hand on the miniature as if he wanted to see proof of Natale's good will before handing over the reward.

"Say no more," Natale said. "I shall go to Chavez and bring you the gift of sweet dreams."

"Your desire to anticipate my wishes is touching, my dear Natale, but it is another matter about which I want to consult you, and I hope you will indulge me."

"Consider it done," Natale said. He tried not to stare at the miniature between them.

"My marriage is going badly," Deodatus said. "I cannot seem to make Luisa happy. She is weeping one moment, defiant and resentful the next. Her family is impatient for an heir. Her resentment and their impatience make for a dangerous mix."

Natale nodded. "Your father-in-law is a fierce man."

"He is a bully! He has threatened to shame me if I cannot do what comes natural to any coarse rascal! He does not know what it is to have a soul."

Natale sighed. He was eager to earn his reward, but he had no idea what Deodatus wanted from him. "My dear Deodatus, you have my sympathy entirely," he said. "You have hinted that I might be of assistance to you, but I do not see how I can help you in this predicament."

"When I last attempted to speak to Luisa, she refused to see me. Now, I am told, she refuses to eat."

"The symptoms of mental suffering."

"Or hysteria."

"Hysteria, if you wish to call it that."

"Or dementia."

"Oh, I don't know about dementia," Natale said, but he began to see Deodatus' drift.

"She raves like a Maenad, like the frenzied huntress of Greek myth, who roams through the woods and tears apart her quarry with bloodied teeth."

"You are waxing poetic," Natale said. "It is the poet's privilege to exaggerate, but surely Luisa will not tear you to pieces."

"You understand perfectly well what I am trying to say," Deodatus said impatiently. "She is oblivious to all human conventions. I cannot be expected to live with a demented woman. Would not the church in such a case provide an annulment of the marriage?"

"And is that the favour you were going to ask me, to set in motion an annulment?" Natale saw the reward slipping from his hands. There was no chance of an annulment in Deodatus' case. The marriage contract was a valid legal document. It had not been signed hastily or under false pretences. Luisa and Deodatus had freely consented to the marriage. The union had been consummated, perhaps not entirely *comme il faut*, but Luisa was no longer a virgin. "Let me be plain, Deodatus," he said. "I do not think you will be successful in this enterprise. My advice is to leave it alone. It is a costly and lengthy legal process. Cardosa will object, you can be sure of it. He will appeal the case all the way to the papal court. It would be a waste of your time and money."

Deodatus looked like Atlas carrying the world on his shoulders. "What am I to do then? My life has become insufferable."

Natale saw his comfortable arrangement with Deodatus fall apart if he proved useless as a purveyor of happiness, or of contentment at any rate. He desperately tried to think of a way out. An idea struck him. "You might call in a physician," he said.

"Is that the sum total of your wisdom?" Deodatus said gloomily.

"A young attractive physician."

Deodatus stared at him, and broke into morbid laughter. "Are you advising me to pander to my own wife?" he said.

That was the gist of Natale's advice. The idea was not perfect. In helping Deodatus, he was being unfair to Luisa. But then an intrigue with a handsome lover was not altogether unpleasant. She would not suffer unduly. "I advise you to give your wife what she needs: love."

"You mean: if the physician should become her lover, she will have what she needs?"

"Indeed. And you will have peace." And their cosy arrangement would remain intact.

"More likely, I will have a scandal on my hands."

"Oh no, we wouldn't allow things to get out of hand. It's fear of scandal that keeps the guilty party quiet and amenable to peace. Of course the whole thing needs careful management."

Deodatus bit his lip. "And where do I get a young and attractive physician without arousing suspicion?"

"Why not consult your colleague, Alonso Malki?" Natale said. His eyes wandered to the miniature on the desk between them.

"You have earned my gratitude," Deodatus said and pushed the little painting in Natale's direction.

Natale took it up reverently and felt the glossy surface with his fingertips. "You are too generous," he said.

Voices could be heard in the courtyard. Deodatus put his hand on Natale's arm. "That will be Doña Catalina on her daily mission of mercy," he said. "Perhaps you will oblige me by receiving my worthy mother-in-law and presenting your idea to her."

Natale clutched the miniature to his chest. "Leave the matter to me," he said.

CHAPTER 9

DOÑA CATALINA WAS IN THE ENTRANCE HALL, handing her mantilla to a servant. Natale bowed and led her to the drawing room, solicitously asking after her health.

She looked at him dolefully. "I am at my wits' end," she said and sank into a chair. Her voice was a wheeze of short breath and agitation. "You are Luisa's spiritual advisor, Fray Natale. My child is languishing in her room, sighing and weeping. It is incumbent upon you to comfort her." Her cheeks were bathed in tears. "You are neglecting your duties."

Natale raised his hands in protest. "I have done my duty, Doña Catalina," he said, "but this is a case for a physician. I have said as much to Deodatus, and he agrees with my view of the matter."

"Dear me!" said Catalina. "So you think it's a case for a physician? I would have said my poor lamb is suffering from a broken heart, and what she needs is love. But if you think we should call in a physician, I will send for Doctor Comenius at once. I have always found his treatment very effective."

"With all due respect, Doña Catalina, Doctor Comenius is an old man and not conversant with modern methods. This is a serious case, and you want the best."

"Only the best," said Catalina, "but I thought Doctor Comenius..."

"I have taken the liberty of raising the question with Deodatus," said Natale, "and his preference is for Doctor Malki."

"Oh!" Catalina said. "But Doctor Malki is a Jew. Do you really think we ought to consult a man of that race?"

"Doctor Malki is a *converso*, Doña Catalina. He has been baptized and is a good Christian. I can vouch for him. Besides, he has been distinguished by the Cardinal's patronage."

"In that case I have no objection," Catalina said. "I always follow the Cardinal's lead."

"If you wish, I shall send for him."

"The sooner the better," Catalina said, "and perhaps you could explain the difficulty to Doctor Malki." She looked at him anxiously. "I would do it myself," she said, "if it were not indelicate for a woman to raise such a subject."

"I will see to everything, my dear lady," Natale said. "There is no need for you to speak to the physician or be present at the consultation. Luisa might be embarrassed to name her concerns in your hearing. Far better to have the doctor attend to the patient in the company of her spiritual advisor."

"Much better," Doña Catalina said. "But is Doctor Malki a discreet man?"

"A doctor is bound to secrecy by his professional oath," Natale said, "and I myself will treat everything I hear as if it had been entrusted to me in confession."

Doña Catalina dried her tears and pressed his hand gratefully. "I never thought I would find another confessor like Fray Ferrero," she said. "I cannot tell you how much I regretted his retirement, but I see you are a worthy successor to the venerable man, Fray Natale. You have my full trust."

"I should think I have earned your trust," Natale said with meaning. "I have kept your own little secret tight, Doña Catalina, and will be equally close-mouthed about Deodatus' sordid practices. I have the honour of the family at heart."

Doña Catalina raised her mortified eyes to him and dissolved in tears at once. "And I am forever in your debt for your discretion, Fray Natale," she said, uttering pitiful sobs and bobbling her head up and down. "Don't I always share with you the presents Don Ramon makes me at Christmas and on my name's day?"

"And many a widow has shared in them as well," Natale said. It was their little conceit. The money was no bribe. It was charity. Natale was very particular about maintaining their pretense. "Your generosity has allowed me to be generous in turn," he said.

"Yes, many a poor widow," Doña Catalina repeated obediently, rummaging in her reticule for a handkerchief. "I know, and I will urge Don Ramon to reward you for supporting us in this predicament and ask him to make his own contribution to your charitable causes." The fear of exposure was writ large in her eyes.

"You are most gracious, Doña Catalina," Natale said. She was pathetic. Natale felt sorry for Doña Catalina and would have left her off the hook long ago, but he had no other source of ready money. He had given up on his vow of poverty and begun to provide against the future. But his nest egg was growing only slowly, the nest egg he hoped would one day pay for a dispensation from his vows and allow him to live as an ordinary priest, enjoying an income from a parish or from a canonry. One day, he hoped to live the life of a cultured gentleman without fear of reprimand. But how fragile such dreams were! His Superior might recall him to Seville, Fonseca might lay another trap for him, the alchemist might be caught in the snares of the Inquisition and leave Deodatus without comfort and himself without patronage. His dream of independence was at the mercy of many vicissitudes.

***

For days Luisa lay on her bed with her head turned toward the window and watched the sky. It seemed very far away, cloudless, out of reach, stretching past the horizon into eternity, shimmering blue in the morning, deepening in the midday sun, turning lilac in the evening, and dropping into lead-blue at night. Every morning she woke, feeling like a swimmer rising from the depth and breaking the surface of the water. She emerged from sleep gasping for air and dizzy with exhaustion. I can't get up, she thought recoiling from the memory of the last weeks, her ears buzzing with voices, the questions of visiting relatives spiralling in her eardrums. Her eyes burned. Keep the shutters closed, she told her maid. The recollection of the quarrel with Deodatus paralyzed her. She tried thinking of herself in the third person, the heroine of a rhetorical exercise, the kind she had practised with Natale. But she soon grew tired of that pretense, and wished she could drop out of the story altogether, leave her body behind on the bed like a slaked skin, and begin a new life.

Her mother had told her of Deodatus' decision to call in a physician. No doctor can help me, she thought. I am sick at heart. But a deep astonishment, like a breath of divine admonition, seized her when she first heard the doctor's voice. He had stopped in the corridor outside Luisa's bedroom and said: "I expected Deodatus Rijs to receive me."

She heard Natale reply: "He thought it was best if you heard about Doña Luisa's troubles from a third party. Her condition was precipitated by a quarrel, and she has been in low spirits ever since." He lowered his voice. The rest of his speech was an indistinct murmur.

Then there was a knock at the door, and the maid showed the two men in.

"The doctor is here to examine you, my dear," Natale said into the semi-darkness of Luisa's shuttered bedroom.

The curtains of her bed were drawn tight, but on the doctor's request, she parted them and saw, standing by her bedside, a young man with handsome elongated features, almond-shaped eyes and dark brows shaped like half moons. He reminded her of St. John baptizing the faithful in the river Jordan, and in a flash of imagination she saw the doctor's body clad only in a loincloth, sinewy like St. John's. The thought made her blush. She wondered: was it the resemblance to the saint that made him look so familiar? But she had heard his voice before as well, speaking words of endearment. Or was that a trick of her ailing mind?

She put out her hand for the doctor to take her pulse and answered his questions with a whispered yes or no to hide the rapturous joy she felt at his touch. But when he suggested bleeding her, she protested. "I loathe leeches," she said. "They are revolting creatures."

"I do not use leeches, madam," the doctor said. "I use what is called a scarificator, a small knife to make an incision in the arm. But I need to see what I am doing. With your permission, I will open the shutters."

She did not object.

He seemed startled when he saw her in the full light of the day. Was he astonished or touched by her suffering?

"Will the procedure hurt?" she said.

"Not much. I hope you will be courageous."

He looked at her steadily as he put a tourniquet on her arm and positioned the bleeding cup underneath.

"The bleeding will purge your body of black humours," he said, making the incision. "It will take care of any stagnation in the veins."

Luisa looked at the blood flowing from the cut and felt purged of all sadness.

He took off the tourniquet and allowed his fingers to rest for a moment on her arm. She felt a current passing between them and noticed a soft withholding of breath when he released her.

"That is all," he said. "It was not very painful, was it?"

"No," she said, faint with pleasure.

The doctor turned to Natale. "The illness may have emotional roots, as you suggested, but we must not neglect the possibility of an underlying physiological cause. Have the maid supply me with a sample of her mistress' urine, and I shall examine it for abnormalities."

He promised Luisa to return in two days' time and departed, leaving her limp with desire for another word from his lips, another touch of his fingertips. At last she remembered where she had seen him before. In her romantic dreams, in an amorous reverie. He was the knight whom she had showered with kisses, to whose fervent declarations of love she had listened with a fluttering heart, whose embraces she had welcomed in a lush garden shimmering with peach blossoms. Was the aya right after all? Could her eyes, indeed, could the eye of her mind attract men? Was it her dream that brought Alonso Malki to her bedside? She resolved to put her powers to the test, but when the doctor returned to report his findings, her attentive gaze and the light pressure of her hand elicited no response from him that could be taken as encouragement. His words were kind, but he politely averted his eyes from Luisa's face and answered her questions unsmilingly. She was left taut with longing.

Perhaps Deodatus' presence inhibits my powers or weakens them, she thought. Alonso had insisted on her husband's presence. Natale was in attendance as well, playing the toady, tilting his head obligingly, pulling up chairs for Deodatus and Alonso, moving between them, smiling and bowing.

"I have found no abnormalities in either blood or urine," Alonso said, addressing Deodatus. "In my considered opinion, Doña Luisa has no physical ailment. She suffers from melancholia. It is a malaise endemic to young brides. If I may be allowed to speak frankly: a young woman of good family has no voice in the selection of her husband. The experience of her elders is thought to be a safer guide than her own fancies, and that may well be so, but the fact remains that she is expected to love at the stroke of a pen. The marriage contract is signed, the rings are exchanged, and those tokens are supposed to translate into love and affection. But the couple soon discovers that their needs and expectations differ, and there is no one to reconcile their differences. He expects obedience, perhaps, while she wants passion. He is a learned man with sophisticated tastes; she is a naive young girl. Is it any wonder that such differences and dis-appointments induce unhappiness?"

Those were plain words, and Luisa expected Deodatus to protest and argue that other young women adapted to their husband's wishes and found happiness, but he answered with equanimity. "You are a discerning man, Doctor Malki. I agree with much of what you said. Luisa is in need of a therapy of words, then, more than a therapy of drugs."

"You might put it that way," the doctor said.

"As you suggested, Luisa is naive and has girlish notions about marriage," Deodatus continued. "She needs someone to talk common sense and convince her that everything is as it should be."

"Or that things might be arranged in a way that pleases both parties," the doctor said.

"It would be good to set up a routine of daily consultations," Natale interjected.

"Quite so," Deodatus said and turned to Luisa. "If you are in agreement, my dear, we might ask Doctor Malki to attend you for an hour every afternoon and speak to you about the emotions proper to a woman and about the expectations a husband may have of his wife."

"And the expectations a wife may have of her husband," she said. "Unless you think those are girlish concerns."

"I meant no offense when I used that word, my dear," Deodatus said. "I meant to say: you are young and inexperienced. Of course I expect you to engage in dialogue with Doctor Malki and ask him questions in turn."

"And he rather than Natale will be my teacher?" Luisa said.

"For a time at any rate. Perhaps Natale and I have been too concerned about your intellectual progress, and there are other areas in which you need instruction which Doctor Malki will be able to provide."

"I am not certain that the kind of instruction you have in mind is within my competence," Alonso said. "The patient's mother, I think, would be in a better position to give Doña Luisa the advice she needs."

"We have tried that expedient, Doctor Malki," Natale said. "Doña Catalina and I have been at Luisa's bedside every day. But despite our best efforts, we have not been able to help her. I do believe there is merit in engaging someone who is not a member of the family or the household." He turned to Luisa. "What is your opinion, my dear?"

Seeing all eyes on her, she said: "I believe talking to Doctor Malki would help me, but..." She blushed. She had meant to say: I must speak to him in private. She found Alonso's presence a tonic more effective than any prescription. His words were like spring water, feeding her parched soul. I am in love with him, she thought, and I wish I could make him fall in love with me in turn.

To Luisa's surprise, Deodatus came to her aid. "You must have a chaperone of course," he said, "but the conversations will necessarily touch on personal matters. It would not do to have a servant present, and I understand you would not be comfortable to speak of our difficulties in my presence. Perhaps Fray Natale could attend the meetings. He is in your confidence, is he not?"

It was by far the most agreeable solution. "He has been very understanding," Luisa said.

Alonso passed a hand over his brow. "I am in two minds about taking on the task," he said.

"I understand that you cannot give us any guarantee of success, Doctor Malki," Deodatus said, "but if the proposed course of action proves effective, the family will be much indebted to you. You may be sure that we shall let the world know of our gratitude."

Alonso did not reply at once, and Deodatus continued pressing him. "Is the hope of professional satisfaction and the prospect of being warmly recommended by a prominent family not worth an attempt at any rate?"

At length, Alonso yielded and agreed to the consultations.

***

At first the doctor seemed proof against all temptation. He was scrupulously correct in his address and spoke to Luisa only in the cool language of reason. It was not for Natale's sake that he observed decorum. If he had wanted to make advances, he could easily have outwitted her chaperone. Natale took up his place in the furthest corner of the room, and was seemingly absorbed in his breviary. Sometimes he stepped out, to fetch a book from the library or to write a letter that could not be put off. He left the door ajar for appearance's sake, but otherwise seemed to trust in their modesty.

One day, when Natale had left the room, Luisa said softly: "Doctor Malki, I feel I have known you forever. We must have met before."

"I do not think I had the honour of your acquaintance, madam, until I came to the house a few weeks ago," he said.

"I must have been dreaming then," she said and blushed violently. Desire sprang up in her as she was looking into his handsome face. She felt the hair prickling on her nape. In vain she told herself: I am a married woman and must suppress foolish longings. The retort was easy: But you are married to a man who has no affection for you. And who can live without love altogether?

"Do you dream often?" Alonso asked.

"Do you, Doctor Malki?"

He did not reply.

"Forgive me," she said. "My question was indiscreet." But she could not keep from searching his eyes in one more attempt to put her powers of attraction to the test. Whether it was magic or natural attraction, Alonso's reserve melted at last.

"My father used to ascribe meaning to dreams," he said. "Perhaps you are right, Doña Luisa, and there is a mysterious connection between us. Not long after my father died, he appeared to me in a dream engulfed by flames, speaking words of warning. By his side was a young woman weeping for my misfortune. I awoke with a sense of foreboding but also with a longing to find my father's companion. When I saw you..." He did not finish the sentence. "No, I must not allow myself to indulge in fanciful notions," he said. His voice had turned sober, but he looked at Luisa wistfully.

She smiled. She could taste success.

"Do you believe that people may be drawn to each other in dreams?" she asked.

"I am a man of science, madam," he said. "I prefer to believe in rational explanations."

But there was something in his eyes that belied his words. He is falling in love with me, she thought, and her intuition was right. Soon their consultations turned into confidential talks.

"There is much I have not told you about myself," she said, "but the heart has many recesses, and I cannot hope to throw them open to you all at once."

"Then we must be patient with each other," he said. He put out his hand and withdrew it again, but his fingertips came so close to her arm that she felt the movement of the air, sensed the heat of his skin. She could hold back no longer. She told him of her aspirations and her disappointments, of Deodatus' failings and her suffering.

"I believe Deodatus has no need for a wife and children. He married because that is what society expected of him. His interests lie elsewhere."

"Perhaps you are seeking in him what no man can give," he said, crossing his arms as if to keep himself forcibly from touching her.

"My expectations may have been a childish dream, but nothing prepared me for the monstrous reality."

"Monstrous?" he asked, but she did not dare to say more. Instead she told him of the aya's advice, the visit to the *bruja*, the scrap of paper the woman had given her, covered with curious characters and inscribed "Capnio's use of the powerful name of Christ".

"A spell, the *bruja* said, but it was quite ineffective," she told him.

"You mustn't believe old wives' tales about spells and love potions," he said. "The woman cheated you of your money and abused the good name of a scholar. Capnio is a well-known Cabalist."

Luisa had never heard of the mystic Cabala, and Alonso was unwilling to say more. He cast a sideways glance at Natale who was enjoying the summer breeze on the balcony outside Luisa's room. He was leaning against the railing and watching them discreetly through the open door.

"It is better not to talk of the ancient Jewish philosophy," the doctor said in a low voice.

Luisa had told him the secrets of her heart, and soon he told her of his tribulations in turn, the denunciations against his family, the inquisitorial trial, the cruel death of his father, his own aspirations, his search for the truth.

"That is my quest," he said, "to find the eternal truth. I spend my evenings reading the philosophers and pondering their meaning."

"And if you find the truth?"

"Then I will know how to order my life. The truth will be my Pole Star, and I will take my bearings from it."

"When you say you are searching for the 'eternal truth', do you mean God?" she asked, trying to following his train of thought.

"You could call it that. Yes, God is Truth."

My longing for him is hopeless, she thought. He is far above considerations of earthly love. But then she remembered a passage in the Epistle of John.

"But St. John says: 'God is love'."

The doctor's eyes softened, and she boldly completed the quote: "'He that does not love, does not know God'."

"And who taught you to argue like a theologian, Doña Luisa?" he said and smiled. It was the first time he smiled on her, and the curve of his lips was irresistible, but their hour of togetherness was over.

Natale returned to the room, and Alonso's smile faded. As he stood to leave, Luisa rose too, and their hands brushed. Was it by chance?

We must continue our talk about God, she said and gave him a meaningful look.

He nodded, but did not return her look. His eyes were on Natale.

There were other confidential talks, and each word and each day brought them closer together. Their hands touched more often, and not by chance. Their fingers remained intertwined. One day their lips touched as well, and Alonso's hand caressed her cheek and her neck. They were in each other's arms. The minutes passed unnoticed, the room became a blur, they no longer owned themselves. Their heartbeat was one, and when their lips parted, their breath warmed the air between them. They felt the truth of the poet's words. *Love's burning rays kindle the soul, and no mortal hand can extinguish the flame.*

Natale's lenience permitted them to indulge in confidences, in whispered confessions of love, in secret embraces. He left the room more often. They became bolder in their love-making, but Alonso was wary of the priest.

"I have every reason to suspect his motives," he said. "Natale used to be a spy for the *Suprema*."

Natale, her smiling tutor an agent of the Inquisition! But there had always been something evasive about him, and now she understood. It was the shadow cast by his secrets. Luisa shuddered at the thought of the Inquisition, which was to her a mysterious creature, *a beast that moves his tail like a cedar and has sinews of stones and bones of brass,* a behemoth in hiding to be unleashed at the command of the Inquisitor General and summoned forth to punish sinners. The Cardinal held the strings of power, she knew, but it seemed the creature had a life of its own, like an unruly beast yoked to a wagon, obedient to the master's whip but pulling the other way when his attention was called elsewhere. The Cardinal is a fair judge, she thought, but he is human and can err. He has erred in choosing Deodatus as my husband. And there must be rogues at the inquisitorial court. Why else did the Malkis suffer persecution? What was their crime? Luisa could not understand why it was wrong to assemble for prayer on a Friday night or cut sinews out of meat.

"And how did you discover Natale's past?" she said.

"He admitted it himself when I confronted him. He shadowed me on the instruction of his superiors, but took a liking to me, or so he said. He claims that he recommended me to the Cardinal. I cannot verify his claim, but it is true that the prelate received me with favour and gave me the dispensation I needed to practise my profession. Still, I cannot regard Natale as a friend. He knew of my father's execution and offered to obtain for me the dossier containing the proceedings of the trial. That is, he offered to procure it at a price. No more than he had to pay an intermediary, he said, but his offer had the ring of blackmail. I knew the mischief that could come of the documents getting into the wrong hands. I made no attempt to haggle with Natale and paid the price he named. He brought me the documents. I read them, wept over the fate of my family, and consigned the papers to the flames."

"But can you be sure that the copy he gave you is the only one in existence?"

"No, I cannot be sure at all, and I believe that Natale is a dangerous man. His mild manners and his harmless smile are deceptive. He may pounce on us one day. He has seen and heard more than he lets on. He will betray our secret if it is to his advantage."

Luisa was startled, but could not persuade herself of Natale's will or power to harm them. She had seen the cowardly flicker in his eyes when he encountered a man's anger and observed his yielding softness when he met firm resistance. He cowed Luisa's mother, but he shrank from her father, and he danced attendance on Deodatus. There was no need to fear such a man.

"I cannot believe that Natale will betray us," she said to Alonso, "and if he informs Deodatus, he will find me defiant. I am not afraid of my husband. His secrets are blacker than mine."

Alonso drew her close and looked into her eyes fondly. "You have changed in the short time I have known you, Luisa," he said. "You were weak and helpless when I first saw you. You have turned into a fearless woman now, but your courage does not lessen the danger we are in. We must be careful in future."

"Or meet elsewhere in secret," she said boldly. The aya had taught her how to escape the confines of the house. "I might slip out at night when everyone is asleep and meet you at the garden door. We'll make the woods and meadows our guardians."

"My darling," he said, "you are a wood nymph yourself, a spirit who draws me irresistibly. But it would be foolish to take such a risk."

"And yet we read in the Bible that *the day utters speech, and the night showeth knowledge*," she said playfully, playing with fire. He wavered, and she stroked his arm. Her soft caress brushed away his reservations.

***

They met at the gate after the house had gone quiet. They walked through the meadows alive with the chirping of cicadas and the light of fireflies, on to the woods that kept their secret under the cover of their leafy canopies. They lay down on the coat Alonso spread on the ground and kissed, hardly daring to look at each other, tasting each other's lips softly at first, then hungrily.

"I should know better," he said, pulling back. "I am a fool for endangering you, for giving in to..."

Luisa put a finger on his lips and silenced him. She cupped his face in her hands and ran her fingers over his neck and chest. She slipped them inside his shirt, feeling the hollows of his armpits, digging her fingers into his back, holding him greedily. She felt his muscles tense under her touch, saw passion sweep over his face like a prayer. His hands tightened on her shoulders, slid down to her breasts, her thighs, every caressing move a raid on her senses. She put aside modesty and allowed him to undo her dress, received him into her body, made love fiercely, furiously, with breathless expectation. They fell into one rhythm, the pulse of desire. She throttled a cry, shivered with delight, and was lost in rapture.

When she came to her senses, the taste of his skin was on her tongue, cinnamon and salt. She felt sweat cooling between her shoulder blades and the touch of his damp hair against her cheek. Curling up against him, she listened to his breathing, fast, then slowing, then just a breath of air grazing her neck. She had expected to feel the exuberance of love, wanted to speak to him softly, sweetly, but when she said "I will love you forever" her words were tinged with sadness, and he said quietly: "Make no vows to me, Luisa. Forbidden love is a delicate flower. Are you not afraid it will soon be touched by the frost of reason?"

"I am," she said, "but for now let us be summer's children."

They wandered back to the house hand in hand like innocents and parted at the gate, kissing as if they had the power to stay the seasons.

As Luisa walked across the terrace, she noticed that the night wind had died down. The sky had changed its hue imperceptibly, from dark ebony to a lustrous shade of blue. She pulled at the French window she had left unlatched, but it refused to give. It was shut tight and locked from the inside. With a beating heart, she went to try the next window, and so on down the row, but her entry into the library was barred. She stood looking up at the windows of Deodatus' room. They were dark, but she felt his presence, saw him in her mind's eye looking down on her, watching her, cruelly enjoying her impotence.

The shutters of the library creaked and opened slowly. A figure emerged from the shadows. Luisa pressed her hands together in mute prayer, desperately searching for words, an explanation to offer Deodatus for her presence on the terrace. But it was Natale, not Deodatus who beckoned to her from the opening and allowed her to slip into the library. He lit a candle and stood before her looking like a jolly uncle in his embroidered robe and matching nightcap. He shook a finger at her as if she was a naughty child. A smile played on his lips. Or was it the rictus of a snake getting ready to strike? The candle in his hand cast a flickering light on the painting of Mary Magdalene, the biblical sinner, and on Luisa, her earthly counterpart.

"Was it you who shut me out?" she said, feigning indifference. She took off her mantilla, smoothing her hair with a light touch to give him the appearance of being at ease. "I could not sleep and went for a turn in the garden," she said, aware that her dress was in disorder and her shoes damp and grass-stained.

He nodded peacefully. "That's what I suspected when I looked out the window and saw you leaving the house. The dear child is restless, I thought, or distressed. I must follow and comfort her. But I need not have worried. You were joined by Doctor Malki, that remarkable man who knows how to cure the vapours. And so there was nothing left for me to do but sit up and wait and give you a warning."

"A warning that you will betray me?"

He inclined his head. "Betray you, my dear?" he said. "I believe it is my duty to admonish you and inform your husband when I see you go astray."

"You have no material proof that I have gone astray," she said. "And I will deny your allegations."

"And who will believe a woman over a man? Who will believe a sinner who has every reason to deny her trespasses over a priest who has the sacred truth at heart?

"And what is the sacred truth, Fray Natale?" she said. "Mortals cannot hope to fathom it. We must trust in God to direct our paths to salvation. And this is not about the sacred truth. It is about human perception: your word against mine. Deodatus will have to choose, and he will choose to believe me, because a scandal is not in his interest."

The smile, which had never left Natale's lips, broadened. "I am delighted to see how well you have learned to reason under my tutelage, my dear Luisa. But as much as I enjoy sparring with you, this is not a suitable time to engage in rhetorical exercises. It is late, or rather early, indeed almost time for the servants to rise. We must not give them an opportunity to gossip. As you say, my dear, scandal is in no one's interest. Let us retire quietly, and take my advice: be more discreet in future."

He looked slyly at Luisa as she brushed by him and ran upstairs to her room.

There was no help for it now. She must make Natale her accomplice and depend on his good will. Alonso agreed when she told him of her misadventure. They had no choice, but their conversations became muted and their gestures constrained, and they resigned themselves to live in danger.

CHAPTER 10

THE SEASONS TURNED. IT WAS WINTER WHEN DOÑA Catalina came to the house, wearing black opal pendants. The lace ruffles on her dress had been replaced with plain bands to honour the memory of the dead. A distant relative, most likely, Luisa thought. She looked at her mother's animated face. Mourning became her. She liked funerals almost as much as weddings. It was all grist for her mother's tear-mill.

"Have you heard the news?" Doña Catalina said. "Has Deodatus told you?"

"I've heard nothing," Luisa said. "Deodatus spends his mornings at the university. I never see him until we sit down to dinner."

"Then let me tell you," Doña Catalina said. "King Ferdinand has passed away, and the Cardinal has gone to look after the affairs of the country. He has been appointed Regent until Prince Carlos can be brought home from the Low Countries."

"And the King's daughter?" Luisa said. "It is Juana who is next in the line of succession, is she not?"

"Juana will be Queen, but Queen in name only. She is mad, they say. The courtiers call her La Loca because of her unpredictable rages. I hope she will behave better at her father's funeral than she did at her husband's. You know what Madam the Duchess told me?" Doña Catalina settled down comfortably, eager to share the most delicious court gossip with her daughter. "The Duke was present when Juana's husband died of the fever – two years ago, I believe it was. On the night of his death, she carried on like a lunatic. Her shrieks and wails gave everyone the shivers. The next day, she refused to give up her husband's corpse. The attendants had to pry her fingers loose to close the coffin. She was beside herself and wept and called his name and would not let the funeral procession depart. She clung to the casket until the King gave orders to have her forcibly removed. They are keeping her locked up in a convent now."

"Poor woman!" Luisa said.

"Poor woman, indeed," Doña Catalina said. "But to make a public spectacle of her grief! Fray Ferrero said it was learning that unhinged Juana."

"Learning has no such effect, Mama."

"It didn't do you any good," Doña Catalina said. "It gave you the vapours. And now that the lessons have stopped, you are suddenly better. Are you at peace again with Deodatus?"

"He leaves me alone," Luisa said.

Her laconic answer did not satisfy Doña Catalina.

"Leaving you alone is no solution," she said. "I thought you had reconciled with him. I was sure I saw love return to your eyes, Luisa." She looked at her probingly, and Luisa turned away to hide her telltale eyes. "In any case," Doña Catalina went on, "you are better. Perhaps it was the combination of ending the lessons and beginning therapy with Doctor Malki. He is a wonderful doctor. I have recommended him to all my acquaintances. Unfortunately he won't be in town much longer."

"What do you mean?" Luisa asked sharply.

"The Cardinal has offered Doctor Malki a position at court and asked him to devise a therapy for the Queen." She stopped. Her sentimental heart had picked up a signal of distress. She saw the look that came into Luisa's eyes at the mention of the doctor's departure, and in a moment understood the true nature of her daughter's cure. "Oh my dear child!" she breathed, tears of shock and apprehension welling up in her eyes, but before she could ask a question, there was a knock, and Natale poked his head in the door.

"I hope I am not disturbing the ladies," he said cheerfully and entered without further encouragement. "I saw your new attendant in the hall, Doña Catalina. How is the aya? Still in poor health?"

"A little better," Doña Catalina said, trying valiantly to recover her composure. "But old age has caught up with her, I'm afraid. Don Ramon will have to find her a comfortable place to live out the rest of her days. Her departure will be a great loss to me." She folded her tears into a sigh. "So much has changed in these last two years. Fray Ferrero retired, Alejandro gone away to university, Luisa married, and now I must get used to a new maid." The tears were back in her eyes. "I don't know how I will manage without the aya. The house will be at sixes and sevens. As it is, the housekeeper does as she pleases, or rather does as little as possible. I'd better be going to make sure she has put black crepe on the doors. The Duke's palace is already decked in mourning. They have covered the balconies with black damask. I only came to tell Luisa that the Cardinal has left Alcala to meet with the court." She turned to Luisa. "He sends you his greetings. He would have liked to say farewell to you himself, my dear, but there was no time. You are the apple of his eye, you know."

"I know," Luisa said, "he has always been like a second father to me."

"Like a father," Fray Natale echoed, and Dona Catalina sniffled. The maid was summoned and brought Catalina's fur-lined wrapper to guard her against the sharp January wind. She departed with meaningful looks and wet kisses.

***

"You look pale, my dear," Natale said when they were alone. "The consequence of love, as Ovid says." He looked at Luisa attentively, running his eyes over her body and allowing them to rest on her midriff. He could see that Luisa was unsettled by his penetrating look and smiled.

"I am tired," she said, "Mama has that effect on me. She goes on and on. I think I will rest for a while." She escaped to her room, but she had to face Natale again in the afternoon. How could she speak to Alonso in his presence and say what was on her mind and in her heart? How would she hide her grief if what her mother said was true? I will be making a public spectacle of myself, like Juana, she thought. I will go mad if I lose my beloved.

When Alonso came at the appointed hour, his grave look confirmed her fears. Natale took a seat in the far corner of the room and turned the pages of his breviary listlessly.

"Have you heard of the Cardinal's appointment?" Alonso asked.

She nodded.

He took her hand and said quietly: "He has asked me to join him at court."

"And attend the Queen. Mama has told me," Luisa said.

"It was unexpected," he said. "The Polyglot project will soon be completed. My own work is almost done. The Hebrew text is ready for printing. I thought the Cardinal would let me go without further ado. Instead, he proposed to reward my services with an appointment at court."

Natale put down his breviary and listened unceremoniously.

"You will go, then?" Luisa cried.

Natale left his chair and put a finger to his lips. "My dear Luisa, lower your voice!"

"I asked for time to reflect," Alonso said. "My heart tells me to stay. My mind tells me not to offend the Cardinal by declining his offer."

"Don't leave me, Alonso," Luisa pleaded.

"You are behaving like children," Natale said, stepping between the lovers. "Alonso has an opportunity to advance his career, and he hesitates for your sake, Luisa. A noble sentiment, to be sure, but you must match his generosity of spirit and sacrifice your interests in turn. Surely you are not thinking of holding Alonso back? It is a great honour to be appointed court physician. You must let him go."

"A great honour if I succeed and a great embarrassment if I don't," Alonso said. "The Cardinal expects me to restore the Queen's health, but only God can work such a miracle."

"You have acquired a reputation for being a miracle worker," Natale said with an ironic smile. "Who is to say that you cannot devise a therapy to calm the Queen and bring peace to her mind? But the main thing is to retain the Cardinal's good will. You are his protégé now, and he means to help you by summoning you to court. Your heart tells you not to go, but you must think of Luisa's reputation as well. I would remind you of the punishment awaiting adulterers in hell if I thought you would listen, but I fear sermons are lost on lovers. Let me appeal to your honour, then. Your affair cannot remain without consequences here on earth, and where would that leave Luisa? You must show consideration for her safety and wellbeing, Alonso."

Luisa trembled at Natale's words. It was too late to consider the consequences now. She thought of the heroic role she had envisaged for herself in her childhood dreams. The learned Luisa. Saint Luisa. The pure and ardent lover. It was time to step out of her dreams and live the heroic life.

"I have no need for your appeals to my honour or to my feelings," Alonso said to Natale. "I know what I owe to Luisa."

"And to God and society," Natale said.

Alonso ignored his interjection. "I have thought of Luisa's position of course, and I will do whatever is best for her and whatever she wishes me to do."

"Then stay," Luisa said. Her eyes were brimming with tears. "Or else take me with you." There was desperation in her voice. "Let us put an end to all deceit and make a new life for ourselves."

"Luisa!" Natale exclaimed, scandalized.

"We shall be outcasts," Alonso said.

"I am prepared to give up everything."

"You may think you are being magnanimous, my dear child," Natale said, "but you are not. You are asking Alonso to throw away his life as well. If you have any regard for him, if you wish to give up anything for him, there is a more sublime sacrifice you can make. Surrender your carnal pleasure and elevate your love to the spiritual plane. The highest form of love is found not in the union of bodies, but in the union of souls. If your love for Alonso is more than base desire, if it is of that higher form, distance will mean nothing. You will remain united with him in a spiritual embrace."

Luisa bit her lip. "I see you have decided to give us a sermon after all," she said, but she could not resist Natale's appeal to her generosity. I must let Alonso go, she thought. I must not involve him in my own troubles.

Natale saw her wavering and said: "I will go one step further and put myself at risk. You may write to each other, my dears. I will be your go-between and relay your letters." He could see from Luisa's tears and from Alonso's resigned silence that he had won the argument, or that love had won the argument. He moved toward the door. "I will linger in the hall and leave you to say your adieus," he said, "but don't be long. The maid will soon come around with the refreshments, and I do not want her to say she found me neglecting my duty." He discreetly withdrew.

Luisa put her arms around Alonso's neck and wept without restraint.

He stroked her hair and said gently. "It would be selfish, indeed unconscionable of me to stay. We have escaped public disgrace so far, but we must not tempt fate any longer."

"If you leave, it will be the death of my soul," she said.

"No, Luisa," he said, "our souls are immortal, and our love is forever. You once asked me about Capnio and the mystical philosophy of the Cabala. As yet I understand it only imperfectly, but I intend to study it more deeply, and we may find in it the spiritual bridge connecting us. The more I read in the books of the Cabalists, the more I am convinced of the powers of the *sefirot*, the divine emanations. The universe consists of words and things and the energy that connects them in a sacred triad. We will experience that energy, Luisa, if we prepare for its reception by cleansing the body, purifying the spirit, and illuminating the mind." He spoke hurriedly and with a strangely lucid passion, but Luisa put her fingers on his lips. The door had opened a crack. Natale was returning to his post.

"Capnio and the *sefirot* will land you in the court of the Inquisition," he said. He had overheard Alonso's last words. "Can you think of nothing better than the old Cabalist? I would have thought the verses of a poet more appropriate to bid Luisa farewell."

"I have said nothing unchristian," Alonso said, "and I will not speak of frivolous things at a profound moment like this."

Voices could be heard in the hall among the clattering of dishes. Alonso pressed Luisa's hand and released it with a sad and sober look.

***

The maids smiled at each other when they saw Luisa pale and retching. The aunts and cousins came to visit and whispered congratulations. "You'll feel better in a month or two," they said, and petted her. Doña Catalina shed tears of joy at the thought of her first grandchild, but she suspected that Luisa's indisposition was not merely a symptom of pregnancy and ventured on little hints and allusions to draw her out.

Luisa had no taste for confidential talks with her mother. She was dispirited but she had no use for sentimental sympathy. Natale, too, put himself in Luisa's way, inviting confidences, offering to convey letters to Alonso. She had expected a note from her lover by now and did not know how to interpret his silence. She hoped it was only caution that kept him from writing and from making use of Natale's offer to be their go-between, but she feared that he had forgotten her now that he was at court. Love was fickle. She wanted to hide from her mother's sympathetic eyes and from Natale's solicitous questions. She wanted to be alone, to think of Alonso and weep in her loneliness, but this was no time to indulge her malaise, no time for languor. For the sake of her unborn child, she must not fall into that abyss again.

And so Luisa's life turned into a staged performance. She responded to cues, desperately trying to keep her wits together. Conversations with her mother followed a script from *The Lady's Treasury of Prudence*. Conversations with Natale followed the rules of Quintilian's manual of rhetoric. And talking to Deodatus was like a game of chess: one move countered by another.

"I see your mother has resumed her daily visits," he said to Luisa one day over dinner. They were on their own. Natale had excused himself, perhaps to allow them to talk freely.

She avoided Deodatus' eyes and continued with the motions of eating, cutting the meat, chewing, swallowing. She wasn't sure where this conversation was going. She was waiting for her cue.

"Your father is looking at me with new benevolence," Deodatus said. "I take it you have given your parents the happy news." His voice was matter of fact, his thin face inscrutable. Was this her cue? Letting her know that he was aware of her pregnancy?

"Yes," she said simply. "I told my parents that I am with child." She was at his mercy now. He knew he could not be the father of the child. He once made me an offer of peace, she thought: dividing our spheres of activity, me playing the chatelaine, him living a celibate life devoted to books. The Abbot and the Lady. Was he still amenable to such an arrangement?

"You are with child. A virgin birth?" he said, his mouth pulled into a mocking smile.

She would have preferred anger to irony. She stared him down.

"Has the archangel Gabriel announced to you the name of the child's father?" he said.

"Angels have nothing to do with it."

"The devil, then."

"You yourself have been playing the devil," she cried. "You must take some of the blame."

"My dear," he said, "let us be calm. There is nothing to be gained from impulsive words. The law says *matrimonium patrem demonstrat*. Marriage establishes the father. I do not intend to challenge the law. I shall make no difficulty about your child." His voice had turned icy. "I expect the same discretion from you. If the truth comes out, I shall be obliged to take your lover to court. You may want to be circumspect for his sake, even if you have been careless about your own reputation and mine, carrying on your affair under the very eyes of the servants."

He has known for a long time, she thought, and wondered whether Deodatus had laid a trap for her, knowing that a pregnancy would put her at his mercy. But she realized: the trap might close on him as easily as on herself. It was a question of whose sin was worse, hers or Deodatus'.

"You fear exposure as much as I," she said.

"I am proposing an arrangement that will benefit us both."

"Something like your earlier proposal?"

"You found fault with my proposal then, but you may be more receptive to it now. The situation has changed."

"It is the nature of the proposal that has changed," she said. "Your last offer was for your own convenience. I had nothing to gain by it. Now, we are speaking of a different kind of understanding, a bargain, a trade-off: my failings against yours."

"I will not quarrel about words. You may call it an arrangement or a trade-off, as long as you agree to keep up appearances and give me a semblance of peace."

"A trade-off, then," she said. But the balance was in her favour. Society sometimes connived with adulterers. It was unforgiving to fornicators of Deodatus' kind.

She left the table, concealing her anger. She was convinced that he had played a trick on her, set a trap, watched her silently, waiting for her to slip up. If silence gives consent, she thought, he has consented to my affair and is using it now to force me into submission. She was determined to get the better of him, to unmask him. Did Deodatus have a lover? She watched his students come to the house to flatter the master, to show him their poems, to take away letters of reference. Was one of them his paramour? But their visits did not have the aspect of trysts. Deodatus' well-modulated speech could be heard in his study above the scraping of chairs and rustling of papers and the stammering tributes of his admirers. Had anyone in the household caught Deodatus' eye? She thought of the gardener, or the ostler. They were handsome young men, but they kept a respectful distance from their master, and he regarded their closely cropped heads and sunburned faces with distaste. And Natale? She thought of his pudgy dimpled hands resting on Deodatus' arm or touching the folds of his mantle, his soft eyes, his mincing steps, the wetting of his lips before he spoke, the smiles and pleasantries he exchanged with Deodatus. Sometimes the two men were closeted in the confessional silence of Natale's room, at other times they sat close together on the cushioned window seat of Deodatus' study, deep in conversation. Could Natale, the man in whom she had foolishly trusted, be Dedodatus' paramour? Were the two men plotting against her, to act with impunity once they had her trapped? Is that why she had received no letters from Alonso? Because now that she was caught, there was no more need to play the game and keep her happy.

***

The maid kindled a fire in the brazier and drew a bath for her mistress. She prepared the bed, folding back the covers. Luisa lay down and listened to the wintry gusts turning the slats of the shutters. The monotonous sound of scraping and creaking made her drowsy. She closed her eyes. When she opened them again, the wind had fallen silent. I must have dozed, she thought. Instead of the melancholy sighs of the wind, she heard the sound of weeping. She got up, stepped into the dark hall, and stood listening. The sound came from Deodatus' room. The weeping stopped, and she heard a murmur of conversation. She could not make out the words, but she heard the despair in Deodatus' voice and the calm tone of Natale's replies, Deodatus' voice raised in anguish, Natale's controlling. Not the voice of a lover, she thought. Perhaps she was wrong, and he was Deodatus' master, holding secrets over his head as he did over hers. A terrible confusion filled Luisa. She thought of Alonso's warning: do not trust Natale. His smile is deceptive. He is a spy, a treacherous man. She walked down the hall to Deodatus' bedroom, unsure of her own motives – to close the trap on Deodatus in turn? To weep with him? To put an end to Natale's sinister dealings? She stopped at the door and listened.

"She was to me the incarnation of St. Catherine," she heard Deodatus say. His voice was despondent, tremulous.

"Come now, my dear," Natale said. "The first sip always makes you maudlin. You must not think of her. What's done is done. You need your sleep." Impatience mixed in his voice with paternal care, the voice of a father about to discipline his wayward child.

Luisa opened the door softly and through the chink saw Natale kneeling on the dishevelled bed, cradling Deodatus in his arms, holding a flask to his lips. "Drink up, my boy. It's time to sleep," he said curtly.

On the table beside the bed, a candle in a brass holder was burning low. Deodatus groaned deeply. His breath made the moribund light flicker.

"Hush," Natale said. "You will wake the household and alarm the servants." He pressed the flask to Deodatus' lips. His embrace turned into a wrestling grip. "Close your eyes and sleep." Natale's voice was commanding now.

Deodatus drank deeply and sank back on the bed. His shoulders were heaving, shaken by sobs. "I have violated my vow to St. Catherine. I am a condemned man," he said. "Why do I go on? Why..."

Luisa's broken cry cut short his question. He raised his head, saw her standing at the door, and contemplated her with sodden eyes. Natale remained motionless, arms stuck around Deodatus' shoulders, mouth frozen in a moué, a picture of unease. Luisa pulled the door shut and ran back to her room. Her heart was pounding. She waited for Natale to come after her, quirking his lips and explaining the scene away, but the house remained silent, a silence that roiled her stomach. She lay down on the bed stiffly, arms wrapped around herself. She had no more tears. An afterimage remained on the insides of her eyelids, of Deodatus in the thrall of a strange sickness, white wrestling arms against a crimson shadow. At last she heard the door of Deodatus' room open and close, and the sound of footsteps receding. Silence prevailed once more. The battle is over, she thought. Tomorrow I shall demand an explanation, and we shall negotiate in earnest. This time I will dictate the terms of the truce.

But there was no tomorrow for Deodatus. When the screams of the servants woke Luisa in the morning, and the weeping maid told her that Deodatus had been found dead, she was gripped by a stabbing pain, a knife turning in her groin. She felt a trickle of wetness between her legs, turned back the coverlet and saw a blood stain spreading on the sheet. Maria followed her gaze and pressed her knuckles to her mouth. "Doña Luisa," she said. "We must get the midwife. I will run to the village myself."

The midwife saw at a glance that nothing could be done. She did not call it a miscarriage. "A clot of blood, a thing without soul," she said in a comforting voice, patting Luisa's arm. Luisa nodded obediently, trying to keep thoughts of tiny fingers and toes from invading her mind, fending off images of what could have been.

The maid had brought a basin with warm water and fresh linen to put on the bed. The midwife wrapped strips of cotton around Luisa's thighs and between her legs, working with practised hands, lifting and turning her gently. "When you are done with the bed, Maria," she said to the maid, "call Fray Natale."

"Why do I need a priest?" Luisa said, alarmed. "Am I dying?"

"No, dearie," the midwife said. "What makes you say that? You are young and strong, and God willing, the bleeding will soon stop. It's nothing, dearie, as long as you keep off your feet and drink the infusion of herbs I have asked the cook to prepare. I'll give you a vinegar soak in a day or two. Make sure you eat properly, drink a little mulled wine once the bleeding has stopped, and you'll be up and around in no time. The worst part is facing the confessor."

Do the domestics know? Luisa thought. Have they been spreading rumours? "I have nothing to confess," she said firmly.

'Oh, I know," the midwife said, "but the priest will be at you like God on Judgment Day. He will want to know: Was it a natural miscarriage, or was it your own fault?"

"How could it be my fault?"

"It isn't. Don't you worry, my dear. It was the shock. Everybody knows it. But the confessor is supposed to ask those questions. Now listen, my sweet, and take my advice. Tell him: as soon as you suspected you were with child, you left off wearing a corselet and kept away from spicy food. If he asks you, has your husband visited your bed lately, say no. And if he asks, have you been walking up or down the stairs, say no, you've been staying in your room. Or he'll say you've been moving too vigorously and have been neglectful of God's gift. And then he will make you pay a thumping penance. But maybe you are in luck. I'm told Fray Natale is lenient and doesn't make a fuss about such things."

"No, he won't be hard on me," Luisa said, and thanked the woman for her advice. "And before you go, let me give you a note for my father."

"I'm not sure it's a good idea to sit up and write, my dear," the midwife said, but Luisa had already signalled Maria to bring her writing desk. "Just a few lines," she said to the midwife and wrote:

"Dear Papa, Deodatus has passed away after taking an overdose of a sleeping draught, they tell me. I am in shock and have suffered a miscarriage. I must consult with you and Mama before speaking to Doctor

Comenius. He will have questions about the manner of Deodatus' death. I want you to know that Natale was the last person to be with Deodatus.

Your loving daughter Luisa."

She asked Maria to help her seal the letter and handed it to the midwife. "You will oblige me by taking this note to my father. He will reward your services well," she said.

The next morning, the midwife returned. She put her hand on Luisa's forehead.

"No fever," she said. "That's good." She changed the bandages. "And the bleeding is only a trickle now," she said. "You are doing very well, Doña Luisa."

I must be out of danger, she thought. She has stopped calling me dearie and treating me like a child. She addresses me like a woman.

"Have you delivered my note?" she asked.

"Oh yes, madam," the midwife said. "Don Ramon will come and visit you this morning. I told him to wait a day or two, but he insisted on coming today. It's not every father who shows such concern for his daughter." She was all smiles.

Father must have been more generous than usual, Luisa thought. Most likely, he was afraid of giving the woman a reason to complain and talk about the case.

CHAPTER 11

A FAMILY COUNCIL CONVENED IN LUISA'S bedroom. Her mother crept into the room, teary-eyed, sniffling. Her father came, steely looking, a man in armour prepared to fight for his family's honour. He asked briskly after Luisa's health and held up his hand when Doña Catalina began to fuss.

"I only meant to ask her..." she said and looked aggrieved, but she shut her mouth obediently.

"There is nothing to fear, Mama," Luisa said. "The midwife is pleased with the speed of my recovery."

Her father nodded curtly and came to the point of his visit: "What do you know about this sorry business?" he said. "What was the cause of Deodatus' death?"

Luisa told him of the scene she had witnessed. Her mother, clutching her handkerchief, made pitiful noises, but swallowed her tears when her husband turned around and glared at her. He rang for the maid and called for Natale.

Doña Catalina looked down into her lap and nervously laced and unlaced her fingers. "Ramon," she said. "I shall faint if I have to listen to more of this. I think I will go downstairs and wait for you in the drawing room."

"Go wherever you please," he said gruffly. "Luisa will do as a witness to what I have to say to Fray Natale."

She slunk away, murmuring disconsolately.

"I curse the day the Cardinal introduced that weasel to me," Cardosa said. "And the day when he presented me with Deodatus' offer for your hand."

"The Cardinal meant well, father. He had my interests at heart."

"He had his own interests at heart. He foisted his protégé on me because it was to his own advantage."

"Father!" She knew he would show no sympathy for Deodatus, but to impugn the Cardinal's motives! "What advantage could Deodatus possibly offer the Cardinal?" she said.

"The advantage of a famous name. The Cardinal wanted to strengthen his ties with Deodatus, to keep him working on that fool project of his, to keep him lecTorinog at the university. Deodatus was his drawing card, and the university is the Cardinal's foundation, his love child. That's what someone told me at any rate. Deodatus wanted to go back to Flanders. I wish to God he had gone, but no, the Cardinal begged him to stay. They were all crazy about him and his books, the Cardinal, the Duke – Ah, there you are."

Natale had come in, looking pasty-faced and fluttering his hands, offering condolences.

Cardosa gave him an implacable stare. "Spare me your platitudes, Fray Natale," he said. "Let's talk about what matters. It seems you abetted Deodatus in his sins."

"As his confessor I was aware of his failings," Natale said. "I admonished him, as was my duty, Don Ramon. I did what I could."

"By procuring drugs for him?"

"You forget that Deodatus was my master," Natale said. "I followed his orders, though not without protest. But why speak of such things, Don Ramon? He is beyond man's judgment now, and we shall commend his soul to God."

"He is beyond man's judgment," Cardosa said wrathfully, "but *we* are not, and the manner of his death is bound to cause speculations detrimental to the honour of my family. If it turns out that Deodatus has taken his own life, there will be no burial in sacred ground, no funeral mass, no eulogy. The Cardosa name will be dragged through the mud."

Natale's pudgy face was impassive.

"What's the truth? What happened? Out with it."

Natale shrugged his shoulders. "He took an overdose of a sleeping potion."

"On purpose?"

"Who can tell?"

"Precisely. Who can tell? When Doctor Comenius asks you, you will say it was an accident."

"What I say will hardly matter."

"It's you who will be questioned. You were the last man to see Deodatus alive."

Natale smiled weakly. "You are right as always, Don Ramon," he said. "All things considered, it will be best to call it an accident."

Cardosa pressed on. "Tell Doctor Comenius it was an accident, and take the blame for it."

"Take the blame? Me?" Natale asked. "You are asking too much, Don Ramon."

"We must reward Fray Natale for his troubles, Papa," Luisa put in, afraid the friar might betray her if he had his back against the wall.

"Aha!" Cardosa said, satisfaction ringing in his voice. "My child is learning the ways of the world." He turned to Natale. "Luisa is right of course. There may be something in it for you, depending on what you are willing to say."

"I might say I mixed the potion for him," Natale said. "And he gave me the wrong formula by mistake."

"Not good enough. Someone could claim Deodatus gave you the wrong formula on purpose because he wanted to kill himself."

Natale sighed. "I have graciously offered to incriminate myself," he said, "and you ask for more."

"Yes, I'm asking for more. You will say that you misunderstood his instructions."

"And how will such a statement benefit me, if I may advert to your earlier offer, Don Ramon? It seems rather dangerous to me. I might be arraigned for murder."

"I will buy you passage to Italy. I'd buy you passage to the New World if it could be arranged tomorrow, but I suppose Italy will have to do. The sooner you leave the country, the better, both for you and for us."

"Allow me to express my profound gratitude," Natale said, "but may I point out that I will be regarded a run-away if I leave without the permission of my superior, that I would have to obtain a dispensation and find a living in Italy? A canonry, for example. I am quite prepared to be exiled for the sake of the family and to bury myself in Italy, but how will I live without ready money?"

"You drive a hard bargain," Cardosa said, but the time was pressing. He was not going to let money stand in the way of saving the reputation of his family. "Passage to Italy and thirty florins in ready money," he said.

Natale pondered the offer. When it looked as if he would hold out for more, Cardosa flew into a rage, and Natale, cowed by the flash of anger in his eyes, agreed to the terms offered.

A little well-timed raging is a useful thing, Luisa noted. She understood the world better by the hour.

"Then let us fetch the physician," her father said and rang the bell.

Doctor Comenius came and cast a concerned look at the patient. "Do I see a little flush on your cheeks, madam?" he said, but after taking Luisa's pulse, he declared himself satisfied. "It's the heat from the brazier, I warrant."

Natale rose to open the doors to the balcony, but the doctor put up a warning hand. "No, Fray Natale, leave the door alone. Fresh air can be dangerous for a convalescent," he said.

Natale sat down again.

"I am very glad Doña Luisa has weathered the crisis so well," Doctor Comenius said. He turned to her father. "Our first concern must be for the living, but we must also speak of the dead, I am afraid. Your son-in-law had a weak heart, Don Ramon. He should not have taken a sleeping potion at all. Who prescribed the physic for him?"

"Perhaps Fray Natale can tell us," her father said.

"I believe he obtained the prescription from a Flemish visitor, who passed through town last week and swore to its efficacy," Natale said.

How readily he makes up his answers, Luisa thought. When he told her that he had received no letters from Alonso, was he lying as well? His mien gave nothing away. His voice was level, his words persuasive.

"I would have thought him a more cautious man," the physician said. "And was Deodatus in the habit of mixing his own potions?"

"I mixed the potion," Natale said slowly and allowed tears to rise to his eyes. He hesitated, then said with just the right mixture of grief and horror: "May God have mercy on me if I misunderstood his instructions and erred in mixing the ingredients!"

A great performance, Luisa thought. So lifelike, so believable.

The physician eyed Natale with pity. "I should not burden myself with such doubts," he said and looked at Luisa's father for support.

"That's right," her father said. "No need to engage in speculations."

"Then we shall bring this sad business to a conclusion," Doctor Comenius said. "Let us say: death by misadventure and God's mercy on Deodatus' soul."

On the day of the funeral, Luisa allowed herself to be carried downstairs. Deodatus' body was laid out on a bier, his emaciated face skeletal already, his hands bony and knotted. The cloying smell of the bouquets set up in the hall barely covered the smell of death and decay.

"I don't think I will be going to the cemetery after all," Luisa said to her mother. "I am not up to it."

"Of course not, my lamb," she said. "In this weather it's far better for you to stay indoors. We don't want anything to hold up your convalescence."

It was a cold, wet day. To Luisa the rain seemed purifying, washing off the patina of lies that had dulled her life. When the servants opened the door for the pall-bearers to carry the coffin out into the courtyard, the rain was like a wall, a pearly sheet of water. The domestics who had gathered on the steps bent their heads low and sheltered under their dripping hoods and tunics. They formed a gray knot in the sluggish daylight. The horses, like the people, kept their heads down. From the hall door, Luisa saw the coffin swaying as the pall-bearers passed the gate. She watched the cortege without regret and closed her ears to the bells faintly ringing from the village church. She felt pity for Deodatus, but no grief. Her heart was light and full of hope. She would find a way to send Alonso a letter. Everything would come right. Did not the poet grant a happy ending to the tangled tale of Elisena and Perion? He did not allow them to suffer *without love, their hearts stripped and naked of all joy.*

CHAPTER 12

The thick stone walls gave a chill to the rooms of the royal residence even as the afternoon sun lit up the façade and gilded the window panes of the room, where Martin contemplated his new responsibilities.

King Ferdinand was dead. The tapestries adorning the royal chamber were covered with black cloth, veiling the merry hunting scenes and the proud heraldic emblems of the Castilian and Aragonese dynasties. The grandees of Spain had come and filed past the King's body resting on a bier garlanded with fragrant myrtle. They made their obeisance first to their dead sire and then to the Cardinal-Regent.

"The King is dead," Cisneros intoned. "Long live the Queen."

"The King is dead. Long live the Queen," they repeated.

There was an air of deference, but Martin knew that the grandees were kept in check only by prudence and ceremony. Their loyalty was threadbare. It would be difficult for the Cardinal to hold his own against the leading families. They were accustomed to bow only to royalty. It remained to be seen whether he could make the majesty of his office count.

The Cardinal had read Ferdinand's last will and testament to the assembly. It designated his grandson, sixteen-year old Carlos, as successor to the throne on the death or abdication of his mother, Juana, the mad Queen. It was the fervent hope of everyone present that Juana could be persuaded to abdicate in favour of her son. But for the time being, it was Cisneros who held the reins of power as regent of Spain.

There was no dissenting voice. Not yet. They professed obedience. They swore to uphold the laws of Spain. Then they went home; no doubt, to hatch their plots.

The Cardinal immediately set about the business of the state. The first letter he dictated to Martin was an urgent message for Prince Carlos in the Low Countries, informing him of his grandfather's will and requesting his presence in Spain at the earliest opportunity.

"It will be a long and dangerous journey," Martin said.

The Cardinal nodded. "We will need to negotiate diplomatic immunity with France before the

Prince sets out. The royal ships will pass along the French coast and require taking in provisions at French harbours. Even if all the preparations go well, it will be months until Carlos arrives."

A weary time lay ahead. The magnates were likely to take advantage of the interregnum to usurp rights that weren't theirs and to encroach on royal privilege. There were dangers from without as well. Navarre was poised to stage an invasion, Sicily prone to fall to revolution. And worst of all, Martin thought, the health of the Cardinal was precarious. Religion and politics had taken a toll on his body. His face had the leathery aspect of an ancient mummy, and his back was bent, as if the burdens of his office had compressed his spine. Yet he was resolved to do his duty to God and his country.

"The Almighty has given the regency into my hands," he said, "and I will stand at the helm of Spain and guide her through this storm. May He preserve me until I deliver the country safely into the hands of Prince Carlos."

But even if God preserved the Cardinal, and the Prince reached Spain without incident, there was one more obstacle to overcome: the mad Queen must agree to hand over the government to her son.

"The poor woman has felt the heavy hand of fate," the Cardinal said. "Her husband died in the flower of his manhood, leaving her a widow. Her young son was kept from her and raised by his aunt in the Netherlands. Now King Ferdinand has died and entrusted her and the country to me, a stranger who cannot even boast of being a member of the royal family."

For some years now, Juana had lived in confinement at Tordesillas, but the Cardinal was wary of conspirators attempting to take her hostage and using the disturbed woman as a political pawn. She was, in a sense, the Cardinal's ward. Her bodily and spiritual wellbeing were his responsibility. And so he surrounded her with men he could trust. He had summoned Alonso Malki to serve as her physician, assigned to Martin the duty of Confessor to the Queen, and charged the governor of Tordesillas with guarding her person.

Martin had first laid eyes on the Queen when he delivered the news of King Ferdinand's death to her at Tordesillas. He was waiting in the audience chamber, when the guard admitted a shabbily dressed woman accompanied by an old attendant. Martin was dismayed. So this was Queen Juana, and everything he had heard about her and dismissed as gossip was true! She lived and looked like a pauper. The hem of her robe was frayed, the black cloth faded. Her matted grey hair was tied in a knot that threatened to unravel.

Martin made a deep obeisance.

"Your Majesty," he said, respectful of her office even if he could not muster respect for her person. The Queen reeked of urine. The hand she held out for him to kiss was scored with scratches, the finger nails jagged and broken.

She listened to Martin's message silently, her eyes devoid of understanding.

"Tell me again," she said at last. "Who is it that died?" Her voice was tinny with disuse.

"The King, Madam. Your father. May God bless his soul."

The Queen sighed. "They all die and desert me."

"Will you deign to look at your father's last will, Madam?" Martin said and placed in her hands the document he had been instructed to deliver.

She looked at him with grave and empty eyes. "What about it?" she said. "It is a piece of paper."

"Your father, Madam, has appointed Cardinal Cisneros regent until the arrival of Prince Carlos, your son. The Prince will assist Your Majesty with the government of the realm."

"Carlos?" she said. "How can a child help me with the government of the realm?"

"He was a child when you left the Low Countries, Madam, but he has reached the age of discretion now."

She looked at him confused. "What do you want from me?" she asked abruptly.

"I need Your Majesty's signature on the document acknowledging the Cardinal's appointment," Martin said. The necessary preparations had been made. A pen, ink stand, and blotting sand were in readiness, set up on a table.

The Queen looked at the spread of writing implements and shook her head despondently. She turned to her attendant. "Beatriz," she said, raising her voice to attract the attention of the old woman who was half-deaf. "I've forgotten how to write."

The attendant raised her rheumy eyes to Juana's face. She was reading the Queen's lips, Martin realized.

"I will guide your hand, Madam," she said, picked up the pen, dipped it into ink, and extended it to the Queen.

Juana clutched the pen, and the old woman gingerly moved the Queen's hand, pressing the nib down on the parchment and shaping the letters for her.

Martin stepped forward, witnessed the signing, and sprinkled sand over the two signatures.

The Queen watched him impatiently. "I think it's time to feed the cats," she said, and turning to face her lady-in-waiting, she repeated the words for the benefit of the deaf woman. "Time to feed the cats, Beatriz!"

The cats? Martin did not know what to make of this surprising announcement, but the old attendant shuffled forward and took her mistress' arm. "Indeed, my lady, it is time to go," she said. "The Cardinal's emissary will excuse us."

Martin bowed and watched the two women leave the room.

And am I to be this woman's spiritual advisor? he thought, recalling the scene now that the Cardinal had appointed him Royal Confessor. The Queen was hardly sentient. How could he give her spiritual counsel, and what need was there for absolving her of sins? She had the mind of a child. She could not be held responsible for her thoughts and actions. Would Alonso be able to improve the Queen's condition? Would medical skills be of any avail, or were prayers the only remedy left?

***

Martin was among the first to welcome Alonso Malki when he arrived at the royal palace and presented himself to the Cardinal to receive his credentials. Since their first encounter in Alcala, when Martin had consulted the doctor about his nightmares, they had become friends. Martin missed his genial company, the evenings they had spent in Alcala, engaged in lively discussion or absorbed in a game of chess. He had made no friends at court. His days were crowded with tiresome work. The Cardinal had delegated his inquisitorial duties to Martin. That was the most burdensome of his tasks: to field the denunciations. Assuming the mantle of the inquisitor, Martin was forced to see only The Accused, not the human being. He blocked the voice of the mother guilty of buying a horoscope for her little boy or the jilted woman accused of witchcraft, or the superstitious old man who had dealings with a necromancer. He shut his mind to their pleas and concentrated instead on the numbered paragraphs of canon law and the dictates of the church, or else he might have felt sorry for them and taken pity on the baptized Jew who ate unleavened bread on Friday or the baptized Moor who was caught praying to Allah. He allowed the law to numb his heart with its incantations of *must not, shall not,* and *circumstances not withstanding.* The interests of the church must be served. The sinners must be fined and publicly humiliated, made to walk barefoot and bareheaded in a procession, in the shaming ritual of the *auto da fe.* They must be banned, sentenced to serve in the galleys, yes, and burned at the stake if they were unrepentant.

Martin's heart was turning to stone. And what was the cure for a stony heart? A friend. When Alonso arrived at the royal palace, he welcomed him with open arms.

The doctor looked around Martin's well-appointed apartment.

"You have begun to live in style at last," he said.

The secretary's rooms were handsomely furnished in the Mudejar style, with candelabras of chased silver illuminating fine tapestries and oriental rugs. A good fire was blazing in the brazier, and was needed to drive out the damp cold. The spring rains had turned the courtyard below into a windswept, watery plain.

"I live the way I do on the Cardinal's orders," Martin said. "We are at court, he says, and you will get no respect unless you adopt the style of the court. You are my representative, and the interests of state and church must take precedence over your likes and dislikes. And so I live like a courtier."

"And soon you will turn into a courtier."

"No, I won't allow my surroundings to change the inner man. I am who I have always been – your companion, your friend, and willing to indulge you even if it means being beaten at chess."

"I'm glad to hear it, my dear Martin, and looking forward to resuming our games."

"And what news do you bring from Alcala? The Cardinal told me that you were called in to treat Doña Luisa. I hope it was no serious illness."

"It was a case of mental exhaustion. She has recovered since."

"To be candid," Martin said. "I thought her marriage was rushed. She was too young to take on the responsibilities of a wife."

"I agree."

"She should have been allowed to follow her own heart."

A reserved look came into Alonso's eyes.

"Don't misunderstand me," Martin said. "I did not mean to suggest that a young woman should be allowed to choose her own husband. I meant to say that she should have been given a choice between marriage and celibacy."

"Is that not a question of vocation?" Alonso said. "Does Doña Luisa have a religious vocation in your opinion?"

"You recall the dream that haunted me?"

"A dream with a puzzling message."

"Which I understand at last. I have resolved the ambiguity of the Latin word *tollenda*. *The bride will be lowered by marriage* – marriage in the conventional sense. But *the bride will be raised up by marriage* if she becomes a bride of Christ."

"Very neatly resolved, my friend. And does the dream apply to Luisa?"

"When she was a girl, the Cardinal told me, it was her wish to become a nun. She yearned for sainthood and even martyrdom. Her parents dismissed it as a childish dream, but it may have been a divine seed, a longing planted in her mind by God. I fear it was wrong to marry her off, and it was marriage that lowered her spirits."

"I would rather not engage in that sort of speculation," Alonso said. His eyes wandered to the window, as if he was trying to discern the truth in the rain beating against the panes. "We see the truth through a glass, darkly, as the Bible says. Let us speak of things that are within our ken. Tell me about your life here, Martin."

Martin was ready to unburden his heart. He was unhappy at court. "The courtiers are a more changeable lot than a troupe of traveling players. They assume many roles, but the most popular is that of the flatterer. They attach themselves to one of the grandees and admire his every move. You remember the words of the parasite in Plautus' comedy: *He says yes, I say yes. He says no, I say no*. That is a perfect description of the courtier."

Alonso laughed. "Flatterers are every where," he said, "not just at court."

"And there is no charity in the grandees. When I ask them to contribute to the support of the poor, they tell me they are short of funds. They are short of funds because they waste their money on jesters, mimes, pimps, and women of ill repute. I find the company here so objectionable that I asked for my dinner to be served in my apartment. The Cardinal agrees with my complaints, but he does not want me to isolate myself. He reminded me that I must not disgruntle the courtiers. My appointment as Royal Confessor has yet to be confirmed by Prince Carlos. To tell you the truth, I do not care for the appointment. I am content to be the Cardinal's secretary. But to oblige him, I take my meals in the great hall on alternate days."

"I share your misgivings about dinners in the great hall," Alonso said. "On the evening of my arrival, they served half-cooked meat with twice-cooked cabbage, and fish that was no longer fresh. The plates and cups were filthy. The company was as unpleasant as the food. The man who sat beside me at table stank of yesterday's vomit and disgusted me with his fetid burps."

"Nothing is clean at court, literally and metaphorically. The Cardinal is immune to corruption, but the court has affected him in other ways. The press of business, the constant worry is damaging to his health. His energy is spent."

"I have noticed it," Alonso said, "and offered him my advice. His first care must be to conserve his energies and avoid the fatigue of travel. He looked at me and said: That is a difficult prescription to follow, doctor. To keep law and order, I must act and be seen to act. I must be omnipresent. I cannot avoid travel."

"As a result, he lives the life of a wandering minstrel, on the road every third day," Martin said. "I can only hope that your royal patient, Queen Juana, will be more receptive to your advice than the Cardinal."

"I am told the Queen's mental health is shaky."

"It is a distressing case. I have been to Tordesillas and witnessed her strange behaviour. And something must be done about her appearance, which speaks of neglect hardly becoming to the dignity of a Queen. She lives with an aged companion and a dozen cats, and is more attached to the latter, I was told. She insists on sharing her dinner with them. She sits among them on the floor and licks her plate in imitation of her pets."

"Dear God!" Alonso said. "It will take more than medical skill to help her. Perhaps you can make your influence felt, Martin. You are her spiritual advisor after all."

"I doubt that I can be of any help," Martin said. "It is a delicate situation. I am afraid I lack the diplomatic touch. I tend to be too severe. I know it, but I cannot soften my face or modulate my voice. In any case, you'll have to manage on your own, Alonso. The Cardinal has decided to keep me by his side until Prince Carlos arrives and relieves him of his duties as regent."

"Then the pleasure of your company will be short. My instructions are to leave for Tordesillas the day after tomorrow."

"And I will join you there before Christmas, God willing."

CHAPTER 13

THE SEASONS TURNED, AND WITH THEM THE rumours about the progress of Prince Carlos' journey: it had been delayed once again. No, he had finally set out for Spain. The royal convoy had been sighted. No, it had been captured by the French. No, it had fallen into the hands of pirates.

When the Cardinal came to Martin's apartment unannounced one evening, he expected to hear new and alarming reports about the progress of the royal flotilla. The prelate was not in the habit of visiting his secretary. Only an extraordinary event would prompt him to break with his routine.

It was late, and the Cardinal had put away the finery of his high office and was wearing the coarse habit of a friar. He stood before his secretary no longer the regent, but a tired old man, gaunt, sallow-faced, and troubled.

He dropped into the chair Martin pulled out for him. The candles in the chandelier were burning low, and shadows were filling the room, sharpening the Cardinal's features and turning his skin to parchment. Martin thought he could discern a faint trembling in the Cardinal's lower lip. When he spoke, his voice was husky as if he wanted to cover up powerful feelings.

"I have come to tell you the sad news in person," he said. "Letters from Alcala inform me of a double tragedy: Deodatus has died unexpectedly, and Luisa has suffered a miscarriage."

Martin exclaimed in dismay. The memory of Luisa's sweet face blended with the image of the woman who had haunted his dreams.

"My cousin tells me that Deodatus died after taking a sleeping potion prepared by Natale," the prelate said.

"Is Natale to be blamed for his death, then?"

"It would not surprise me. He is an unsavoury man."

"You will excuse my presumptuous question," Martin said, "but did he not become Luisa's tutor on Your Eminence's recommendation?"

The Cardinals' face showed his tiredness. "I am sorry I recommended him," he said somberly. "As for his involvement in Deodatus' death, my cousin, Doña Catalina, informs me that he misunderstood Deodatus' instructions and used the wrong ratio in mixing the ingredients of the sleeping potion. Yet another informant tells me that Deodatus ended his own life, and Natale assumed responsibility for his death to spare the family. When you last saw Deodatus, did he seem disturbed? Did he have reason to be disturbed?"

"He was his usual self, that is to say, volatile. It will not have escaped Your Eminence's attention that he was subject to rapid changes of mood."

"But do you give credence to the rumour that he ended his own life?"

"I cannot say. I have never been in Deodatus' confidence."

"Natale left for Italy in great haste, I am told, and without obtaining his Superior's permission to depart, which would indicate complicity in Deodatus' death."

"Your Eminence has no doubt formed his own opinion," Martin said. He thought of his ominous dream. It would have been better if Luisa had never married. The Cardinal should have known better than to promote her marriage to Deodatus.

For a long time, Cisneros had been Martin's lodestar. His life seemed a pattern of perfection. His immense certainty, his determination had buoyed him. But he had overestimated the Cardinal. He was not the solid rock he had imagined him to be. He made mistakes. He introduced a corrupt man into Cardosa's household. He chose the wrong husband for Luisa. And what Martin had taken to be certainty of mind was no more than a stubborn clinging to routine. The Cardinal's world was a tidy place, where each virtue and vice had its place, arranged in an immovable order. But was the world immovable, or was it a stream, as Heraclitus said, and *no one can step into the same river twice*?

"And how does Doña Luisa bear her misfortune?" Martin asked.

"Let us hope that God will give her strength in her affliction."

Yes, his dream had come true. The sinister meaning of the Latin word *tollenda* had governed Luisa's marriage. She had been lowered by her union with Deodatus. Martin prayed that the second, auspicious meaning of the word would come true as well, that she might find happiness as a bride of Christ.

"Marriage has not turned out well for your niece," he said. "As St. Paul says of unmarried women and widows: *It is good for them if they abide in celibacy, even as I do*. Luisa might take the apostle's words to heart now, and seek eternal bliss in the arms of the heavenly bridegroom, Christ."

The Cardinal's face reverted to its former determination. He straightened his back and rose to his feet.

"I quite agree with you, my dear Martin, or rather with St. Paul," he said. "It is never good for a young woman to be left to her own devices. A wife can look to her husband for guidance. A widow will do well to submit to the discipline of a convent."

"Luisa's fortune will create a substantial endowment for the religious house of her choice. Where will you advise her to go if she chooses to take that path?"

"Her father will have something to say about the matter, and I fear he will not favour my opinion. Luisa's marriage contract provides for the dowry to revert to the widow, and since the marriage has remained without issue, Deodatus' possessions will devolve on her as well. No doubt Ramon Cardosa has given thought to his daughter's wealth and will take steps to divert it to his own purposes. He will want Luisa to remarry and enhance the family's fortunes and his own connections."

"In that case," Martin said, "there is no time to lose. You must give Doña Luisa the immediate benefit of your counsel. She must be removed from Cardosa's influence if she is to be won for the glory of Christ and his church."

The Cardinal nodded in agreement. "Indeed it would be best for Luisa to take up residence here with me if she is fit to travel. Suitable arrangements can be made for her in due course. To begin with, she might join the Queen as a lady-in-waiting. The secluded life at Tordesillas will allow her to reflect on her vocation. If she chooses to take the veil, she may enter the convent of the Clares which adjoins the Queen's residence. It has an impeccable reputation and would provide Luisa with a place of spiritual repose. I shall write to her immediately."

"And the courier who has brought your letters today can take back your reply to Alcala tomorrow."

"I am afraid the business is too important to be left to the agency of others. You will have to be my courier, Martin, and add your voice to mine. You must go to Alcala at once and, if Luisa agrees to our plan, escort her here."

Martin thought of the imminent arrival of Prince Carlos. "But is it wise for me to leave your side at this time?" he asked.

"I can ill afford to dispense with your assistance," the Cardinal said, "but we must venture it and hope that you will return in time to lend me support when I need it most. I feel the weight of old age and fear my shoulders can no longer bear the burden fate has laid on them, but time is of the essence in Luisa's affairs as well, and her welfare is of the greatest importance to me."

The message of his prophetic dream was uppermost in Martin's mind as well.

"I shall be your faithful agent in Doña Luisa's affairs," he said to the Cardinal. "And with God's help I will persuade her to embrace a life of holiness and convey her safely into your presence." He hesitated before continuing: "Your Eminence has alluded to the heavy burden God has laid on your shoulders. You will not be angry with me if I take the liberty of suggesting that you put yourself into the competent hands of Alonso during my absence. His skill will ensure that your physical strength matches your mental vigour."

Knowing the Cardinal's stubbornness, Martin had couched his words in discreet language, but the prelate frowned.

"I shall entrust myself to God first," he said, "and to a physician thereafter." He paused. "And to a Jew last."

"Allow me to say that Alonso is a man of uncommon spiritual gifts, a man with a philosophical bent of mind. I have come to regard him as a friend, and I need not remind Your Eminence that he is a *baptized* Jew."

"He has been baptized, yes, but I doubt that he can ever be purged of the poison he imbibed as a child growing up in a household of unbelievers," the Cardinal said. "His father died at the stake, an unrepentant sinner. Can a man growing up in such moral filth be redeemed? Does not God visit the sins of the fathers on their sons, even to the third generation?"

"And does Alonso's conduct go for nothing?"

"Indeed," the Cardinal said, "when I observe the man's modesty and his courteous manner, when I consider his scholarship and his medical skills, I feel that I am doing him wrong. As for the doctor's philosophical bent, I fear that he loves knowledge more than he loves God and looks for the truth in the books of the ancient philosophers rather than in the Bible." Doubt remained written on the Cardinal's face, when he added: "However, to put your mind at ease and show you that I value your counsel, I will summon Alonso and ask him to attend me during your absence. Does that satisfy you?"

"Your Eminence is very kind to indulge me," Martin said.

Although he had spoken with confidence of Alonso, the Cardinal's reservations about "the Jew" disconcerted Martin. Was the influence of Christ-denying parents on their children really irreversible? He had touched on the subject once in conversation with Alonso, raising the question: "What makes us the men we are?"

"Memory," Alonso had said without hesitation. "The customs we grow up with, the instruction we receive in the bosom of our families. Those memories determine the choice of a man's companions and allow him to overcome misfortune or make use of good fortune."

"You mean experience, then?"

"Let us say experience internalized, experience transformed into our own flesh and blood."

"You are right," Martin said. "At the Last Supper Jesus transformed the bread and wine into his flesh and blood and told the apostles: Do this in memory of me. That act of memory is what makes us Christians: our communion with Christ."

"When my family converted to Christianity," Alonso said, "my father gathered up the Hebrew books in his library and carried them to the central square of Seville, where the friars had made a bonfire, calling on all Jews to cast away the symbols of idolatry. I was a boy then. My father placed the books on the pyre, and we watched in silence as the pages curled at the edges, blackened and turned to ashes. Sometimes when I sit in my room on a quiet winter evening and look into the blazing fire, I see that bonfire again and realize that it has become a part of me, entered my flesh and blood. It has made me who I am."

"No, it was baptism that made you who you are, Alonso, a new man turned from a Jew into a Christian; baptism and the memory of Christ, the communion with Christ's flesh and blood."

"Christ was a Jew," Alonso said quietly.

***

Martin set out for Alcala the following morning. A light drizzle blew up against his face as the gelding fell into an easy trot. The visionary dream and its mysterious message were on his mind. Although the ambiguity of the Latin was resolved, Martin's dilemma was not. He felt the same disquiet thinking of Luisa, the same temptation he had tried to subdue with fasting and flagellations and even with dialectical reasoning. He could not subdue his sinful passion and did not know how to conduct his meeting with Luisa.

He pulled down the dripping hood of his cloak and tried to think of the scene as it might unfold: a well appointed drawing room, Luisa putting out her hand to greet him, but the scenario was dated. Luisa was wearing a bridal smile. He had last seen her on her wedding day.

He tried to imagine her as a widow, but he saw only the dream woman, her cheeks misted with tears. He had never seen Luisa's house in Arelate. Her present-day surroundings were a blur, like a painting left unfinished by the artist. Martin tried to marshal his arguments, addressing words to a widow of indistinct qualities. There was no response. His shadowy partner remained silent.

When he reached the city walls of Alcala, he still had not devised a plan or composed a speech in his mind. How was he to fulfill his mission and persuade Luisa to join the Cardinal and thereafter live a cloistered life? And even if he had the words at his command, would he be able to look into her eyes without seeing the woman in her? He had fought hard to suppress his desires, to turn his love for earthly beauty into a divine flame burning only for God, to make the church his beloved. Would the temptations of the flesh return to haunt him when he laid eyes on Luisa?

He arrived at the villa in Arelate. A servant ushered him into the library. The scenario was unfolding at last. He was able to fill in the missing pieces: glass-fronted bookcases, a writing desk with a painting of Mary Magdalene above it, elegant settees with tasseled silk cushions, French windows overlooking the garden.

The door opened. He turned and saw her, a slender figure in a rustle of black silk. Luisa welcomed him with a smile that was aloof, a pale ghost of a smile, and even so he was afraid of looking into her eyes. Grief had not impaired her beauty. She was a child-bride when he saw her last, a skinny girl with burning eyes. She had blossomed into a woman now. The fire of her eyes had deepened.

"I have come to convey the Cardinal's condolences, Doña Luisa," he said, "and to tell you that his prayers are with you."

Luisa had stopped under the painting of Mary Magdalene. Her eyes have the same disconcerting depth as the biblical sinner, he thought and reproved himself. He was the sinner. He was the one who could not discipline his mind.

"It is kind of the Cardinal to keep me in his thoughts," Luisa said. "I wish I could converse with him in person, but I know his duties keep him at court."

"I am here in his stead, Doña Luisa. He asks you to open your heart to me," Martin said, but a monstrous fear took hold of him, that she would take him up on the offer and grant him an intimate glimpse of her self. He looked at the rise and fall of her breasts under the black silk and felt his heart racing. A vein began pulsing in his neck. He was deafened by the rush of blood in his ears, but he went on talking, forming the words with difficulty. "The Cardinal has been thinking about your future," he said.

"I have been thinking about it myself," she said. Her voice was firm, as if she had been pondering her fate, decided on a course of action, and had no need of advice. Grief, he thought, has matured her and filled the well of her heart to the brim. *She has put away childish things*, and has become even more dangerous to me in her dark beauty.

He caught his breath. He tried to think dull thoughts to lower his pulse – he thought of canon laws in their leatherbound codices, the numbered paragraphs, the maze of legal phrases. Think of the Byzantine clauses, he told himself, follow their meandering path, the measured flow of formulaic words repeated over and over. His heart beat slowed.

"No doubt you have given thought to the future, Doña Luisa, but you must not make rash decisions," he said. "Life has removed you from the tutelage of a father, and death from that of a husband, but you are still in need of counsel. Indeed the law requires you to seek counsel and adopt a legal representative."

She took a seat on the sofa, and motioned him to a chair opposite. "I can hear the Cardinal's voice in yours," she said.

He had fallen into the Cardinal's mannered speech, turned into a preacher. Entrust yourself to God was his next line. He pulled back and said instead: "Trust in the advice of the Cardinal." Was it wise to refer Luisa to the counsel of a fallible man? But he could not say to her: Trust in my dream vision.

As if she had guessed his misgivings, she said: "Trust the Cardinal's advice rather than the advice of my father?"

"I do not wish to make odious comparisons, Doña Luisa, but the Cardinal is not guided by worldly thoughts. In giving you advice, he does not think of estates or power or the aggrandizement of his family. He will consider only your happiness."

"My father's advice is to remarry," she said. "What is the Cardinal's counsel?"

"You may read his own words," Martin said, handing her the Cardinal's letter.

She quickly broke the seal, unfolded the sheet, and ran her eyes over the lines. They barely filled half a page. She looked up impatiently. "His letter is full of riddles," she said and read out his message. *The first dignity is assigned to virginity, the next to widowhood, and the third to marriage. Virginity surpasses marriage as a precious stone surpasses gold, and widowhood gives place to virginity only as onyx yields to pearl.* And how does this apply to me? I suppose you have come as his exegete, Fray Martin."

"Do you wish me to expound the lines?"

"First let me tell you what my father thinks about marriage and widowhood. Widows, especially young widows, he said to me, make a nuisance of themselves. They spend their days prying and gossiping. The authority of a husband will bring a woman's natural levity under control, and the responsibilities of a new family will keep her from idleness, which is the devil's helper." An ironic smile played on her lips. "Clearly my father ranks marriage above widowhood."

"That does not surprise me," Martin said. "You will be besieged by suitors when the mourning period is over. Deodatus' death has made you a woman of means." He wanted to say: and you are young and beautiful, but he choked back the words. They were too close to his heart. "You will have your choice of suitors, and your father will urge you to think of the interests of your family and choose accordingly."

"I shall determine my own fate."

"God determines our fate."

"God helps those who help themselves."

"A frivolous adage, Doña Luisa, coined to excuse the inexcusable," Martin said as severely as he could. "Now let me comment on the meaning of the Cardinal's words, or rather, the meaning of Saint Paul, whose words he paraphrases. Virginity is the noblest calling but it is not for everyone. Marriage, too, has much to commend itself. Christ honoured the wedding at Cana with his presence after all, but a widow must choose carefully between celibacy and remarriage. The Cardinal counsels celibacy. He invites you to join him and place yourself under his protection. Trust to his guidance, Doña Luisa." He was sermonizing again. He could find no middle ground, between falling into the trap of her beauty and falling into sanctimonious speech. The safeguards in which he had trusted—his vows, the habit of the Franciscan, the discipline of his mind—were weak defenses against temptation. He needed another barrier between Luisa and his desires: *her* discipline, *her* vows.

"I do not doubt the Cardinal's good will," Luisa began, and broke off again. She looked at Martin uneasily. "What are the Cardinal's plans for me?" she said. "For I believe he has a plan."

"He wishes you to find peace."

"In the arms of a suitor who is to his liking?" she said sharply.

"Yes, in the arms of a suitor who is to his liking: Jesus Christ. But you must go into that marriage prepared with a full understanding of the vows you take, the promises you make to the heavenly bridegroom, the heavenly joy and the earthly deprivations you may expect as a bride of Christ."

She looked down on her hands.

"Return with me, Doña Luisa," Martin said urgently. His heart was aflame again, he could not help it. His breath was hot, his words fervent. He was speaking of things that mattered. "Entrust yourself to the Cardinal," he said, his speech fluid, the words coming unbidden. "He will arrange for you to join the household of Queen Juana as a lady-in-waiting. She lives a retired life, and you will have leisure to consider your future without anyone exerting undue influence on you."

"That is all very well," Luisa said, "but the Cardinal is ailing and carrying the burden of old age. He may not be able to protect me for long. Where shall I turn for counsel then? You will forgive my plain speaking, Fray Martin, but you yourself urged me to be circumspect."

"You are right to raise that question, Doña Luisa. I assure you I will be your friend." *I will be your knight-errant*, he wanted to say. *I will lay down my life for you.* "I shall stand by you and look after your interests if anything untoward should happen to the

Cardinal." He was ready to make any promise. "The Cardinal has put my name forth for the post of Royal Confessor," he said desperately. "I shall have some influence at court." Perhaps the offer was made too eagerly. Perhaps it promised too much. She was smiling.

"Our conversation gives me an odd sense of déjà vu, Fray Martin," she said. "When I was a girl, I read the Lives of the Saints and wanted to become one of them. I had visions of taking the veil, of living in a lonely cell, of devoting myself to prayer and fasting. In my daydreams, I had only one confidant, my confessor, a gaunt Franciscan with a long, narrow face and gray eyes, a fervent preacher." She stopped and regarded him attentively. "Yes, you do look a great deal like the confessor of my dreams, Fray Martin, and so I trust your offer of friendship."

"A meeting of dreams!" he said astonished, but she took his exclamation as an expression of incredulity.

"Don't laugh at me, Fray Martin," she said. "It was a childish dream, I know."

He was helpless under her eyes. "I would not dare to ridicule your dream, Doña Luisa," he said. "Dreams come from God, and I am honoured by your trust in me." His voice was rough with feeling. "But we are speaking of contingencies. May God preserve the Cardinal's strength for many years to come, for the sake of the church and for our country."

"And for my sake," she said.

"You have another friend at court as well," Martin said, thinking that his friend might become his ally in persuading Luisa to fall in with the Cardinal's wishes. "Doctor Malki, who attended you when you were ill and is now the Queen's physician."

"Ah, yes, Alonso Malki," she said and put her hand up to her eyes as if a sudden emotion had overcome her – the memory of another time when Deodatus was live, when she was with child? "He has written me a letter of condolence."

She took a letter from her writing desk and handed it to Martin. "This is what he wrote."

Martin ran his eye over it, although he already knew its contents. The Cardinal had informers everywhere who copied for him all correspondence that left the court or the Queen's residence. It was his responsibility as Regent to guard against any plots, and as Inquisitor General to guard against infidels. Of course he carefully vetted "the Jew's" letter. The contents passed muster. Martin had expected nothing else. He thought it was a model of Christian consideration.

To Doña Luisa, with my respects,

Dear Madam, I have received the grievous news of your husband's demise. Allow me to express my condolences and, as your physician, express my concern for your wellbeing. A wife may easily blame herself for the troubles of her husband, ascribing them to her own negligence. I beseech you not to torment yourself needlessly, saying: If only I had done this or not done that. I know you are blameless and must see your misfortune, not as divine punishment for your sins, but as part of God's mysterious plans which we humans cannot hope to fathom.

I have been told that your misfortune has been doubled by a miscarriage. Believe me, Madam, when I say: I grieve with you as if it had been the death of my own child. In the course of the treatment I devised for you, Madam, I came to know your thoughts. I conceived a deep respect for your courage and a glowing admiration for your spirit which, I pray God, may now guide your actions.

As for myself, I am successful in my profession but cannot overcome a sense of loss, being separated from the society of those who were dear to me and whose company I valued in Alcala.

I am desirous to hear how you are faring, Madam, and would regard it a token of unmerited favour if you honoured me with a reply.

I remain, Madam, your loyal servant, Alonso.

Alonso understands a woman's soul, Martin thought as he returned the letter to Luisa and saw the page tremble in her hands. Alonso had the words to move her. He would have been a better messenger than I, he thought.

"There is so much to consider," Luisa said softly.

Martin wanted to feel the softness of her breath on his skin. I cannot escape the sinful temptation of those lips, he thought, until they have been purified by a vow of chastity. His body ached with the effort of staving off temptation. He felt the fires of purgatory. His mouth was dry with longing. "You must search your heart, Doña Luisa," he said, breathing roughly, "and give the Cardinal an answer soon."

She moved to the window and looked across the lawn, as if the panorama of trees could inspire her. She turned, and Martin saw the sweetness of her smile. "You shall have my answer now," she said. "I will come with you."

Martin felt the muscles in his arms unknotting. The seething and fluttering in his heart abated. She will take the vow, he thought, and the strong walls of a cloister will shield me from her eyes.

"You have made the right decision," he said with relief. What remained to be done was lawyer's work, the sober work of parchment and sealing wax which was his natural element. "There is another decision to be made," he said. "It concerns your property. Is your father acting as your legal representative, Doña Luisa?"

"We have not yet discussed the matter," she said. "The truth is, I have held him off. I was not ready to speak to him of my future."

"Then it may be to your advantage to appoint the Cardinal your attorney. Indeed it is appropriate to choose a man of the cloth as your legal representative if you intend to enter the church."

"It may be appropriate and to my advantage," Luisa said, "but my father will object."

"I shall speak to him on your behalf. But I advise you to send the power of attorney to the Cardinal at once. The royal couriers travel between Alcala and the court every day. They will carry the papers safely to the Cardinal."

"You are right," Luisa said. "It will be best to confront my father with the accomplished fact. And I trust the Cardinal. He has my interests at heart and will listen to me with a sympathetic ear."

It was as if the decision to accompany him had undone all her reservations and established a natural progression of things, or so it appeared to Martin. She walked to the desk, took out pen and paper, and invited him to draw up the power of attorney. When she had signed it, she wrote a note to her father asking him to come the next morning and discuss the settlement of her estate. Martin looked at her determined figure. She had passed through misfortune as steel passes through fire. He thanked God for endowing her with a fearless spirit and giving her the determination to act. Surely it is the hand of God, he thought. My words alone have no power to sway her.

***

When Martin came to Luisa's house the next morning, there was no time to talk and devise a strategy, as he had hoped. Don Ramon was early. He stepped into the room, eyes unblinking, a burly man with a threatening presence, his energy barely contained. He nodded curtly at the secretary and took both of Luisa's hands, seizing possession of his daughter.

"My dear Luisa, I am glad to see you so well," he said, shrewdness behind his cordial manner. "When last I came, your maid told me you were ill and could not receive me."

"I am feeling better," she said, extracting her fingers from his grasp, "and wanted to talk to you about the estate."

"We shall do that presently, my dear," he said and strafed the secretary with an impatient look. "But we must not keep Fray Martin from going about the Cardinal's business."

"The Cardinal sent me to advise Doña Luisa," Martin said. "I have no other business in Alcala."

"That is very kind of the Cardinal," Ramon said. His voice betrayed irritation. "He means well of course, but I am quite capable of advising Luisa myself. You may tell the Cardinal from me: I have followed his advice in the matter of Luisa's first marriage, with tragic results. I shall keep my own counsel when it comes to considering her remarriage." He made a significant pause before continuing: "A connection with an aristocratic family is not out of the question."

"The Cardinal has set his hopes higher than that," Martin said. "He hopes for a union with Christ. The heavenly bridegroom surpasses all in glory, and he bestows on his bride the most valuable wedding gift of all: eternal happiness."

An angry flash appeared in Ramon's eyes, but he let the fire die out and said evenly. "The Cardinal is a man of the church, and it behooves him to look to eternal happiness. Luisa is a young woman and might reasonably look to happiness here on earth." He turned to her. "In saying that, I am sure I express your opinion as well, my dear."

Luisa did not respond to his prompt. "The Cardinal asked me to reflect on his advice and search my heart," she said. "He is well aware that a woman must not take the veil without considering her vocation."

Ramon was as tense as a bowstring now, gathering force to spring. "Luisa is a sensible woman," he said to Martin. "I'm sure she knows her vocation is marriage."

"The Cardinal believes it will be best for Luisa to ponder that question in an atmosphere conducive to reflection and free of worldly dis-tractions," Martin said, and ended the diplomatic dance. "He has invited Doña Luisa to join him at court."

"And I have accepted his invitation," she said, as if they had practised part singing and she knew her response.

Her father's eyes narrowed to pin points. A painful contraction swept his face and smoothed out again.

"You are right, my dear," he said. "A little holiday will do you good. I will ask your mother to accompany you."

"There is no need to inconvenience Doña Catalina," Martin said. "Duke Gonzalo Fernandez, as you may know, is presently in Alcala and will rejoin the Cardinal in a week's time. He will extend his protection to Doña Luisa. As you may have heard, he acquired two carriages on his last mission to France. We will travel safely and comfortably in his company."

"Carriages!" Luisa said. "We shall travel in luxury."

"I wish you were not travelling at all, much less in one of those contraptions," Cardosa said. "It's a foolish apery of French fashion, or rather Flemish fashion, because I believe it was Philip who introduced them first."

"For one thing-," Luisa said, but her father cut her off.

"For one thing, it's an excuse to waste money. But it's not my money, and I dare say you will have a pleasant holiday in the company of the duke's family."

"I do not mean it to be a holiday," Luisa said, "I mean it to be a permanent arrangement."

Ramon's face curdled. "An arrangement without my permission?"

"You must not be angry, Don Ramon," Martin said. He kept his voice quiet and reassuring. "The Cardinal is looking after Luisa's interests. He has arranged for her to serve the Queen as a lady-in-waiting. It is a great honour to be taken into the royal household, an honour for the Cardosa family, as you are well aware."

Ramon could no longer keep still and began stumping around the room. "An honour it may be," he said, "but the Queen is a crazy woman. Luisa, have you considered what it means to join the retinue of Juana the Mad?"

"I have considered it," she said. "The Queen is a pious woman and lives a retired life. I will have an opportunity to reflect on my vocation."

"Very well, Luisa," her father said and stopped his march. His fitful mouth belied the conciliatory tone of his voice. He is redrawing his battle lines, Martin thought as he followed Ramon's gaze. He was looking around the room as if to gauge the value of the furniture.

"In that case, my dear, you will want me to dispose of the house and look after your affairs here in your absence," Ramon said, raising his head, his nose testing the air. He was willing to let Luisa go in exchange for her property.

"I have thought about that, Papa," she said. "The Cardinal has consented to look after my affairs. I sent him a power of attorney yesterday. It is only appropriate for him to be my legal representative if my wealth is to endow the church."

Ramon's anger exploded. He looked like a fighting cock, a black rooster, his head snapping from side to side. "With your assets you can buy the convent of Montserrat and its abbess!" he shouted. "If you waste your money like that, Luisa, I must disown you. You are no daughter of mine!"

"She is a child of God, Don Ramon," Martin said, facing him calmly. "Jesus says: *Leave your father and mother and follow me.* That is the meaning of becoming the bride of Christ."

Ramon glowered at the secretary. "Keep your sermons for the pulpit," he said, and turned to Luisa for a final appeal. "Luisa," he began, but her defiant look made him shut his mouth.

"We will talk another time," he said, pretending that he had another chance, that the battle was not lost. He yanked the bell with a brutish move and waited for the servant to show him out, bearing the silence of his daughter with a stony face. He offered Martin no more than a polite nod when he left.

CHAPTER 14

THE COACHES CARRYING DUKE FERNANDEZ' FAMILY and his guests got under way in the morning. Nightfall found them still on the road, miles from the inn that was to offer them shelter. Rain had turned the road to rutted mud, and the convoy was crawling along at a snail's pace.

The honour of riding in a carriage had been urged on Martin as the Cardinal's representative. He would have preferred to ride his horse, but he could not reject the duke's offer without giving offense. He shared the carriage with a large painting and a young kinsman of the duke, who introduced himself as Sebastian Fernandez. The duke had acquired the painting at great expense and thought it too valuable to entrust to a rattling cart or expose it to the elements. It was covered with a protective cloth of felt and sat on one of the benches like a guest of honour, taking up almost the whole width of the coach and cramping the men's legroom.

The young man was garrulous.

"I've just returned from the Netherlands," he told the secretary, "fighting on the Habsburg side against the rebellious Gelderlanders. They are a vicious band, but we trounced them. It took razing a village or two and cutting down a dozen orchards, but in the end the peasants stopped providing cover for the rebels, and we rounded them up and hung them by their feet, every single man of them. For good measure, we gouged out their eyes and cut off their hands and a few more appendages. It sets a good example to the rest of the population. Everything has gone quiet now."

Sebastian had the raw speech and crude manners of a mercenary. Martin listened to his brutal tales silently and gave only monosyllabic replies to his questions. Seeing that his military exploits failed to make an impression, Sebastian shut his mouth at last. The rain had stopped, and the fields were bathed in the pale white light of the moon. Sebastian looked out at the ghostly landscape for a while, then took a flagon from his coat pocket and offered a swig to Martin.

"Burns your gut," he said, "and cures what ails you."

When Martin declined, he put the flask to his own lips and emptied it with one long pull. He upended the bottle with a silly grin, sprinkled the last drops on the carriage floor, and gave out a loud belch. Satisfied, he leaned back into his seat. But his peace of mind did not last. He began to fidget, sat up and lifted a corner of the felt cover to inspect the painting the duke had bought. It was a canvas depicting Eve offering the forbidden fruit to Adam. Sebastian ogled the naked figures and laughed lasciviously. He expressed his delight at Eve's rounded breasts and speculated about what the painter had modestly covered with a fig leaf.

"No wonder, she got Adam where she wanted him," he snorted. "She looks juicy enough to be eaten herself." He saw the Franciscan's disapproving look and added: "*You* may be proof against such things, Father, but a young fellow like myself ain't."

"Everyone is subject to temptations," Martin said. "It is our duty as Christians to do battle against them."

"I acquitted myself very well in the war against the rebels," Sebastian said, "but I'm afraid I lost the battle against Eve last night. Perhaps I should make a confession to you."

Martin frowned at the young rake. "A confession is a serious matter," he said, "and requires an examination of conscience. So I would not counsel you to confess lightly."

"Oh, I've examined my conscience. Believe me, I've been thinking about it all day, wondering whether the wench has given me a little more than pleasure and left me with a present I didn't want, filthy slut that she was."

"You should be sorry for what you have done, not just for the consequences of your actions."

"I'm sorry in every way, Father, but the wench made like Eve here in the painting. She allowed me a good look at her titties, and brushed up against me like a cat. I'm not made of marble, you know, and what with the wine I'd been drinking, next thing I knew I was rolling in bed with her. So, let me tell you I'm mightily sorry, and am asking to be absolved from my sin. I don't want my soul to suffer in Purgatory for the sake of that stinking whore."

"I cannot give you absolution unless you are penitent, and you do not sound penitent to me."

"Oho!" Sebastian exclaimed. "Are you refusing me absolution? What kind of holy man are you?" It looked as if he was getting ready to obtain absolution with his fists, when they were interrupted by shouts coming from the rear. The carriage stopped, and the driver jumped down into the muddy road, cursing.

"What the hell is going on?" the young man said. "I hope we haven't run into an ambush, but that's not bloody likely. The guards would have intercepted anyone trying to rob the convoy." He slung his coat over his shoulders, grasped his sword, and jumped down from the coach, crouching low. "Now I see," he said, straightening up. "The second carriage is stuck. I'd better see if I can make myself useful. It's the carriage of the duchess, and she has that pretty young widow with her, Luisa de Rijs."

Martin hastily pulled on his coat and was getting ready to see whether his assistance was wanted, when the door opened, and the driver handed in Luisa, followed by her maid. The two women had been obliged to wade through the morass on the road. Their frocks were splattered with mud and their shoes soaked through.

"One of the wheels has cracked," the driver said laconically. "Don Sebastian has agreed to stay behind with a few men to guard the carriage while it's being repaired."

"And he has graciously offered us his seat," Luisa said. "The duchess insists on being carried in a litter for the rest of the way, or go on horseback. She took the carriage only to oblige her husband."

The maid tittered. "She said the carriage was invented by the devil expressly to torment her."

Luisa turned to the girl. "Settle down, Paulina," she said. "There isn't much space here, but it will have to do."

"I'll get in beside that thing," the girl said, pointing to the canvas, and squeezed into the narrow space between the frame and the side of the carriage. Luisa took her seat by Martin's side.

The driver meanwhile had climbed back up on his seat. The carriage lurched forward and resumed its tortuous progress, bouncing and swaying.

"I'm wet through," the maid said and nonchalantly began pulling off her shoes and stockings, giving Martin a generous view of her calves.

"Paulina!" Luisa said. "What do you think you are doing?"

"Better to take those wet things off than to catch a cold," the girl said.

"And better still to keep them on and preserve your modesty," Luisa said. "You might show a little more discretion in the presence of Fray Martin."

"Oh, I'm not worried, Doña Luisa. He'll avert his eyes, won't you, Father?"

Martin smiled at her innocence. "You might have warned me before you started, my girl," he said.

"Don't mind the silly little goose, Fray Martin," Luisa said. Her voice betrayed irritation and embarrassment. "She doesn't know any better. She has been with me only three weeks, and I have yet to teach her manners. I wish I could have brought my old maid, but her mother is ailing, and she was loath to leave the old woman."

"Loath to leave her sweetheart, more likely," Paulina said.

"You are too forward, my girl," Luisa said. "Give your tongue a rest and close your eyes, and I will try to get a little sleep myself. It will be after midnight by the time we reach the inn."

"As you please, Doña Luisa," the girl said, yawning, and crawled into the space behind the canvas. Luisa settled into the far corner of the carriage, pulling her coat tightly around herself and resting her head on a pillow fashioned from a rolled-up shawl. Soon her breath came evenly. A slight snore emanated from the corner, where the girl had holed up. Martin closed his eyes but could not sleep. The jerking and shaking carriage moved Luisa's body closer to his, until their thighs touched.

Martin's senses were inflamed by Sebastian's lewd talk and Paulina's immodest display. Luisa's thigh was burning against his own, and his member began to swell, becoming indecently firm. The duchess was right. The carriage was an invention of the devil. Martin placed his hand on the bench, meaning it to be a barrier of sorts between his body and Luisa's, but that only increased his difficulties. The rumbling carriage made his hand rub up against Luisa's thigh, and in a rush of ecstasy he spent himself. He was mortified. A spicy scent spread through the carriage like a cloud. It seemed strong enough to tickle the nostrils of a dead man, but the sleeping women did not stir, and Martin shrank into his corner of the carriage, shamed and humiliated by his furtive lust.

An hour later they entered the courtyard of a large inn. Martin clambered down from the carriage and was glad to see a servant handing out Luisa. He felt too unclean to touch her hand, and could not bear to look into her face. He excused himself and retired to his room, but he was sleepless with remorse and bitterly repented the sinful thoughts that had made him spend his seed. It was a painful lesson. God had tried him, and the crucible revealed the base metal of his soul. He had failed the test.

***

Two letters from the Cardinal awaited Martin on his arrival at the royal palace. One informed him that Prince Carlos' flotilla was expected to make port at Santander. The prelate had gone there to prepare a royal welcome for the heir to the throne and present him to the assembled court.

A second letter informed Martin that a storm had driven the royal fleet off course. The ship carrying the prince and his retinue had drifted ashore on the rocky beach of Villaviciosa, the Cardinal wrote. When the villagers saw the ship approach, they feared a pirate attack. The women and children fled to the mountains, and the men took up position on the shore, armed with pitchforks, scythes, and knives. They realized their error and put down their weapons when they saw the royal colours run up on the main mast. The prince and his retinue came ashore and were received into the peasants' huts. It was a wretched welcome for the future king.

News that the royal party was now approaching by the land route reached him the following day, the Cardinal wrote. He was not disposed to wait for the arrival of the Prince, however. He was about to saddle up and meet the Prince and his retinue half-way, in Llanes. This would give him an opportunity to have a private interview with the future King and press his own concerns before he was inundated with petitions by the grandees.

The news will disappoint Luisa, Martin thought. No doubt, she expected to be welcomed by the Cardinal in person.

"Prince Carlos has landed in Spain," he told her. "The Cardinal has gone to meet him. It is a strenuous journey for an old man. Doctor Malki was concerned about his health even before he set out. He specifically advised him against unnecessary travel, but the Cardinal can be single-minded sometimes. Fortunately the doctor is attending him. At least he is in good hands."

But unknown to Martin, the Cardinal was beyond the help of human hands. The next morning, a haggard courier, who had ridden through the night, brought the news that the Regent was dead. With the dust of the road still on his boots and his face burnished by the wind, he told Martin that the prelate's heart had given out on the journey to Llanes. The welcome for the royal party overshadowed the funeral preparations for Cisneros, he reported. The prince planned to meet with the assembled nobles and listen to their concerns. He would then proceed to Tordesillas to receive the blessing of his mother. The royal party was expected to arrive in Tordesillas in two weeks' time. Martin's instructions were to go there directly and prepare the ground for the all-important meeting.

It was more than a simple reunion of mother and son, who had not seen each other in fifteen years. It was an opportunity to persuade the Queen to abdicate in favour of her son. The Prince expected the Queen's confessor to set the mood and play his part in the diplomatic dance.

The mission filled Martin with dread. He had travelled to Tordesillas repeatedly after the Cardinal designated him Royal Confessor, but his pastoral efforts had been futile. The Queen balked at confessing to him, carried on scurrilous conversations, and even accused him of being disrespectful to her cats. In short, Martin failed to establish any rapport with the Queen. Diplomacy had never been his forte, and he had little hope of being more successful in the present circumstances. The news of the Cardinal's death had left him unmoored. The grief he felt was that of an orphaned child. Even as he had become aware of the prelate's fallibility, he continued to admire his integrity. And Cisneros had always been a generous patron to Martin. His appointment as Royal Confessor was meant to establish his position at court. Fear swept through Martin when he thought of the rash promise he had made to Luisa in Alcala, the assurance that he would look after her interests should anything happen to Cisneros. He remembered his boast: "The Cardinal has designated me Confessor to the Queen. Once the appointment is confirmed by Prince Carlos, I shall have some influence at court." There was little prospect of that now. He no longer had a patron to promote his career. He was unknown to the Prince and had no hope of impressing him with his abilities. The mission he had been given—to prepare the meeting in Tordesillas—was no doubt a test. If he failed, the appointment would go to one of

Carlos' protégés. Nor could he fall back on his post as secretary to the Cardinal. Whoever succeeded Cisneros as Inquisitor General was likely to replace Martin with a favourite of his own. Luisa's prospects were better than his. She would soon take the veil and be safely ensconced in a convent. Her wealth assured her a warm welcome in any community. Nuns were not immune to the glitter of gold, alas. Of course, now that the Cardinal was dead, there was the risk of Ramon Cardosa re-establishing his influence over his daughter. That would spell the end of her freedom to choose the manner of her life.

Or had the Cardinal made definite arrangements for Luisa before his death? He had at any rate written to the abbess of the Clares in Tordesillas and set the process in motion. Those were Martin's thoughts when he delivered the news of the Cardinal's death to Luisa.

***

The journey to Tordesillas was very different from the humiliating coach ride, which had exposed Martin's moral weakness. Luisa was riding by his side, but this time no effort was needed to subdue his unruly passions. Grief over the Cardinal's death kept them in natural check. The composure Luisa had shown in the face of adversity astonished Martin. She heard the news of the Cardinal's passing with quiet resignation. She did not protest when Martin informed her of the necessity to resume their travels and set out for Tordesillas at once.

On the contrary, she seemed almost eager to depart and begin her new life in the service of the Queen, but as they neared the end of their journey, she became quiet and thoughtful. They had been reminiscing about the Cardinal and talked about his advice to Luisa.

"I respect his wishes of course," Luisa said, "but I wonder what kind of reception I will get from the Queen. Paulina who loves gossip has told me some very odd stories – empty tales, I hope. She heard that the Queen chased her ladies-in-waiting with a broom and told them to leave her alone. She wants no one about her except one old companion who has been with her for many years."

"I have heard the same story," Martin said. "It seems the governor of the palace obtruded his daughters on the Queen. She objected vigorously and made her opinion known in rather drastic fashion. The young ladies, I understand, are quite content to stay away from her as long as they continue to draw their stipend as ladies-in-waiting."

"I fear I may suffer the same fate as the governor's daughters."

"I in turn hope you will win the Queen's affection, and I trust that her disposition has improved under Dr. Malki's influence. I assume he has already returned to Tordesillas and is back at his post now. He may be able to give you some guidance."

Luisa seemed content with this answer. "We will put our trust in God and Dr. Malki, then," she said and even mustered a gentle smile.

Martin admired Luisa's fortitude. On the road she had never once complained of fatigue, even though the ground was rough and they were in the saddle for many hours. She was a sure rider, who needed no more rest than the horses. On the last leg of the journey, it was she who spurred on her mare and made them all pick up their pace and outride the storm clouds gathering in the sky. They reached Tordesillas before the rain broke.

The walls surrounding the royal palace rose steeply from the river, fortress-like, but Luisa seemed undaunted by the forbidding appearance of the citadel, indeed almost cheerful.

The gateway of the palace was flanked by a guardhouse on one side and the residence of the governor on the other. The governor himself, resplendent in a black cape and lace collar, came out to welcome Martin and his party and showed them to their quarters. Alonso was with him, and gave them a hearty welcome.

A repast had been prepared for them. The governor's wife led Luisa to a seat next to one of her daughters, and Alonso took his seat beside Martin. After the travelers had answered the polite inquiries of the governor about their journey, the talk turned to the Queen's health.

"I was relieved to find her in a more settled mood," Alonso said. "I was concerned that the routine I prescribed for her would be neglected. But her attendant, who is devoted to her mistress, agrees with my advice and does all she can to make it palatable to the Queen."

"Indeed, the Queen's condition has improved greatly under your care, Doctor Malki," the governor said. "She doesn't look quite as mad as before. It seems a miracle. I don't how you managed it."

"I never thought of the Queen as mad," Alonso said. "She is a broken woman, her mind unbalanced by the misfortunes she suffered. Her pets are the only joy she has left in life. I have tried to use her love for them as an inducement. I praised her for looking after the cats so well and said to her: Have you observed the sleekness of their fur, Madam? Should you not honour your companions in turn by keeping your dress as neat as they are keeping their coats? I could not tell how much she understood, but she looked down on her dress with surprise, as if she noted its shabbiness for the first time. Then I said to her attendant: And you must brush your mistress' hair until it is as smooth as a cat's pelt. And the Queen nodded eagerly."

As Martin listened to Alonso, he noticed that the doctor's eyes had wandered to Luisa, and there was something in his look that made her blush.

"Ah, Dr. Malki, you have the right touch," she said, lowering her eyes.

"Then your lessons in cleanliness have been successful?" Martin said.

"They are slowly taking effect."

The governor's wife laughed. "To begin with, Doctor Malki's advice did not have the intended effect. When he asked the Queen to follow the example of her cats and practice cleanliness, the Queen began to lick her arms. Or so I was told by one of the maids. It would be better to use a sponge, Madam, old Beatriz said to her, but it took a long time to persuade her to adopt that method."

While the company laughed at the poor Queen's expense, Alonso's eyes settled on Luisa again, and Martin diagnosed the doctor's condition. He recognized that look. He knew those feelings first-hand, and he pitied his friend. It was a hopeless situation. The doctor would never realize his desires. His place in society was as much of a stumbling block as Martin's vows of chastity. It was folly for a converso to aspire to the hand of a woman of Luisa's position. Cardosa would never consent to such a union. Indeed, Luisa herself was bound to reject Alonso's advances. She had as good as pledged her life to Christ. She certainly avoided the doctor's admiring looks now, and quietly asked to be excused to retire to her room.

As she left the table, Martin resolved to warn his friend at the first opportunity. But what could he say to Alonso? Don't make a fool of yourself? Don't torment and humiliate yourself, as I have done? And if he was wrong after all and saw desire where there was none? No, it was better to leave the first step to Alonso, if he wanted to open his heart to him. For now he preferred to talk about another matter. Alonso had been with the Cardinal on the fateful journey to Llanes. He had witnessed his death.

"You must tell me about the Cardinal's last moments when we have some privacy," he said to

Alonso, as the governor rose and the company made ready to leave the table and go to their separate quarters.

"We'll have privacy in my consultorium," the doctor said and led Martin across the hall.

***

The doctor's office had the look of a library rather than a consulting room. There was a reading chair placed by the window and the shelves along the wall were filled with books and manuscripts. There were no adornments, except for a painting above the doctor's desk, which depicted the creator soaring above the void like a swirling cloud. Through an open door behind the desk, Martin could see the doctor's dispensary, stocked with ceramic jars and rows of stoppered bottles.

Alonso invited him to sit in the chair by the window, drew up another chair for himself and began to relate the sad story of the Cardinal's last days.

"His health took a turn for the worse while we waited for the arrival of the Prince," he said. "Indeed rumours circulated that someone had tried to poison him."

"The Cardinal had many enemies. Was there any truth to the rumour, you think?"

"I examined him and concluded there was no need to look beyond age and fatigue to explain his feeble condition. I prescribed complete rest, but the Cardinal would not hear of it. The royal party had landed, and he was going to ride out to meet Prince Carlos. It was an unexpected opportunity for a private audience, he said. I objected to the journey of course, but he was unwilling to slacken his pace. Too much was at stake, he told me. All I could do was join him and remain at his side."

"You could do no more, I know."

"We set out for Llanes accordingly. After we had ridden an hour or so, I saw the Cardinal motion to me. I drew up beside him. His forehead was drenched with sweat in spite of the chill in the morning air. He looked at me but could not speak. I seized the reins of his horse and eased him to the ground, massaged his chest and told him to breathe deeply. He shook his head, as if I was asking the impossible. I tried to rally his spirits. You must make an effort, I said. The prince is expecting you. It is Christ, the heavenly prince, who is expecting me, he answered, and closed his eyes as if he wanted to shut me out of his thoughts. I put a flask of water to his lips. He took a few sips with difficulty. After a while he recovered his breath and said: I wish Martin were here with me."

"He asked for me?"

"For you. To comfort him and hear his confession."

Martin sighed. "I wish I could have been at his side. But in the absence of a priest, a Christian may make his last confession to a layman."

"That is what he said. And so he confessed to me and made his peace with God. Then he told me of his concerns for Luisa." Alonso paused. He drew a deep breath, as if he was bracing himself for what he had to say next. His words stunned Martin: "The Cardinal asked me to be Luisa's guardian."

Martin half-rose from his chair. "You!" he exclaimed, searching his friend's eyes. He found it hard to give credence to Alonso's words. Was that the meaning of the doctor's attention to Luisa during dinner? Had Martin mistaken the considerate look of a guardian for that of a hopeful lover? "The Cardinal wanted *you* to be Luisa's guardian?" he asked as if repeating the prelate's last wish would make it more plausible.

"Those were his instructions," Alonso said. "He had been expecting death for some time, he told me, and was carrying with him the tokens of love he wished to pass on to you and Luisa. In his saddle bag, he said, I would find his prayer book, which he wanted Luisa to have as a memento, and a medallion of St. Francis, which was meant for you. The power of attorney Luisa had sent him was there as well, he said. He asked me to remove it and keep it safe until Luisa could transfer the powers to me." Alonso rose, unlocked a drawer in his desk and took out a wooden box. "And here it is, together with the mementos," he said, showing Martin the contents and picking out the medallion of St. Francis.

Martin received it silently. He could not disguise his anguish at the Cardinal's preference.

"You are surprised?" Alonso said. "Dismayed?"

Ashamed of his feelings, Martin said: "I would have expected the Cardinal to return the power of attorney to Luisa's father. He is her natural guardian after all."

"Perhaps he did not think Cardosa would act in her best interest." Alonso paused. "But you mean, why did he choose *me* rather than *you*? The answer is simple. Because I was there with him."

Martin wrangled with his discontent. "I admit it. I am disappointed that the Cardinal did not entrust Luisa to my care. But of course he realized that I would not be able to protect her interests. My position at court is uncertain now." And I am morally unfit for the task, he thought. My soul is riddled with sin. I am jealous. I am envious. I was unable to overcome my lascivious thoughts. How lewdly he had behaved in the carriage! No, he was not worthy of being Luisa's guardian. God had seen his sinful heart and guided the Cardinal's decision.

"I am in no position to help Luisa," he said to Alonso. "You have a profession at least, and will likely be confirmed by the heir as Royal Physician. You need no patron. Your medical skills speak for themselves."

"Some of that may have gone through the Cardinal's mind," Alonso said, "I can only tell you what he said. I suggest we inform Luisa of the Cardinal's last wishes together, when we have an opportunity."

"In any case, your guardianship will be brief," Martin said. "The Cardinal has written to the Convent of the Clares here, and the abbess has agreed to accept Luisa as a postulant. I expect the arrangements to be completed in the near future."

"If that is Luisa's wish, I shall respect it of course," Alonso said.

***

The next morning Martin called at Luisa's rooms to present her to the Queen. He plied her with polite questions. Had she slept well? Did she like her accommodation? But all he could think of was the Cardinal's last instruction. The prelate had entrusted Luisa to Alonso. It was as if the distance between them had grown overnight, and she was slipping away from him already. Better so, he reasoned, but his mind was a poor match for his soul, and he could not overcome his sadness.

They reached the Queen's apartment and were shown in by a servant. The effects of the doctor's treatment were evident when the Queen received them in her audience chamber.

She had changed since Martin had seen her last, at least in appearance. Her face and hands were clean. Her hair was pulled back in a tidy chignon, and she was dressed in a new black frock, but her face was as blank as always.

She sat in a gilded chair, clutching a rosary. The old attendant stood at her back, pressing close, as if she was holding the strings of a puppet and was waiting to set her in motion.

The Queen's face remained expressionless as Martin introduced Luisa, but when he mentioned that she had been widowed recently, a glimmer of interest entered her eyes, and she looked at Luisa with childlike curiosity. She motioned her to approach, touched her black taffeta gown, and looked down on her own gown as if she were comparing her fate with Luisa's.

"Tell me your name again," she said in her thin voice.

"Luisa Cardosa de Rijs, Your Majesty."

"Rijs," the Queen said, her eyes wide and swimming now. "Are you from the Low Countries?"

"My late husband hailed from the Low Countries, Your Majesty."

"Like Philip, like my beloved Philip!" Juana said, and her eyes filled with tears. For a moment she was lost in thought, but then she rose and said, as if coming out of a trance: "What now, Beatriz? Shall we go and walk in the cloister?"

"Not while we have visitors, my lady," her attendant said.

"Tell them to go away."

"Doña Luisa is your new lady-in-waiting, Madam," the old woman said. "She is supposed to stay with you."

"Oh well, she may stay for supper then. See that a plate is set out for her at the table," the Queen said. She turned to Luisa. "Do you like cats?"

"I do, Madam," Luisa said. "When I was a girl, kittens were my favourite playthings."

"And did you take care of them?" the Queen said. "You see I take very good care of my cats. There are eleven of them, and you must learn their names if you are to stay here. I used to keep them with me at all times, but the doctor said they must have a room of their own. He is a nice young man, and so I agreed, but I think the cats miss me. Don't you think the cats miss me, Beatriz?"

"The doctor says they need time to themselves," Beatriz said. "And he is right."

"But I can hardly bear to be away from my little angels," the Queen said, looking pained. "They are my children, you know," she said to Luisa. "Do you have children?"

"God has not granted me that joy, Madam," Luisa said. "I suffered a miscarriage."

"My poor dear," the Queen said. "I know how you must feel. They made me leave my son, my sweet little boy. They made him stay with his aunt in the Netherlands."

Martin stepped forward. "You will be united with Prince Carlos soon, Your Majesty," he said and gave her the news of the Prince's arrival in Spain.

She listened to him silently. The lines in her face deepened.

"He is expected to be here within two weeks, Your Majesty," Martin said.

The Queen sucked in her breath and shook her head in a drifting wave. "I will never see him again. They made me leave him behind. And now Philip is gone too. Both of them gone, never to return."

"But you *will* see Prince Carlos again, Madam," Martin said with determination, wrangling with the Queen's disturbed mind.

The old servant gave him a warning glance and shook her head. The Queen ducked down into her chair, like a rabbit squeezing into the underbrush. She looked at Martin anxiously, her imagination busy.

"The Prince is on his way here," he said emphatically.

Juana's face contorted. "No!" she cried. The rosary clattered to the floor, and the old attendant stepped forward in alarm and put a hand on her arm. The Queen shook her off. "You are lying!" she screamed at Martin, as he stepped back, appalled by the effects of his words. The screams kept coming in relentless dark waves, rolling out into sobs. "Don't you dare raise my hopes!" she burbled. "There will be death. There is always death." Tears were streaming down her face. She pushed up from her chair. "Tell him to go away, Beatriz," she said. Her voice had fallen to a breathy whisper.

"Your Majesty," Luisa said softly, as if they were sharing a secret. "There is death, and there is resurrection." She put a hand out to the distraught woman, and Juana clutched it.

The old attendant motioned Martin to leave the room. See what you've done, her eyes said, as he retreated, flushed with embarrassment at the scene he had created.

Before stepping into the corridor, he looked back. Luisa was leading the Queen toward the inner apartment.

"Your Majesty must rest," she was saying, and Beatriz followed the two women, making soothing noises.

I am a hopeless fool, Martin thought, standing alone in the corridor. I don't know how to talk to people, except in a crude and straightforward manner. But the human heart is not straightforward. It is full of dark corners and recesses. How did Luisa come by her understanding? Who taught her wisdom? I have been looking for it in the wrong places, I suppose. Books and lecture halls. Monasteries and rites. They have taught me nothing. But even if I had lived in society among ordinary people, I doubt I would have benefited from them. I was friendless as a child. I was friendless until the Cardinal took me in like a stray dog. In all the years I lived in Alcala, I made only one friend, Alonso, and it was a connection of the mind, not the heart. Do I know anything about feelings? What of my feelings for Luisa? No, there is nothing of the heart in them! They are base appetites like hunger or thirst and do not deserve the name of feelings. It is best for me to live a solitary life. Human beings give love in exchange for love. God alone loves unconditionally. He cares for the birds in the air and the lilies in the field, and he cares even for a mongrel like me.

CHAPTER 15

TWO SHORT WEEKS TO PREPARE FOR THE meeting between Prince Carlos and his royal mother! Martin made no headway with the Queen. Her mind was set against him. She took a liking to Luisa, however, if those vacant eyes of hers could be said to convey liking. She accepted her presence at any rate, addressed her occasionally, and permitted her to read to her or play the lute for her entertainment. Martin was obliged to watch from the sidelines as Luisa and Beatriz gently broached the subject of the Prince's impending arrival and tried to make the Queen understand the import of the meeting.

In the days leading up to the great event, Martin had asked himself many times: What if Juana refused to hand over the government to her son or share it with him at any rate? What if she fell into a raving, shrieking, clawing fit? He consoled himself with the thought that the dramatic scene would play out behind closed doors, and the world would not be the wiser.

When Carlos and his retinue finally rode into the courtyard and the time came for the Prince to greet his mother, only a handful of witnesses were allowed into the audience chamber. They were carefully selected for their loyalty and discretion. Adrian of Utrecht, the Prince's First Minister, had picked half a dozen courtiers that made up his inner circle. The Queen came with Beatriz and Luisa in attendance. Martin was admitted by virtue of his office.

The single seat of honour in the audience chamber had been replaced with two carved and gilded thrones set on a dais and roofed by tasseled velvet baldachins. An embroidered wall hanging formed the backdrop, depicting an allegory of Spain holding out the palm of victory, surrounded by the four cardinal virtues, Prudence, Justice, Temperance and Fortitude.

Carlos looked the part of the future king, dressed in white hose and padded doublet with a short skirt covering his thighs. The Prince was not handsome, Martin noted. He had inherited neither his father's pleasant features nor his mother's dark beauty. Instead he recalled his paternal grandfather and bore the Habsburg features: narrow-set eyes and a long curved nose that almost touched his voluptuous lips. He had a penchant to cast down his eyes and leave his mouth hanging open, which gave him the appearance of an idiot. Appearances were deceiving, however, for the prince had a razor sharp mind, a precise memory for facts, and an unusually mature judgment for a young man of sixteen.

A frisson of excitement passed through the courtiers when the Queen entered. She was dressed, as usual, in a black gown of old-fashioned cut that draped her figure like a protective covering thrown over unused furniture. She had been persuaded, however, to wear a tempette that held back her hair and framed her face tightly, coming down over her forehead.

Much depended on what happened next. Would the Queen recognize her son, would there be a meaningful exchange of conversation, would she agree to resign her authority or share it with her son and allow him to take the reins of government? The assembled courtiers stood in breathless expectation, as Luisa and Beatriz led the Queen to her seat. The two attendants stepped back but stayed by her side, in case an intervention was necessary. Every step of the meeting was planned. Nothing had been left to chance.

"Who is this young man?" the Queen asked as Carlos came forward, approached the throne, and made a respectful bow.

"His Highness Prince Carlos, who has come from the Low Countries," Luisa said softly. "He begs to be received by Your Majesty."

The Queen regarded Carlos silently. Her fingers rested on Luisa's arm, digging into her velvet sleeve, leaving matted indentations.

"Your son," Luisa repeated in a steadfast voice. "Prince Carlos, the heir to the throne, whom Your Majesty relinquished to the care of his aunt in the Netherlands, when he was a child."

"My child," the Queen said, making it sound like a question.

"Your child, Madam," Luisa said, "who has come to embrace his mother."

Juana nodded uncertainly. She rose and took a halting step forward and, at Luisa's prompting, stiffly embraced her son.

"And what now?" she said, releasing Carlos, and sinking back into her seat.

"Now that Prince Carlos has come, Your Majesty no longer need shoulder the burden of government alone," Luisa said.

"Oh yes, it is a great burden," the Queen said. "And tedious." She eyed her son. "And so you would govern for me?"

"If that is your wish, Madam," Carlos said.

Juana shrugged. "Well?" she said to Luisa. "Why is he looking at me like that? What is everyone waiting for? He can govern or not. I don't care one way or another."

"If Prince Carlos is to govern, Madam, your signature is required."

"My signature! Always my signature. Papers, papers, papers."

The relief was palpable, when she continued: "One more paper then. What does it matter? Let them bring it on."

Carlos took his seat by the side of his mother. A table was placed in front of the majesties. It had been decided that the Queen's Confessor would tender the document readied for her signature. The Prince was counting on his priestly authority, but the Queen balked as soon as Martin stepped up to the table.

"I know you," she said sharply, "but tell me your name again."

"Martin Casalius," he said with a deep bow.

"Oh, yes," she said. "I don't like you."

Martin blanched at hearing her words. Such words spelled death for a man's career.

"Great knuckles on his fingers and a dour face," the Queen murmured, looking at Martin with disapproval. "Like a man on stilts, like a judge. The Inquisitor. Yes, that's what he is. The Inquisitor."

"Madam," the Prince said. "Martin Casalius is your Father Confessor."

"Not the Inquisitor?" the Queen said. "Then I'll make him so. I'll make him the Inquisitor General and send him away to his palace."

Carlos' courtiers shuffled uneasily.

"Madam," the Prince said. "The Inquisitor General has many grave duties to attend to. He is responsible for the purity of our faith. He is the overseer of sixteen regional tribunals with numerous judges, assessors, and commissaries. The position of Inquisitor

General requires a man of experience and authority, such as Doctor Adrian of Utrecht"–he motioned the minister forward—"whom I beg your Majesty to consider for the post."

"Sixteen tribunals and sixteen regional inquisitors," the Queen said and gave the Prince a look of annoyance. "What of them?"

"It is a position of great responsibility, for which Adrian of Utrecht is well qualified. He has served me loyally for many years, and has served my father before that."

The Queen stared at the tall greying figure of the First Minister, who looked back at her quietly with sagacious eyes, standing the trial of her uneasy glance. "I had the great honour of serving Prince Philip, Your Majesty," he said.

"Ah, Philip," she said. "How I miss my dear husband!" She looked at Adrian again. "So be it," she said with a sigh. "Let him be Inquisitor General. But what will I do with the other one?" She pointed at Martin, who had remained standing before her, document in hand, wincing under her gaze.

"I know," she said. "I'll make him one of those sixteen regional inquisitors. Then he will leave me alone." She looked at the Prince with sudden resolve. "You may draw up the papers."

There was a stir among the courtiers. A look of consternation came into the Prince's eyes.

"We have drawn up a document for your signature, Madam," he said. On his discreet move,

Adrian took the document from Martin's hand and presented it to the Queen.

"Does it say that this man"—Juana pointed to Martin – "will be regional inquisitor?"

"The document assigns plenipotentiary power to me, Madam, and will allow me to make such an appointment," the Prince said.

"But does it say that he will be the regional inquisitor and must leave me alone?" the Queen said doggedly.

The First Minister bent down and whispered into the Prince's ear.

"What is he whispering?" the Queen said sharply, pursing her lips and giving Adrian a suspicious look.

"The minister has asked permission to draw up an undertaking to that effect – to appoint Martin Casalius to the post of regional inquisitor, at the next vacancy, that is, according to your wishes, Madam," the Prince said, and nodded to Adrian.

"Will this take long?" the Queen said. "I cannot allow any delay. My cats are waiting."

A murmur arose among the courtiers witnessing the scene. Paper and ink was brought to Adrian. He drew up a few lines and presented them to the Queen for her signature.

"Where is Luisa?" the Queen said irritably. "Hand me the pen, child. And hold my hand. It trembles so when I write."

With Luisa supporting her arm, she put the nib to the paper and scrawled her name in a spidery hand.

"And may I present to you the other document as well, Your Majesty?" Luisa said. "The one assigning authority to his Highness, Prince Carlos?"

"Will they leave me in peace then?" the Queen asked.

"There is only one more signature required," Luisa said.

"Ah, a great deal of sacrifice is required from us widows," the Queen said, but she allowed Luisa to guide her arm and, to the relief of those present, signed the document that would open the way for Carlos to govern the country.

"And now I will look after my cats," the Queen said with finality, and pushed herself up from the chair.

Carlos honoured Luisa with a gracious smile that promised favours in return for her dexterous handling of the situation. The Queen's Confessor was relieved of an honour he had never wanted, and burdened with the prospect of another – the office of a regional inquisitor. Martin's heart heaved and buckled. God in his wisdom deigns to punish sinful men in various ways, he thought. Some he destroys outright, others he allows to languish in sickness or poverty or in a foul dungeon. For me he has reserved a higher form of punishment: success – success in the eyes of the world, but a crushing burden to me. God has fettered me with the law, and every day I will have to pass judgment on sinners, reminding me that

I am a sinner myself and will one day stand before the judgment seat of the Almighty.

CHAPTER 16

While the Spanish courtiers were trimming their sails to the new wind, Natale had already found a safe harbor at the house of the merchant banker Jacopo Rodriga.

"Venice, amidst the billowing waves of the sea, stands on the crest of the main like a queen," Rodriga quoted with patriotic fervour.

Natale agreed readily. Venice was a splendid city, and the banker a splendid host. Natale had presented Cardosa's letter of introduction and was welcomed to the banker's house and shown around the city.

He admired the pastel-coloured palazzi rising from the Grand Canal like painted flats inviting the onlooker to watch the theatre of life. Sleek boats were tied up at the piers and water gates. Their shining hulls were lacquered black and their cabins hung with green and purple satin to protect the passengers from the sun and the eyes of the curious.

Natale was in rapture, savouring the beauty of Venice. He breathed in the magnificence of San Marco like sweet perfume and greedily eyed the mosaics, the pavement of smooth stones inlaid with marble, wishing he could own every square his foot touched. He listened dreamily to the *marangona,* the chiming bells of the Campanile, which seemed to him beauty set to music. In the evening, at the entertainments given by Rodriga, he regaled his eyes on the elegant dress of the guests and was ready to lay a wager that there was not a single woman at table who did not have five hundred ducats' worth of rings on her fingers: diamonds, rubies, sapphires, and emeralds. The city fathers had introduced sumptuary laws, afraid that such conspicuous wealth would cause unrest among the poor, but the laws were flouted everywhere.

Rodriga and his family lived in a palazzo in the northern part of the city. The windows of their stately drawing room looked out on the island of Murano and on the calm sea teeming with boats, their white sails tacking against the wind. Natale marveled at the coffered ceilings, the inlaid marble floors, the rich Persian hangings, and the finely chiseled silverware gleaming on the sideboards, but there was not a single portrait on the walls to commemorate Rodriga's ancestors. That's because he is a *converso,* Natale thought. He had heard that Jews disapproved of portraits. To them, displaying the images of forefathers smacked of idolatry. Oh, well, Natale thought. Once a Jew always a Jew. The baptismal waters hadn't purged Rodriga of the old superstitions, it seems, but that was none of his business. In all other respects, his host's way of life was not much different from the life of a wealthy merchant in Spain.

At dinner, Natale sat across from his young hostess. Her jewels exceeded in beauty anything he had seen in Spain. Her hair was exquisitely dressed with pearls and the sleeves of her dress embroidered with golden thread.

"Your Isabelita is a sweet little creature," he said by way of starting the conversation, flattering his hostess, who was the proud mother of a toddler.

Her red lips curved into an animated smile. She talked of the child volubly, twittering about her cute nose, her cute little fingers, her cute little belly button, then remembered her hostess duties. "And how do you like our city, Fray Natale?" she asked. "What do you think of the piazzas and the houses along the Grand Canal? Are they not handsome?"

"Miracles of beauty," Natale said, "but they cannot rival your own home, madam. I have never seen a more beautifully appointed drawing room."

His hostess' eyes sparkled as she thanked him for the compliment. "Yes, but it is nothing compared to the palace of Messer Zorzi Cornaro, which cost 20,000 ducats to build, or that of the Foscari family, which is rented out to a patrician for 120 ducats a month, they say. And you must ask my husband to take you to the

Merceria. There isn't a thing in the world that you can't find in the shops along the Merceria. Brocades, tapestry, hangings of every imaginable design, carpets, camlets, silks, pearls, gems; there are warehouses full of every thing you heart desires!"

In the evening, Natale sat at the window of his elegant bedroom and watched the sun set in a scorched sky. How much more beautiful this room was than his quarters in Arelate, which overlooked only a dusty road and furze-covered hills. The comparison redoubled his pleasure. He looked down on the darkening sea and listened to the soft lapping of the waves, and let the satisfaction settle in his chest. Who was living in the house in Arelate now, he wondered. Luisa had moved to Tordesillas, that much he knew. "She has the honour of serving the Queen as a lady-in-waiting," Cardosa said in his last letter. Honour! In thrall to a mad woman and living in dreary surroundings, as far as he had heard! Cardosa probably wanted his daughter locked away until the scandal of Deodatus' death blew over. The doctor's verdict "Death by misadventure", the consecrated earth of the cemetery, the unctuous eulogy at graveside, none of them could quell the rumours that Deodatus had committed suicide. There was nothing Cardosa could do about it except wait a year or two and let time work the miracle of oblivion. Then he could find a wealthy suitor for Luisa and make up for the connections he lost with the Cardinal's death. It must have been a heavy blow to him. And not only to Cardosa. Natale wondered how the other protégés of the Cardinal were getting on, whether

Alonso Malki could cling to his career at court in the circumstances. Martin at any rate had landed on his feet. He had been appointed inquisitor. A remarkable career for the Cardinal's secretary, but Martin always had an inquisitorial streak, a zealous mind, and the dour face and judgmental eyes to go with it. Not a human blink in those gray eyes! Yes, Martin was well suited for the post. Still, who would have thought it! Mother Church was looking after her children, and Natale hoped he too would experience her bounty now that his dispensation had come through. His hands were no longer tied by the vows of poverty. Many careers were open to a priest free of monastic strictures – if you did things properly, that is, paid the lawyers, and the secretaries, and the scribes. Otherwise you'd end up like that run-away monk Luther, holed up in a castle somewhere and under threat of excommunication. Natale had used Cardosa's money wisely. He paid his dues and was free at last to move whenever and wherever he pleased and take any employment as long as it was compatible with his priestly office.

He had no income at present, but he was not overly worried. Rodriga's house was his cushioned seat in the caravan of life. True, he had noticed a certain impatience creeping into his host's voice lately, a tick of irritation. Rodriga did not withdraw his hospitality, but he began throwing out hints and introducing Natale to potential employers. Natale saw that he would soon have to shift for himself. Fortunately, one of the men to whom Rodriga introduced him was Aldo Manuzio. The books produced by the famous printer were in great demand among scholars. The printer perked up when Natale told him that he had lived in Deodatus' household, "as his associate," he said, adding adroitly, "and dare I say, his friend."

"I have in mind to publish an edition of the collected works of Deodatus," Manuzio said to Natale. "You strike me as the right man to check the texts and write a short biography to be placed at the beginning of the volume, if that is a task that interests you."

Checking the text was tedious work and did not appeal to Natale, but he feigned an interest. "You have come to the right man," he said. "I happen to have an unpublished manuscript in Deodatus' hand, a collection of dialogues entitled How To Live One's Life." He had taken the manuscript from Deodatus' bedside on the morning his lifeless body was discovered by a servant. Some people might call it theft, but Natale thought of it as a rescue. Who knows what would have happened to the manuscript in all the confusion?

"I rescued the pages from destruction," he said. "His widow would have discarded them. She is a woman quite lacking in literary sensibilities, I am afraid."

The twinkle in Manuzio's eyes told Natale that he could put a higher price on his services now. "I am willing to write the biography," he said, skirting the question of proofreading which he loathed. As for the manuscript, he said he would put it at Manuzio's disposal at once, except that he had one or two enquiries from other printers.

Manuzio took the bait. He was ready to outbid the competitors and offer Natale favourable terms of employment. He insisted on including the task of proofreading, but the contract he dangled before Natale also offered the prospect of pleasant accommodation.

"I will arrange lodgings for you at the house of a friend, the art dealer Paolo Dovizi."

Natale accepted the post and soon settled into a comfortable routine. He pored over the texts for two hours in the morning and advanced the biography by a few paragraphs, the official version of Deodatus' life, that is. Too bad he couldn't tell the real story. Writing about Deodatus' eye for male beauty, his dependence on the alchemist's art, and his willingness to pander Luisa to a Jew would have been so much more interesting than the pale, expurgated version he was preparing for the printer. An idea struck Natale: why not write his own memoirs? He had heard so many spicy tales in the confessional and seen so much crime and violence in the service of the Inquisition. Of course he couldn't name names, but he was sure a printer could be found for his recollections. Who knows, they might rival the infamous *Decameron* in popularity. And so he put Deodatus' biography aside and spent the afternoons jotting down his own memories.

Natale's leisurely progress on the collected works of Deodatus Rijs was not to his employer's liking, but the contract was signed, and Manuzio could not renege on it now. The manuscript in Deodatus' hand, which Natale had promised the printer, turned out to be disappointing. It was a first draft and had nothing of the polished style and elegant wit for which Deodatus was famous. Natale finally supplied the biography as stipulated, but Manuzio found it vague and short on insights. The priest also lacked the discipline which made for a good proofreader. All round it was a bad bargain for Manuzio, and he did not hide his displeasure, but Natale paid little attention to his grumbling.

***

Rodriga had shown Natale the bright side of Venice. The priest soon discovered a seedier part which offered no visions of splendor. No boats were moored there, and the gates of the houses were walled off. It was the site of a disused foundry, where the Jews of Venice lived. The Ghetto was like a fort, enclosed by high walls and linked with the city by a gated bridge which was shut at sunset and opened in the morning at the sound of San Marco's bells. The walls had been built a year earlier because, as the decree of the senate said, *no God-fearing citizen would wish the detested race of the Jews to live throughout the city and to go wherever they choose by day and by night and perpetrate shameful acts that give grave offense to Christians. Be it resolved therefore, to prevent any unseemly deeds and occurrences, to oblige them to go and dwell within the Ghetto at San Hieronimo. If by chance a Jew is found by the officials outside the Ghetto after the hours specified, he shall be arrested at once for his disobedience.*

It did not take long before Natale became acquainted with the Ghetto's denizens. He made it his custom to visit the pawnbrokers from time to time to look for trinkets that had been left unredeemed. There were exquisite pieces among their wares that could be had for very little money.

Natale had learned Italian at his mother's knee and had no difficulty understanding the shopkeepers or making himself understood, but one day he entered a shop that had been recommended to him, and the owner answered his inquiries in Spanish. He was a native of Seville, he said, and invited Natale to take a seat. Business was slow, and the two men sat in idle conversation over a cup of fragrant mint tea.

The pawnbroker's name was Otniel Malki.

Malki! Could it be that he was a relative of Alonso? Natale wondered, but his long career in the service of the Inquisition had taught him to keep his mouth shut and let others tell their tale.

"I left Seville more than twenty years ago," Malki said.

Natale had no need to inquire into the circumstances. No doubt, the pawnbroker had left in 1492 when the edict was issued expelling Jews from Spain.

"But I still have family there: two nieces in Las Palmas, and a nephew who is Queen Juana's personal physician."

The man was Alonso's uncle!

"An illustrious post," Natale said. "You must be proud of him."

"He did well for himself while he was in the service of Cardinal Cisneros, but after his patron's death, he was obliged to join the Queen's household in Tordesillas, a wretched place full of small-minded people. They regard him as the very spawn of the Devil. *Conversos* suffer discrimination everywhere in Spain, but especially in small towns which have no experience of the larger world."

Venice was more tolerant, Natale conceded. "Remarkably tolerant. I had occasion to stay at the house of the banker Rodriga, who seems to have done very well for himself."

Malki shrugged his shoulders. "The bankers do well of course," he said, "whether they are *conversos* or Jews. The city needs them and the council gives them special status. The rest of us are confined to these cramped quarters now, but at least we are allowed to practice our religion and are not forced to convert to Christianity."

"Ah, prejudice is a terrible thing," Natale said smoothly. "After all, a man does not choose his forefathers. So why not look to character rather than family when assessing a man's worth?"

"If that is your view, you are a rare bird," the pawnbroker said drily. "But I do think that a Jew has better prospects here than in Spain, and I advised my nephew to pull up his roots and join me. He is about to marry a wealthy widow. What better place to start their life together than Venice?"

A wealthy widow? How very interesting.

The talk turned to Natale's prospects next.

"And what brings you to our city?" Malki asked.

"Like your nephew," Natale said. "I found myself at a disadvantage after my patron's death, but his family was kind enough to recommend me to Rodriga here. Rodriga in turn introduced me to the printer Aldo Manuzio. Or perhaps I should say, the name of my late patron recommended me to him. You may have heard of Deodatus Rijs – he was a famous man of letters."

"I'm afraid I know little about books," Malki said, "unless they are ledgers."

Their conversation lapsed, and Natale took his leave, not without expressing his regret that the salt cellar the pawnbroker had shown him was beyond his means at present. It was a fine piece of craftsmanship, a dainty gondola of chased silver holding a crystal bowl, and would have complemented his little collection. Natale lingered on the threshold of the shop and looked back at the exquisite piece, feeling a rush of longing, but the price was quite out of his reach.

***

Making his way home, Natale turned his mind to the information the pawnbroker had given him inadvertently. So Alonso was in Tordesillas. And about to marry a wealthy widow. And Luisa, too, happened to be in that town. Were the two love birds making their nest there? Natale considered the value of his information. Who knows what advantage might be gotten out of it. He decided to store it away for future use, for his memoir, perhaps—he had started jotting down the salient points—but destiny soon prodded him into action.

Not long after his conversation with the pawnbroker, a child's body was found near the Ghetto, stabbed to death and mutilated. A rumour started, no one knew where or by whom, that a Jew had committed the murder. An angry mob rushed into the Ghetto, stormed the synagogue, tore open the ark, trampled on the Torah, and set the wooden portals of the temple on fire. It was Passion Tide, when feelings against the "murderers of Christ" were running high and any spark could kindle a conflagration. The murder of the child roused an inferno, a churning, licking, yellow-tongued fury that threatened to devour the Jews. The merchants closed their shops and retreated behind the walls of the Ghetto, finding it for once a bulwark rather than prison. They decided to wait out Holy Week and hunker down in their quarters until the authorities had restored order in the city.

It was late at night, when a servant came to Natale's room at Dovizi's house to announce that a gentleman wished to speak to him.

The servant hesitated as he spoke, shuffling his feet in a dance of indecision. "A fellow, I mean," he said, amending his words, hinting that the individual waiting below was no gentleman in his estimation.

"What kind of fellow?" Natale said, raising his eyebrows.

"A Jew," the servant said. "You'd better watch out, Fra Natale. They are a blood-thirsty people."

The only Jew, who might know where to find me, is Malki, Natale thought. And he would not run the risk of coming here if he did not have urgent business, or rather, an urgent request. A vision of the crystal salt cellar in Malki's shop tempered any apprehension Natale might have felt to meet with the man.

"Show him in," he said to the servant. "I can fend for myself."

The man who ducked in was indeed Otniel Malki. "I come at peril to my life to ask you a favour," he said without bothering with polite preliminaries, "and I mean to show my gratitude for it."

"What can I do for you then, my dear Malki?" Natale said.

"My nephew has accepted my advice and is preparing to leave Spain," Malki said.

"Then I wish him and his bride well," Natale said.

"But the time is not propitious. He will get a rude welcome here. I must warn him to delay his journey a little," Malki said. "The business is urgent, but I cannot show my face in the city and have no means of finding a courier to take a letter to Spain. If you can make the necessary arrangements, I am willing to give you a good price on the salt cellar you admired. I'll sell it to you half price, let's say."

Natale cleared his throat and put on a clouded face. "I'm not sure I want to be involved in this business," he said. "You are asking a lot from me, my dear Malki, and offering very little in return. First you put me at risk, coming here. What if my servant goes tattling to people and makes out that I'm colluding with a Jew? And if I agreed, I would have to spend the better part of a day running around and finding a courier. Then, when I've gone through the whole rigmarole, I'd have to go back to you and haggle about the salt cellar. I am not suggesting that you will cheat me, but you will admit that our acquaintance is of very recent standing."

Malki cut his arguments short. "What would you consider adequate compensation, then?" he asked. "Name your price."

"I am not keen on the task at all," Natale said, "but I thought you might have offered me the salt cellar outright. It seems a small present for a day's work, when you consider the risk I am running."

The pawnbroker threw up his hands in a fluid gesture as if to sweep away Natale's objections. "I won't endanger my nephew's life for the sake of a salt cellar," he said. "I'll give it to you, once you show me the courier's receipt. Only make haste."

"Don't misunderstand me," Natale said, his voice reassuring now, "it's not that I am unwilling to do you a favour or think less of you because you are a Jew. It's just that a man has to weigh his risks. But I'll venture it."

He would not do it, however, without drawing up a memorandum specifying the terms: his service in exchange for the salt cellar. After the Jew had written him a hasty note, he took charge of the letter and assured the pawnbroker:

"I'll see that it is dispatched without delay."

Except for the delay of reading what you have to say to Alonso, he thought as he showed Malki out himself. The less his servant saw the better.

He returned to his room, broke the seal, and read:

My dear Alonso,

You will soon embark on your journey, and may God make it a speedy and safe crossing. I long to converse with you in person, but it will be advisable to delay your arrival in Venice until after Easter. Holy Week is always a precarious time for us because preachers whip the people into frenzy, making us out as the murderers of Jesu Nozeri, but this year the danger is acute. A few days ago a boy was found dead, and the people have accused Rabbi Jehiel Basola of slaughtering the child in ritual sacrifice. The discovery of the crime caused outrage and cries for revenge.

I need not tell you that the accusation is a monstrous lie, but the mob is vicious in their hatred for the Jews. Alas for our race! They give every man the benefit of doubt until he reveals himself a scoundrel or a mountebank, but they consider the Jew guilty until proven innocent.

I know that you have been baptized and your bride is a Christian. Nevertheless it is better to be cautious in these trying times.

With my best wishes and the hope to embrace you soon,

Otniel Malki.

Natale twisted the letter into a wick and held it into the flame of his candle. As he watched the paper burn, he thought: And who was Alonso's bride, the wealthy widow? Luisa, no doubt. The pair must be contemplating a clandestine marriage. Natale was certain that Cardosa would never agree to his daughter's union with a Jew.

Next morning Natale found a courier who was on the point of departure for Spain, but the letter he gave him was not Malki's. It was one of his own, and it was addressed to Martin Casalius. He had carefully considered the question: Who should be the recipient of this bit of information – Ramon Cardosa or Martin Casalius? The father, in whose interest it was to prevent an undesirable union, or the Inquisitor whose duty it was to sniff out relapsed Jews? Who would offer the greater reward to the informer? In the end Natale addressed his letter to Martin. His contract with Manuzio had not been renewed. Dovizi employed him occasionally, sending him out in search of curios. He appreciated Natale's knack for finding interesting pieces, but he did not pay well. Dovizi was a skinflint, and Venice, that golden city, had lost its sheen. In the circumstances, Natale thought, it was best to return to Spain. Martin, he hoped, would recommend him for a post if he showed sufficient zeal for the purity of faith. A letter with valuable information might do the trick. He chose his words carefully:

> *I am writing from Venice, where I am assisting the printer Aldo Manuzio in preparing an edition of Deodatus' collected works. Busy as I am, I must not neglect this occasion to congratulate you on your appointment as inquisitor of Valladolid. There is another, less happy reason compelling me to write at this time. A few days ago a piece of information came my way, of which I regard it my duty to inform you. I chanced to speak to a pawnbroker, who left Spain in 1492 to settle in Venice, where the Jews are allowed to practise their faith but are now, thank God, confined to one area of the city. The pawnbroker's name is Otniel Malki. He is a brother of Alonso's father. I asked him what news he had of his nephew. To my surprise he told me that Alonso was about to be married and was planning to leave Spain with his wife and*

settle in Venice. The local Jews have misgivings about the Spanish anusim, *as they call the* conversos, *and encourage them to return to their old faith. Most of them need no encouragement and readily revert to the practices of their forefathers. I fear Alonso will be one of them. But this is not the worst of my fears. Alonso attended Luisa in Arelate some years ago when I was her tutor. There were rumours at the time that doctor and patient had formed a tender attachment, and some people did not scruple to say that Deodatus took his life because of the affair. It was for this reason that I sacrificed my own reputation and let it be known that I administered a sleeping potion to him on the night of his death. My testimony allowed the family to silence the rumour mongers, and you may believe me when I say that they offered me the most touching tokens of their gratitude.*

I understand that Luisa has joined the Queen's household at Tordesillas and that Alonso, being the Queen's physician, is there as well. Need I elaborate on my fears? You will judge whether the matter warrants action against a man who may be a heretic and a fortune hunter.

As for myself: Although my work gives me great satisfaction, I long for Spain. An ancient adage says ubi bene ibi patria, *"where we do well, we make our home," but I cannot subscribe to it. Spain is ever in my heart. Should you have an opening for me in your administration or be able to recommend me to a family needing a tutor, I would come with all speed and remain forever your grateful servant,*

Natale Benvenuto.

He asked the courier for a receipt. "Kindly make it out as "One letter to Doctor Alonso Malki, royal physician at Tordesillas," he said.

The courier checked the address. "But it says here: Martin Casalius..." he began.

Natale put a hand on his arm. "Do as I say, and you may charge me a little extra for the favour," he said.

That night Natale ate a dinner of Indian cock, a delicacy forbidden by the sumptuary laws of the city yet easily procured on the black market. He enjoyed an excellent bottle of Valpolicella, allowing it to burnish his throat, and finished the meal with a plate of almonds and marzipan. He went to bed, well pleased with his day's work, and soon lay on his back snoring and caught up in a curious dream.

He dreamed that he was a dog resting on an embroidered cushion in a lady's boudoir. A soft breeze made the muslin curtains billow. He was lazily contemplating the remnants of his dinner. Suddenly he became aware of an elegant white hand tugging on the chain around his neck. It was a finely wrought chain of gold, more like a necklace than a dog's collar, but a restraint nevertheless, and it cut into the soft flesh of his nape, choking him. When he looked up, he saw that it was Luisa, who was pulling at the chain. She looked at him with cruel eyes and, wordlessly, tightened her grip until he felt his eyes bulging and his breath coming in gasps.

He woke up with a jolt and said to himself: What a strange dream! It's as if Luisa wanted to take me to task for tearing up Malki's letter and putting her bridegroom at risk. The aya, that pathetic old woman, used to say that Luisa had magic powers, but those powers would have to be far-reaching indeed, if she could pursue me across the sea and punish me with a dream. Besides, don't certain voluptuaries swear that a bit of choking is a delicious sensation and thrilling to the heart? So it isn't punishment at all, he thought, and turned over on his soft bed. He fell asleep once more, smiling, and this time he dreamed of a splendid position offered him by Martin Casalius.

**

THE EASTER CELEBRATIONS HAD DISSIPATED THE public wrath against the Jews. It was no longer dangerous to visit the Ghetto, and Natale made his way to Malki's shop to collect his prize. The Jew greeted him with alacrity.

"I trust you were able to find a courier for my letter," he said.

"I did, on the very next morning after your visit," Natale said and presented the receipt. "You haven't heard back from your nephew?"

"Not yet. But perhaps it's too early to expect a reply."

The salt cellar was a generous reward for Natale's service, *if* he had rendered it, that is, and he half expected Malki to start haggling again. But the old man kept to his side of the bargain and fetched the salt cellar from his storeroom.

"Here it is," he said. "You should have come earlier in the day. It will be dark before you get back to Dovizi's house, and you'll have to walk through a rough patch of town. I would send my servant with you, but the gates of the Ghetto are about to be closed for the night. Why not come back tomorrow morning?"

He doesn't want to part with his treasure, Natale thought. He doesn't show it, but he is peeved. I won't get another bargain from him, that's for sure. He eyed the little silver gondola greedily. "No need to worry about me," he said. "It's a small thing, and I'll keep it well-covered under my cloak."

Malki handed over the salt cellar, but not without another warning: "Some people kill for gold and silver, you know."

Natale did not bother to reply. He grasped his little treasure and hurried toward the gate. As he crossed the bridge, he heard the gates close behind him. The streets on the other side of the water were deserted. He had buried the salt cellar in the inside pocket of his coat, sheltering it from view. Dusk descended. In the gloom of the narrow streets, every recess, every dark doorway presented a menacing aspect. Natale picked up his pace, and put his hand on the spot where the salt cellar was hidden, passing his fingers lovingly over its contours and pressing it against his chest, keeping it close to his heart.

As he passed a covered stairwell, he saw a face peering up at him. It was the face of a beggar, no more than a bundle of rags, a bruised shadow. Out of the corner of his eye, Natale saw the man creeping up the stairs and heard him fall in step. At the corner, the man slowed as if he was about to abandon the pursuit. Natale breathed a sigh of relief, but soon the steps started up again. He broke into a run. If he could only reach the piazza, a tavern was sure to offer him refuge. His pursuer was speeding up, too. Natale heard his breathing now, smelled his festering body, his rancid stinking breath. His heart started to hammer. A rough arm seized him from behind, a knee pushed into the small of his back like an anvil. The man pressed his body against Natale's, clasping him like a lover, a partner in a spastic dance to the wild music of his beating heart. Natale fell forward. His head hit the broken pavement with a crack, his face was pressed against the bottom of a musty wall. The fellow was on his back. Natale wanted to cry out for help, but his throat closed sharply, tightened, garroted. In a flash he saw Luisa's hand holding the leash. Then he heard the salt cellar drop to the pavement with a tinkle and saw a skinny hand close over the silver gondola.

CHAPTER 17

A square tower rose above the chapel of the Clares at Tordesillas and threw its shadow over the cloistered walk, where the nuns took the air. The religious order was the refuge of a dozen gentlewomen too impoverished or too ill favoured to succeed in the marriage market. They were housed in the eastern part of the old palace built by King Alfonso XI to commemorate his victory in the Battle of Salado. The apartments of Juana and her retinue occupied a nearby building to the west.

When Luisa first came to Tordesillas in Martin's company and dismounted in the courtyard, she looked up at the walls broken only by a row of windows with iron bars and felt the cold breath of despondence, but she consoled herself with the thought of seeing Alonso again and living in close proximity to him.

Before the doctor took over Juana's care, her apartments, though spacious and adorned in the Mudejar style, had been as dingy and bedraggled as the Queen herself. Cobwebs and dust darkened the corners, the floors were sticky with spills and smeared with excrement, the tapestries faded, the upholstery matted with cat hair and the chair legs streaked with claw marks. On the doctor's instructions, the rooms were scrubbed clean, aired, and refurbished. He banished the cats to a separate room and had a servant regularly tidy and clean after them.

Thus Luisa found her surroundings more pleasant and her duties less onerous than she had been led to expect. When Queen Isabella reigned at court, she had never been surrounded by fewer than a dozen ladies-in-waiting. Juana lived the life of a nun. She sent away her ladies-in-waiting, "those witches", as she called them, and refused to have more than two attendants. Beatriz, her old retainer, watched over her by night, sleeping on a couch at the foot end of her bed, and Luisa was her sole attendant during the day. She was on call during the Queen's waking hours, but Juana was not demanding. In former years, when she lived at court, she had been agitated by the tumultuous life of the regal household, her mind unmoored by the events and the ceaseless flow of people around her. In the solitude of Tordesillas, she sank into a gentle languor from which she was seldom roused. There were no banquets, no dances, no charades to be played or tournaments to be watched. It would have been a dull life for Luisa if it had not been for the thrill of being near her love, the rapture of being in Alonso's arms, the sweetness of his company.

The Queen began her day hearing mass in the chapel where her husband had been laid to rest. She kneeled at the foot of his catafalque, which stood before the main altar, covered with a pall of black brocade. Sometimes she remained to listen to the organ. On Alonso's insistence, she walked for half an hour every day. The doctor had argued with the governor–the jailer, as the Queen called him–to allow her the use of the loggia overlooking the river, but he refused. The Queen must not be seen by her subjects except in royal robes, he said. It would not do for her to appear to them in the simple dress of a nun. But who would see her? Alonso said. Who, looking up at the balcony from the other side of the river or from a passing boat, could possibly tell that the figure high up there was the Queen? A rumour would be bad enough, the governor said, and absolutely vetoed her use of the loggia. And so Juana took her walk in the pillared arcade surrounding the nuns' patio. The rest of the day she spent sitting in an alcove of her drawing room, working at her embroidery frame or gazing out the window. Luisa kept her company, working on her own embroidery or reading a book, while the Queen watched the comings and goings in the courtyard below, the carts delivering supplies, horses being saddled or unsaddled, the tradesmen and servants going about their business. But Juana watched them with unseeing eyes. The courtyard was a tableau for the scenes playing in her mind.

There were times, however, when the Queen rallied and played her harpsichord or struck up a conversation with Luisa.

"Do you have sisters?" she asked Luisa one day.

"I have an older brother, Madam, but no sisters."

"I had three sisters. What a cheerful life we had together until they sent us away, Catalina to marry the King of England, Isabella to marry the King of Portugal, and when she died, Maria to take her place. And I followed Philip to Flanders. We all went our separate ways." The sheen of tears was in Juana's eyes, and she launched into the dirge that ended all her reminiscences: "They die and leave me behind. First my brother, then Isabella, then my husband. My mother and father died next, and now Maria has gone to the grave as well. Yes, they all die. And I am left behind."

Luisa kept a respectful silence while the Queen wept. After a little while she calmed down, dabbed her eyes with a handkerchief and asked: "Do you have children, Luisa?"

"I am childless, Madam."

"Oh, yes, you told me. You had a miscarriage, poor thing. I had six children, two boys and four girls. They took them away from me, one after the other. Carlos has come back now, but I don't know. What do you think, Luisa? Does he look like me?"

"The Prince has your husband's features, if I may say so, Madam," Luisa said.

"The long Habsburg chin, alas, but not his good features. No, Carlos isn't handsome at all. Now *you* have a handsome husband," she said, and stopped in confusion. "No, what am I saying? For a moment there I thought the doctor was your husband. But now I remember. You are a widow. Well, better so, my dear, because good-looking men have a roving eye. The doctor—I can never remember his name..."

"Doctor Malki."

"Doctor Malki. Is he married?"

"He lives on his own."

"He has his eye on you, Luisa. Mark my words. I've seen the way he looks at you. I can tell he is in love."

Luisa could not help blushing and lowered her eyes.

"Ah, I see how it is," the Queen said, lifting up Luisa's chin and peering into her face. "You love him in turn. Then be steadfast, my dear, and don't let anyone take him away from you. Or you'll end up like me, all alone. But I wonder what your father will say. Do you get along with him?"

"I respect him, Your Majesty."

"As you should, my dear. I respected my father but I didn't get along with him. He was too domineering, you know. He wanted me to remarry after Philip's death. How can I remarry? There is no love left in my heart, except the love I feel for my cats, which reminds me that

I should go and pay my darlings a visit. You needn't come along, Luisa."

"It is my duty to attend you, Madam."

"I don't like being watched when I'm with my cats. Did the doctor tell you to keep an eye on me? I don't mind having Beatriz around because she's half blind and quite deaf. She's supposed to look after my wardrobe, but sometimes I have to fasten the hooks myself. She says her fingers are too stiff to help me. Poor old dear. I don't mind her staying with me at night. I'm used to her. And if you have been told to attend me by day, Luisa, so be it. Only I'd rather be alone with my cats."

"I won't disturb you, Madam. I will take my seat in the corner, as always, and keep quiet."

"I know the doctor doesn't want me to sit on the floor with the cats. You won't tell on me, Luisa, will you?"

Luisa promised not to tell.

"What if he comes in and catches me in the act? Where does he go after he has examined me, do you know, Luisa? What does he do all day?"

"He visits the hospice of the nuns, Madam. He goes to the little gate, where the nuns hand out alms in Your Majesty's name. He listens to the poor people's complaints and gives them medicine. And he visits the sick in the outlying farms and in the fishermen's huts along the river."

"He won't get much for his services there."

"He does not ask for payment, Madam. He serves the poor for the love of God and is rewarded by the gratitude they show him."

"Then he is an even kinder man than I thought. But he is so very serious. And it's always: Don't do this, Madam. Don't do that. Well, you won't betray me, Luisa."

She gave her a pleading look before getting down on hands and knees to play with her cats. She chased after them, lifted them up by their paws and danced with them.

"I was a very good dancer in my youth," she said to Luisa, who looked on from her chair in the corner. "Everyone admired me. I inherited my mother's strawberry blond hair, you know." She touched her hair thoughtfully. "But look at me now. Thirty-nine years old." Her hair was streaked with grey, her cheeks were pendulous. "An old woman, who will never bear children again." She got up from the floor and straightened her dress.

"Now all I have is memories. Ah, what bliss it is to be young, to love and be loved. Luisa! Are you blushing again? I do believe you are in love with Dr. Malki."

The Queen's outbursts and her childlike candor could be embarrassing.

"I am afraid the rest of the world does not regard love as tenderly as Your Majesty," Luisa said. "My father takes a more practical view. He looks at a suitor's wealth and influence rather than his feelings, or mine."

"I know the world is mercenary, my dear. But love conquers all. *Amor vincit omnia.*" She tugged at the thin chain of gold around her neck—the only piece of jewelry she wore on her person—and revealed a pendant: a heart of gold, inscribed with the Latin motto. She held it up to Luisa like a sacrament.

"*Amor vincit omnia.* That has always been my guiding principle," she said.

She carried on like that when she had one of her talkative days. More often she was silent and stared out the window for hours without moving, without saying a word. If Luisa asked "Would you like me to read to you, Madam?" she nodded glumly.

"Shall I read from the new book my brother sent me, Thomas More's *Utopia*? It is very amusing, Madam."

She shook her head. She wanted no amusement.

"Perhaps Your Majesty would prefer a devotional book?" Luisa fetched Thomas of Kempten's *Imitatio Christi* and began to read, but the Queen soon became restless. When Luisa turned the page, she drew a deep breath, and said:

"Now stop, dear, and keep silent. I can't hear a word he is saying if you keep making so much noise. Philip I mean. And don't look at me like that. I know he is dead. They all die and leave me behind."

***

Not long after Luisa's arrival, the abbess of the Clares paid her a visit. In the last days of his regency, Cisneros had written to say that Luisa wished to enter the convent as a postulant. No doubt the abbess already thought of the wealth that would flow into the coffers of her convent if Luisa decided to take the veil.

She was a tall woman with angular features and shrewd eyes. Dressed in the coarse grey tunic and black cape of her order, she stood with her back to the gilded mirror on the wall, as if she wanted to block the vanities of the world with her body. In a prim voice, she inquired into Luisa's life and inclinations.

"I was married at sixteen," Luisa said, "and widowed before I turned eighteen. My mother's cousin, Cardinal Cisneros—may God rest his soul—always took a kindly interest in my life. It was he who advised me to take the veil."

"And do you feel an answering call in your heart?" the abbess said.

"Alas, God has not deigned to enlighten me, Holy Mother. I hardly know my heart."

Oh, but I do, she thought. My heart belongs to Alonso. How easy it had become to disguise her mind, to speak half-truths, and go on loving Alonso in defiance of the laws of God and men.

Looking into the probing eyes of the abbess, Luisa felt a stab of conscience and was tempted for a moment to confess, ask forgiveness for her sins, and return to the innocence of her childhood. Turn back the time and give up Alonso? One was as impossible as the other!

"I am a sinner, Holy Mother," she said. "I am not worthy of joining your holy congregation."

The abbess listened with her head inclined as if she had heard a small sound, something softer than words, the whisper of Luisa's unspoken thoughts. Her hearing was fine enough to detect Luisa's prevarications and to understand that she was not made for the contemplative life. Such fine eyes, such proud bearing, such abundance of hair roped with seed pearls, such elegance in the narrow sleeves of her dress embroidered with silver thread! Pearls and silver when she was barely out of mourning; Luisa's adornments spoke of worldliness and answered the questions of the abbess better than her words.

"I advise you to seek spiritual counsel," she said, but she did not press for a commitment. Luisa's hunger for life was written too plainly on her face. The abbess did not call again.

There was nothing to fear from that quarter, then, and nothing from the Queen. There was no one to keep Luisa from indulging her sinful heart. Only etiquette prevented her from spending time in Alonso's company. She kept her distance from him in public and met with him in private. The old palace was made for trysts. There were half a dozen guest bedrooms on the second floor, overlooking a pine forest and the banks of the Duero River, but no visitors had been entertained at Tordesillas for some time. When Prince Carlos and his retinue came, the local aristocracy had provided lodgings for the royal party because Juana's palace offered no suitable quarters. The guest rooms had been shuttered for years, and the curtains and carpets were threadbare and faded with disuse. On the top floor was a warren of small rooms of uncertain purpose that no one ever entered. They were piled with old furniture and broken ornaments and dusty with neglect.

There was no shortage of places where the lovers could meet. Their hands and lips touched in the stillness of the abandoned rooms, their hot breath and beating hearts the only signs of life. They made love on ancient poster beds under the watchful eyes of embroidered griffins looking down on their naked bodies from the thicket of the canopy. Soft sheets that had lain untouched for years, tangled and frayed under the thrust of their bodies. Pillows shed their tufted velvet in the grip of their frenzied hands, and the ornate coverlets slipped to the floor and came to rest on the carpet in a silky, shimmering mound. Afterwards, when their moans turned into whispered endearments, when their desire was exhausted, Luisa rested her head on Alonso's chest and listened to the rise and fall of her lover's breathing. She lay back, looked up to the dusky ceiling and saw the brass arms of the chandelier glint as if moved by his breath, but it was only the sunlight glancing off the metal, rays piercing the loose shutters, reminding her of the outside world. Shame spread through her then, as she looked down on her nakedness and thought of her gasps and cries, of her sinful pleasure.

To the chaplain of the Clares she confessed only venial sins. The mortal sins she kept to herself: making love to a man who was not her husband, spilling his seed often, receiving it into her body once or twice when passion overcame them. And yet her womb had not quickened. Was she barren now? Was that God's punishment for her sins?

In the cool autumn evenings, she sought the warmth of the brazier in Alonso's study. His consulting room adjoined the apartment of the Queen, but the longing to be in his arms had loosened all fear in Luisa. She trusted in the remoteness of the servants' quarters, in the knowledge that Juana was oblivious to her surroundings and old Beatriz too deaf to take notice.

She slipped into Alonso's room after the Queen retired. She was hungry for his caresses and his words. Their talk was far removed from the rhetorical exercises she had composed under Natale's ironic eye, from the round phrases she had practised under Deodatus' condescending smile, from the dinner conversations that had made her feel superfluous. Her conversations with Alonso were of the heart and mind. He told her about his visits to peasant huts, where men and beasts huddled together in a common shelter. He told her of the starved bodies he had seen, the suppurating boils, the mangled fingers and crooked limbs, the fevered cries he had heard, the moans, the struggles of a newborn child fighting for breath, a woman's death rattle, and when the ugliness of life became too much for them, they talked of the beauty of art. Alonso took the Book of Hours from his shelf and opened it at the frontispiece.

"Touch your fingers to the goldleaf," he said to her, and she passed her fingertips lightly over the smooth, shiny surface, smiling with pleasure.

"Now the indigo and the carmine red," he said. It was as if he was teaching her the colours anew. She moved her fingertips up to his cheek and stroked his hair. A thrill ran through her, as if he was renewing her sense of touch as well and teaching her fingers a lesson in love. She looked into his eyes, and felt his love like the rays of the sun warming her face.

He kissed her hands then and asked about *her* day. She had brought along the book disdained by the Queen, Thomas More's *Utopia*.

"Juana has no taste for literature," she said. "I wanted to read More's new book to her, but she closes her ears to the living and converses only with the dead."

"Is her dwelling on the past more fantastic than More's dwelling on a utopian city?"

"I think it is, Alonso. The future is possible after all. The past is irretrievably lost. More's utopian city offers an escape to dreamers, the past offers only graves."

"Perhaps you and I should journey to another world then. It need not be an exotic island, like Utopia. We might escape to Italy or France."

She smiled. "What, and put up with flawed societies when we could live in More's ideal society *knit together by the common ties of humanity*?"

"I wonder if you would not tire of his city," Alonso said. He took the book from her hands and leafed through it. "Listen to this," he said and read out the passage about lovers, their *vagrant appetites* and *forbidden embraces, severely to be punished.*

"I grant you the Utopians were hard on lovers," Luisa said, "but I did like their practice of presenting the bridegroom naked for the bride's inspection. I would not have married Deodatus then."

"But is it not more important to reveal the bridegroom's soul to his future wife?"

Luisa thought of Deodatus' tortured spirit. "Ah, he was wretched in his ambition and the uneasiness of his soul!" she said. "Would I have married him out of pity, I wonder?"

Their talk turned to the nature of the soul then, to the theories of the ancient philosophers, the mysticism of the Cabala. Alonso's words were like oracles to Luisa's ears, mysterious, tempting and alien, trailing the edge of heresy.

***

It was a winter full of passion for the lovers, and a spring of magical thinking, until a letter from Martin Casalius to Luisa pulled them up short and showed them the necessity to plot a future beyond trysts.

Luisa had never been at ease with Martin Casalius, but Alonso considered him a friend.

"A friend?" she said. "Martin Casalius is no one's friend. He loves God. He was loyal to the Cardinal. But being a friend means showing warmth, showing sympathy. Fray Martin is incapable of warmth."

There was something austere about him, something almost inhuman. The office of inquisitor suited him, she thought. He had the probing mind and the penetrating eye of a judge. He had a rigid and unbending sense of duty.

As always, his letter was full of religious fervor. As always, he urged Luisa to take the veil.

"I had a dream once," he had written in an earlier letter, "a dream in which you appeared to me as a weeping bride. At your side was a priest who spoke the ominous words: *Sponsae vita nuptiis tollenda*. I have thought a great deal about the ambiguity of the verb *tollenda*. Does is mean destroy or uplift? I believe God meant me to ponder its meaning and warn you against remarriage. Both meanings of *tollenda* apply in your case. Your marriage to Deodatus was unhappy and cast you down. Conversely, if you follow the Cardinal's advice and become a bride of Christ, God's grace will lift you up."

Luisa had neither encouraged nor discouraged Martin's expectations and hoped that he, like the abbess of the Clares, would draw his own conclusions. But his latest missive was alarming. It ended with a warning. "Your father wants to see you remarried. I am told he is determined to wrestle the power of attorney from

Alonso. He will use the force of law if necessary." Again he urged Luisa to take the veil and put an end to the uncertainty of her position.

Martin's warning was timely. Soon afterwards, Alonso received a threatening letter from Ramon Cardosa. The doctor's study had become Luisa's haven, but it lost its soothing aura when she saw the letter in Alonso's hand and read the lines in her father's firm handwriting. "The undersigned gives notice of his intention to seek the protection of the law against Alonso Malki, royal physician, the usurper of his paternal rights."

"Usurper!" Luisa said. "How dare he call you a usurper, when the Cardinal himself entrusted me to your care!"

"Perhaps I misinterpreted the Cardinal's intention," Alonso said quietly.

"But you told me..."

"I did not tell you everything, Luisa."

She looked at him, confused. What had he left unsaid? Could there be secrets between lovers? Was she not the repository of his hopes and fears, of his thoughts and meditations?

"But why did you not tell me everything?" she asked.

"To spare you what is in the past and cannot be changed. But it is always wrong to suppress the truth." He got up and took a turn around the room, as if the twists and turns of fortune were cramping his limbs and he must stretch and straighten them. "You know that the

Cardinal asked me to safeguard the power of attorney when he was on the point of death. He spoke to me in gasps, in fragments, in whispers. I had to put my ear to his mouth to hear what he was saying. His last words, as far as I could make them out, were 'Luisa' and 'guardian.' But it is hard to say what he meant."

"He wanted you to be my guardian," Luisa said firmly, refusing to admit of alternatives. "I am sure that is what he meant to say."

"And what if he meant Martin to be your guardian?"

She stopped her ears. "No!" she said, but it was too late to shut out the inquisitor's name. "No, not him! The Cardinal trusted you."

"He trusted me enough to confess and make his peace with God through me."

That's what Alonso is holding back, then, she thought: a confessional secret. That's why he has not told me everything. That's why he is hesitating even now, she thought. He is weighing the evidence, considering the whole and its parts.

Alonso took her hand in his. "I did not speak up sooner because I did not want to impugn the Cardinal's honour," he said. "And I would not speak up now if it was not necessary, and if he had not given me leave to tell you what concerns you intimately."

Another hedging moment went by.

"You mean he regretted the role he played in my unhappy marriage?" Luisa said. "He regretted foisting Deodatus on me to serve his own purpose, to keep a prominent scholar at the university. That's what my father said at any rate. It must have weighed on his conscience, but it was an error of judgment rather than a sin."

"It was another matter that weighed on his conscience, Luisa. As a youth, he told me, he was infatuated with your mother, but he could not make her his wife because the laws of the Church forbid marriage between cousins."

Luisa thought of her own trespasses into forbidden territory. "I have heard rumours that the Cardinal was in love with my mother once," she said. "But love is no sin."

"Is it not?" Alonso said softly as if he agreed with her, yet could not refute the scruples of others.

Luisa hesitated. She felt the pricks of conscience, suppressed but never deadened. Conscience led a ghostlife in the depth of her mind, surfacing unbidden to whisper and hum. Yes, she had broken her marriage vows when Deodatus was alive, and she was living in sin now. Alas, she knew what it meant to feel a passion condemned by all. She was culpable, but to think of the Cardinal in the same vein! "I cannot believe that the Cardinal..."

"He confessed that he sinned gravely—heinously, he called it. He confessed that he committed an act debasing his holy office. He could not overcome his passion for your mother even after he entered the church." Alonso's voice shifted. Luisa sensed something momentous. It was ringing in his voice already. "He loved your mother even then."

In his eyes she saw that there was more, a truth half-guessed and half-known. The man she had revered like a saint was a sinner. The man she had loved like a father, was he her father?

"And if," she said, stopped by a formidable thought. "And if my mother bore me in sin?"

"Then Ramon Cardosa has no right to direct your life. Yes, but we will never know the truth of the matter."

"My mother knows. I will ask her," she said. With every word, she became more convinced that Ramon Cardosa was her father in name only, that he was her keeper, the lock and chain human laws put on her heart.

"And you think Doña Catalina will incriminate herself? You expect her to confess and bring shame on her family's name?"

Luisa thought of her mother's frequent tears, the quivering lips and the look of helplessness in her eyes, the way she cringed and cowered under her husband's stormy eye. She was a feeble woman and had never given Luisa the motherly support a daughter needs. She had abdicated her duties to the aya. She did not have the strength to stand up to the truth.

"You are right," she said to Alonso. "She will never risk it. And I pity her. Her love was doomed. The Cardinal was fettered by religious vows, she was tied by the bonds of marriage. But we are free to become husband and wife, in a clandestine marriage at any rate. I am not afraid of balking the man who calls himself my father."

They had talked of clandestine marriage before, but it was a narrow path to lead them out of their troubles, and hardly safe. Once Alonso was Luisa's husband, the law made him her natural guardian, but the church frowned on clandestine marriages. Ecclesiastical law required the consent of the father and the presence of a congregation to witness the marital union. A private marriage lacking parental consent was unlawful. If they informed Ramon Cardosa after the fact, would he acquiesce to avoid scandal?

"Or would he try to have the marriage annulled?" Alonso said.

Ramon Cardosa was a stubborn man, who insisted on his rights, who clung to his possessions. Already he had seized the house in Arelate and the income from the land, masking his theft by calling it care-taking. He had not been able to get his hands on the annuity Prince Carlos had granted Luisa as the Queen's lady-in-waiting or on Deodatus' investments in Antwerp and the dividends paid to his widow.

"Then let us leave Spain," Luisa said, "and begin a new life elsewhere." It was not the first time the lovers had considered that alternative. The arm of the law was long, but it did not reach across borders. There was no one to hold Luisa in Spain, no one who had a claim on her affections, except her brother. She was fond of Alejandro. His letters were a comfort to her. But nothing would change if she left Spain. She missed his company now, and she would miss it if they left the country. She was separated from Alejadro by a great distance already. Soon the passing years and the claims of others – a wife, children, duties at court perhaps – would widen the gap between them even if she stayed in Tordesillas.

Alonso took Luisa into his arms and kissed her gently. "My sweet love," he said, "You once offered to leave Alcala and follow me. You were ready to defy society and be an outcast. I could not accept your sacrifice then, but fate may favour us at last."

"I would follow you to the end of the world, Alonso, if I could do away with all secrets and deceits and live openly as your wife."

"That would be happiness indeed," he said and took both of her hands in his. "I have taken the first step, Luisa, and written to my uncle in Venice." Adventure ghosted in his eyes, and the courage that comes of passion.

She trusted him. Alonso will find a way, she thought, and Martin's dream will come true in a sense that he could not anticipate. *Sponsae vita nuptiis tollenda.* Marriage to Alonso will lift me up and make me happy.

Over the next weeks, Alonso's plan took shape. The taste of freedom was on Luisa's lips when he told her that he had received an encouraging reply from his uncle. "He urges us to come," he said, "and settle in Italy. He promises to help us in every way he can. Now we must find a way to leave here without arousing suspicion, for we will not be safe until we are married. It will be easy to find a reason for my going away – a visit to a patient, who lives at a distance."

"And I might ask for leave to visit my family over Easter."

The last lie, the last act of deception!

"Once you have left Tordesillas behind,"he said, "we shall meet up and continue our journey together. How glorious it will be to live a life of truth thereafter."

Ah, Italy!

CHAPTER 18

IT WAS THE END OF LENT AND THE BEGINNING OF Passion Tide. The liturgical year matched Luisa's mood. A time of anticipation had begun. There were trials ahead and suffering, but also delivery. It was the season that held the promise of resurrection.

    The lovers were in Alonso's study. He had dismissed his servant for the day, shed his professional skin and become the man Luisa loved. His eyes promised surpassing sweetness. The certainty of his voice melted into the delicious uncertainty of longing, his measured gestures gave way to the disorientation of desire, the flurry of love. He was wrapping his arms around Luisa, when they heard a commotion in the courtyard – the heavy gate turning on its hinges, the beating of hooves on the cobblestones, the clanking of weapons.

Alonso stepped up to the window. Dusk was draining the colour from the sky. The walls cast long shadows on the courtyard below and tinted the walls mauve. In the dim light, he saw the governor greeting Martin Casalius and pointing him to the house. But the scene did not have the appearance of a friendly visit. The two guards who had come with the inquisitor dismounted. A stable boy was leading the horses away.

"It's Martin Casalius," he said, turning to Luisa.

She blanched. The inquisitor must not find her here. She quickly moved to the door, but Alonso held her back.

"Too late," he said. "They will see you coming out of my room."

Martin and his guards had entered the hall. Their footfall was audible on the stairs.

"Hide in the dispensary," Alonso said, and Luisa quickly retreated behind the narrow door.

A moment later, there was a knock.

Luisa's refuge—no larger than a closet—was a converted pantry, with the shelves holding medicine bottles now instead of provisions. Through a chink in the ill-fitting door, she saw Martin enter. He was alone. His guards must be waiting in the corridor, she thought. Waiting for what?

The two men embraced, Alonso with the natural inclination of a friend, Martin stiffly.

"You should have told me you were coming," Alonso said. "I might have talked the cook into giving us a respectable dinner."

"I came on the spur of the moment."

"Welcome then to the wilderness of Tordesillas."

Martin looked around the room, a spy training his mind on details, Luisa thought. She felt the vertigo of fear, as if the objects in the room could give Martin a clue to the words she had spoken, as if her hands had left visible marks on the furniture and on Alonso's shoulders.

"You chose wilderness over a life at court," Martin said. Luisa could no longer see his face. He had turned to Alonso. "I take it, the company rather than the place attracts you," he said.

"The company of my books?" Alonso said, waving his hands at the well-stocked shelves.

Martin walked across the room and cocked his head to read the titles on the spines. Medical handbooks, the classics, the Church Fathers. He stopped.

"Capnio's *De arte cabalistica*?" he said.

Natale's voice echoed in Luisa's mind when she heard Martin read out the title of the book. *The art of the Cabala.* The Inquisition will take an interest in you if you talk carelessly about the Cabala, Natale had told Alonso, smiling his slippery smile.

"Capnio is a learned author," Alonso said.

"Learned but dangerous. He is under investigation for heresy."

Martin continued his inspection of Alonso's shelves.

"You have a large number of Hebrew books, I notice."

There was a dawning watchfulness in Alonso's face when he said: "They are biblical commentaries for the most part. They served me well when I was working on the Polyglot text."

The evening closed in on the two men. The objects in the room lost their contours. Alonso lit a candle. A flame sprang up, and Luisa saw that Martin had placed his hand on a large volume.

"And that one?" he said, pulling the tome back and forth as if he needed to find the right place for it on the shelf.

"The Talmud," Alonso said.

Martin's eyes were on him with unsettling concentration. "A book abhorred by Magister Raimundus and called shameful in Petrus Nigri's *Star of Messiah*," he said. "A book forbidden by the church."

His words sucked the air from Luisa's throat. A forbidden book. A touch of heresy. She felt her chest tighten and a grey malaise take hold. If it was true...

"Forbidden to the public, but not to scholars, who study the interpretions of the law found in the Talmud," Alonso said. "Have you come to pass judgment on my books, Martin?"

"I shall make no pretenses," Martin said, taking a step closer to Alonso, so close he might have laid hands on him. "I have come here in fulfillment of my duties as inquisitor. You have been denounced as a Judaizer."

He rapped out the words. They struck Luisa like the blow of an axe. She made a gag of her fists, pressed them against her mouth to keep from howling out her anguish.

"The evidence against you is strong, and if placed before qualifying judges, will suffice to indict you, Alonso. I am here as a friend, to give you warning. But my first duty is to God: I cannot allow you to contaminate the minds of those with whom you are in daily contact." He spoke without taking a breath, reciting the words like a speech he had rehearsed many times.

"Who is my accuser?"

One of the servants? Luisa thought. The governor? The chaplain of the Clares? Who had denounced Alonso?

"You know very well that the Inquisition does not reveal its sources. And it is not the first time suspicions have been raised about you, Alonso. So far I have given them no credence, but the new evidence is irrefutable. I can no longer close my eyes to the accusations. I am in duty bound to act. I have been candid with you and I expect candid answers to my questions in turn." Martin paused. "Is it true that you are entertaining a liaison with Luisa? And that you have made plans to leave Spain together with her and settle in Venice?"

How did Martin know of their plans? Had Alonso's letters to his uncle been intercepted?

"And is it true that you are in contact with the Jewish community there?" Martin continued.

In the light of the candle, Alonso's skin appeared bloodless. Martin's questions hung heavily in the air.

"The word liaison has a sordid ring," Alonso said. "My love for Luisa is honourable. As for your second question, I have indeed made plans to leave Spain. You know that *conversos* do not always fare well in this country, and I believe my services will be better rewarded in Italy. I have corresponded about this matter with my uncle, who left Spain in 1492 under the terms extended to the Jews by the Crown. I believe it is not against the laws of the Church to maintain contact with one's relatives or consult with Jews concerning non-religious matters."

"You have answered prudently, or shall I say, cleverly," Martin said. "I will put it to you another way, then: Do you feel drawn to the religion of your forefathers? Answer me truthfully, Alonso."

"Am I under interrogation?"

"Have I not told you that I am motivated by friendship?"

The more often Martin used the word friendship, the more Luisa doubted his goodwill. Even if they had been friends once, Martin's duties stood between them now, a solid wall.

"I could have hauled you before a tribunal," Martin said. "What I am doing is against the protocol of the *Suprema*."

Alonso hesitated. "I invoke the laws of friendship, then, in telling you the truth. I have been studying the Cabala to settle certain questions in my mind and to look for answers that God has not granted me to find in the gospel."

"You have done well to invoke the laws of friendship," Martin said. "A judge would say that your answer smacks of Judaism."

"I have done nothing wrong," Alonso said. "God has made us rational beings. He has given us a mind to reason with and to ask questions in our quest for the truth."

"A devout believer finds his reasons and his answers and his truth in the Bible. Your questions amount to doubt, which is an unpardonable sin against the Holy Spirit. I came as a friend, hoping that the accusations against you would prove groundless, but you are a sinner, and recalcitrant at that. I can do nothing further for you, Alonso. I must do my duty."

Luisa felt as if her body was trapped under water. She no longer saw Alonso. She heard only Martin's threatening words. His voice seemed to ring from the rafters of the ceiling.

"My servants are waiting in the corridor. On my instruction they will apprehend you and put you in chains."

Alonso did not lower his gaze. He looked the inquisitor in the eye. "You must do your duty, then."

"You leave me no choice." Martin drew a deep breath and straightened his back. "I charge you with relapsing into Judaism," he said, using the customary formula, which made the charge valid before the law: "Being a baptized Christian you have left our Catholic faith and have gone over to the Law of Moses. You are a heretic and apostate of our holy faith. The penalty for such a heinous crime is excommunication with confiscation of property and the handing over to the secular arm for capital punishment. But I invite you to repent and abjure your errors and be received once again into the fold of Holy Mother Church, that in her mercy she may absolve you from your sins, instruct you in the mysteries of faith necessary for the salvation of the soul, and pardon you."

Heresy and excommunication! Luisa silently joined Martin's prayer. Holy Mother Church, instruct me in the mysteries of faith. Give me strength. How can I stand by a man who is charged with Judaism, how can I love a heretic? No, no, that was the wrong question. How could Alonso be a heretic? God give me strength to stand by the man I love, she prayed.

When Alonso made no reply to the official charge, Martin said: "You will spend the night in confinement. In the morning you will be be taken to Valladolid and put before a tribunal."

He opened the door, called to his guards and gave orders for Alonso to be arrested and taken to the dungeon below the palace.

From her hiding place, Luisa saw the soldiers shackle Alonso and march him off. Martin stood in the room for a moment longer, his head bowed, like a man defeated. When he looked up his eyes were on the door that shielded Luisa. The candle light made them look like hollows. Could those inquisitorial eyes penetrate walls? Luisa trembled at the thought of Martin searching the room and finding her in the dispensary, but he only placed his hand on Alonso's desk with a gesture of farewell and followed the guards down the stairs.

Their receding footsteps set off a drum roll in Luisa's mind. The pain that had been waiting behind her eyes broke loose and hammered her head with brutal force, set her teeth on edge and her skin on fire. She could taste the pain on her tongue. Nothing made sense. Shackle a man's courage? Punish his principles? Alonso had acted like a man of honour. He refused to use his beliefs as a bargaining chit. And if his beliefs were heretical? But what did that dreaded word really mean? It seemed to be a large and fluid term. She knew only that Alonso was prepared to die rather than renounce his beliefs. Was death the inevitable return for his courage?

No. There must be a way to save his life.

***

Luisa crept out of her hiding place.

The candle Alonso had lit earlier was guttering in its holder, thick with wax. The chair, pulled out from his desk, stood at an angle, as if Alonso had gotten up and stepped out of the room only for a moment.

A plan was forming in Luisa's mind. She walked to the desk, opened one of the drawers, pulled back the lining, and took a golden signet ring from a hidden compartment. It was a gift from Alonso's father, she knew, a curious piece with a hollow bezel containing stun-powder. For a moment she was tempted to release the spring and ascertain that the powder was there, but she could not risk breathing its paralyzing fumes. The ring fit loosely on Luisa's middle finger. She closed her hand over it to keep it in place.

The corridor was empty when she stepped out of Alonso's room and walked softly across the landing to her own apartment.

Paulina was asleep, curled up on the window seat, her cotton skirt bunched up around the knees. When Luisa entered, she stirred and rubbed her eyes.

"Doña Luisa," she said wearily, sitting up and pulling her skirt down over her solid peasant legs. "The Queen should not keep you up so late."

"Hush, Paulina. Mind of whom you are speaking."

"I'm only repeating what they say in the servants' hall. It isn't fair..."

"It isn't fair to keep *you* up late, you mean?"

Paulina twisted her apron, plucking the fabric between her thumb and middle finger. "And there was a lot of commotion in the hall earlier on. I peeked out and saw two armed guards standing there. I got all scared."

"You should mind you own business, Paulina, and not spy on other people and on what does not concern you."

"But I didn't spy, Doña Luisa. I shut the door as soon as I saw the guards, and I went about my business. I turned down the covers of your bed and brought a basin of hot water, but it's cold now."

Could Paulina be trusted? Luisa looked into the girl's face, gauging her honesty. Perhaps she was honest, but she was not discreet. She was a silly girl who couldn't keep her mouth shut, who was a poor helper for what Luisa had in mind. But she had no choice.

"No sleep for me tonight, Paulina," she said. "The inquisitor has come from Valladolid, and I shall have to accompany him on a mission that concerns Her Majesty."

A frightened look came into Paulina's eyes. "The inquisitor?"

"Yes, and you don't want to run afoul of him. So listen carefully, my dear. I want you to go to the stable and wake up Antonio, who is your special friend, is he not?"

The girl lowered her eyes. "We've done nothing wrong, Doña Luisa," she said.

"I know, Paulina. Go and wake Antonio. Take care not to wake anyone else, and if you do, make them believe that your visit to Antonio is a matter of the heart. Do you understand?"

The girl blushed and nodded.

"Tell Antonio to saddle my horse and the horse of the inquisitor and to lead the animals out by the small gate, the one where the poor are given alms, and wait for us there. Tell him to wrap the horses' hooves in rags so that they won't clatter on the cobblestones of the courtyard. We are going on the Queen's business, and it is of the greatest importance to keep our departure confidential."

The girl's mouth was hanging open. "I don't know that I understand you rightly, Doña Luisa," she said.

"Repeat the instructions to me, then."

"I am to wake up Antonio and tell him to saddle up your and the Lord Inquisitor's horse and sneak them out by the small gate." Her voice went up in a question mark. She was round-eyed with wonder.

"That's right, Paulina. And tell Antonio: The inquisitor will not take it kindly if word of my departure leaks out."

The girl nodded. Her face was dark now and freighted with secrecy.

"Go then, my dear. Do as you are told and come straight back to me when you're done."

She listened for the girl's steps on the stairs, went into her bedroom, and began to gather up her things. She took a hooded coat from the carved chest at the bottom of her bed. She took the money she had on hand, and anything that could be turned into ready cash, a pearl necklace, a bracelet and earrings set with amethysts, a golden locket, a spray of diamonds, a jeweled cross. She wrapped them up in a bundle. She wished she could lay her hands on provisions as well, but a plateful of dates and almond tarts was all she had in her room.

Then she sat listlessly on her bed and waited for Paulina's return, going through the preparations in her mind until she was confident she could carry off her plan and felt the levitating power of certainty.

"Done?" she asked when the girl came back.

Paulina nodded. Her eyes were full of excitement and self-importance now. "Antonio didn't believe me at first. He thought I was playing a game, but I told him you had been very particular about it, and you don't play games when the inquisitor is in it. So he believed me at last and went off to saddle the horses."

Luisa put a coin into her hand. "You did well, Paulina. Take this with my thanks." She did not dare to give Paulina a more generous present for fear of raising her curiosity. "Now go to bed, my dear," she said, "and in the morning, if anyone asks about me, say you don't know, that I left while you were asleep. Then no one will pester you with questions, and you will not be tempted to say what must remain a secret."

"And will you come back soon, Doña Luisa?" the girl asked.

"In a day or two."

"Will there be anything else, Doña Luisa?"

"That's all. You may go."

She waited until she could be sure that the girl had gone downstairs to the house servants' quarters, and listened to the unbroken silence of the night. Then she took the candle from the table and descended the stairs to the dungeon. She had heard the governor complain about the cost of keeping a jailer there. "Why pay a drunken lout for doing a few days' work once in a while?" he said. "The last time we needed him was a year ago, when a robber was kept in the dungeon until a public hanging could be arranged. Another time, two peasants were thrown into the hole. Rebel leaders. I would have given them short shrift. No need to keep such vermin alive and pay a guard to watch over them."

Luisa had seen the jailer only once, a dirty brute, emerging from that dark stairway like the devil from the mouth of hell. And now she was descending to that hellhole herself.

***

The candlelight fell on the worn stone steps, the scuffed walls, the angles and arches leading to a heavy oaken door at the bottom, a door set in iron bars. A track of rust was bleeding from the key hole, as if it had been stained with the prisoners' blood.

With a beating heart, Luisa knocked on the door. There was no response. She knocked again, more loudly, afraid now of rousing the household. At last she heard steps approaching.

A key turned in the lock and the door was thrust open by the jailer. He gave Luisa a goggle-eyed stare. "What is it, my lady?" he said, yanking at a bunch of keys at his belt. The respect in his voice was provisionary. What business did a lady have here, at this hour of the night? His muscular arm was on the iron handle of the door, ready to shut her out if her answer did not satisfy him.

Luisa's courage gave way before his thuggish presence. She suppressed a gibber of panic. Her hands trembled with a life of their own. She hid them under her shawl and mustered a spurious courage.

"You are holding a prisoner here, I believe. Doctor Malki?"

"The Jew? What do you want with him?"

"He is my husband," she said.

He gave her a wolfish grin. "Your husband, is he?"

She looked at him steadily, willing her eyes to work their magic once more and tame the beast.

"Release him," she said to the jailer, "and I will make it worth your while. If you oblige me, you shall have this ring."

She held up her hand, turning the signet ring to make it shine in the light of the jailer's torch.

He raised his bushy brows and screwed up his mouth. "Is that so?" he said and caught up Luisa's hand in his paw to examine the ring. A glimmer of greed appeared in his eyes. "And what about your earrings?" he said, leaning in close to look at her emerald pendants, breathing throat-catching fumes.

"You may have them, too," she said, turning her head.

He waved her in and shut the oaken door after her.

"Nice trinkets," he said and bared his lips in a sneering grin.

"They will be yours, as soon as you have released my husband."

"Not so fast," he said. His voice had lost all respect. She was a supplicant, someone who depended on his good will. A woman married, she claimed, to a man who was in trouble with the Inquisition. He sneered. "I can see you are impatient to embrace your husband and the ring and the pendants are nice enough, but not worth risking my neck. What will I say to the inquisitor when he comes tomorrow and the prisoner is gone? He will have me up before a tribunal. Next thing the noose is around my neck."

"Say that the prisoner lured you into the cell feigning illness and then overpowered you," Luisa said, looking down a narrow flight of steps that seemed to lead to an abyss.

"Is he down there?" she said.

She could see a grating at the bottom of the steps and beyond it a wall of coarse masonry shadowed with the ghosts of absence and loss.

"Down there, in the hole," the man said, grinning.

"Let me speak to him," she pleaded, edging past him and beginning her descent, as if he had given her permission already.

The jailer followed her, drawn by the glitter of the earrings or by the magic of her eyes. But he still objected to her plan.

"Overpowered me? Who'll believe that? With all due respect, lady, your husband isn't the man to overpower me." He pounded his burly chest. The fists looked hard like anvils.

The scrunching of the guard's boots and the scraping of Luisa's shoes on the stairs was the only sound to disturb the funereal silence.

"I'll let you see him," the guard said. His voice echoed in the cave-like hollow. "That's all I can do for you."

They came to the grating at the bottom of the steps. The jailer pulled back an iron bar and admitted Luisa to a vile and fetid hole, a lair too beastly even for wild animals. He set the torch in an iron bracket halfway up the wall. It cast a yellow beam of light on the slimy walls and the figure of a man: Alonso, sitting on a narrow wooden bench that was the only piece of furniture in the cell.

He had heard the jailer's objections to Luisa's pleading. A discerning light appeared in his eyes when he glimpsed the signet ring on her finger.

"You are right," he said to the jailer. "I'm no match for you, but if you'll say I struck you with a piece of iron I kept concealed under the bench, they'll believe you."

"They won't believe me," the jailer said, "and I won't risk my neck for a dirty Jew."

"Think of what you stand to gain," Luisa said. "Think of the value of the ring and the emerald pendants."

"A pawnbroker will give you twenty florins for them," Alonso said.

"I bet you know all about pawnbrokers," the guard said with a great rotting laugh. "I warrant you've grown up among the greedy pigs."

He looked at Alonso with a bully's joy gleaming in his eye. Luisa took a step closer. An intense desire seized her, to touch Alonso's hand and comfort him.

"Release him, I beg you," she said to the jailer.

"I tell you what. You give me the ring, lady, and I let you spend the night with your man. Your husband if you say so. I won't ask any questions. I'll shut my ears to your love-making. I won't disturb you, as long as I get my reward in advance. I won't tell them you were here. Is it a deal? Because if it ain't, I might just tell them that I had a visitor tonight. You know what I mean? So, let's have the ring."

He grinned maliciously and stretched out his grimy hand for his reward.

"So be it," Luisa said. She slipped the ring from her finger, pressed the hidden spring unlatching the bezel and threw the ring into the jailer's face. She saw the black powder catch in his eyebrows and quickly stepped back, turning away and covering her mouth and nose with the ends of her shawl. Alonso had already moved to the back of his cell and turned his face to the wall, shielding it from the poison cloud.

The turnkey blinked bewildered and wiped his cheek and lips on his sleeve. The powder left a charred residue, a concentric smear on his face and a dusty mustache under his bulbous nose. His face was contorted with rage as he took a step forward, reeling like a drunken man. The powder was beginning to take effect. His mouth was gaping open. He moaned and groped for the wall, seeking support. His knees buckled. His fingers slipped, and he collapsed on the packed earth floor. The ring fell from his hand and clattered on the floor.

Alonso looked at Luisa through toxic tears.

"We have no time to lose," he said. "The effect of the power will wear off in an hour or two."

They left the sprawling body where it had come to rest, barred the grating to keep the jailer in his prison hole, where no one could hear his cries for help, and rushed up the stairs.

There was time only for a few hurried explanations as they shut the outer door behind them. The rank air in the corridor seemed pure by comparison with the fetid dungeon. They hastened up the steps to the main floor and made their way through the silent hall to the courtyard. The night air filled their lungs. They clung to each other for a moment in the shadow of the stone walls, then hurried on. At the side gate, they found Antonio waiting with the horses; and beside him Beatriz, looking at them rheumy-eyed.

Alonso's fingers tightened on Luisa's arm and let go again. They moved apart, but the shock of having been discovered by the Queen's confidante froze their steps. Neither of them ventured to speak. Indeed words could not explain away their action. Luisa was about to prostrate herself before Beatriz and implore her mercy, when the old woman took a shuffling step forward and said:

"Her Majesty prays for a prosperous outcome to your journey and sends you this token of her affection."

She pulled from her shawl a small object wrapped in a handkerchief of cambric and put it into Luisa's hand.

Luisa saw that the corner of the fabric was marked with Juana's initials. A golden heart nestled in its folds. *Amor vincit omnia.* She lowered her eyes to hide from Antonio the tears of relief and gratitude flooding them. She should have known. The Queen was a champion of love.

"Please convey to her Majesty my most hearfelt thanks for taking so kind an interest in my safety." She would have liked to say more, but was afraid of betraying the true circumstances to Antonio.

Beatriz eyed the groom soberly. "You shouldn't put your trust in the likes of him," she said. "He is a bold and overconfident lad. Wanted to know whether it was true that the Queen had sent you on a mission and told us all sorts of empty tales. Luckily Her Majesty knows how to plumb the human heart and can tell the difference between truth and malicious gossip."

"We are reassured by the trust Her Majesty places in us," Alonso put in.

Beatriz turned to him. "I need not tell you, Doctor Malki, that the Queen is forgetful. You have often noted it yourself. I doubt she will be able to recall any of this if they ask her tomorrow."

Antonio's eyes kept wandering from Beatriz to Alonso and Luisa, and back again. His mouth was hanging open, ready to devour every word escaping their lips.

Alonso was afraid the groom might guess the hidden import of their conversation or, worse, that Beatriz might rouse the guards. She spoke in a loud voice as persons hard of hearing often do.

"May I speak with you in private for a moment, Doña Beatriz?" he said.

The old woman read his lips and caught his meaning. She nodded, and allowed him to lead her away to the other end of the courtyard. There the two stood, looking into each other's faces like lovers declaring their undying devotion, standing so close you could think they were about to embrace. Then the old woman stepped away from the doctor and made her way back into the house, and Alonso returned to where Antonio was waiting with Luisa.

"I thought the Lord Inquisitor would accompany Doña Luisa," the groom said, still baffled.

Alonso answered him with authority. "There has been a change of plans. Keep what you have seen and heard to yourself, on pain of treason."

Alonso's firm voice cowed the groom, but the expression on his face clearly betrayed his thoughts: The Queen is mad, and someone ought to inform the governor that she has sent the doctor and her lady-in-waiting on a madcap mission.

Meanwhile Alonso had helped Luisa into the saddle and mounted Martin's horse. He gave the groom a steady look.

"I hope the road to Barcelona has not suffered from the rains last week," he said.

"Can't tell you, sir," Antonio said. "Nobody's been to Barcelona lately as far as I know."

The question was a dodge to make the groom believe they were heading for the coast. Their intention was to go north and cross into France. If Antonio was questioned tomorrow, he would remember that the doctor had asked about the road to Barcelona. That would set the pursuers on the wrong track, or so they hoped. But the incredulous look remained in Antonio's eyes, and they knew it was by no means certain that he would wait until questioned. More likely, he would guess that something was afoot and raise the alarm before long.

"And what did Beatriz say to you?" Luisa asked Alonso as they rode off into the night.

"The Queen heard the commotion in the corridor and feared a conspiracy against her own person. For a long time she waited, kneeling by her bed and praying silently. At last, she plucked up her courage and sent Beatriz to investigate. She found Antonio lurking in the hall. Apparently he had second thoughts about following Paulina's instructions. He was going to speak to you in person, but no one answered the door, and he was uncertain what to do next. There is a God in heaven, Luisa, for we were delivered twice tonight. First from that beast in the dungeon, and again from Antonio, who nearly discovered our plan. Surely it was divine providence that sent him into the path of Beatriz. When the Queen heard his garbled story, she thought we were planning an elopement. Fortunately, her romantic sympathies were with us."

The Queen may have a dim understanding of the world, Luisa thought, but she has an unerring sense of love. She looked up into the night sky and said a silent prayer for her royal benefactress since she could not kneel and kiss her hand, as she would have liked to do.

CHAPTER 19

ALONSO KNEW THE FOREST OF TORDESILLAS WELL. He had hunted there with the governor and his sons. He had visited the huts of woodcutters and the homesteads of peasants in the clearings and on the outskirts of the wood. He knew every footpath, but there was no moon to light their way, just a slab of black night above them. They feared brigands as much as Martin's henchmen. Trusting the horses to find their own footing, they rode in silence. Once they heard the lugubrious hoot of an owl. Was it a bird or was it a human voice imitating the bird, a robber signaling to his accomplice the sighting of a prey? They rode on, alert to every rustle, to every creaking branch. Soon they became aware that the noises they heard were not random. They were the dull thud of galloping hooves. They quickened their pace and made their way to a clearing. A sheep pen came in sight and Alonso reined in his horse.

"An old man and his grandson live here," he said to Luisa. "He is one of my patients. I looked after him when he was ill last winter. Perhaps they will give us shelter."

A rutted path led to the peasant's house. The walls were wattled and smeared with mud, horsehair, and sheep-dung. The daub had not yet lost its native odour and overpowered the scent of the pinetrees surrounding it. The doctor knocked and called out softly.

"Who is it?" a hoarse voice said. When the doctor said his name, an old man opened the door and let them in. A boy was about to throw some faggots on the dying embers of the hearth, but Alonso arrested his hand.

"Don't," he said. "The light will show through the window." He turned to the old man. "Hide us, Mateo, for the love of God and if ever I have done you a good deed."

"Who is after you, doctor?" the old man said.

"I have no time to explain," Alonso said. "Hide us and our horses before it's too late."

The old man gave Luisa a curious glance. "Running away?" he said. "Well, I was young once, and foolish."

She could not make out the expression on the old man's face in the semi-darkness of the hut, but he said to the boy: "Take the horses round the sheep pen, Guille, and keep them out of sight."

The boy ducked though the door and led the horses away.

The forest was alive now with rough calls and the hoofbeats of horses.

"Get under the bed," the old man said, pointing to a plank bed covered with a straw mattress.

He moved two earthen pots that had been stored underneath. The fugitives squeezed into the narrow space below the planks and hitched their bodies against the wall. Luisa felt the earth against her skin, cold and dank. Her fingers curled over Alonso's hand in a tight squeeze.

The old man barely had time to rearrange the pots and pull the straw mattress back into place before their pursuers pounded on the door.

"In the name of the Inquisition, open up," a commanding voice called out.

Luisa heard the door thrust open and bang against the wall. The trampling of boots shook the dirt floor and rang through her bones. Voices mingled curses with rough questions.

"Have you seen or heard anyone pass by during the past hour? Have you? Out with it, you old fool. What are you staring at me? Has the devil sewn up your mouth?"

"I've seen no one," Luisa heard the old man say. His voice sounded strangled. Were they holding him by the throat, twisting up his shirt, sneering into his face? "For God's sake," he said, pleading with the intruders, "take away your torches. You are going to set my hut on fire."

"Let go of the wretch, Eduardo," one of riders said. "We are wasting our time here. God knows what we chased after; the devil, for all I know."

"Devil take *you*!" the other man said. "You take me for a fool, Benito? I heard horses. Let's check the man's barn."

"I have no barn," the old man said. "Only a lean-to at the back of the house."

"I tell you, we are wasting our time," Benito said. "They didn't come through here. You heard what the ostler told us. They asked about the road to Barcelona."

"I don't trust that boy," the other man said. "Maybe he's in cahoots with them and wants to put us on the wrong track."

"We are on the wrong track now. Let's turn back and try the road to Barcelona."

Luisa heard them rush out, remount their horses and gallop away. For a moment there was silence, broken only by her own breathing.

Then the old man moved the pots to allow them to skid out of their hiding place and rise as from a grave, dust and earth clinging to their garments.

"It's a good thing, doctor, you didn't to tell me the Inquisition is after you," the peasant said. "Because I wouldn't have helped you then. Not me. I'm an old man. It will not be long until God calls me before his judgment seat. What will I say if he asks me: Why did you help a heretic?"

An ember flared up among the ashes. Luisa saw his face for a moment, the yellow of his eyes, the corners of his cracked lips.

"God knows we are innocent," Alonso said. "Why would you believe that we are heretics?"

"I know nothing about heresy, doctor, and I hope I never will, but I know that the Inquisition is God's instrument. And a Christian must not go against it. So get out of my hut, you and your woman, and God help your soul."

"Don't betray us, I beg you," Luisa said, clutching the old man's arm. She felt the frayed sleeve of his peasant coat, the rough hand and broken fingernails as he pulled away from her.

"I won't betray you, lady." His voice was suddenly knife-edged. "For my own sake I won't, and for the sake of my grandson. They'd kill us both if they found out that we sheltered heretics."

"But we are no..."

He cut her off. "The sooner you are gone the better."

***

They rode on until dawn came and roused the song birds. Their horses had begun to flag and stumble over the rough path. They halted by a creek and relieved the animals of their gear. Their backs steamed in the cool morning air as they lowered their heads to graze.

Alonso spread a saddle blanket under a pine tree. They sat close, leaning against the trunk of the tree, shoulders touching, looking at each other, their faces pale with fear and lack of sleep.

"Is it true, Alonso? Are we heretics?" Luisa said, daring herself to ask the question, to say the dreadful word. She was no wiser than the peasant who had disowned all knowledge of this greatest of great sins.

"There are a hundred definitions for heresy," Alonso said. "I'll give you mine." He picked up a fallen branch and sketched out a circle in the pine needles that covered the ground under the tree. The air filled with the delicate scent of resin.

He pointed at the centre of the circle.

"This is orthodoxy, as defined by the laws of the church," he said. "It is hallowed ground. Beyond its borders lies heresy." His hands moved outside the circle he had drawn. "I dared to raise questions. I have gone beyond the pale."

He took Luisa's hand into his. "When we talked about the Cardinal, Luisa, you said *Love is no sin*. You were standing at the very edge of the circle when you said that. You were about to cross into heresy. Church law does not permit love outside of marriage. Would you recant your love to stay within the circle? Would you renounce me, Luisa?"

"I will never renounce you," she said, "and I cannot believe that God will condemn me as a heretic for loving you."

"God in his mercy may not condemn us, but men will," Alonso said and pulled her into his embrace. In his arms, Luisa felt the shadow of fear lifting from her mind. She felt her senses stir, felt the happiness of love again. In Alonso's embrace, she began to think of heresy as a mirage, of their escape as a past adventure. But in the soberness that followed his caresses, she knew that heresy was a deadly sin and that the distance they had covered during the night was not enough to make for a safe escape.

They slaked their thirst with water from the creek and their hunger with the scant provisions Luisa had brought, and set out again. The spikes of the midday sun were glinting through the trees when they reached the edge of the forest and came to the well-travelled road leading to Burgos. Fields stretched on both sides. There were no byways here or forests to shield them from discovery.

Luisa pulled her shawl over her head, but Alonso could not avoid the eyes of the cart drivers on the road, the pedlars hauling their wares, the peasants walking beside shaggy donkeys. And he could not entirely put off fellow travelers on horse eager to strike up a conversation and overcome the boredom of a long journey. Nor did the inquisitor's horse, a splendid black gelding, escape notice and comment.

The day was wearing on, and the horses slowed their pace. Luisa's palfrey became restless, shook her mane and began to drift to the edge of the road. It was time to rest the horses, but stopping at an inn along the main road was not safe. Fortunately, another, less travelled road branched off at this point. It led to the monastery of San Esteban.

"We'll turn here," Alonso said. "The monks will give us shelter."

San Esteban was famous for its reliquary, a crystal flask containing three drops of Christ's precious blood. It drew a crowd of worshippers during Holy Week. The stony road leading to the monastery would soon be filled with pilgrims, but for now Alonso and Luisa were the only travellers. There was no one to observe them and carry news back to Tordesillas.

They arrived at the monastery and were shown to the guesthouse. After a frugal meal, one of the monks offered to show them the reliquary. He took them to the underground vault where the precious flask was kept on a lace-covered altar. A coffin, trimmed in silver and gold sat on a low trestle before the altar.

"The body of San Esteban, miraculously preserved from putrefaction by the power of the holy blood," their guide explained.

The sanctuary was lit by yellow wax tapers placed at the head and foot of the coffin and by an iron chandelier suspended from above, which held a dozen flickering candles. The rough walls, the low arched entrance, and the cracked pavement of uneven flagstones made Luisa shiver. It had the same shadowy look and musty smell as the dungeon they had escaped.

The guide motioned them to approach the trestle and lifted the lid of the coffin by a hand's breadth, revealing an inky blackness suggestive of marvels. They peered through the opening which gave off a stale odour of earth and rotten fruit. The monk shut the lid again and looked at them triumphantly, like a magician who had just performed a successful trick. "It is a great miracle," he said, "and now you have seen it with your own eyes."

"I could barely discern the body," Luisa said. "But perhaps the saint is meant to be seen with the eyes of the mind."

The monk pursed his lips. The colour of his face heightened disagreeably. "Do you believe in the miraculous powers of the saints, my lady?" he said.

"I believe in sainthood," she said quickly, "and I pray to be touched by the spirit of San Esteban." She saw his wondering look, and felt uneasy in her own heart, as if she had stepped outside the safe circle, and the shadow of the Inquisition had once again fallen on her.

There was a collection plate on the altar. Alonso dropped a coin on the salver, and the tinkle eased the frown on the monk's face.

"The saint's hair and nails continue to grow," he said, going on with his tour. "They require yearly trimming." He pointed to a set of canisters much like spice boxes containing saffron or turmeric. "We keep the trimmings there to be venerated on the saint's name day or to give away to generous donors as keepsakes." He looked at them meaningfully and compressed his lips when they said nothing in reply.

Next morning, when the time came to pay for their night's accommodation, Alonso explained that they had been the victims of trickery. Their servant had absconded with their pack mule, he said, and a purse of money.

"I was wondering why you were traveling without baggage and without a servant," the abbot said coldly. He was afraid of losing out on a night's lodging, or worse, being asked for charity, but he began to smile when Luisa showed him her jeweled cross and declared her willingness to part with it in exchange for a sum sufficient to continue on their pilgrimage.

"The cross has been in my family for a long time," she said. "I was told that a Templar brought it back from Jerusalem during the last crusade. Of course I cannot vouch for the story."

But the abbot needed no persuading. He had already taken a fancy to the cross.

"It will look handsome above the altar in the sanctuary," he said. "A cross hailing from Jerusalem will give a special aura to the vault containing the holy blood of Christ." No doubt he would think up a romantic story to open the pilgrims' wallets. He supplied them with a pack mule, provisions, and a man to accompany them as far as Vitoria. "The backroads are lonely," he said. "It's good to have a companion, especially a brawny fellow like Pedro who will make any rogue think twice before tangling with you."

They thanked the abbot for his concern.

"And you must stop at St. Bolonis," he said, "and visit the collection of precious reliquaries in the church there: three thorns from the crown of Jesus, two splinters from the wood of the holy cross, the hand of Mary Magdalene, the head of one of the thousand martyrs, two heads of the twelve thousand virgins – oh, and I almost forgot: the eyes of St. Mithrius. A prayer and a small offering at each reliquary will yield 18,000 years in indulgences. Think about it: 18,000 years off purgatory!"

"St. Bolonis is rather out of our way, isn't it?" Alonso said.

"Delivering your soul from the fires of purgatory is worth the detour," the abbot said with conviction.

***

Their brawny companion turned out to be more threat than protection.

"I've heard about you, Doctor Malki," he said as they rode through the gate and out into the road. "My brother lives in Tordesillas, and on my last visit there, his neighbour praised your skill and your generosity. He said you are in the habit of visiting the old and the poor and charge them nothing for your labours."

"I'm glad to hear I have a good name among your friends and family," Alonso said.

Pedro's eyes wandered to Luisa. He stared at her impudently, but she lowered her eyes and turned away, and he asked no questions.

They followed the winding path along the ridge until it dropped steeply down to the main road leading to Vitoria. The afternoon was turning into evening when they stopped for the night. They dismounted under the painted sign of a goggle-eyed lamb announcing the inn's name: La cabeza del cordero. In the yard, two young fellows in high spirits jostled and boxed each other, laughing and jeering. They interrupted their sparring to ogle Luisa and made way reluctantly under Alonso's impatient eye. Although they moved off to a corner of the yard, their braying voices were loud enough for Luisa to hear their bawdy talk and make her blush and blanch in turn.

"You heard the news from Tordesillas?" one of them said. "A woman ran off with her lover. She's a nun, they say."

His companion guffawed. "And you believe that? Those nuns are old and wrinkled like plums."

"What do you know, Silvano? Maybe there's juice in those plums. If you have the right tool..."

The man lowered his voice, but his lewd gestures, his pumping fists made it clear what was on his mind, and his companion exploded with laughter.

"You know who her lover is?" his friend crowed. "The devil in the guise of a Jew. The inquisitor himself came from Valladolid to purify the nuns' featherbeds."

Pedro, who was leading their horses away, looked back at Alonso and gave him a sly grin. "The stories people come up with," he said, shaking his head. "Did you hear what he said, doctor?"

"I'm not in the habit of listening to drunks," Alonso said.

"No, of course not. They are talking nonsense," Pedro said with mock respect, but the irreverent grin stayed on his face. "I bet you could set those fellows straight, doctor." His grin broadened into a sneer.

Alonso did not answer the insolent fellow. He took Luisa's arm and led her into the house. The innkeeper stood at the door. He had come out to see what the shouting and laughter was all about.

"My wife is indisposed," Alonso said to him. "It's nothing to worry about, but do oblige us and have our dinner brought up to our room."

It was better to keep out of sight, and the reason Alonso gave was not entirely spurious. Luisa had been feeling queasy.

The innkeeper eyed her. "Nothing to worry about, eh?" he said, hiding a grin. He could guess what the lady was suffering from. Nothing that nine months couldn't cure.

In their room, Luisa sank on the bed, exhausted. When she first felt the familiar symptoms, she was relieved that God had not struck her down with barrenness, but she was also afraid to think of the future in store for the child of an unmarried mother.

"Of course Pedro has put two and two together," she said. "What will we do now?"

"Discharge him tomorrow morning and hire another servant in Vitoria."

"Some dimwitted fellow who is deaf to the world and communes only with horses and donkeys?"

"Yet is clever enough to know the road and keep track of our provisions? I know, Luisa. The news of our flight has spread, but we will be out of danger soon, as soon as we cross into France."

They spent a restless night. Luisa's sleep was disturbed by fear, which turned into an oppressive dream of being bound and blind-folded, of her fingers trawling dirt, coming upon unspeakable horrors. Sometimes sounds broke into her dream, hacking coughs and tuneless voices, a grating that set her teeth on edge. The night limped on until she woke in the early dawn and saw Alonso sitting on the edge of their bed, ready to get dressed.

"I couldn't sleep," he said when he heard her move. "I thought I'd get up."

She reached out to him and pulled him close. They lay in the quiet comfort of each other's arms a little longer, until their bad dreams and churning thoughts dissolved and they heard the household stir.

After breakfast, Alonso paid their guide off and sent him on his way.

Pedro did not immediately pocket the coins Alonso handed him. He jingled them in the hollow of his palm.

"Is that all, doctor?" he said. "I thought you would be more generous, considering."

"I don't know what you are considering," Alonso said. "You want me to add a thrashing? You look like a fellow in need of the horse whip."

Pedro scowled. "And you look like a Jew," he said and spat on the ground, but he finally pocketed his pay and moved off.

"It was a mistake to quarrel with him," Luisa said when they were on the road again.

"I know," Alonso said, "but I cannot always be meek. And even if I had been gracious to that cur, it would have done us no good. He will betray us. The Inquisition pays its informers well."

"It will take him two days to reach Tordesillas and put the bloodhounds on our track."

"By then we will be in France, I hope. But to be on the safe side, we'll change our route."

They had told Pedro they were going to take the coastal road through Fuentarrabia, the route most travelers chose because it was the easiest way to reach France, but if Pedro made their route known to their pursuers, they might overtake them before they reached France. It was better to take the more arduous route through the mountains.

They continued as far as Vitoria, dreading every horseman who rode at a hurried pace, every cart rumbling by with a curious driver staring at them. In Vitoria, they stopped only long enough to rest their horses and hire a guide to conduct them through the mountains. He was a taciturn Basque who knew the route well. He had crossed from Gasteiz (as he called Vitoria) to France many times, he said.

Before long they had left the walled city behind and rode along the road climbing up into the Pyrenees. The path inclined gently at first, then became steeper and narrower. They rode in the shadow of snow-covered peaks, surmounting crest after crest, looking down into the blue shadows of deep valleys. As they followed the stony path, all talk ceased. They were afraid of the horses losing their footing and tumbling into the pathless ravines. The clatter of hooves on stone, the hollow snorts of the pack mules and the groan of cart wheels were the only sound in their ears now. In the early evening they reached the summit. It was so far above the world it seemed to touch the canopy of heaven, and so cold and lonely it made them think of the end of time. But their guide led them to the safety of a shelter, a sturdy lodge built of rocks and timber, where they spent the night in the company of other travellers, and where they were lulled to sleep by the dark melody of howling winds and the warmth of the fire in the hearth.

The next day they descended into France and stopped in the border town of Saint Jean Pied de Port. They were out of the reach of their pursuers at last, and free to become man and wife. Alonso called on the local parish priest and made his request. Luisa's father was dead, he said, and had entrusted his daughter to the doctor's care. They loved each other and wished to be united before God. The priest nodded, glanced at the power-of-attorney Alonso showed him, but shook his head when Alonso asked for a private wedding that very evening.

"You are in a great hurry," the priest said. Of course, people who wanted private weddings were always in a hurry, but the sacrament of matrimony could not be doled out like a loaf of bread or a bumper of beer. The vows were not to be taken rashly. "I would like to oblige you," he said, "but the banns must be published first. I'll marry you in two weeks."

"We cannot stay in Saint Jean for two weeks," Alonso said. "We are expected in Montpellier."

"If you want to get married here, you will have to wait, my son," the priest said.

Alonso pulled out his purse, and the holy man found that he could accommodate Alonso's request after all. Alonso thought of the Queen's gift to Luisa. *Love conquers all,* but only if joined by its powerful ally, money. The priest gave a suitable interpretation to the conventions and injunctions of the Church and married the pair outside the city walls in a chapel not much larger than a roadside sanctuary.

The nave, solid and whitewashed, was unadorned except for a wooden cross. The altar was covered with a lace cloth tatted by a peasant hand and lit by a single candle. The chapel had a simple grace that pleased Luisa. It was like her love for Alonso, plain and artless.

They walked down the flagstone aisle to the altar, hand in hand. The priest had invited a congregation of two to witness the wedding, an old, weak-headed man and his doddering wife. How different this pledge was from the pomp and ceremony that had accompanied her wedding to Deodatus, a staged performance in which the bride and groom had been the puppets of fate. Standing in this rustic house of God, the priest and the witnesses seemed incidental. They stood before a higher power for whom their love was sufficient testimony.

The old couple had taken their seats in a pew at the back and sat, confused by the ceremonial whisper at the altar. Their grey heads nodded, while Alonso and Luisa pledged their troth and became husband and wife.

***

At the inn, Luisa and Alonso sat down to dinner with a company that had come from Montpellier and was on their way back to Spain. Alonso struck up a conversation with his neighbour at the table, a jurist from Toledo.

"They say that travel is dangerous to your health," the jurist said, when he heard that Alonso was a physician, "but you need an antidote against vice as much as against the infectious air of France. We encountered a great deal of crime and immorality on the road."

"I tried to close my ears and eyes against it," his wife chimed in, "but it was no use. I could not overlook the harlots at the roadside inns with their gaudy rags and their shrill laughter." She turned to Luisa. "To think there are women who defile the sacred institution of marriage with their sordid practices and bring shame on our sex!"

"Indeed," said the lawyer and quoted the canon law prohibiting pre- and extramarital relations, using Latin to protect the ears of his innocent audience, but translating for their benefit the fines threatened by the church.

There was lively agreement around the table about the ineffectiveness of the church laws and the decline of morals, of which many examples were given with the most interesting details that made the jurist's wife burn with eagerness and righteous indignation.

The conversation turned back to the adventures of the road.

"Is it business that takes you to Montpellier?" the jurist asked.

"It is only a stopover," Alonso aid. "We have a long journey before us. Our destination is Venice. I hope to settle and practise my profession there."

"You should stay a while in Montpellier," the jurist said. "The faculty of medicine is famous. I understand the university attracts students from all over Europe who wish to hear lectures on anatomy and observe the dissection of bodies."

"My dear," his wife said. "Don't speak of such gruesome things." She turned to Luisa. "Never mind the university," she said. "You should visit Balaruc, which is just outside of Montpellier and famous for its hot springs. A great many fashionable people go there to bathe and drink the water, although I cannot recommend it myself. It is rather salty and disagreeable to the taste, like bad soup highly seasoned, but it possesses curative powers, and I must say I did sleep wonderfully well at Balaruc. And speaking of which, dear madam, I believe I shall retire."

She got up and bid the company good night, but lowered her rump again. "Oh, but I almost forgot to tell you. If you have any time at all in Montpellier, you must secure an invitation to the Comte de Tournon's castle. Your husband merely needs to send up his name. The Count is eager for the company of physicians. He is suffering from the gout and forever hopeful that one of them will provide him with an effective cure. He gives the most fashionable balls. You should have seen the gown Madame la Comtesse wore on one occasion, of green and amber taffeta, edged with silver braids. There is only one warning I must give you. The French dances are scandalous. Those voles, courantes, and gaillards are positively sinful. No respectable lady in Spain would want to be seen moving in that undignified and forward manner. I did enjoy watching the Comte's son, though, a boy of six, dancing with his sister. Such dainty steps and elegant bows – but here I'm going on and it's getting late." She rose and delivered Luisa of her company at last.

In the meantime, others had risen from the table as well and were scraping back their chairs. The company was breaking up for the night. One of the men took Alonso aside.

"Daniel da Segni at your service," he said. "I could not help overhearing your plan to travel to Venice. I would advise you not to go there just now."

"And the reason for your warning?" Alonso said.

"When I left Genoa three days ago, I heard rumours about riots in Venice, people storming the Jewish quarter in retaliation for a heinous crime. A rabbi had committed ritual murder, they said. He had slaughtered a Christian infant. The crime was denounced from the pulpits of the Genovese churches." He looked at Alonso sideways. "You know the priests' cant," he said. "They carry on about the 'detestable and abominable murderers of Christ.' They whip the people into a frenzy with their burning rhetoric. In Genoa they exhorted the congregation to go out and sack the Jews' houses. I would not go to Venice now if I were you. Wait until tempers cool. In a week, after Easter, matters will return to normal."

"But I have nothing to fear. I am a Christian," Alonso said.

"So am I," Da Segni said, "but my father had the courtesy of keeping his Jewish nose to himself and my French mother was kind enough to bequeath me a light complexion. Your face says you are a Jew, and you will be treated like one. You know what the ambassador of Urbino said to me the other day when I sat next to him at dinner? 'The Spanish *marranos*, those baptized Jews, ought to be kept out of Italy. They are faithless people, neither Christian nor Jew.' And he said a great deal more in the same vein, which I will spare you. But take care and do not think you are safe because you are baptized. If you are not afraid for your own person, you should delay your journey for the sake of your charming wife."

Alonso thanked Da Segni for his warning and caught up with Luisa.

She took his arm. "What have you been talking about so earnestly?" she said.

"Gruesome stuff, as the jurist's wife would say."

"Oh, about the anatomy lectures?" she said. "I suppose you want to attend them."

"Perhaps we should stay a few days in Montpellier. Would that please you?"

Luisa gave him a vivid smile. "It would please me very much."

They reached their room. She shut the door and put her arms around him.

"I've been thinking, Alonso," she said. "If we stop in Montpellier, why don't you see if you can get us an invitation to Tournon Castle? I'm dying to see the frivolous dances that gave so much offense to the jurist's wife."

"And to take a turn at them yourself?"

"If you will ask me to dance with you."

"Are you not afraid of cutting an undignified figure?"

She slapped his wrist playfully. "I'm afraid of cutting a silly figure because I haven't danced in such a long time. I don't know the new steps, and I have forgotten all the old ones."

"We must practise, then," he said. He took his place opposite Luisa, bowed, and said: "Allow me, madam."

She took his hand, and they pranced and capered up and down the room, turning and curtsying, humming the melodies they remembered, until Luisa was out of breath and fell into Alonso's arms, laughing.

She was giddy with happiness. To love without feeling the pangs of conscience or the fear of discovery! She touched the golden heart, the Queen's keepsake which adorned her neck now.

"Life is very sweet," she said. "*Amor vincit omnia.*"

CHAPTER 20

AT LAST: VENICE, THAT ENCHANTING, GLORIOUS, mythical city! Erasmus called it *the most splendid stage of Italy,* but so far Luisa had seen very little of it beyond the view from the window of the inn where they lodged: a grey canal crowded with gondolas, a narrow landing, the handsome but dank facades of the houses across the water, and in the distance a tantalizing glimpse of splendor, the cupola of San Marco and the tiled roofs of noble palaces.

Alonso spent long hours every day making the rounds of the great houses and waiting in the antechambers of important men. So far his search for patronage had been in vain, and a physician new in town could not hope to attract much custom without letters of introduction. No patient would put his trust in a foreigner, at least none who had the means to pay for his services. Charitable cases were plentiful. Alonso was not averse to making a contribution to the common weal, but he had to make a living, to satisfy his own pride and to provide for Luisa. And for their child, as her rounded body reminded him every day. Their situation was precarious. Luisa had forfeited her stipend as lady-in-waiting, and had no hopes of extracting her landed property from the iron grip of her father. The payment of dividends from the investments in Antwerp had to be redirected to Venice, but had not reached them yet. In any case, Alonso was unwilling to live on Luisa's money. Or on the generosity of his uncle.

"I do not want to depend on him for longer than necessary," he said a week after their arrival in Venice.

Otniel Malki had more than once declared his willingness to support his nephew however long it took to establish himself.

"Regard my home as your home," he said, "and make use of my money as you would of your own."

He was the most open-handed of men, but he was also a devout Jew and rarely visited them at the inn without steering the conversation to the question of religion. He spoke with discretion, but it was clear that he expected Alonso to return to the beliefs of his fathers and that he was hoping for Luisa's conversion as well.

Alonso answered him with quiet resolve.

"I have been studying the books of the great rabbis and the foremost Christian theologians," he said, "and am left with many questions. It was for that reason, principally, that I was imprisoned in Spain. I am a man in quest of the truth, uncle, and I fear it will be a life-long quest. I have not always stayed the course. I freely confess: I have practiced deceit for love's sake when it was necessary, but Luisa and I have come here so that we may live in accordance with our conscience, and I hope I will never have to choose again between my love of Luisa and my love of the truth."

Disappointment showed on Otniel's face, but he found it difficult to challenge his nephew's reply. He turned to Luisa next, thinking perhaps that her fortress was easier to breach.

She kept a respectful silence, however, and at last Alonso answered on her behalf.

"You must understand, uncle," he said, "that Luisa cherishes the religion of her forefathers as much as you do your own. You will not fault in her the virtue you practise yourself: fidelity to your traditions."

After that, Otniel Malki allowed the conversation to flow into other channels. He was saddened but undeterred from his purpose. On his next visit he returned to the subject which was so close to his heart: the conversion of the newcomers. It was hard, Luisa thought, that Alonso should be persecuted in Spain on suspicion of Judaism, and regarded with dissatisfaction by his uncle for remaining a Christian. Italy had not turned out to be the haven she had imagined in her desire to escape the strictures of Spanish society.

After weeks of trying every avenue of finding employment, Alonso's efforts finally bore fruit. He had good hopes of obtaining a position at a charity hospital. The trustees were willing to hire him. Alonso had impressed them with his knowledge and his agreeable manners and, most of all, he told Luisa, with his readiness to accept the modest salary they offered. Of course, they needed letters of reference before signing a contract with him. And so he was cast back on that hard rock. Where was a newcomer in town to get references? A newcomer who had cut his ties with Spain and could not fall back on his old connections?

The answer was: From Natale Benvenuto.

When Otniel Malki welcomed Alonso and Luisa in Venice, they told him of their narrow escape and perilous flight. He in turn told them of the warning letter he had sent to Tordesillas through a Spanish priest.

"Natale Benvenuto!" Alonso exclaimed when his uncle named the priest. "I am not surprised your letter never reached me," he said. "Natale is a treacherous man."

He explained their connection to his astonished uncle.

"He may be all you say, but I don't know whether he is to blame for the loss of the letter," Otniel Malki said. "He sent it off at any rate. I saw the receipt. The fact that the letter did not arrive is another story. It may have been intercepted and put into the inquisitor's hands. It happens often enough."

They left it at that, but Natale's name cropped up again when the trustees of the charity hospital requested a letter of reference from Alonso.

"Why not ask the priest?" Otniel Malki said to his nephew. "He will write you a reference if you pay him for it. He is a venal man."

"Say rather, a scoundrel."

"But a useful scoundrel. It will do no harm to look him up at any rate. He lives at the house of the art dealer Dovizi."

"Natale has crossed me before and will betray me again. What keeps him from informing the inquisitor of my whereabouts?"

"The fact that it will not benefit him. You are no longer under Spanish jurisdiction. The priest will take your money and write the letter, mark my word."

***

Alonso did not relish the idea of bargaining with Natale, but necessity forced his hand. He saw no other means of obtaining a letter of reference that would carry weight with the trustees of the hospital. Natale was a member of the church. The cloth, if not the man, commanded respect and gave him authority. Reluctantly, he made his way to Dovizi's house in the Campo dei Frari.

The piazza was all but deserted when Alonso passed the church of the Franciscans. Time had dulled the delicate trace work of Santa Maria Gloriosa and left the stone portal looking grey and dingy.

Dovizi's house stood next to the church. It was a handsome building, three stories high, with a travertine front and pillared balconies. A servant answered the door and announced Alonso's presence to his master. On such occasions it was good to have a handle to one's name. "Doctor" has a fine ring, and Dovizi himself emerged from his study to greet Alonso.

"This way, *dottore*," he said, leading the way through a warehouse of bronze and marble statues, past walls hung with ornately framed paintings, and prints stacked against the wainscoting.

"Are you a friend of Fra Natale?" he said, preceding Alonso up the stairs.

"A compatriot and an acquaintance of long standing."

"I wish you had been at hand, when that good Samaritan brought Fra Natale home – but I doubt you could have helped him even then." He stopped when he saw the baffled look on Alonso's face. "You don't know?" he said. "You have not come to attend him?"

"I know nothing. I've only recently arrived in Venice. Is Fra Natale ill?"

"He is in a bad way, I'm sorry to say. He was attacked and robbed some weeks ago and left for dead in the street. I don't know what he was doing in that godforsaken part of the city. What can I say? It was very unwise to walk there unattended at night. A friend of mine, an apothecary, came and examined the gash in his head, but he could do nothing for him. Pray for the man, he said to me. Pray for his quick death or for a miracle.

He is hanging on to his life, but I fear there will be no miracle."

At the door of Natale's room Dovizi stopped and said in a lower voice. "He hasn't recovered his wits. You will find him raving."

Natale was indeed a wretched sight, his face suffused with the unhealthy glow of fever, his tonsure glistening with sweat above the thick bandage that was wound around his temples. He was attended by an old woman holding a basin of vinegary water in her lap and sponging his cheeks. At Dovizi's nod, she got up and left the room.

Alonso took a seat at the bedside and gently put two fingers on Natale's pulse. It was racing.

At the touch of his hand, the sick man's eyelids fluttered open, but he saw only the ghosts of his fevered dream.

"No one to help me," he groaned. "No one coming to the rescue. I tried to call out – but he was choking me." His hand went up to his throat, as if wrestling with an imaginary rope. He coughed through parched lips.

"You are safe now, Fra Natale," Dovizi said, laying a calming hand on the patient's shoulder, but the nightmare kept its grip on Natale.

"How could he know about my little treasure?" he mumbled. "I kept it well hidden under my cloak." He opened his eyes wide and stared up at the ceiling. "But I know where he was hiding," he went on, talking fast now, as if he had to get the story off his chest before it was too late. "He was cowering in that stairwell. I saw him out of the corner of my eyes. He was creeping after me."

"I don't know what treasure he is talking about," Dovizi said.

Natale arched his back and cried out: "Help me!" Under the pressure of Dovizi's hand, he sunk back again and murmured feverishly: "If I could only reach the piazza."

"He tells the story over and over again," Dovizi said, "in the same words exactly, like a man reading from a book."

As if prompted, the sick man went on: "At the corner, I look back. He's still after me. I run. I can hear him breathing. I can feel his bony fingers around my neck. He is pushing me. I am falling, falling." He gripped his chest and clawed at his shirt convulsively. "My heart, my poor heart, it's like a hammer. But wait, there is light coming. High up in the sky. The stars are so radiant." His lips parted. "So radiant," he said and fell back on the pillow, silenced by the beauty of his vision.

"Your apothecary friend was right," Alonso said. "He is beyond human help."

"Then I'll leave you to say a prayer for him," Dovizi said.

The room was quiet after Dovizi left. Natale was no longer rambling. He had fallen into the comatose state preceding death. Alonso looked around the room. It was capacious and neatly kept. On a ledge running along the wall was a row of salt cellars, curiously wrought of chased silver. A lacquered scrignetto held half a dozen gilded books. Above the bed, which was set up in a recess, was a triangular mirror with an elaborate golden frame that gave it the appearance of a tabernacle. Natale has done well for himself here, Alonso thought. No doubt, he found Venice as fertile a field for blackmailing as Alcala. Did such a man deserve God's mercy? Could a prayer save his black soul?

After a while Dovizi returned and accompanied Alonso downstairs with a great show of civility, which Alonso recognized as the usual preamble to cadging medical advice. It was a common experience. As soon as people discovered Alonso's profession, they tried to benefit from his knowledge and coax a free consultation from him. He did not begrudge his advice to people of slender means, but Dovizi was a wealthy man.

He hemmed and hawed a little before saying: "By the way, *dottore*, could you recommend an effective cure for flatulence – it's on behalf of my wife I'm asking. Her health is poor, and we are often obliged to seek the services of my apothecary friend or of a physician. But she's embarrassed to consult anyone about that disorder. It seems a small thing, yet very awkward, you understand."

"I quite understand," Alonso said. "Ask your cook to compound crushed egg shells with nutmeg, cloves, and rue. Infuse in boiling water, allow to cool, and serve before meals."

He was sure the cook knew the treatment, but coming from the mouth of a doctor, the simple remedy took on a scientific sheen.

"Much obliged for your advice, *dottore*," the art dealer said, pleased to have gotten something for nothing.

***

The next morning Alonso went back to Dovizi's house, to see what could be done to ease Natale's last agony, but he was too late. The priest had died during the night, Dovizi told him.

In Natale's room, the bed was already stripped. The body, wrapped in a shroud, was lying on a gurney, ready to be taken to the cemetery. The gilded books Alonso had seen on his first visit were gone. The collection of antique salt cellars was sitting in a motley group on the table.

"I thought it was my duty to look after the funeral arrangements," Dovizi said when he saw the doctor looking around the bare room. "As for Natale's possessions – I hope there is enough here to cover what he owes me, to pay a priest and a gravedigger and to commission a headstone."

"The collection of salt cellars looks valuable to me," Alonso said. "Natale had a good eye for treasures."

"Quite so," Dovizi said, "but first I will have to find a buyer for them, and in the meantime I have to lay out ready cash for the burial, unless you know of friends or family who would defray the cost. I ask, because, sad to say, you are the only friend who called on Natale during the time he lived here."

"I know nothing of his family," Alonso said. "Natale was my wife's tutor once, but my present position does not allow me to assist you in defraying the cost of his burial, if that was the point of your question."

"Not at all," Dovizi said. Alonso could tell he was embarrassed and wished he had not raised the subject. He could well afford to pay for the burial. "If Natale was your wife's tutor, take a keepsake," he said quickly to make up for his faux pas. "One of the salt cellars perhaps?"

Alonso thanked Dovizi for his offer. He wanted no keepsake. He wanted nothing at all to remind him of Natale.

The conversation turned to Alonso's medical skills and the ailments of Dovizi's wife. By now, Alonso had sized him up as man who was fond of his money. He expected another attempt to extract free services from him. It was not long in coming. Would the doctor be kind enough to take a look at his wife and give his opinion on her condition, Dovizi said.

"I won't impose on your time, *dottore*. But if you could spare a minute-"

"I will gladly put my services at your disposal," Alonso said, "if I may ask a favour in turn. You have been kind enough to offer me a keepsake, but what I need is a letter of reference. Indeed, that was the purpose of my visit to Fra Natale before I knew he was ill: to ask him for a recommendation." He told Dovizi of his chance to obtain a post at a charity hospital.

Dovizi was all smiles. "But of course, *dottore*. I cannot tell you how much I value your skill. The concoction you prescribed the other day worked wonderfully well."

The bargain was soon concluded. Alonso attended the lady of the house, whose chief ailment, it seemed, was a surfeit of fat about her body. Dovizi meanwhile went to his study and wrote a letter of recommendation.

***

Luisa fingered the heart-shaped pendant hanging from the gold chain around her neck—the Queen's gift, her talisman. Would love conquer all?

Left to herself in their lodgings at the inn, she felt a numbing idleness. In Tordesillas her duties as a lady-in-waiting had kept her occupied for much of the day. Now the hours dragged on and turned her mind into a hall of echoes. She asked herself the same questions over and over again, and the difficulties life posed appeared more sinister with every turn: their straitened circumstances, the uncertainties of Alonso's career, the disap-pointment of his uncle, the treacherous mind of Natale. The obstacles to her happiness seemed insurmountable.

She closed the book she had been studying, a manual of the Italian language. Her worries would not let her concentrate. She got up and paced the room, came to a halt at the window, and looked out on the gray silhouettes of the houses across the narrow canal. In Tordesillas she had breathed the salutary air of pine forests. Here the air was rank and putrid in the noon heat, brackish and salty when a breeze blew in from the sea in the evening. The cries of the boatsmen floated up to Luisa, drifted into her head, and settled there like soot, colouring her mood black.

Alonso had been out all morning. She was impatient for his return. Was she longing for his body or his mind, wanting to be sheltered in his arms, or comforted by his words? His lucid reasoning did not solve their problems, but it contained them neatly, hedged them in with logic until they no longer appeared so formidable. His words were a comfort to Luisa. She remembered when they were first parted, when he was called away to join the court. He had spoken to her of the mystic Cabala then and promised they would never be parted in spirit. Luisa wished she could call on those sacred powers now and find the mystical bridge between their souls. Then she reproached herself. Really, she had no reason to feel so dejected. A few months ago, marriage to Alonso seemed an impossible dream. Now her dream had come true. How quickly she had taken that happiness for granted, and was looking for more: not content with Alonso's body and mind, she also wanted his mystical soul! Not content with spending a few hours in his presence, she wanted to be with him always. She begrudged his company to others. He is too kind, too generous, she thought, always making himself available to those in need, even to a despicable man like Natale, who didn't deserve such goodness.

    Her thoughts were interrupted by a knock.

    Donna Maddalena, the landlady was at the door. Her lips were wreathed in a smile as she stepped into the room, holding out a tray to Luisa. On it was a plate of *buzoladi* pastry and a dish of tripe supposed to be of special benefit to pregnant women. Donna Maddalena was solicitous for Luisa's wellbeing. It was her way of thanking Alonso after he prescribed an effective cough syrup for her little boy.

    And how was her dear Madonna Luisa? Was everything in order?

    "*Tutto bene,*" Luisa said, a small offering from her limited stock of Italian.

    Donna Maddalena burbled on, patting her arm.

    "My first pregnancy was difficult. I almost died giving birth to Marta," she said, as far as Luisa could understand. After that, she could make out only names, the names of Donna Maddalena's younger children: Maurizio, Anna, Matteo, and Raffaele, all of whom had survived. Her good fortune was connected with the medallion of Santa Margarita of Antioch, which she now pulled out from under her neckcloth and held up to Luisa. To kiss? To admire? Santa Margarita was the most powerful patron a pregnant woman could have, the landlady said. "You must pray to her." *Ora, ora*, was her advice.

The smell of tripe was in Luisa's nostrils and made her stomach heave. *Estoy cansada*, she said in Spanish, hoping the Italian word for "tired" sounded similar. *Flaca*, she said, when the landlady gave her a blank look.

"*Ah, si, si, fiacca. Poverina!*" Tired. Of course! She left with many apologies. She hadn't meant to disturb Luisa.

Alas, the landlady's visits were no cure for Luisa's restless mind. The swarm of unintelligible words she poured out offered no comfort.

Luisa opened the door to the little balcony and set the dish of tripe on the floor, hoping that pigeons or seagulls would take care of it. Looking down, she saw a gondola at the landing, and there he was! Alonso. He looked up and waved to Luisa. She threw him a kiss – if only he brought good news! She turned back into the room. His footfall was on the stairs. The door opened, and he came in. Good news or bad? She searched his face, so familiar in every line, in every contour. It was curiously changeable, a mixture of sadness and joy.

"Natale has passed away," he said quietly after embracing her.

Luisa said a silent prayer of thanks. God had delivered them from that blackguard. Good news, surely.

Alonso, too, was smiling now, and flourishing a folded sheet of paper.

"A letter of reference," he said triumphantly. "From Dovizi, in return for my services. Read it, my dear."

She quickly perused the lines and gave Alonso a joyful kiss. "Honeyed words!" she said. "Sure to satisfy the trustees. Fortune is on our side, at last."

"But fortune can be fickle," he said.

There was a time for reason, and a time for the heart, to rejoice. "Oh don't be so wise, Alonso," she said, throwing her arms around his neck. He held her tight, and she felt the golden heart press against her chest. "Or only as wise as the Mad Queen," she said.

He kissed her fondly. "Madly in love, you mean? I am, my darling, and I promise I will always be a fool for you."

"Will you?" she said and was overcome with happiness.

The golden heart was working its magic. *Love conquers all.*

ABOUT THE AUTHOR

Winner of the Random House Creative Writing Award in 2011, Erika Rummel is the author of more than a dozen non-fiction books (social history, biography, translation) and three novels: *Playing Naomi* (2009), *Head Games* (2012), and *The Effects of Isolation on the Brain* (forthcoming). Erika grew up in Vienna and came to Canada in 1965, where she obtained a doctorate from the University of Toronto. She taught history at Wilfrid Laurier University, Waterloo, and at the University of Toronto. She divides her time between Toronto and Los Angeles and has lived in small villages in Argentina, Romania, and Bulgaria.

Erika Rummel maintains a website at:
www.erikarummel.com.
She can also be followed on Facebook at:
https://www.facebook.com/erika.rummel.1
and Twitter: @historycracks

More Great Historical Fiction from Bygone Era Books:

And the Wind Whispered by Dan Jorgensen

Bittersweet Tavern by S. Copperstone

Divine Vengeance by D. W. Koons

Girl in the River by Patricia Kullberg

The Harlot Saint by Susan McGregor

Immortal Betrayal by Daniel A. Willis
Immortal Duplicity by Daniel A. Willis

Into the Hidden Valley by Stuart Blackburn

Kilpara by Patricia Hopper

Nazi Love by Michael Phayer

The Other Side of Courage by Robert Nordmeyer

Primitive Passions by John M. Cahill

The Prince of Prigs by Anthony Anglorus

The Sands of Kedar by Diana Khalil

A Storm Before the War by Phillip Otts

Whispers of Liberty by Heidi Sprouse

CPSIA information can be obtained at www.ICGtesting.com
Printed in the USA
LVOW10s0003270216

476905LV00012B/37/P